Also by Michael McBride

NOVELS

Ancient Enemy
Bloodletting
Burial Ground
Fearful Symmetry
Innocents Lost
Predatory Instinct
The Coyote

NOVELLAS

F9
Remains
Snowblind
The Event

COLLECTIONS

Category V

MICHAEL McBRIDE

VECTOR BORNE

A THRILLER

FACTOR V MEDIA

For Blake...This, and the World

Special Thanks to Roy and Liz at Bad Moon Books, Jeff Strand, Gene O'Neill, Bill Rasmussen, Brian Keene, my family, and all of my loyal readers, without whom none of this would be possible.

The reason why the universe is eternal is that it does not live for itself; it gives life to others as it transforms.

— Lao Tzu

All gods are homemade, and it is we who pull their strings, and so, give them the power to pull ours.

— Aldous Huxley

Life is simply the reification of the process of living.

— Ernst Mayr

One

Pueblo Bonito
Chaco Canyon, New Mexico
June 17th
7:36 p.m. MDT

Twelve Years Ago

Dr. Graham Bradley waited for the rooster tail of dust that had followed them for the last twenty miles to pass over the forest-green Cherokee before he finally opened the door and stepped down onto the sun-baked earth. His chief of security, Roland Pike, remained rigid behind the wheel, staring fixedly through the dirty windshield. The setting sun bled the sandstone escarpments crimson and cast long shadows from the sparse pockets of sage and creosote that spotted the sandy valley. A faint breeze ruffled Bradley's hair and returned the dust, forcing him to shield his azure eyes. His custom-tailored Caraceni slacks and calfskin shoes were already gray with accumulation. At least he'd had enough foresight to shed his jacket in the car, just not enough to have packed a change of clothes in his hurry to reach the site. When the call came from Dr. Brendan Reaves eight hours ago, Bradley had been in the middle of a board meeting. The anthropologist had refused to divulge the nature of his discovery over the phone and had insisted that Bradley needed to see what he had found in person. Considering the scope of Reaves's research, Bradley couldn't imagine why he would be summoned in such a fashion, which only served to heighten his curiosity. The corporate jet had been fueled and waiting at Sea-Tac when he arrived. Four hours in the air and three more wending through the New Mexico desert in the rental Jeep, and here he was, parched and irritated, and tingling with anticipation.

"This had better be good," he said, and struck off toward the cluster of khaki tents at the edge of the Pueblo Bonito ruins.

The rubble formed a D-shape, straight in front and rounded where it abutted the sheer cliff. Walls composed of stacked layers of flat rocks climbed three stories up the sandstone face to where petroglyphs had been carved by long-dead hands nearly a thousand years prior. Where once more than six hundred rooms and thirty-nine ceremonial kivas had surrounded a broad central courtyard, now only the framework remained. Some walls still stood thirty feet high, while others had crumbled to the ground. A large portion was buried under tons of sandstone where "Threatening Rock" had broken away from the embankment.

For nearly two hundred years, this had been the capital of the thriving Anasazi culture and could have housed as many as five thousand people. Until, abruptly, they abandoned the entire canyon and embarked upon a northwestward migration that would prove to be the end of this once flourishing society.

And no one knew why.

A ring of halogen lights blossomed to life just beyond the tents, turning half a dozen men and women to silhouettes. One of them raised an arm to hail him and broke away from the group. Dr. Brendan Reaves, Regent's Professor of Cultural and Evolutionary Anthropology at Washington State University, strode directly toward him. He wore a dusty ball cap over his unkempt, sun-bleached hair. The bill hid his face in shadows. He extended a dirty hand, then thought better of it and swiped it on his filthy shorts. Instead, he tipped up his chin and offered a beaming smile, which made his sharp hazel eyes positively sparkle. He barely looked out of his teens.

"Thank you for getting down here so quickly," Reaves said. "I honestly didn't think you'd be willing to make the trip in person."

Bradley gave his best boardroom smile to hide his annoyance. GeNext Biosystems was his baby and he was intimately involved on every level from research and development through marketing and distribution. He wasn't the kind of COO who pandered to shareholders or spent his days swilling martinis on tropical shores. His vision was of a forward-thinking, revolutionary company that remained on the cutting edge of biotechnology through a nontraditional approach to research all over the globe, which meant that even he needed to roll up his sleeves from time to time.

"So, Dr. Reaves. Right to business. What could possibly be important enough to drag me across the country on a moment's notice?"

"You wouldn't believe me if I told you." Reaves turned and guided Bradley toward an old pickup painted tan by the desert. "Like I said, you have to see it with your own eyes."

Pike eased out of the Cherokee and stood at attention, but Bradley dismissed him with a subtle wave. He climbed up into the passenger seat of the professor's truck and kicked aside a pile of garbage to make room for his feet. The truck reeked of body odor and dust, and shook when Reaves started the engine.

"Where are we going?" Bradley asked.

He watched the ill-defined dirt road in the bouncing headlights.

"Not far. Just across the wash to Casa Rinconada. It's the largest, and only freestanding kiva in the Pueblo Bonito complex."

"You found more remains?"

"You could say that."

Reaves glanced over and gave a cryptic smile.

Bradley was in no mood for games. He was tired and famished, and had reached the end of his patience. Reaves must have recognized as much from his expression and started talking to fill the tense silence.

"Okay. Let me set the stage. In case you don't remember, I'm an evolutionary anthropologist. I study the changes—both cultural and physiological—in a society over time. My primary focus is the tribes of the American Southwest, specifically the Anasazi, who inhabited this amazing primitive mecca here in Chaco Canyon from about 800 to 1150 C.E.. We're talking about more than four hundred separate villages clustered around a dozen or so major pueblos like Bonito back there, all within a twenty-five thousand square-mile territory, the majority between these very canyon walls. They mastered agriculture, even in this hostile terrain, and set up a system of commerce that was beyond advanced for the time. And then, one day, they just up and abandon this community that took hundreds of years to build, by hand, stone by stone."

The tires grumbled over a bridge that shuddered under the truck's weight. The creek bed below them didn't appear as though it had ever held water. Ahead, a low mesa crowned by a tall stone ring resolved from the cliffs behind it.

"Next thing we know," Reaves said, "the Anasazi reappear in the Four Corners area, only their entire architectural style has changed. Instead of building at the bottom of valleys like this one, they're erecting fortresses hundreds of feet up on the cliffs. We're talking about the kinds of places that someone can only enter if a ladder is lowered down from the village or if they can scale the sandstone like Spider-Man. Places like Mesa Verde in Colorado and the White House in Arizona. We speculated that the mass exodus was caused by a prolonged period of drought in the middle of the twelfth century, which killed all of their crops and drove the wild game from the area, but that didn't explain the necessity for the fortified villages carved into niches that only birds could reach. It was almost as though they feared something, as though they were preparing to defend themselves against some kind of invading force."

"I know all of this, Dr. Reaves. I'm the one underwriting your research. Tell me how all of this pertains to the project I'm funding."

The plateau rose above them to their right as the road wound around it. From their vantage point, the circular walls of the kiva appeared remarkably well preserved.

"Right. We know that the Anasazi had an absurdly high incidence of anemia. Nearly forty percent of the remains exhumed here in Chaco exhibit *porotic hyperostosis*, which is a destructive pathological condition caused by iron-deficiency anemia that erodes the bones of the skull and orbits, and the ends of long bones. We assume that this was caused by a shift in diet over time as the Anasazi came to rely almost exclusively on plants and grains rather than the increasingly rare native game animals. They essentially cut out the iron that the human body needs to function, which it extracts from meat. That's why it made reasonable sense when we found evidence of cannibalism. The body always knows what it needs to survive, and instinctively determines how to get it. It's the same reason that pregnant women have cravings. Their bodies are telling them exactly what they need, both for themselves and their unborn fetuses, from fundamental nutrition to vitamins and trace minerals."

"What GeNext is paying you for, Dr. Reaves, is to determine if the Anasazi had a genetic predilection toward anemia or if it was truly dietary. We need detailed physical assays of the structural and physiological damage in order to understand how to counteract it. And considering the prevalence of anemia diminished significantly within this same population over the next two hundred years as it migrated away from this canyon and into Colorado, we need to identify the mechanism by which it decreased, be it genetic or environmental. Nearly three percent of the population of the United States has converted to vegetarianism, which opens a huge market for targeted dietary supplements. Not to mention the intrinsic value of this information as it pertains to cultivating artificial plasma and blood."

Reaves stared straight through the windshield as they rounded the mesa into a makeshift dirt lot wedged between Casa Rinconada and the canyon wall.

"While we appreciate and respect your expertise in matters anthropological, and would be thrilled if our shared venture afforded you the opportunity to advance your own theories in regard to the demise of the Anasazi, it is of secondary concern to our vested interest in your anemia research. GeNext *is* a biotechnology firm after all."

Reaves killed the engine, which died with a *clunk* that rattled the entire frame. He turned to face Bradley and offered a sly smirk.

"Prepare to forget all about that."

Reaves clambered out of the pickup, grabbed his backpack from behind his seat, and slammed the door.

Bradley climbed out and followed the professor up a steep dirt trail toward the ruins. It struck him as odd that this one sacred kiva would be built all the way across the canyon when there were nearly forty within the fortification walls. They scaled a crumbling mound of stones and dropped down to the level ground on the other side.

Reaves removed a long black Maglite from his backpack. He clicked it on and slung his pack over his shoulders. The beam illuminated a T-shaped opening in the tall circular wall, which framed a staircase that descended into the kiva. It reminded

Bradley of a miniature coliseum with the rings of stone bleachers that encircled the main ceremonial stage. Three rectangles of flat rocks had been stacked a foot high to either side and toward the rear of the weed-riddled earth like primitive planting boxes roughly the size of graves. A mound of dirt and sandstone chunks lorded over the one directly ahead of them. The flashlight stained the pall of dust seeping from the hole.

"We found the first stair about three feet down." Reaves nodded toward the pit and shined his light onto a stone staircase that vanished into the darkness. He hopped down into the hole and spotlighted the narrow channel. Bradley covered his mouth and nose with his handkerchief to keep from breathing the dust and followed Reaves underground. "It took nearly another month to excavate the remainder of the staircase and remove the stones they had used to seal off this chamber."

Reaves led him into what appeared to be a natural cave. The walls and ceiling were rounded and scarred by dozens of petroglyphs, all of which featured massive centipedes with enormous pincers attacking stick-figure representations of men and animals alike.

"The Anasazi considered depictions of the centipede to be taboo," Reaves said. "They believed it to be a powerful symbol of the transition between the world of the living and the land of the dead. The mere act of drawing it on these walls would have been considered sacrilegious."

Bradley stared at the violent images for a moment before pressing on. Cobwebs swayed overhead and hung to either side where they'd been severed. Potsherds littered the floor amid a scattering of grains and gravel. Reaves stepped to his right and directed the beam at a heap of bones at his feet. They were disarticulated, shattered, and scattered in no discernible order.

"They're human," Bradley said.

"This wasn't a burial," Reaves said. "This was a willful desecration."

"Who would have done something like this?"

"They did it themselves. We believe it was part of a ritual designed to trap the evil spirits down here when they sealed the kiva."

Bradley knelt and inspected the bones. There was no residual blood or tissue, and the marrow had been scraped out. He couldn't fathom the correlation to their project.

"That's not what I brought you here to see." Reaves pointed the beam at the back wall, where a jumble of rocks marked a shadowed orifice. He turned the Maglite around and offered it to Bradley. "I'll let you do the honors."

Bradley took the heavy flashlight and started toward the opening. He had to scale the fallen stones and duck his head to enter. Fractured segments of bone guided him deeper into the tunnel, which constricted around him, forcing him to stoop.

"We found the rock barricade exactly like you saw it," Reaves said from behind him, his voice made hollow by the acoustics. "Not neatly unstacked, but toppled. We suspect it was knocked down from this side, by something that desperately wanted to get to the meat inside the main chamber."

"They buried live animals down here?"

"Just keep going," Reaves said.

Bones cracked under Bradley's tread and threw uneven shadows across the stone floor. He ran his fingertips along the wall, which had distinct ridges as though carved by sharp, thin implements. The leading edge of the beam diffused into a larger cave ahead of him. The faintest hint of the orange sunset slanted through gaps in the low ceiling. It appeared as though a rockslide had sealed a natural entrance. Motes of dust sparkled all around him.

The ground was covered with piles of bones. Entire ribcages. Cracked skulls. Shattered pelvises and femora. Both human and animal. The mounds were tangled with hair and fur. It looked like a bear's den.

Time had leeched the stench of fresh kill, leaving the musty, mildewed smell of a crypt.

"At the back of the chamber," Reaves whispered. "On the other side of the remains."

Bradley had to remove the handkerchief from his face to balance on the bones. The flashlight beam swept across the desiccated figures propped against the cavern wall, casting vaguely hominid shadows onto the sandstone.

"They sealed them in here when they abandoned the pueblo," Reaves said softly, almost reverentially. "And shortly thereafter started building high up on the sheer cliffs to the northwest."

"There are more than enough bones here to assemble fifty skeletons," Bradley said.

He crouched in front of the only two intact carcasses in the chamber. They were gaunt, their flesh mummified, parchment skin stretched across knobby bones, cloaked in shadows. He raised the flashlight toward their faces—

"Jesus!"

Bradley toppled backward onto the bones and scrabbled away from the bodies.

"This is why the Anasazi fled Chaco Canyon," Reaves said. He clapped Bradley on the shoulder. "Like I said, you wouldn't have believed me if I'd told you."

Two

Kilinailau Trench
South Pacific Ocean
176 km East of New Ireland Island, Papua New Guinea
November 26th
11:58 a.m. PGT

Present Day

The deep sea submersible cruised over a mat of gray lava pillows the size of boulders, twenty-two hundred meters beneath the surface of the Pacific Ocean. Far off in the murky black distance rose the rugged rim of the Kilinailau Trench, formed by the subduction of the Pacific tectonic plate beneath the Bismarck microplate. Their movement resulted in a steady flow of magma and geothermal heat from the Earth's molten core. Forty-five hundred watts of HMI lights mounted on an array of booms, enough to nearly illuminate an entire football stadium, turned the water a midnight blue. Jagged crests of mineral and ore deposits appeared at the extent of the light's reach, where they abruptly climbed hundreds of meters back toward the sun.

After close to four hours of freefall in absolute blackness and another two skimming the bottom of the world, they had finally reached their destination.

The Basilisk Vent Field was a hotbed of geological activity. Seawater that leeched through the silt was superheated, suffused with toxic chemicals and minerals, and funneled back into the ocean at more than seven hundred degrees Fahrenheit through tall chimneys called hydrothermal vents. Seven main chimneys, nicknamed black smokers for the noxious plumes of water that poured out of them like the smoke from a tire fire, were staggered across Basilisk. It was one such formation, a more recent eruption named Medusa, that had summoned them more than a mile down to where the pressure could crumple a man in tin can fashion. Over the last twenty days, intermittent seismic activity had already toppled two of the older chimneys and increased the ambient water temperature by two degrees, which may not have seemed significant to the average man on the street, but reflected a massive expulsion of hydrothermal energy at nearly twice its previous rate. An opportunity like this might not come along again.

The submersible *Corellian*, named after the fictional manufacturer of the escape pod used by R2-D2 and C-3PO in *Star Wars* due to its striking physical resemblance, slowed to zero-point-eight knots as it closed in on the ridge. Its thirty-foot, twenty-eight ton body was primarily fabricated from fiberglass and foam attached to a titanium frame that served as housing for the rear thruster assembly, a series of lights and cameras on forward-facing booms, and the two-inch-thick titanium personnel sphere that accommodated a dedicated pilot and two scientific observers. Patterned after the Woods Hole Oceanographic Institution's Deep Submergence vehicle *Alvin*, which had set the standard for nearly half a century, the *Corellian* had cost GeNext Biosystems more than thirty millions dollars to build for its own personal use. Factor in the cost of its mobile berth, the one-hundred-and-seventy-foot Research Vessel *Ernst Mayr* and the salaries of the eighteen scientific researchers and twenty-eight officers and crew, and this was a two hundred million dollar private venture that amounted to little more than deep sea prospecting.

"Medusa rears her ugly head," John Bishop said. The pilot could have passed for a beach bum with his unkempt blonde hair, deep tan, and lazy surfer drawl, but the former Navy Seaman was all business when he assumed the helm. He eased back on the throttle and watched through the foot-wide porthole as they approached the hellish eight-story behemoth. The *Corellian* had been equipped with a thirty-six inch LCD screen that relayed the footage from the digital video assembly mounted above the window so that the pilot no longer had to press his face against the reinforced glass to see where he was going, but Bishop was old-school. His motto was *I didn't come all the way down here to watch it on TV.*

Dr. Tyler Martin shifted his lanky six-foot frame. His unruly chestnut hair fell in front of his brown eyes. He tucked his bangs behind his ears and leaned back from the port view window, where he had been watching the lava fields transform into sharp crests that came to life with scuttling crabs and shrimp, and turned to face the monitor. The digital clarity surpassed even what he could see with his own eyes.

The live feed focused on the chimney, a great branching trunk composed of anhydrite, and copper, iron, and zinc sulfide precipitates. Black smoke poured out of various openings reminiscent of the pipes on some bizarre Dr. Seuss machination and roiled toward the sky. Six-foot tube worms that looked like crimson tulips bloomed from chitinous tunnels, filtering the hydrogen sulfide from the scalding water, which fueled the chemosynthetic bacteria in their guts, the source of all life in this strange ecosystem. White Yeti crabs snapped at the worms while clouds of ghostly shrimp swirled from one toxic flume to the next. Golden mussels and pale anemones staked claim to every spare inch of space. An octopus squirmed away from their lights.

"You guys ready to get to work?" Bishop asked.

"Might as well, you know, since we're already down here and all," Dr. Courtney Martin said. With her long auburn hair and emerald eyes, it was nearly impossible to tell that she and Tyler were related. His little sister snuggled up to the starboard viewport, where she could use the control panel to her right to manipulate the retractable armature. The monitor above her head displayed footage from the camera affixed to its hydraulic claw.

"How close can you get us?" Tyler asked.

He dimmed the screens that displayed their GPS data and bathymetric maps to better see the monitor for his own armature.

"Close enough to count the hairs on a crab's ass."

Bishop smirked. He had logged more than four thousand hours in this very submersible over the last three years and took his job so seriously that he even catheterized himself prior to launch so that nothing would distract him from his duties. He maneuvered the *Corellian* with such fluidity that it seemed like an extension of his body, an exoskeleton of sorts.

"Take us up about thirty feet," Courtney said. "You see where the chimney forks like a cactus? Right there by those two vents where all the smoke's coming from. That work for you, Ty?"

"Perfectly," he said.

He fiddled with the armature controls, flexing the elbow, testing the clamps. Satisfied, he used it to pinch the handle of his collecting device, a tubular bioreactor that looked like an industrial coffee dispenser, and drew it out of its housing beneath the sphere.

"Sonar's registering seismic activity," Courtney said. "Looks like a swarm of mini-quakes."

"It's been like that for the last three weeks," Bishop said. "It comes and goes."

As Bishop watched, several of the fluted pipes broke away from the chimney and tumbled toward the sea floor, dragging crabs and anemones with them. There was a flicker of light as magma oozed out of the ground and immediately cooled to a gray crust.

Courtney bumped him from behind, knocking him forward against the glass. Three of them in that diminutive metal ball was like keeping a trio of goldfish in a wine glass. With the rounded walls racked with equipment and monitors of all kinds, it barely left room for them to squat on top of each other in what amounted to an uncomfortable, padded pit. There was barely space for them to kneel. The air was damp and sweaty. Fortunately, that was one luxury they had in abundance. There was enough oxygen for forty hours, while their dive was timed for only ten. Of course, that wouldn't matter if the sphere breached. The pressure would compress the titanium shell and the equipment, with them right there in the middle, into a metallic tomb the size of a basketball.

Three

My Son Ruins
69 km Southwest of Da Nang
Quang Nam Province, Vietnam
March 12ᵗʰ
9:46 a.m. ICT

Seven Years Ago

Dr. Brendan Reaves shoved through the overgrowth of fan-leafed dipterocarps, palm trees, and conifers and stepped out into a small clearing, if it indeed qualified as such. The blazing sun reached the moldering detritus in slanted columns that stained the early morning mist like penlights shined through the dense canopy. Before him stood a knoll upon which a stone *linga*, a symbol of the worship of Bhadresvara, the local variant of the Hindu god Shiva, had been erected. The sculpted red stone was furry with moss and shrouded by a proliferation of vines and grasses, most of which had been ripped away and lay in brown tangles at its foot. Four identical life-size faces of Shiva had been sculpted to mark the cardinal directions of the compass on the three-foot-tall pedestal. The diety's slender face tapered to a point at his chin, where a garland of snakes encircled his neck. A crescent moon framed his braided hair, which was coiled into a conch shape on top of his head. His flat eyes, of which there were three, stared indifferently into the jungle. Excavated dirt and stones ringed a dark opening in the base of the hill.

He wiped the sheen of sweat from his brow and tried not to think about whatever was crawling on his skin beneath his damp khakis. The assault of the insects had begun the moment he stepped out of the rental Jeep at the My Son ruins, arguably the crown jewel of the Champa Empire, which ruled Central Vietnam from the fourth through fourteenth centuries. Phuong Dinh, a former student who had been with him on the Chaco dig, had been waiting at the A1 temple as she had said she would be, leaning against what little remained after it was shelled during the war, the first rays of dawn caressing her tan skin and making her rich hair glimmer with reddish highlights. She had smiled so broadly when she saw him that he couldn't help but reciprocate. She was no longer the shy and unassuming girl she had once been, but a confident woman, now a colleague, whose dark eyes lit up when she bounded down the slope and gave him a hug. He remembered the splay of freckles dotting the bridge of her nose.

"Look at you," Reaves had said. "All grown up."

"I can tie my own shoes now and everything." She smirked. "You haven't aged a day, Dr. Reaves."

He tried not to blush.

"It's Brendan to you now, Dr. Dinh." His relationship with Phuong had always been somewhat unique. She'd been closer to his age than that of her classmates, and had been driven by an inner fire that often eclipsed his own. As the daughter of an American soldier who had quite possibly died somewhere in these very hills, she had been raised in poverty by a single mother who spoke only Vietnamese, yet she had risen above her circumstances thanks to the desire to better understand the two dichotomous worlds that she felt both a part of and alienated from at the same time. It gave Reaves no small pleasure to see that she was now totally in her element. "I can't tell you how proud I am that you're doing exactly what you set out to do."

It was Phuong's turn to blush.

"We're burning daylight," she said. "We have a long hike ahead of us."

He donned his backpack and followed her into the jungle on a path the trees seemed desperate to reclaim even as they traversed it. During the three-hour hike in the dim twilight provided by the dense canopy, they had caught up with each others' lives and the accomplishments of the intervening years, while swarms of insects hummed and buzzed around them, finches and wrens chirped, and snub-nosed monkeys screeched. He'd been somewhat embarrassed to explain why he had left his post at Washington State to work exclusively for GeNext. It still felt like a betrayal of the anthropological tenets he had preached to his students, but Phuong understood. After all, she was one of the select few who'd seen the remains beneath Casa Rinconada, a sight that no one who witnessed it would ever forget. GeNext had given him the opportunity of a lifetime. He had carte blanche to travel anywhere in the world, to dig wherever he wanted, without having to beg for grants or even give a second thought to the financial side, and rather than focus on the evolution of a single society, he had the unprecedented chance to broaden his scope to encompass the entirety of the human species.

He approached the hole in the ground slowly, taking in even the most seemingly insignificant sights and sounds with each step. This was the part that he loved the most, those first eager steps toward a discovery held captive by the earth for hundreds, maybe thousands of years, as if patiently waiting for the perfect moment to reveal her secrets. Or perhaps for the perfect person to whom to reveal them. So what if he hadn't instigated the dig or troweled out the loam one scoop at a time? It still belonged to him. Of that there was no doubt. It called to him like a mother's song only remembered subconsciously through the memory of a child.

His hands trembled as he shed his backpack and withdrew his digital camera.

"We discovered it almost by accident," Phuong said. "A monsoon swept through here just over a month ago. The rain exposed the hint of a brick wall built into the hill. It took a while to clear the dirt from around it, but after that, the bricks were easy enough to unstack."

"What am I looking at?"

Reaves walked a slow circle around the clearing, taking pictures of the *linga* from every possible angle.

"It's a *Sivalinga*, which symbolically represents the god Shiva himself. The Champa built these all across the countryside before they abandoned the region in the early fifteenth century to the Viet. This one's similar to those back at the ruins where you met me, only much more elaborate. The chamber beneath it, however, is completely unique."

"The photographs you sent me...they were taken down there?"

Phuong nodded and gestured toward the shadowed orifice. Reaves couldn't quite read the expression on her face.

He leaned over the hole and took several quick pictures. The flash limned decomposing brick walls crawling with roots and spider webs, and a decrepit stone staircase leading downward into the pitch black. He removed his flashlight from his pack and followed the beam underground. Dust swirled in the column of light, which spread across the brick-tiled floor riddled with moss and fungal growth a dozen steps down. He smelled damp earth and mildew; the faintly organic scent of the tomb. His rapid breathing echoed back at him from the hollow chamber.

When he reached the bottom, he snapped several more shots. The brief strobes highlighted stone walls sculpted with ornate friezes, a scattering of bones on the ground, and a central altar of some kind, upon which rested what he had traveled all this way to see in person. He walked slowly toward it, taking pictures with each step. The carvings on the wall were savage. Each depicted a malevolent Shiva lording over a scene of carnage with his adversaries lifeless at his feet or suspended from one of his many arms. The bones on the floor were broken and disarticulated and heaped into mounds, aged to the color of rust, and woven together by webs that housed the carcasses of countless generations of insects.

His heart rate accelerated. This chamber was similar in so many ways to the one back in Chaco Canyon, which had dominated all of his thoughts during the last five years.

He finally brought the flashlight to bear on the altar.

"It gives me the chills every time I see it," Phuong said.

Reaves felt it too, almost as though the object seated on the rounded platform radiated a coldness that was released by the exposure to light.

"Carbon dating confirms that it was sealed in here more than five hundred years ago, about the time that the Champa vacated the area." She wrapped her arms around her chest and shivered. "It's just like the others, isn't it?"

Reaves could only nod as he approached. His beam focused on the skull seated on the dusty platform and threw its shadow onto the far wall, which made the hellish designs waver as though the many Shivas were laughing with a sound his mind interpreted as the crackle of flames.

"Jesus Christ," he whispered.

Fissures transected the frontal bone, the orbital sockets given sentience by the reflected light from the spider webs inside. A large stone had been thrust between its jaws with such force that the mandibular rami to either side had cracked.

And then, of course, there were its teeth.

Four

Kilinailau Trench
South Pacific Ocean
176 km East of New Ireland Island, Papua New Guinea
November 26ᵗʰ
12:13 p.m. PGT

Present Day

The *Corellian* leveled off and Bishop pivoted the light and camera arrays to focus on the chimney through the roiling black smoke, which was really a toxic soup of tiny metallic sulfide particles.

Dr. Tyler Martin could barely contain his excitement. For the last six years, since completing his doctorate in Molecular and Cellular Biology at Dartmouth, he'd been studying microorganisms classified as extremophiles, prokaryotic bacteria that were not only capable of surviving the harshest conditions on the planet, but of thriving in environments that killed all other types of life. They formed the bottom of the deep sea food chain, and provided theoretical proof that life could flourish under any conditions. These were microscopic bugs that functioned in the same capacity as plants on dry land, but while plants used the process of photosynthesis to essentially capture the power of the sun and produce the oxygen necessary to sustain terrestrial life, extremophiles chemosynthesized hydrogen sulfide to generate energy. Some scientists went so far as to speculate that these very organisms he now prepared to capture and bring to the surface were the origin of life on Earth, from which all higher orders of animals evolved. The recent surge in seismic activity offered him the rare opportunity to potentially collect new species that might be forced nearer the oceanic crust from where they dwelled in the deeper strata. Such a discovery would not only afford him the chance to be the first to study them; it would allow him to put his stamp on the entire field.

While extremophiles in general were capable of surviving everywhere from beneath the frozen Antarctic ice caps to the fiery heart of a volcano, it was the facultative thermophilic branch, those that thrived with intense heat and pH levels, but could survive lower temperatures, that intrigued him. Most people weren't even aware of their existence, yet these bacteria were part of their everyday lives. They were used in the manufacture of detergents and perfume, in food processing plants, and to clean up oil spills. There was even a species called *thermus aquaticus*, discovered in a hot spring in Yellowstone National Park, that produced an enzyme called Taq I, which made it possible using restriction fragment length polymorphism technology to create human genomic fingerprints, the kind used in forensic science to match DNA and solve crimes. This enzyme could copy billions of strands of DNA in just a few short hours. That one species alone had already generated more than two billion dollars in royalties for the company that held the patent, which was where GeNext came into the picture. The race was on between biotech firms to harness the power of these bacteria. Research teams were being dispatched all across the globe, to the highest mountaintops, the densest jungles, and in Tyler's case, the deepest oceanic trenches, in the name of progress and profit.

He manipulated the armature to position the bioreactor, which would allow him to maintain the proper temperature and chemical concentrations while agitating the sample to prevent sedimentation, directly into the black smoke.

"Come here, little guy," Courtney said. "Stick that head out just a bit farther."

Tyler glanced over Courtney's shoulder at her monitor. She had nearly coaxed one of the long worms out of its tube and into a collection bin similar to his. The worm owed its scarlet coloration to the presence of hemoglobin, the very same constituent of blood that flowed through human veins. Courtney was peripherally involved with the creation of a synthetic blood substitute, another multi-billion dollar industry. With shortages in blood banks and the dwindling number of donors, artificial plasma would save hundreds of thousands of lives, and while there was legislation in place to prevent the cloning of human blood cells, there were no such restrictions for this odd invertebrate.

He tilted the bioreactor and allowed the smoke to flow directly up into it.

With a lurch, the *Corellian* canted nose down. A screen of bubbles flooded up across his line of sight.

"What was that?" Courtney asked.

"The water temperature just shot up nearly two degrees," Bishop said. "Sonar confirms we've got ourselves a trembler."

"It felt like we were hit by a truck."

"Strap on your seatbelts, kids. These quakes can make maneuvering a little dicey."

Tyler's screen filled with black smoke. He lost sight of his armature and the controls became unresponsive. The submersible swung sideways and collided with the chimney, slamming him against his viewport. Through the superheated water, he watched a fissure race across the width of the smokestack.

"Oh, God."

The crack expanded and a black cloud billowed up against the glass. A curtain of bubbles cleared his porthole and he saw only a column of churning black water where the hydrothermal vent had once been. Where was the rest—?

Something slammed into the submersible from above, driving them down toward the ocean floor. Chunks of the shattered chimney rained past them on the monitors.

The thrusters whined as Bishop fought to reverse their rapid descent with the weight of the upper half of the chimney lodged against their hull.

"Come on, baby," Bishop said.

The jagged sea bed raced toward them. They were going to impact head on. The ground cracked like an eggshell, only the crevices glowed red. Magma poured out of the earth. As soon as it met with the water, it began to darken and issue bubbles and smoke. Rock formations crumbled and toppled into the lava in slow motion.

They were going to die.

"Come on, baby. Come on!"

Tyler pressed his hands against the glass as though he could prevent it from shattering or melting in the burbling cauldron. He heard screams and vaguely recognized them as his own.

His armature swung across his view, whipping the bioreactor past like a lure on a fishing line.

Another thud against the submersible from behind. The personnel sphere swung upward toward a mile of empty water and he was thrown away from the window. Courtney slammed into him, pounding his back against a rack of equipment. He wrapped his arms around her and tried to shield her with his body.

They were going to die.

He was certain that at any moment the sphere would collapse in upon itself. Would he feel it when his body was compressed to nearly the atomic level?

Bishop stood on top of them and piloted the craft straight up. At least they were headed in the right direction, but if he didn't level it off quickly, the engine would stall and drop them down to their deaths.

"Come on, baby!"

Slowly, Bishop righted the *Corellian* fifty meters above where Medusa had once stood. All that remained now was a jumble of rubble sinking into the molten abyss. The black smoke no longer funneled but exploded from the crater. Ribbons of magma spread across the field below them. The entire topography had been dramatically altered in less than a minute.

Another shudder and an expulsion of bubbles and scalding water propelled them toward the surface.

The dysfunctional robotic arm hung lifeless in front of Tyler's viewport.

The bioreactor was still clamped in its hydraulic pincers.

Five

6 km North of the Bilbao Ruins
Escuintla Department, Guatemala
December 9th
2:29 p.m. CST

Four Years Ago

Bradley didn't see the crevice until he was nearly upon it. After close to half a day of battling his way through the seemingly impregnable forest of ceiba and kapok trees on a path that barely qualified as an animal trail with the weight of his pack on his back, he nearly collapsed to his knees in relief. Roland Pike appeared unfazed by the exertion. He merely set down his rucksack, returned his GPS unit to the side pouch, and removed the hydro bladder, which he passed to Bradley before taking a long drink himself. The branches of the canopy overhead were woven together to hide the sky, save for one shifting gap through which the gray cone of Mt. Fuego rose over them like a thorn prodding heaven's gut. An intricate network of climbing ropes had been strung around the trunks and up into the branches where carabiners glinted through the leaves. The remainder of the ropes, hardly distinguishable from the vines, trailed down into the ground, where a lightning bolt-fracture in the limestone coursed through the detritus. A faint clamor of clattering tools and muffled voices echoed hollowly from below.

A dozen eight-foot-tall obsidian statues surrounded them. The branches of the lower canopy had been cut back and the moss had been scraped away to expose the identical black volcanic stone sculptures. Elaborate headdresses adorned the crowns of their skeletal faces, beneath which they wore collars made of bells. All of them had been turned so that they looked down upon the hole, as though keeping eternal watch. In the email he had received with the pictures of the site, Reaves had identified this disturbing character as Ah Puch, the Mayan god of death, who ruled their version of hell, Xibalba.

His exhaustion replaced by a growing sense of excitement, Bradley shed his burden and walked to the edge of the fissure. A cool breeze gusted up into his face, chilling the sweat that matted his prematurely graying hair. Vines and roots cascaded down through the opening in a vegetative waterfall that reached nearly a hundred feet down to the placid black water. A ring of lights had been affixed to the rock walls of the pit and directed toward the middle, where they hardly penetrated the deep lake, which was part of an underground river system that extended for hundreds of kilometers through a honeycomb of impassable tunnels in the strata. Several men-made-shadows by the fierce halogens stood on the rocky ledge of the pool amid stalagmites nearly as tall as they were. Portable generators provided a humming drone barely distinguishable from the whine of the mosquitoes that had followed them from the Mayan ruins at Bilbao.

Bradley smiled and turned back to Pike, who had already hauled up the harness and held it at the ready.

"You want to go down there, or should I make some sandwiches first?" Pike asked through a faint smile that looked unnatural on his ordinarily impassive face. The diffused sunlight washed out his features and whitened his hair. His blue eyes stood out like amethysts stomped into snow.

"I was debating a siesta, but since we've come all this way…"

Bradley clapped his longtime associate on the shoulder and slipped his legs into the harness. Once it was tightened to his satisfaction, he again approached the sharp-edged orifice. With a glance back at Pike, who nodded his readiness, Bradley took hold of the rope and stepped out over the nothingness. He twirled in slow circles as Pike belayed him down into the earth. Flies buzzed around his head and the roots brushed at him as he dropped in smooth increments. Soon, the ragged hole above him was a faint scar of shadow against what little he could see of the domed ceiling through the tube of roots, which swayed gently on the planet's breath. It grew more humid as he descended, yet it smelled more like a mountain stream, crisp and cold, than a guano-riddled sinkhole under the primal jungle. The lights became brighter and words spoken in Spanish resolved from the din.

Twenty-four hours ago, he had been the keynote speaker at a biotechnology symposium in Stockholm when Reaves had called. Pike had motioned him to the side of the stage, and after a moment of whispered conversation, they had simply hurried out of the hall, leaving behind a packed house of the world's greatest scientific minds to blink at each other in confusion. Two hours later they had been on the corporate Challenger 300 Super Midjet, streaking toward the southern hemisphere. A Land Rover had been waiting for them at the airport in Puerto San José, and had whisked them through the pre-dawn fog to the old ruins.

They had caught a break on this one. An archaeologist from the University of Liverpool in England, who had been restoring the statuary in Monument Plaza at the Bilbao ruins, had discovered the Ah Puch ring almost by chance and had posted pictures of it on the university's website. Reaves had recognized it as potentially more than just a random creation in the middle of the vast forest and had gambled that there was greater significance. The statues had been arranged as though they were guarding something, not simply forced to stare at each other for eternity, which was contrary to the more traditional motif of posting them to face outward. While Reaves had guessed wrong in the past, most notably on expensive digs in the raised peat bogs of central Ireland and in the Godavari River basin of India, he had at least learned from each failure. Both of their previous findings had been discovered in the ruins of societies that were historically notorious for instances of cannibalism, and that had abruptly abandoned primitive meccas at the height of their prowess. The revelation that both of them had been spurred to flight shortly after verifiable volcanic events—in the case of the Anasazi, the eruption of the Sunset Cone in 1150, and for the Champa, the surge in activity in the Haut Dong Nai volcanic field mere kilometers from Mỹ Sơn—allowed him to narrow their focus even more. Of course, advances in technology helped, as well. When Reaves located an area of interest, all they had to do now was send an aircraft fitted with remote sensing devices over the treetops. The multispectral imaging equipment collected the signals and translated them into three-dimensional digital elevation and digital terrain models that showed every detail of the ground, right down to the individual blades of grass, and below. If there was anything buried in the soil, be it ancient ruins reclaimed by the earth or a mass burial site, the sensors would detect it and create detailed representations. And while nothing of greater importance than the Ah Puch statues had been detected aboveground, something intriguing had been visualized forty-two feet below the surface of the subterranean pool, something that caused Bradley's pulse to race and his palms to dampen on the cord as he was lowered down into the blinding field of light.

"I was starting to think you weren't going to make it in time," Reaves called up to him.

"Wouldn't have missed it for the world." Bradley dropped below the convergence of the spotlights. Reaves's silhouette resolved from the shadows to his left as he leaned out over the water, grabbed Bradley's harness, and hauled him over to the rock ledge. "Have you seen it yet?"

Reaves flashed a devious smile. His wet suit still glistened with beaded water.

"So you're sure it's one of ours?" Bradley asked. He stepped out of the rope seat and heard it zip up away from him while he readjusted his cargo pants.

"Without a doubt."

There was a splashing sound behind him. Bradley turned to see a scuba diver breach the surface. He couldn't recognize the man for the mask and the mouthpiece, but he did recognize the acetylene torch he clutched to his chest.

"There's no way we're getting it out of there without cutting the chain," the man said. Bradley finally identified him as Barrett Walker, a young geologist they had lured away from the United States Geological Survey for his field experience. "That boulder it's attached to is wedged down there pretty tight. We'd need a crane—"

"Cut it," Bradley said.

Walker grinned, shoved the regulator back into his mouth, and dove back under the water. Bradley watched the dark pool until what looked like a distant star flared into being. The digital elevation model had shown a human form pinned to the bottom, its arms sprawled beside its head. A length of chain was wrapped around its torso and legs.

"The body isn't just bound in chains as we initially thought," Reaves said. "They're also coiled around a rock the size of a file cabinet. My guess is they somehow lassoed her with the chain and rolled the rock down through the opening up there in the jungle floor, dragging her right along with it."

"'Her'?"

"The pubic bones and sciatic notches seem to think so."

With a whizzing sound, Pike plummeted down toward them before effortlessly halting his progress. He swung over to the ledge and slipped out of the harness.

A rush of bubbles popped on the pool, making the surface appear to boil. The ghostly light faded from below and a dark shape slowly rose toward them.

Bradley was so excited he could barely think straight, let alone speak. He realized he was holding his breath when he saw sparkles in his peripheral vision.

Walker spit out the regulator when his head crested the surface.

"Someone want to give me a hand with this thing?"

Bradley threw himself to all fours and reached down into the water as Walker paddled toward them, cradling the skeleton in his arms.

"The chain's rusted solid," he said. "I just cut the whole thing away from the boulder. I didn't want to risk the integrity of the body by trying to cut it off down there."

The two locals they had hired to help rig the lines and run the lighting cursed in Spanish and scuttled back into the shadows when the light caught the remains. Reaves and Pike knelt to either side of Bradley and helped raise the skeleton out onto a flat section of limestone.

All of the flesh had long since dissolved, leaving the stark white bones tenuously articulated by knots of cartilage. The left foot was gone, as were the fingers on the right hand. The ribs were cracked and rust-stained where the chain constricted the chest. A single loop was tightened around the neck. The legs and pelvis displayed only minor remodeling: a healed spiral fracture of the left lateral malleolus, and periosteal deformities where the outer sheath of bone had been peeled slightly away from the medial femoral condyles and greater trochanters. There was mild reversal of the normal lumbar curvature and exaggerated cervical lordosis, which combined suggested a markedly hunched posture.

But, as with the others they had found, it was the head that immediately drew their attention. The foramen magnum, the hole in the base of the skull through which the spinal cord passed to the brain, was widened and elongated, and patterned with a faint network of stress fractures that reflected slow but steady outward force. The cranial sutures were abnormally deep and clearly defined. And the teeth…the alveolar sockets into which the roots plugged had ossified into sharp hook-like protuberances.

"The centipede, Shiva, Ah Puch," Reaves whispered. His brow furrowed as he pressed the pad of his index finger against one of the pointed growths. A bead of blood swelled from the skin as he drew it away. "They believed these people were the physical manifestations of their most vengeful gods, sent from the fiery heart of the Earth to punish them."

Bradley looked up into Reaves's face. The anthropologist's eyes grew distant and he could see Reaves mentally struggling to grasp an elusive thought. His lips moved silently with some inner dialogue. After a long moment, an expression of calmness washed over his face. The corners of his lips curled up into a smile as he met each of their eyes in turn.

"I think I've deciphered the pattern."

Bradley could only pray Reaves was right. He returned his attention to the mouth of the skeleton on the ground before him.

It was like looking into the jaws of a shark.

Six

Kilinailau Trench
South Pacific Ocean
176 km East of New Ireland Island, Papua New Guinea
November 26ᵗʰ
4:32 p.m. PGT

Present Day

Dr. Courtney Martin had never been so happy to see the sun in her entire life. She thought she was going to die down there, and by all rights, would have were it not for Bishop's almost superhuman maneuvering. They should have known better than to proceed into the Basilisk Field with the level of seismic activity and the unstable nature of the ridge, but the temptation had just been too great. When would anyone ever have that kind of opportunity again? Her hands still shook, even after hours of trying to steady her nerves as the *Corellian* slowly floated back to the surface. Or maybe it was the excitement of realizing that despite everything that had happened, she had managed to secure a prime example of *Riftia pachyptila*, the tube worm that now resided coiled in the canister she lugged at her side down the hallway away from the submersible hanger.

"Wait up!" Ty called from behind her. He tried to jog, but with the weight of his dented bioreactor, it was more of a shamble.

The main deck of the Research Vessel *Ernst Mayr* housed the majority of the scientific suites. There were machine and electronics shops, and a divers locker nearest the hanger, a two-story garage with a sled on rails to slide the *Corellian* back and forth from its launch. Moving toward the bow, there were fully equipped laboratories of all kinds: hydrologic, computer, a massive general lab, and a biology/analytical clean lab. GeNext had spared no expense in equipping what amounted to the most advanced mobile research platform ever put to sea.

There were four functional decks above them. The 01 Deck housed the mess and galley, the emergency generator room, lounge, library, and the scientific personnel quarters, while the remainder of the crew boarded on the 02 Deck with the hospital suite. The Master Quarters on the smaller 03 Deck were reserved for the Captain, his officers, and the chief scientists. Above that on the 04 Deck were the radio/chart room, the surface control station, and the pilothouse, from the top which the communications tower reached another twenty-five feet into the sky.

Ty caught up to her and threw his arm around her shoulder. He smelled of brine and sweat, a scent that reminded her of his pigsty of a bedroom as a teenager in Wildwood, New Jersey. She imagined she was pretty ripe herself.

"It's crazy back there," he said. "Pretty much the entire crew's in the hanger preparing to disassemble the *Corellian*. They're going to have to strip her and basically rebuild her from scratch. Did you see how badly beat up she was?"

Courtney shook her head. She had climbed out the hatch and refused to look at the battered vessel even as it was hauled out of the ocean by a massive A-frame crane and taxied into the hanger. She knew how close they had come to dying without the visual confirmation.

Both of them landing the assignment on the *Mayr* had been a real coup. It was the opportunity of a lifetime, and they had needed to sell themselves as the very best in their fields to beat out dozens of applicants from the many GeNext-funded research labs filled with the most brilliant and ambitious scientists in the world. It was the first time that she had ever stood on level ground with her brother. Ty was the golden child, for whom everything had always come so easily. All of her life, she had dwelled in his shadow. All of her teachers had expected better from her than she could deliver based on their experiences with her brother. How many times had she seen that same expression on their faces, the one that begged the question, "Are you *sure* you're related to Tyler Martin?" Even her parents, in their loving yet condescending way, had always treated her as though she needed an extra boost to succeed, while expecting less of her in the process. She couldn't blame any of them, though. Ty was a genius and had never been anything other than wonderful to her, or anyone else for that matter.

It wasn't until her college years at Rutgers that she had stepped into a spotlight of her own. Not only had she graduated at the top of her class from one of the most prestigious marine biology programs in the nation, but she had been able to forge an identity of her own, entirely independent of his. Now, here she was on a commission so many of her colleagues would have given an arm for, preparing to isolate the hemoglobin from a deep sea worm few even knew existed in hopes of revolutionizing the health care industry, and her brother couldn't have been happier for her. She could see it in his eyes, hear it in his voice. Ty had never felt the same need to compete with her. He had always believed in her, and had been there every step of the way to protect her from the big bad world, even when she didn't need it. There was no one else on earth she would rather have working at her side right now. Even if he *was* in desperate need of a shower.

"What do you say to a late dinner tonight once we're done in the lab?" she asked.

"Sounds good to me. I can't imagine it'll take me more than a couple of hours to transfer samples to the main batch reactor and the continuous culture module."

They reached the door labeled "Biology/ Clean Lab." Ty pressed his thumb to the scanner on the security panel, then lifted it away from the pink digital representation of his print. The lock disengaged with a click and the stainless steel door slid back into the recessed wall. Once they passed through, it closed again behind them with little more than a whisper.

The lights were bright enough to shame the sun. It always took Courtney several moments for her eyes to adjust. There were several hooded microarray work stations where isolates were heated, centrifuged, and incubated in the center of the room on an island surrounded by stools. Beside them were various matching off-white machines attached to computer keypads and monitors: a dual absorbance detector, a separation module, an auto sampler, a refraction index detector, a continuous culture module, a gas chromatograph/mass spectrometer, and a real time PCR machine. There were buttons, wires, tubes, and blinking lights everywhere.

Their lab assistants were already there, warming up the equipment and running through the transfer protocols. Both were graduate students paying their dues and hoping to weasel their names into print when the time came to publish. Both of them glanced up from their tasks, then resumed them with renewed vigor.

Ty branched to the right and made his way to the far right corner of the laboratory while Courtney headed toward the back of the room. A one thousand gallon aquarium made from the same glass as the portholes of the submersible waited for her. The heated seawater inside was pressurized to one hundred and fifty atmospheres and flooded with hydrogen sulfide gas that funneled up through a salvaged section of the collapsed hydrothermal vent Godzilla, complete with empty tubes from the worms that had abandoned it.

"We heard what happened down there," her assistant said. Kim Stanley was a graduate student at the Scripps Institute of Oceanography working on her PhD in Marine Biology. With her diminutive size and stunning traditional Asian features, she looked like a geisha in baggy overalls. "I'm so glad that you're all right."

"There was never any doubt." Courtney forced a smile and latched her collection canister onto the airlock built into the side of the tank. The seal disengaged with a hiss. Water from the aquarium raced into a chamber that surrounded the inner housing where the worm rested. Once the pressure and temperature equalized, she would open the inner gasket and allow the worm to wriggle out into its new home. "I don't think Bishop even broke a sweat."

"We could feel the quake all the way up here. It was like the ocean just dropped out from under the ship."

"It wasn't that bad down there." Courtney didn't want to talk about it anymore. She was still shaken up. It was all she could do to steady her hands. "Can you monitor the gauges and flood the bin when everything's stabilized?"

She turned away without waiting for a response. While she had time to kill, she might as well see if there was something she could do to help Ty. He crouched at the far end of the room next to an industrial-size batch reactor that reminded her of a beer vat. Hoses snaked from the side of the unit to wall-mounted nozzles that issued steady streams of compressed gasses. Devin Wallace, a

Microbiology and Virology doctoral candidate from the University of Pennsylvania, monitored the power, enthalpy, heat transfer coefficient, and wall temperature gauges on a touchscreen display. His shaggy brown hair kept falling over his glasses, which triggered his annoying habit of jutting forth his lower jaw so he could blow his bangs aside. He wore a thin, patchy beard in an effort to look older than his twenty-four years. His six and a half feet of little more than skin and bones had earned him the nickname Lurch.

Ty glanced up and winked as she neared. He was kneeling beside the portable bioreactor, coupling the transfer tubing. He stood and wiped his palms on his pants.

"Shall we do this?" he asked through a smirk.

"Ready when you are," Devin said. He tapped the screen with a long, bony finger. "Initiating sequence."

With a whirring sound, the batch reactor began to inhale the contents of the bioreactor. Courtney felt the vibrations through her feet. She was ten steps away when she heard a loud *crack* and something metallic pinged off into the corner of the lab. Pressurized steam fired from the bioreactor's ruptured seal directly at Ty's head. He shouted and threw himself to the ground, where he rolled onto his side and pawed at his face.

The smell of rotten eggs filled the air, signaling the release of poisonous hydrogen sulfide gas.

"Ty!" Courtney screamed, and broke into a sprint.

Devin was faster. He slapped the emergency button on the wall. A Plexiglas barrier shot down from the ceiling and embedded itself in the floor, effectively sealing off that entire portion of the lab. The ceiling vents kicked on and a klaxon blared.

"Ty!" Courtney threw herself against the barrier over and over. "Ty!"

She was helpless but to watch as the steam intensified and filled the cordoned chamber like a sauna. Devin's silhouette ran to Ty's side, hauled him to his feet, and dragged him in the direction of the emergency shower stall. For a long moment, she could see nothing through the roiling haze and condensation, and could only pace and scream in futility. When the overhead fans finally sucked the steam through the hoods, she saw both men squeezed together in the clear glass emergency shower stall, fully clothed, soaked to the bone. Both of them held oxygen masks over their mouths and noses, connecting them to the wall by long tubes. Ty offered a wave of assurance, but she could clearly see the pain in his eyes as he walked toward her. When he reached her, he raised his hand and pressed his palm to the Plexiglas.

Courtney matched the gesture. Her hand looked like a child's against his. The entire left half of his face was lobster-red, but she didn't see any sign of blisters or lesions. He struggled to keep his left eye open. It was shot through with irritated vessels and issued a constant dribble of tears.

She sobbed with relief and reached helplessly toward his cheek.

The Hazmat crew stampeded into the room, still shrugging into their gear. Hands seized her shoulders and dragged her away from Ty. She strained to free herself, all the while watching Ty's pained expression fade into the distance until she was shoved into the hallway and the steel lab door whooshed closed in her face.

Seven

Makambu Village
Great Rift Valley
East African Rift System
28 km Southwest of Lake Tanganyika
Zambia
June 24ᵗʰ
5:10 p.m. CAT

Five Months Ago

The Bell UH-1 Iroquois helicopter crested the jagged western edge of the valley and swooped down toward the distinct demarcation where the forest gave way to the eternal savannah that stretched as far as the eye could see. Roland Pike scrutinized the topography as they thundered low across the plains. Tall red plateaus lorded over fields of wild grasses interspersed with clusters of Borassus palms, the occasional baobab behemoth, and prickly mopane shrubs. A sulfurous scent rose from the hot springs off to his right, a series of oblong ponds set into a landscape of barren earth, skeletal trees, and swirling steam. Orange and gold colonies of photosynthetic bacterial growth ringed the shallows of the acidic bodies of water, which turned a deep amethyst-blue toward the center where the hydrothermal vents expelled scalding water from the mantle. Two men clad entirely in white Hazmat gear appeared as specters through the mist, silver collection canisters at their feet. They shielded their eyes against the blazing African sun and watched the chopper pass before resuming their tasks. A tan Jeep glinted against the scorched ground.

Pike adjusted the flow of air through the respirator tank attached to the back of his own isolation suit. He was already wet with sweat underneath the high-density polyethylene fiber fabric. Even with the wind rushing in through the open side doors, he felt as though he were being baked alive.

A plume of black smoke funneled into the sky from a ring of trees on the horizon, replacing the smell of rotten eggs with the charnel stench of burning flesh.

The Huey descended, raising a riot of dust in its wake.

Pike recognized the village from the pictures that had been forwarded to his laptop while he was in transit. A wall of lashed straw had been erected around a circular area roughly an eighth of a mile in diameter, in the middle of which were a good dozen circular huts made of mud packed over a framework of branches with conical thatch roofs. Palms and agave trees with their broad, leathery leaves grew from gray dirt packed by countless generations of bare feet. A weather-beaten Jeep and a panel truck that appeared to have been assembled from World War II scrap were parked in the shade of a single baobab tree. Several more men in Hazmat suits stepped out of the pall of smoke that clung to the village and headed toward where the chopper landed in a wash of flattened grasses and stirred dust.

With a nod to the pilot, Pike grabbed his leather overnight bag and an oversize stainless steel briefcase and hopped down onto the Zambian soil. He was barely out from beneath the rotors when the helicopter took to the air again. Its mechanical heartbeat echoed into infinity as it vanished into the eastern sky.

The two men rushed to greet him and led him to the village.

"Give me the details," Pike said. He passed through the entrance and surveyed the scene through steel-gray eyes. Rivulets of sweat trickled down his rugged, leathered face from under his blonde hair. Although the wrinkles around his eyes and mouth betrayed his fifty years, he was better conditioned than most men half his age. "We're wasting time we don't have."

"Twenty-six dead over the course of three days," Avery Brazelton, an Army-trained biochemist, said. "Primarily women, children, and their elderly. There are six survivors. We've been systematically evaluating the remains and taking blood and tissue samples. We're also collecting bacterial growth from the hot springs in order to prepare cultures, as you requested."

"Show me the bodies."

Brazelton and the other man, whom Pike recognized as James Van Horn, a geneticist they had lured away from the Navy, guided him toward the rear of the village. Over the last five years, GeNext had slowly assembled an inner circle of the most brilliant scientific minds to solve the riddle of what they had nicknamed Chaco Man. That brain trust was further divided into two teams, one that convened at irregular intervals at the corporate headquarters as a kind of think tank, and another that worked full-time under Pike's direction. His unit was officially on the books as private security, but that was only a small component of its duties. Pike's men were hand-selected for their experience in the field, preferably under the kind of supervision that only the military could provide. His were men of discretion, who would not betray the secrets of their discoveries and who, most importantly, would follow his orders without question, under any circumstances. These men were chosen for more than their mental acuity. One never knew what kind of trouble one might encounter thousands of miles from civilization.

The smoke thickened as they passed between dwellings with threadbare blankets draped over their open doorways. Rotting agave fruit dotted the ground. The dirt was spattered with dried blood in long arcs and wide blotches, and scarred by the trails left by the corpses that had been dragged to where Pike could now see the flicker of flames consuming what at first looked like a mass of stacked wood. Charred skeletal remains burned black, arms curled to their chests, jaws opened in soundless screams, piled one on top of the other. Two of his men labored over a heap of bodies beside it, photographing and cataloguing the various wounds before tossing the carcasses onto the pyre.

Pike crouched beside one of the cadavers, a woman of no more than thirty. She wore the tatters of a sunflower-yellow dress, presumably donated by one of the wandering missions. The fabric was crisp with blood darker even than her skin. There were scrapes and abrasions on her face, arms, and legs. A deep laceration bisected her left thigh. Her entire backside was distended by putrefaction. And where her abdomen had once been was a gaping maw of crusted blood and severed vessels. Pike noted the exposed lumbar vertebrae and posterior ribs.

"They were all like this," Brazelton said. "Some had more dramatic defensive wounds, but all of them were similarly eviscerated."

"Looks like some kind of animal had its way with her." Pike used a slender stick to peel the edges of the macerated flesh away from her lower anterior ribs. "These are definitely teeth marks."

"We ran off a pack of wild dogs when we arrived, but not all of the teeth imprints are definitively canine."

"Where were the bodies?"

"Just lying there on the ground. We documented where we found each and every one of them."

"No attempt had been made to bury them?"

"Apparently not. The survivors weren't even in the village when we got here. We assume they saw the smoke and followed it here from wherever they were hiding. Just materialized out of the savannah. We have a translator with them now."

Pike studied the other corpses. There were raggedly torn throats, compound fractures of all kinds, and parallel gashes that appeared to have been inflicted by claws. All of them were sunken in the midsection where they had been absolved of their intestines.

"Have they said anything useful?"

"So far, we haven't been able to get a whole lot out of them beyond the same talk of demons."

Pike rose and walked away from the fire to where he could see several natives clad in ill-fitting polo shirts and dirty jeans gathered near a hut to the north with one of his men in soot-stained protective gear. Upon closer inspection, he saw that the mud walls of the dwellings were cracked and had crumbled in sections.

Over the past month, the Western Rift of the Great Rift Valley had been rocked by a series of mini-earthquakes that culminated in a giant quake that tipped the Richter scale at seven-point-four five days ago as the Somalian tectonic plate slowly broke away from the Nubian plate. The Western Rift itself, a monstrous oblong crater formed by the resultant gap, cradled Lake Tanganyika, the world's second deepest freshwater body, which featured more than eighteen hundred kilometers of shoreline shared by Burundi, the Democratic Republic of the Congo, Tanzania, and Zambia. Hydrothermal vents released scalding water from small chimneys in the lake and numerous geothermal springs scattered throughout the countryside. Monitoring stations had registered a four degree increase in the lake's temperature within hours of the quake. Thousands of rainbow-colored cichlids had washed up onto the banks. Wildfires had broken out in the forests along the southwestern fringe of the lake. GeNext had dispatched a scientific team the moment the news crossed the wire, but it wasn't until a native stumbled into the port town of Mpulungu just over forty-eight hours later, carrying his wife's bleeding body and holding closed an abdominal wound that appeared to have been torn by teeth, that Pike had received the call. He had been airborne on a corporate jet in a matter of hours. They had landed at Kilimanjaro International Airport in Tanzania, where he transferred to the contracted Huey.

The man who had escaped this fate had died in a hospital bed next to the one in which his wife had passed, but not before babbling in his delirium about his village coming under siege by demons during the night.

A dark-skinned man Pike didn't recognize emerged from the hut wearing Hazmat gear. This was presumably their Lunda translator. Another man with no such protection followed. His wide eyes and shocked expression spoke volumes about what he had endured over the previous days.

"He says they trapped the demons in a cave," the translator said with a stilted British accent. "In that plateau over there to the northeast."

"Keys," Pike snapped.

"They're still in the ignition," Brazelton said.

Pike sprinted away from the others toward where the Jeep waited. The oxygen tank on his back dramatically slowed him and made it difficult to situate himself behind the wheel. He cranked the ignition and pinned the gas pedal. Brazelton barely had time to lunge into the passenger seat. In the distance to the right, the other Jeep was returning from the geothermal springs at the edge of the forest. Pike found a footpath that led in the direction of the high rock plateau, a great red crown thrust up from the terra, and straddled it with the tires. The entire vehicle bounced and bucked. Mopane bushes scraped through the paint with a screeching sound. Dust bloomed behind them. Pike sighted the escarpment down the rusted hood and urged the vehicle faster.

The shadow of the stone monolith settled over them. Vultures wheeled overhead. Pike saw a fan-shaped swatch of carbon scoring on the sandstone face and made a beeline for it. The golden grass was trampled in lines darkened by blood.

He slammed the brakes when he reached the plateau and leapt out. What at first appeared to be a haphazard jumble of rocks from a landslide resolved into a hurriedly stacked pyramid of soot-stained stones. The ground was gray with ash, highlighting bare human footprints.

"Clear these rocks!" Pike shouted. He threw himself against the pile and tossed the stones aside as quickly as he could. They were still warm to the touch. Fingers of smoke drifted out from the gaps behind them, issuing a scent not dissimilar to the one they had left behind in the village, only with the undercurrent of an alcohol-based accelerant. They hauled the rocks away to reveal a black maw in the stone, a dark tunnel filled with swirling smoke rushing to escape to the outside world. Pike couldn't see a blasted thing. "I need light."

He heard Brazelton's footsteps recede toward the car as he cleared a section large enough to squeeze through.

"Here."

Brazelton held out a long Maglite.

Pike grabbed it, clicked it on, and scrabbled over the stones. Beam pointed ahead of him, he shimmied into the mountain. The earthen walls were coated with charcoal, the ground with ash and burned kindling. There was just enough room to advance on his hands and knees. His light merely stained the smoke. He tried to piece together what had happened. The men had tracked their demons to this cave. They had then piled debris in the tunnel, doused it with alcohol, and set it on fire, which had served to pin their adversaries deeper in the cave while they barricaded it from the outside and listened to those trapped inside burn even as they suffocated in the smoke. That could only mean one thing.

The bodies were still here.

That revelation spurred him to crawl faster. His tank clanged from the solid stone overhead. Singed bones and pebbles pressed into his palms and knees. His light flashed across a charred ribcage where the tunnel widened. He saw branch-like arms and a skull in profile. There were more skeletons in a heap to his left, saved from the worst of the blaze, their flesh desiccated by the smoke and heat. More victims. Bones broken. Gutted.

His rapid breathing echoed inside his helmet in time with his racing pulse.

He swung the light to his right, and there they were. Pressed back into the corner. Two bodies. What little remained of their flesh was crisp and charcoaled, crumbling away from bones that had obviously undergone a degree of remodeling. He crawled closer and shined the beam onto their bared teeth, into their vacant black eye sockets. The sandstone behind them was carved and bloodstained.

Pike cursed in frustration and hurled a disarticulated tibia against the wall.

He heard a scraping sound and glanced behind him in time to see Brazelton scuttle into the cave. The biochemist looked past him at where the light was focused on the two corpses that had tried to claw their way through the rock.

"Jesus," Brazelton whispered. "We were so close this time."

Pike returned his gaze to the corpses.

"I want these two bodies out of here. Seal and box them, and get them on that truck right now."

Brazelton turned around and started back down the tunnel.

"We were never here. Do you understand?"

"Yes, sir. No evidence. No witnesses. And the village?"

"Burn it to the ground."

Brazelton scurried away. Pike listened to the man bark orders into microphone on his headset until his voice faded and he heard the roar of the Jeep's engine.

He directed the beam back onto the remains he had traveled thousands of miles to find. They hadn't gotten here quickly enough. Forty-eight hours earlier and these baked carcasses would have still been alive. Regardless, Dr. Bradley was going to be pleased. Their theory about the method of exposure had proven correct, but they were still no closer to isolating the microorganism that was responsible than they were before.

With any luck, the samples from the hot springs would bear fruit, although he didn't hold out much hope. The damn natives had cost them what he feared might have been their one best chance.

Turning his back on the vacuous stares of the dead, he crawled the length of the tunnel and emerged into the ferocious heat. The cloud of smoke over the village had darkened. Flames rose from the straw perimeter and roofs.

There was a crack of rifle fire, then another. Pike counted six shots and knew the deed was done.

The final report echoed across the savannah like the harbinger of a coming storm.

Eight

Feni Islands
South Pacific Ocean
52 km East of New Ireland Island, Papua New Guinea
November 30th
10:16 a.m. PGT

Present Day

The old harbor tugboat, its hull more rust than metal, rose and fell on the rough sea, the breakers slamming the ancient tractor tires chained to the gunwales with the sound of thunder and throwing arcs of spray over the bow. Bare steel showed through what was left of the white paint on the cabin. Half of the windows of the wheelhouse were boarded over with warped plywood. All that mattered was that the forty-ton tension winch was functional. With most of the local seafaring vessels out of commission and the rest commandeered to aid in the disaster relief efforts, they'd been fortunate to find even this piece of junk on such short notice. A cold wind battered them first from one direction, then another, assaulting the old vessel with blinding sheets of rain. The normally aquamarine South Pacific was a muddy brown. Tatters of vegetation tumbled beneath the waves. Gray clouds hung low over the bay, an oppressive ceiling reminiscent of smoke. Through the swirling mist and the sheeting rain, Roland Pike watched Ambitle Island, the larger of the Feni Islands, alternately appear then disappear a thousand meters to the east. Steep, densely forested slopes climbed up into the clouds where its long-dormant caldera hid from sight. The beaches were strewn with debris. Tangles of metal littered the sand like dinosaur bones amid the trunks of uprooted trees and the carpet of severed branches and withered leaves. A satellite tower and warped steel panels clung to the skeletal arms of the kapok, batai, and rosewood trees lining the shore, the yellowed trunks of which marked the level of the ferocious tide high up into the stripped canopy. The smaller Babase Island to the north, separated from its sister by the one hundred meter-wide Salat Strait, had fared little better.

Just over forty hours ago, a submarine megathrust earthquake that tipped the Richter Scale at 8.4 had rocked the region. From its epicenter at the subduction zone of the Pacific tectonic plate and the Bismarck microplate in the notorious Pacific Ring of Fire, it had generated a tsunami that raced outward toward Oceania at a rate of nearly one thousand kilometers per hour, fueled by the smaller quakes of 7.3 and 6.8 that followed three minutes apart. By the time the massive wave hit the Feni Islands and the rest of the Bismarck Archipelago, the easternmost land masses in its path, the wall of water was more than twenty-five meters high. It slammed New Ireland Island, fifty kilometers to the west, on a westward course that tore a swath of destruction across Papua New Guinea and Indonesia. Reports of flooding had come in from as far south as Brisbane, Australia and as far north as Hong Kong. A picture of a capsized trawler riding a wave that towered over the treetops, preparing to crash down upon a park filled with panicked, motion-blurred men and women fleeing for their lives in the coastal city of Madang, led off every global newscast and typified the horror of the worst catastrophe to strike this region since the Indian Ocean Earthquake of 2004. While corpses were still being prized from the muck and untangled from trees, the confirmed death toll had nearly reached forty thousand with estimates of doom-and-gloom forecasting as many as three times that amount still to be culled from the ranks of the missing. Relief workers from all across the globe had converged upon Oceania, establishing makeshift triage and treatment centers in areas still flooded nearly knee-deep. And identifying and burying the dead, of course. There were no such relief efforts here on Ambitle, which was inhabited only by a lone small Tolai village on the northwestern shore of the teardrop-shaped volcanic island. The vast majority of the island was leased to a mining corporation out of Sydney that had only recently begun geological surveys. So while the rest of the world held its breath as it watched the disturbing footage rolling in from west of here and every free hand was sifting through the detritus in search of bloated remains, Pike and his men had this bay all to themselves.

Pike could barely feel the cold through his neoprene wetsuit. He confirmed that the SART transponder beacon was stationary fifty meters beneath them on the shipboard radar for the hundredth time and joined the others at the stern. Avery Brazelton and Barrett Walker sat with their legs dangling over the brine, their fins cutting through the foamy waves. Both men were already clad in black scuba gear, diving helmets drawn over their heads, compact free-shaft spear guns strapped to one thigh and knives to the other. Mounted to either side of their helmets were a spotlight and an underwater digital video camera, the feeds from which were being relayed eastward across the Pacific to where the twin to the research vessel torn apart on the reef below them raced in their direction.

He seated his helmet over his Norwegian-blonde hair, adjusted the clear shield over his face, and readied his video recorder. His gut tingled with anticipation. After more than thirty-five hours in transit from Washington to New Ireland Island, where the old tug and its even older Papuan captain had been waiting in the ruined harbor, it was finally time to get down to work and see what could be salvaged. The Research Vessel *Ernst Mayr*, part of the global exploration fleet owned and operated exclusively by GeNext Biosystems, had been investigating a surge in seismic and geologic activity at the Kilinailau Trench more than one hundred and twenty kilometers to the east-southeast of the Feni Islands when the earthquake had struck. Their last communication had been more than forty-eight hours earlier, and all attempts to hail them had proven futile. The pulse from the *Mayr*'s EPIRB distress beacon had allowed for satellite triangulation to this bay, far from its last charted location. Aerial footage had shown nothing but open sea and beaches strewn with metallic debris. Pike and the two members of his team had been dispatched to serve as the forward party that would begin the investigation into its sinking while awaiting the arrival of the mobile research platform. Forty-six souls had been commissioned to the *Mayr*. While he intended to make sure that each and every one of their corpses were recovered, that endeavor was secondary to his mission. The way he saw it, the chaos on the more populous islands had bought them roughly four days with the wreckage before the world would turn its eye upon the loss of life here and the families back home would demand answers. He would need every bit of that time to search the sunken ship and strip it of all of the proprietary research and equipment housed in the submerged laboratories. What had befallen the crew was a tragedy, but he was still responsible for the security of a multi-billion dollar pharmaceutical corporation. Protecting its secrets and vested interests was paramount.

There would be plenty of time to mourn the deceased afterward.

Pike seated the rebreathing mask over his mouth and nose and dialed up the flow. He nodded to his men, who followed his example, then dropped over the edge and splashed into the roiling brown sea.

Nine

The Research Vessel *Ernst Mayr* had struck the reef on its side and been dragged along the ocean floor until it ultimately lodged against the jagged rocks and coral. Debris covered the seafloor as far as Pike had been able to see to the east. Brazelton and Walker were now searching what remained of the upper three decks while Pike worked his way into the hold. The plan was to clear the peripheral areas and meet back on the main level where all of the research suites were housed once they were through.

Pike raised his head toward the stairwell and the spotlight affixed to the right side of his helmet followed. The scales of fish flashed through the murky haze. Crabs already scuttled across the silt that had settled on the starboard side of the main corridor below him. The stainless steel airlocks to the science labs all stood open; dark, gaping pits filled with millions of dollars worth of useless electrical equipment and shattered glass that glittered like submerged jewels. He paddled upward, conscious of the constricting metal around him and the weight of the tons of water overhead. His respirations echoed hollowly in his ears. The entire ship groaned as it settled, punctuated by the wrenching sounds of buckling seams and rivets. A silvertip shark cruised languidly past him from the shadows with a swish of the muscular tailfin that brushed his hip. The fact that it showed no interest in him confirmed what he suspected. The beast was already sated.

He followed the stairs up to the landing, then bent around and upward once more before emerging into a hallway framed by the doorways to the engineering rooms both above and below him. A dark shape drifted through the cloudy brine toward him, arms splayed to its sides, legs hanging limply. Long hair wavered around its head like kelp. He shined his beam toward its face and glimpsed pale, bloated features with milky eyes before forcing himself to look away. Straps of flesh had been torn from the woman's high Asian cheekbones by scavengers to expose her teeth in a macabre grin. Her entire abdominal cavity had been absolved of its contents, leaving a macerated maw surrounded by shreds of clothing through which he could see the white hint of her spine. Shouldering past her, he kicked deeper into the darkness, away from the stairwell.

The corridor walls fell away as he swam into a forest of large white and gray pipes with pressure gauges and release valves that funneled fuel and lube oil, coolants, bilge, and air throughout the vessel. Electrical conduits lined walls with circuit boxes and generator controls. Hooks dotted the pegboards above workbenches where tools had once hung.

With a metallic shriek, the entire vessel shifted toward him as the tide drew its metallic carcass inexorably toward the shore. He could see pulverized coral, stone fragments, and mud through tears in the steel hull below him, through which schools of orange and red fish darted back and forth. Past the maze of pipes, the door to the cold storage hold stood open. He turned in that direction and his beam cast shadows from more floating forms against the steel wall. Another shark startled at his presence, its eyes reflecting gold, before it cruised out of sight. A ragdoll man twisted in its wake, pointing with his lone remaining arm as if in accusation. He'd been similarly disemboweled. Pike's pulse raced as his mind flashed back to the accursed Zambian village. Was it possible…?

Between the scientific staff and the ship's crew, nearly fifty men and women had been aboard when the research vessel set sail from Seattle. As he pressed deeper into the hold, he found the majority of them.

A mass of humanity twisted and writhed in the water as though performing a dance choreographed in the fires of hell. A pall of silt swirled around them. Arms and legs tangled. Bodies bumped against each other only to twirl away and ricochet from the next. Blanched, swollen faces. Blue lips parted by cracked teeth and engorged tongues. Haloes of stringy hair. Lab coats fluttered from researchers, stained with Rorschach blots of suffering. The navy blue uniforms of the crew were nearly black. Some were missing shoes and articles of clothing, others digits and entire appendages. Broken bones poked through sloughed flesh. And all of them—each and every one—had been gutted. Ropes of bowel still trailed from a few, frayed and severed.

Pike could only stare in confusion.

"Are you guys seeing this?" he whispered for the benefit of those watching the feed.

There had to be at least thirty of them down here, hidden away in a dank corner of the engine room. Why had all of their corpses congregated here? There was no way they would have been hauled back here by scavengers, nor were the currents such that they could have all floated to this one point. They must have already been down here when the ship foundered, but why? The logic was contrary to established human behavior patterns. If the crew had seen their fate coming in that towering wall of water, the last thing they would have done was herd into most secluded corner of the lowest level from which there was no means of escape. None of them would have strayed far from the lifeboats, and the captain would have ensured they were all well versed with the evacuation procedures. The fact that Captain Ryan Cartwright hadn't sent out an SOS spoke volumes about how swiftly death had descended upon the *Mayr*. Thus far, Pike's exploration had generated more questions than answers. He only hoped that they'd have the explanation they needed when it came time to face the world, the mourning relatives of these poor souls, and the inevitable lawsuits.

Pike panned his camera slowly across the carnage for documentation's sake. He imagined the team on the other research vessel steaming across the ocean clustered around their monitors, watching in abject horror as he spotlighted every face like waxen moons against the pitch black. No longer did he pay conscious attention to them, but instead let the camera be his eyes while he emotionally distanced himself.

"Pike," Brazelton's voice, marred by static, crackled into his ear. "We're just off the main corridor. There's something…There's something you need to see down here."

"You already cleared the upper decks?" He spoke into his microphone as he swam away from the remains and kicked back toward the stairwell, following his column of light through the haze.

"The Oh-Four deck's gone. The wheelhouse. The chart room. Torn right off and scattered across the reef. All of the officers' and the chief scientists' staterooms on the Oh-Three are empty."

"Same for the Oh-Two," Walker said. "The cabins are vacant, as are the mess and the lounge. There was one body in the hospital suite. Old guy. Doctor if you believe the stitching on the lab coat. The fish had already started in on him." He paused. "So where are the rest of them? They can't have all washed over the deck and we would have seen their rafts on the shore if they'd made it that far."

"They're down here," Pike said. He ducked his head under the threshold and kicked back down the staircase. An ugly scorpion fish covered with venomous spikes brushed against his arm.

"Not all of them," Brazelton whispered.

Pike recognized the reluctance to elaborate in the man's voice. Their communications were monitored on the same feed as the images. Apparently this was something that needed to be *seen*.

He flippered his way forward toward where a faint glow emanated from the darkened doorway above him. Below him, the signs on the wall beside the dented and buckled stainless steel doors passed. Divers Locker, Electronics Shop, Main Lab. He glanced up to orient himself. The signs read: Hydro Lab, Electronics/Computer Lab, Climate Control Chamber. He passed below the open orifice marked "Biology/Analytical Clean Lab." The door was warped and jammed partially open. There were deep scratches in the metal. It was a tight squeeze, but he managed to flatten his chest and squirm through with the tank on his back.

Long worktables were bolted to the now-vertical floor to his left, the machines and glassware that had once rested upon them shattered on the wall in front of him that now served as the floor. Above him, the port wall, now the ceiling, was covered with racks and shelves emptied of their contents. An enormous aquarium was still bolted in place, the water inside as black as tar.

He followed the source of the amber glow across the room, over jumbled mounds of unrecognizable equipment, computer towers, stainless steel and shards of glass to where Brazelton and Walker floated. Both men faced away from him, palms pressed flat against what appeared to be an algae- and sediment-covered wall. Their lights formed coronae around their heads like twin eclipsed suns. The wall must have been made from some opaque material, for their beams diffused ahead of them.

One of the divers turned toward him and Pike heard Brazelton's voice in his ear.

"Check this out."

Brazelton swiped his palm across the wall and produced a cloud of dust. Pike focused his light upon an orange design he recognized immediately. ☣ The biohazard symbol. He thought back to the *Mayr*'s schematics, which he had studied on the flight to New Guinea. This lab had an isolation shield that dropped from the ceiling to seal off the rear quarter of the room where the hooded stations and the batch reactor were installed. He swam closer and smeared away more of the sludge until he could see through the Plexiglas barrier.

Even in the darkness barely lightened by his headlamp, he could tell the ocean hadn't flooded the other side. A massive stainless steel vat glistened in the center of the chamber, jutting forth from what had once been the floor like a tumor. A spider-webbed glass emergency chemical shower filled the corner overhead, a long pull-cord dangling over its open top.

"Down there," Walker said. "In the corner."

"What—?" Pike started, but then he saw them. Little more than silhouettes against the back wall, nearly buried under broken gear and sparkling slivers of glass.

He leaned closer, struggling to discern the details. Water dripped from above onto the accumulation on the floor, which looked to be about a foot deep. He deciphered the human shapes: the bulbs of the slumped heads, the ridges of the shoulders.

Pike's breath caught in his throat. For a second, he thought he'd seen—there it was again. Hardly visible. Slow. Rhythmic.

"Jesus Christ," he said.

"Yeah," Brazelton whispered. "They're still alive in there."

Ten

Consciousness returned by degree with a red aura that burned through her eyelids. She tried to open them, but the effort was just too great. Her heavy body was unresponsive, her torso frozen, her extremities leaden. The fog that shrouded her mind made it impossible to generate a single coherent thought. Each breath was a burden her chest seemed increasingly willing to forsake, each autonomic exertion a feat of superhuman resilience with the weight on her body that felt as though it were compressing her, attempting to merge her with the cold steel beneath her she could no more feel than the frigid water pooling around her. Droplets pattered the accumulation in a dysrhythmic timpani in counterpoint to the throbbing in her temples. The darkness inside of her beckoned. No longer was her life defined by sleeping and waking cycles, but by the myriad shades of gray that separated them, where she was neither aware nor oblivious, floating in the space between heartbeats, which grew wider with each labored breath.

The crimson glare prodded her eyes like needles, gouging channels through which it could flow into her brain like blood, bringing with it a pain that began as an ache before blossoming into agony beyond anything she had ever experienced. Every vessel in her body pumped ground glass, every attempted thought the slash of a razor blade through gray matter. Her frozen fingers and toes felt as though the skin were being flayed from the bones. She opened her mouth to scream, but was unable to draw enough air to produce more than a choking sound. She wanted to cry, desired nothing more than to slip back into the realm of numbness from which the light had summoned her, where there had been no self and time had been both fleeting and eternal, the here and now a figment of an imagination not her own.

Her eyelids parted with the sensation of tearing lashes to reveal an unfocused crescent of blinding light that seared her retinas. The glare was no longer a scarlet hue, but rather a brilliant amber that she drew into herself through the vacuum of her stare. Her eyelids slid closed again. Too late. The damage was done. When they opened again, the forgotten panic awakened inside of her.

Dr. Courtney Martin's eyes snapped wide and she screamed, a shrill sound coated with barbs that tore at her parched throat. Comprehension struck her like a tire iron to the skull. Her chest heaved. Her body trembled. She tried to move her arms and failed, tried to push herself up from the floor and out of the water to no avail. Imprisoned within her unresponsive flesh, clarity of thought momentarily returned.

She was going to die.

Courtney screamed again, dotting the inside of the oxygen mask strapped over her mouth and nose with the last of her precious moisture. The attached tubing connected her to the port on the wall. The flow of air had ceased long ago when the heart of the ship had stilled. She had felt the thrum of the engine fade through the floor, watched as the blue sparks raining from the broken electrical conduits overhead petered like the last flakes of falling snow, the red emergency lights dimming until the darkness without became the darkness within. Cowering in this chamber as the wall became the floor and the rending sound of steel, a discordant choir of the damned burning in the fires of hell, signaled the advance of the flood that raced into her lab and hit the isolation barrier with the sound of thunder. She remembered watching the silt aggregate on the Plexiglas until she could no longer see the destruction, trying in vain to wipe it away from her side of the barricade while she screamed in futility. Each miniature grain of sand, each microscopic alga that adhered to the opposite surface was a nail driven into her coffin. Her salvation had become her tomb. How long had she been trapped in the blackness, waiting for her oxygen to run out, watching the droplets of seawater dripping through the seams in the hull and wondering which fate would claim her first? At what point had the gasping for air given way to unconsciousness? When had her body shut down to preserve only her most vital functions?

The light became many, all of which now moved, their glow diffusing around her, limning the equipment, casting long shadows that shivered on the wall behind her, highlighting the shape of the man crumpled against the wall beside her. She had only the vaguest recollection of his presence.

Starfish—no, they were hands—smeared back and forth across the isolation shield. They cleared wider and wider swatches through which she could see blurry silhouettes in the sparkling clouds caused by their disturbance. The shifting glare focused to the distinct circles of flashlight beams.

There was someone out there.

Courtney screamed with the last of her energy, and again retreated into the insensate darkness.

Eleven

"There's no time to wait!" Pike snapped into the satellite phone. "How much oxygen can that chamber possibly hold? They've already been trapped in there for more than forty-eight hours. They were barely breathing for Christ's sake! By the time you get here, they'll be long since dead!"

He rummaged around on the deck until he found what he was looking for. They were ill-prepared for this contingency. Worst case scenario, they had expected to find any survivors beached on one of the islands in the life rafts. None of them had foreseen the possibility they could have used the isolation cordon to stay alive.

Pike was only peripherally aware of the voice on the other end of the line. They'd already wasted too much time arguing, time they didn't have. If they wanted to learn what had happened to the ship, then they needed these people alive. Besides, he was in charge, and whatever the consequences, they were his to bear.

"We don't know if it's even possible to retract the shield. For all we know, its track is so warped we couldn't make it rise if we did somehow find a way to power the mechanism to raise it. And by then we'd just be extracting corpses!"

The boat lurched beneath him and he grabbed the gunwale. An enormous wave followed, hitting the tug like a truck and throwing spray across the deck. Miniquakes continued to rip apart the Kilinailau Trench, sending monstrous waves outward in all directions. There was no time for this argument. With the instability of the ocean floor, the *Mayr* could shift, the hull buckle, and those sealed inside could end up drowned before they reached them.

"We're going in," Pike said over the objections from the other end. "Wish us luck."

He disconnected the call and hurled the phone through the doorway into the cabin, where already several inches of water covered the floor. Donning his helmet once more, he cradled the acetylene torch to his chest under his left arm, and plunged down into the ocean. The waves had stirred the silt into a shifting cloud through which he could barely see the wreckage. He kicked downward toward the bowed A-frame winch at the stern of the *Mayr* and followed the warped track of the submersible launch toward the open doorway beside the hanger. A light bloomed from the corridor as Walker emerged and took the torch from him. They flippered deeper into the unstable vessel, the groaning of metal all around them.

"What did the engineer say?" Walker asked through the com-link inside his helmet.

"Does it matter?"

Walker chuckled in response.

They swam upward into the lab and back toward where Brazelton waited. He'd cleared all of the sludge from the Plexiglas barrier so they could clearly see inside. Their lights made the refractions of water on the wall inside the chamber waver. The bodies were still slouched in the corner where Pike had last seen them.

"They haven't moved since you left," Brazelton said. "I can't even tell if they're breathing anymore."

"Then we don't have time to screw around."

The torch flared to life to his left, a ferocious blue-white that blinded him for several seconds. Walker braced his feet and leaned toward the shield as high and as far away from those inside as he could get, poised to set to work. He glanced back at Pike for final approval.

Pike understood the man's hesitation. If there were any kind of flammable gas inside, the torch would ignite it and they'd be blown to pieces. It was a calculated risk. Surely any combustible gas would have killed the people in there long ago, and the oxygen mounts on the wall couldn't flow once the tanks were dry. The greater concern was that they had dropped the shield because of the release of some biological contaminant Walker now prepared to release into the water.

"We're going to have to move fast," Pike said. "Once that water starts to rush in there, it's going to flood in a matter of seconds."

Walker nodded and brought the flame to the isolation barrier. The glare grew even brighter. The plastic melted and turned an orange-red. Molten gobs dripped to the ground before turning ashen and issuing bubbling tendrils of steam. Water fired through the rough cut with such velocity that it struck the inner wall on the opposite side of the chamber like a stream of bullets that visibly warped the steel and immediately started to pool on the floor.

"Hurry up," Pike whispered. "Hurry up!"

He watched the water level rise on the other side as Walker burned a circle wide enough for them to squeeze through. The shadows inside were already submerged to their waists and Walker wasn't even halfway done.

"Hurry up!"

"I'm going as fast as I can!"

"This was a bad idea…" Brazelton said.

Pike turned on the flow of air through the ancillary octopus regulator attached to his scuba tank and watched the bubbles rise from the mouthpiece. His legs tensed in anticipation of the first solid kick. He glanced at Brazelton to make sure he was ready. When the time came to move, there could be no hesitation.

Multiple streams of water now fired into the chamber, boring into the steel across the room with the pressure of the entire ocean behind them, filling the room with spray. Pike could barely see the people through the mist and the droplets on the interior of the Plexiglas. Their heads were barely above the rising water. Any second it would eclipse their mouths.

"Hurry up!"

The torch continued its glowing orange arc upward toward where Walker had started, but it was moving too slowly. They had killed the survivors as surely as if they'd sat back and watched them suffocate while they waited for help to arrive.

"There go their heads," Brazelton said. "They aren't even making an effort to raise them out of the water."

"There's still time," Pike said.

"All it takes is one breath and their lungs will fill—"

"I said there's still time!"

With a resounding crack, the circle of thick Plexiglas snapped away from the barrier and struck the interior wall with enough force to bury itself in the metal.

Pike launched himself forward toward the hole, propelled by the awesome current, which sucked him through and spit him out along the vicious flume. He hit the wall and was driven to the floor. The chamber was completely full by the time he gathered his bearings and righted himself. His headlamp played across the nearest figure, a woman, her hair twisting around her head in the swirling current. He swam toward her as fast as he could. He forced the rescue regulator into her mouth, pried her from the debris, and pulled her to his chest.

If she'd already aspirated enough seawater, no amount of oxygen would save her on the long journey back to the surface.

He flippered past Brazelton, who struggled to lift a man from the floor, toward the opening and felt hands grab his shoulders and pull him through. His rapid breathing echoed inside his helmet as he raced across the room and down into the main corridor, urging himself faster. He tried to feel for the woman's heartbeat against her ribs, but the neoprene gloves made it impossible. He willed her to live through sheer force of thought.

The doorways blew past and before he knew it, they'd cleared the stern and were hurtling toward the lighter water and the surface.

They breached the waves and paddled toward the boat. Walker and Brazelton surfaced a moment later, the limp man supported between them. Walker transferred the man's weight to Brazelton, pulled himself up onto the tug, and reached back down for the woman. Together, he and Pike hauled her up onto the deck. Pike tore off his helmet and hurled it aside. Behind him, he heard them heave the other survivor onto the boat.

"Get them some blankets!" He fell upon the woman, pulled the regulator from her mouth, and lowered his ear to her lips. "Now!"

No exhalations tickled the fine hairs or made the slightest sound. He could see standing water behind her parted teeth.

"Damn it!" he shouted.

Pike started CPR with the compressions to pump the water out of her chest. Fluid burbled from her mouth and spilled onto the planks, but still she made no attempt to gasp for air. He tugged off his right glove with his teeth and felt for a carotid pulse. Her skin was tinged blue and ice-cold to the touch. His own fingers were frozen and wrinkled, yet, whether real or imagined, he thought he felt a weak, thready pulse.

Brazelton threw himself to the deck beside them and ripped off the woman's drenched clothes. White patches of frostbite stood out against her blue-marbled skin. He covered her in dry blankets from the cabin.

Pike continued thrusting against her breast as the wind and rain assaulted them in gusts. The entire ship bucked under them on the choppy waves.

He leaned over her head and peeled apart her eyelids. The pupils constricted ever so subtly.

"She's still alive!" Pike said, pumping with renewed vigor.

A geyser of fluid shot from her mouth and spattered back down onto her face. She choked and sputtered. Pike rolled her into the rescue position to allow the fluid to drain.

She made no effort to move, or even open her eyes, but her chest swelled visibly with each inspiration.

With a retching sound, the man Walker had been resuscitating vomited a puddle of seawater behind him.

After watching her breathe for a long moment, Pike carefully lifted the woman from the deck and carried her out of the storm and into the cabin.

Twelve

Redmond, Washington
7:56 p.m. PST Local Time (January 29th)
1:56 p.m. PGT (January 30th)

This was a catastrophe beyond anything Bradley had dealt with in all of his years at the helm of GeNext. He was responsible for sending forty-some people to their deaths. Good men and women who had only been doing their jobs. He felt a bone-deep sorrow as he watched the nightmare images from the South Pacific flash past on the plasma screen mounted to his office wall. Buildings demolished to such a degree that it was impossible to tell what they had once been. The wreckage of ships perched on the remains of structures that had once stood ten stories tall. Bodies draped with stained sheets lining the streets while more and more were pulled out of the rubble. Children wearing masks of glistening blood carried in the arms of rescue workers while they screamed for the parents they would never find. Across the bottom of the screen scrolled the number for the International Red Cross and another number to which to text donations. Fading celebrities were already using the disaster to gain face-time. Every channel showed the same apocalyptic visions of suffering as he flipped through them, faster and faster, until he finally hurled the remote across the room and stood from his desk.

He loosened his collar and used his tie to wipe the sweat from his brow. This office that he had spent so many years perfectly appointing, to be his home away from home, was suddenly suffocating him. The sheepskins on the walls and the leather furnishings became nothing more than the hides of dead animals, the journals and tomes in the bookcases filled with useless words that were obsolete by the time they were published. His desk, purchased from the estate of Harry S. Truman and upon which the famous "The Buck Stops Here" sign had rested, reminded him that the man who had once sat there was now dead, as were the hundreds of thousands of Japanese whose lives had become expendable in the mind of the former president who quite possibly made that decision while sitting at this very desk. All of the crystal, brass, and gold awards and plaques, all of the priceless paintings and framed photographs of him with heads of state, all of the polished marble and electronic gadgets were the trappings of a vain man, come to haunt the young idealist who had set out to save the world from itself and had instead become imprisoned in a Brioni suit, a slave to the fortune and responsibility that sapped his very soul.

His office started to spin around him. He needed to get out of here. Right now. Clear his head. And there was one place that no matter the stress and the chaos always brought the world back into focus.

He staggered out of his suite and down the corridor, signaled the elevator, and prepared to descend to the lowest level. The three subbasements were reserved exclusively for research and development. The lone elevator at the rear of the complex that accessed them wouldn't descend without proper clearance, as enforced by the retinal scanner built into the control panel. None of them was open to the public and only the cream of the scientific crop would ever set foot on the two uppermost. As for the deepest level, only a select few men and women were even aware of its existence, several of whom were down here now in their own private labs, while the rest were crossing the Pacific aboard the R/V *Aldous Huxley* or already at the site of the *Mayr*'s sinking.

Bradley stepped out of the elevator and into the central hallway. He passed the entrances to the various laboratories and clean rooms, each of them sealed by a pressurized stainless steel airlock. His destination was at the end of the corridor, where it abruptly terminated at a door that reflected his approach. He caught a glimpse of the same disheveled suit he had worn the day before, the heavy bags beneath his blue eyes, and a mussed head of hair gone prematurely white. He leaned toward the black screen and opened his eye wide for the laser to scan his retina. With a hiss, the door slid into the wall and he stepped into what his elite team of researchers had affectionately nicknamed The Crypt.

Eight Plexiglas cases stood to either side of the main aisle, spaced every ten feet. Each unit was roughly three feet deep, six feet tall, and sized to accommodate its occupant, with a stainless steel base that housed the humidity and temperature controls that maintained the precise atmospheric conditions required to arrest further decomposition. Inside of each were corpses in various states of decay. Some were nearly intact and mummified, while others were mere collections of bones. He had spent the last twelve years collecting them following the discovery of the first pair in Chaco Canyon, and a fortune hiring the most brilliant and discreet group of scientists in the world to scour the globe for more examples and to break the code of their impossible existence. There was still so much they didn't understand, but he was certain they were close now.

He could remember the details of the acquisition of each one of them with perfect clarity, even without the aid of the enlarged photographs that hung on the walls behind them, which documented where the body had been found and the surrounding area. The two cases at the front of the room housed the very first: the gaunt, desiccated forms of little more than crisp skin stretched over knots of bone that his flashlight had shown him on that fateful day, the same day the first shock of white had appeared in his bangs. Even after all this time, they made his stomach flutter every time he walked into the room. Beside the picture of the ruins of Casa Rinconada and the carcass-riddled cave hung x-rays and CT scans, magnified images of bone matrices and tissue samples, and all sorts of lab printouts from radiocarbon dating to RFLP genomic profiles.

The second case on the right contained the skull they had found beneath the Bhadresvara *linga*. It had cost a pretty penny to secret it out of Vietnam, along with a generous sampling of the bones that had been scattered on the ground around it. They were scored with teeth marks a forensic odontologist had confirmed matched those of the skull.

Across the aisle were the skeletal remains of the woman they had fished out of the subterranean pool in Guatemala, whose bones were almost blindingly white in contrast to the others after thirteen hundred years in the cold water.

In the case beside her rested the cadaver they had removed from a cliff-side tomb on Rapa Nui fourteen months ago, where it had been walled behind several tons of basalt. The stone walls had been scarred with gouges from fingertips and still rimed with brown flakes of dried blood like lichen. He had been entombed alive. His dehydrated corpse had been slumped in the back, his calves and thighs stripped nearly to the bone. The prevailing theory in the lab was that he had attempted to sustain himself on his own flesh after being sealed in there more than two thousand years ago. The pictures that covered the wall behind it were of a serene white beach with just the crown of one of the famous statues' heads against the backdrop of a sheer cliff of volcanic rock, a dark hole in the mounded stones, and the crumpled form with its skeletal legs stretched out before it.

Their most recent arrival prior to the events in Africa, a diminutive man exhumed near Beppu, Japan at the foot of Mt. Tsurumi in 2008, was reassembled in the third case to the right. He had been dismembered, his parts packed in sulfurous precipitates and wrapped in bamboo leaves, and buried near the natural hot spring known as Blood Pond. The location was memorialized in pictures filled with steam and boiling crimson water, lush fields of emerald grasses that crawled up the steep volcanic cone, and the bundled remains on the fertile soil at the bottom of a deep pit. Carbon dating of the remains and the trace amounts of ash in the hole placed his interment at somewhere between eleven and twelve hundred years ago.

The final two cases housed the charred remains from Zambia, which had been burned so badly that despite their best efforts, the bones continued to crumble. Had they arrived just forty-eight hours sooner, they would possibly have still been alive, or at least there would have been enough flesh remaining to unlock Pandora's Box. Since there had been nothing left but charcoal, the DNA samples had been corrupted and whatever mutagenic agent had caused the violent transformation had been lost. The bacterial samples from the hot springs had demonstrated nothing out of the ordinary. They had blown the one shot they had been given thanks to the natives, whom he could hardly blame for saving their own skins. It was regrettable that Pike's team hadn't been able to track down any of the survivors. Perhaps their testimony might have at least helped narrow the possible sources of exposure. As it stood now, the historical precedent suggested that such an event would never happen again in their lifetimes.

Bradley sighed.

Here they had eight individuals from the furthest reaches of the globe and from different points in time, all of which coincided with major geothermal and sociological upheavals. The eruption of the Sunset Cone in Arizona in 1150 C.E. and the mass migration of the Anasazi that immediately followed. The surge in activity in the Haut Dong Nai volcanic fields in the fourteenth century and the subsequent abandonment of My Son by the Champa. The eruption of the Guatemalan volcano Fuego mere miles from Bilbao, in the early eighth century, when the Maya abruptly vanished from the face of the earth. The birth of the Hiva-Hiva lava flow on Easter Island and the sharp decline in the native Polynesian population nearly two millennia ago. The eruption of Mt. Tsurumi in 867 C.E. and the flight of a group of Buddhist monks from their ruined temple. In all instances, they left behind archaeological evidence of cannibalism. But those weren't the only threads that bound them together. All of the corpses shared several remarkable physical attributes. If GeNext could have isolated the origin of these truly amazing genetic traits, Bradley was convinced they could have unraveled the very mystery of life itself.

They had been so close...

Thirteen

Bradley heard footsteps behind him and turned around to find Brendan Reaves staring at him.

"I thought that might be you," the anthropologist said. While his stubbled cheeks were now flecked with gray and his formerly smooth skin had become the texture of a saddle, the fire in his eyes was that of the much younger man who had summoned him to Chaco Canyon so many years ago. "How are you holding up?"

"About as well as one might expect."

Reaves offered a sympathetic smile and a gentle squeeze on the shoulder.

Bradley wasn't surprised to find Reaves down here so late. Their shared obsession had given Reaves the unprecedented opportunity to broaden the spectrum of his research in hopes of isolating the catalyst for the next step in the evolution of mankind and the possible link back to his origins in the primordial ooze. Reaves had been the one who intuited the connection between the bodies and taken the leap of logic that had led them to all of the others. He had combined two of the more controversial theories of evolution to generate a hypothesis of his own.

The fundamental principle was that an organism must either adapt to its environment or perish. At the heart of this notion was the belief that a single cataclysmic event could trigger radical and rapid physical changes within a species, contrary to the slow-motion premise of natural selection.

The second, and most critical factor, had been only recently put forth. A meteorite that scientists speculated had originated on Mars was pried from the Antarctic tundra, but more than just a chunk of iron and minerals had made the journey through space. Fossilized evidence confirmed the presence of microorganisms nearly identical to a type of extremophilic bacteria called *Archaea*, a discovery that supported the idea that life could indeed exist on even the most inhospitable planets. These bacteria, which could survive atmospheres lacking oxygen and temperature extremes that would either freeze or cook all other known life forms, provided the basis for the idea that life hadn't begun in an idyllic garden in Mesopotamia, but rather deep within the molten core of the Earth. Eons of geologic activity had forced these bacteria to the surface where they had helped to convert a hydrogen atmosphere to oxygen as a byproduct of their chemosynthetic processes, theoretically giving birth to terrestrial life.

Reaves had combined two factors that adhered to a single, if circumstantial, theory. With the verifiable cataclysmic events of the sudden eruption of the Sunset Cone in Arizona and the increased volcanic activity on the Indochina Peninsula, the environment had suddenly placed increased pressure on its inhabitants while simultaneously forcing organisms that had never been meant to dwell aboveground to the surface. There was no incontrovertible proof of any kind, however. None of the remains showed any sort of bacterial infestation, nor had more than two individuals been changed dramatically by the geothermal events, but the theory had held together well enough for them to recognize the significance of the Ah Puch statues and the Mayan cenote. From that point on, they hadn't sat back like vultures waiting for news of a potentially intriguing dig. They had actively instigated excavations in regions where geologic disaster and the collapse or rapid relocation of a culture had occurred at the same time, which had led them to Easter Island and the Inland Sea of Japan. And Reaves had coordinated both of those digs, in addition to a dozen others on every continent at the exact same time.

It had been at Reaves's insistence that they started to track modern geothermal activity. After all, if such cases had appeared sporadically throughout recorded history, who was to say that the same thing couldn't happen right now. And once that lone refugee from Makambu Village had stumbled into Mpulungu carrying his dying wife and rambling about demons, Reaves had plucked the report from the wire and his team had been in the air to bolster the research forces already on the ground.

And still they had been too late.

Bradley had cured diseases and enhanced the lives of his entire generation, conquered the business world, made billions of dollars, and yet the only mystery that had ever really mattered to him personally would be the one to haunt him from beyond the grave.

"There's something you need to see," Reaves said.

Bradley noticed a curious spark in the man's eyes. He was about to say that he was in no mood, but he would have been saying it to Reaves's back.

He followed Reaves down the hallway and into the anthropologist's office. Maps highlighted with circles, notes, and various-colored pushpins covered the walls between shelves overflowing with books about nearly every conceivable culture. Scraps of paper curled from the bindings where Reaves had marked countless passages. File cabinets stood in the rear corners, drawers open, manila folders askew. The chairs were heaped with open tomes, files, and stacks of paper. Amid the bedlam were trappings of Reaves's former life: potsherds, arrowheads, and carved bones in Lucite cubes; framed photographs of various excavations and newspaper clippings; Southwestern sand art designs and ephemera of all sorts.

Reaves stepped behind a desk heaped with leaning stacks of research materials that appeared on the brink of toppling to the floor and gestured to the lone chair. Bradley eased through the clutter and sat in the proffered seat. The screen of the laptop in front of him was framed with sticky-notes, the scrawl illegible. Reaves leaned over his shoulder and tapped the mouse pad. The screensaver faded to reveal a rectangular video display and the control bar beneath it.

"The recording you're about to watch was forwarded about twenty minutes ago from the wreckage of the *Mayr* via the *Huxley*."

A fist clenched in Bradley's gut. He winced at the sudden discomfort.

"Tell me there are survivors."

"See for yourself."

Reaves clicked the "Play" button and the footage began to roll.

It took Bradley a moment to rationalize what he was seeing. A blinding glare burned in the upper left corner of the screen, throwing the rest of the image into shadow. He was barely able to discern a man's silhouette at the heart of the fiery glow of a blowtorch, which he appeared to be using to cut through a wall.

No, not a wall. He recognized the biohazard warning symbol on what he suddenly realized was the isolation shield in the clean lab. The view panned downward and to the right. Two human shapes sat slumped in the corner while the water flooded up to their chests.

"Jesus," Bradley whispered.

The following minutes were filled with scenes of thrashing appendages and movements too rapid for the camera to properly capture. Doors and hallways blurred past. The voices of the divers were so jumbled by static and their heavy breathing that their words were incoherent. Eventually, the recording lightened and the view abruptly became bright and clear. Choppy brown waves filled the screen. He saw the crown of a woman's head and then the rusted hulk of a ship. In a matter of seconds, the scuba-clad divers hauled a man and a woman up onto the deck and set to work resuscitating them.

Reaves reached in front of him, stopped the video, and closed the window.

"Apparently neither of them has regained consciousness yet, but at least they're still among the living."

"Thank God." Bradley released a pent-up sigh. "Do we know if there are more of them?"

"I'm getting to that." Reaves scrolled through the index of video files that had been forwarded from the *Huxley*. "We're dealing with a considerable lag time in communication while they chop and bundle the live digital feeds, so all of this happened more than an hour ago. There's one clip in particular I know you'll want to see. Here." He double-clicked the file and the video screen once again appeared. "Are you ready?"

Bradley nodded. He prayed there were more survivors. For a heartbeat, he felt a swell of hope. Rather than standing in front of a gathering of reporters at a press conference to tell them that the entire crew of the *Mayr* had been lost as he had been imagining all day, he envisioned himself triumphantly declaring that the forty-six men and women were still alive despite the worst that nature could throw at them.

Just as quickly, his hopes were dashed when Reaves pushed "Play."

A woman floated in the water, her bloated features whitewashed by the diver's light. There was no doubt that she was dead.

Bradley turned away and closed his eyes. A tear crept down his cheek.

"You need to keep watching," Reaves said softly. He rested a consolatory hand on Bradley's shoulder.

When Bradley looked back again, the view was of a dark channel through a maze of pipes. A human form materialized from the darkness at the extent of the light's reach. Scales flashed as a shark darted away. The diver swam closer and brought the form into focus, behind and to the right of which more bodies hung suspended in the water.

"They're all dead," Bradley whispered.

"Look closely." There was a ghoulish note of excitement in Reaves's voice that made Bradley's skin crawl. How could he possibly—?

And then Bradley saw it.

All of the corpses had been disemboweled. His mind jumped to the pictures of the deceased found scattered around Mpulungu Village in Zambia that hung on the wall behind the encased remains in The Crypt. He had stared at them so often and for so long that he'd memorized every detail of the macerated wounds and every inch of the carved flesh.

Pike's voice from the laptop echoed Bradley's thoughts.

"Are you guys seeing this?"

The condition of the bodies in the hold of the *Mayr* was nearly identical to that of the victims in the African savannah.

Bradley's heart thundered in his chest. He clenched his trembling hands in his lap.

"Do you think…?"

"That's why I called you in here to see it."

"If those two people could survive, then…"

"It's a distinct possibility."

"And if not—"

"It could be either somewhere in that ship, on the ocean floor, or maybe it even reached the shore."

"Either way, do you know what this means?"

"Bear in mind, it's possible we're only seeing what we want to see. Any number of scavengers could have done that to them. You saw the shark."

Bradley could barely contain his excitement. All thoughts of the loss of life fled him. He paused the recording and stared at the waterlogged carcass of one of the researchers, the tattered edges of his lab coat forming parentheses around the maw in his abdomen.

"There's only one way to know for sure." Bradley leapt from the chair and hurried out of Reaves's office. "Meet me in the lobby in ten minutes. We have a plane to catch."

Fourteen

Feni Islands
South Pacific Ocean
52 km East of New Ireland Island, Papua New Guinea
November 30th
3:06 p.m. PGT

Pike breached the surface and bobbed on the rolling waves. Raindrops snapped and popped all around him like water on hot oil. The winch grumbled as it ratcheted its payload, the watertight data storage unit from the communications room that Walker had found in the rubble, battered and half-buried in silt, up onto the deck. If the security cameras on the *Mayr* had captured anything worthwhile, the footage would be somewhere inside of that massive black cabinet, but they would have to wait for the data analysis team on the *Huxley* to arrive before they could crack it open, considering they currently had neither the proper equipment nor the skills. With any luck, the research vessel should be crossing the horizon within the next couple of hours. In the meantime, Pike and his men needed to exhume everything of importance from the ruined ship on the seafloor.

He had spent the last hour and a half swimming through what remained of the *Mayr*, scouring every nook and cranny for clues to its demise while Walker combed the surrounding reef. Since Brazelton was the only one of them with even rudimentary medical training, he had been tasked with monitoring the survivors from the submerged laboratory, neither of whom had yet to awaken. It was still too early for Pike to share his suspicions, even with the members of his unit, who may or may not have recognized what he had, so he continued to gather corroborative footage via the camera on his dive helmet. Including the physician, Dr. Walter Partridge, whose body floated in the hospital suite, and those gathered in the hold, there had been a total of thirty corpses aboard the ship. All of the other rooms had been empty, confirming what they had found on the first pass. Walker had encountered the crumpled remains of five others trapped in the reef amid the wreckage of the pilothouse and the chart room from the decapitated 04 Deck. Four men and a woman, all wearing crew uniforms. The master of the ship, Ryan Cartwright, had been identifiable, despite what the crabs had done to his face, by his jacket. That left nine souls unaccounted for to go with the workboat Pike had determined was missing from the main deck of the *Mayr*. If their SART rescue beacon had been activated upon launch, then a sweep through the radar bands on the tug would be able to locate it as a series of dots, which was exactly what he prepared to do right now.

He hauled himself up onto the stern, removed his helmet, and walked around the cabin to the bow where he helped Walker land and unhook the data cabinet. The geologist appeared to be lost in thought. He had been with the team long enough now that he was undoubtedly at least pondering the possible significance of what they had seen. Sure, a shark or any number of scavengers could have feasted on the entrails of the dead, but none of them had the kind of claws that could inflict the superficial lacerations on the bodies or the deep scratches in the steel doors lining the main corridor.

"I hate leaving them down there for the crabs and fish to work over," Walker said.

"Would you rather we pile them up here on the deck? Have you ever smelled a drowned body as the flesh begins to dissolve away from the bone, leaving puddles of putrefaction—"

"Christ, Pike. I didn't say I wanted to share a bunk with them. I was just commenting on how...wrong it is."

"We'll get them into cold storage on the *Huxley* when it finally arrives."

"There's something to look forward to." Walker shook his head. "Cold storage..."

Pike had no patience for this line of conversation. He clambered up the steps into the wheelhouse and scrolled through the radar bands. Their ancient captain seized the opportunity to make himself scarce. The workboat could easily have washed off the deck during the sinking with no one on board to activate the search and rescue transponder. It could be sunken in this very bay or it could have ridden the tsunami all the way to New Ireland for all he knew. There was the distinct possibility that the nine missing people might never be—

A series of white dots appeared on the radar in the X-band range.

Pike waited another complete cycle. There it was again. Roughly two nautical miles off their stern. He turned around and stared through the cracked, rain-beaded rear window. The forested slopes of Ambitle Island were barely visible through the dark storm clouds. Could they possibly have made it to land and dragged the small craft up past the tree line? It was more likely the vessel had been pulverized on the reef and its remains scattered on the beach, but he had to find out for sure.

Grabbing the field glasses from a hook beside the door, he hurried down the stairs and ran to the end of the tug. He steadied himself on the canting deck and raised the binoculars. The distant shore lurched up and down. It was so overgrown with trees that it appeared to be a solid wall of foliage beyond the debris-strewn white sands. He panned across the rows of trunks, between which he hoped to spot the small boat, but instead only found more trunks and snarls of skeletal shrubs draped with shadows. Broken branches hung vertically, burdened by limp brown leaves. Intricate lattices of vines connected the trees. Warped steel panels nested in the canopy with the twisted remnants of the *Mayr*'s satellite tower. He imagined the monstrous tidal wave rising up over the shore like a cobra preparing to strike, and directed his gaze higher into the canopy.

Pike steadied the binoculars and toyed with the focus until the image was as sharp as he could make it. With the rolling deck, it was nearly impossible to maintain his field of view and he was so far away that he couldn't be entirely positive, but he was confident that he had found what he was looking for.

"Must've been some wave." He lowered the field glasses and strode back around the deck and into the cabin under the wheelhouse, where he interrupted a conversation between his men. "Walker…you're coming with me."

He glanced at the two forms in the lone bunk to the right, heaped beneath mounds of blankets. Their exposed faces were still a ghastly shade of pale. Were it not for the subtle movement of the covers in time with their shallow breathing, they could have been as dead as their shipmates beneath his feet.

"We identified them from their personnel files," Brazelton said. "Dr. Courtney Martin, a marine biologist, and John Bishop, the submersible pilot."

"Keep them alive. We need to hear what they know."

"Where are we going?" Walker asked.

Pike smirked.

"Grab your boots. We're going to climb some trees."

Fifteen

Ambitle Island

Pike and Walker hopped out into the shallows and dragged the Zodiac up onto the beach to the tree line, past bent girders and folded sheets of steel, electrical components and broken glass that glittered indigo when the lightning flashed, and a rainbow of coral gravel sheared from the reef. The waves broke against the debris with the sound of unrequited destructive potential. Raindrops lay siege to the forest, which raged against the whipping monsoon winds. Trunks and branches groaned and snapped with the weight of the satellite tower that would inevitably succumb to the will of gravity.

"You saw something from the ship, didn't you?" Walker asked. "That's why we brought the tarps."

In answer, Pike led him under the arms of the batai and rosewood trees and out of the torrent. Droplets and streams poured from above them to spatter on the exposed ground, stripped of the detritus that had been swept higher onto the island by the wall of water. Serpentine roots snaked in and out of the mud around bare shrubs, the sparse clusters of leaves that clung to them withered and yellow. Pike turned back toward the tug to gather his bearings, then struck off to the south until he found the massive kapok tree he had seen through the field glasses. Mud and shredded vegetation were crusted to the eastern face of its trunk clear up past its stripped lower branches. He looked skyward until he saw the body, swarming with black flies, more than thirty feet above his head.

"Get him down from there."

He could feel Walker's eyes on his back. The geologist hesitated and Pike heard an intake of air as though in preparation of voicing his protests, but the moment passed and Walker approached the tree. The trunk was as broad as he was tall, but with his vast climbing experience, Walker scurried almost effortlessly up into the canopy. Pike watched Walker navigate through the limbs until he reached a pair of legs that swung gently on the gale winds, attenuated to a soft breeze by the jungle. A wet sock hung from one foot. The laces dangled from the Nike on the other. The dirty jeans identified the man as part of the scientific crew. He was folded backward over a thick bough like a roll of carpet, his back obviously broken. His torso rested on the adjacent limb, his bruised arms draped across the smaller branches. The flesh on his face had been gnawed to the bone, his eyes pecked from their sockets. Pike could only assume the man had been on deck when the earthquake struck and the resultant tsunami had cleaved him from the ship and carried him along on its crest as though he were a piece of Styrofoam.

"You should probably step back a little," Walker called down to him.

With the sound of tearing fabric, Walker pulled the corpse by the legs until it tumbled from its perch. It broke through the branches in a cartwheeling descent until it struck the ground with a sickening thud and the *crack* of breaking bones.

Pike crouched over the remains and arranged the heap so that the man was sprawled flat on his back. The flies that had claimed him as their own tracked him in a buzzing cloud.

"Eight more to go," Pike said.

Walker swung from the tree and dismounted with a gymnastic flourish.

"Drag him back down to the beach and double-time it back here." Pike removed the ship-to-shore transceiver from its holster on his diving vest, pressed the button, and spoke into the microphone. "Brazelton."

A moment of crackling static.

"Copy, Pike."

"Where am I in relation to the SART beacon?" Through the foliage and the rain, he glimpsed the wheelhouse of the tug far out to sea.

"It's impossible...pinpoint on the radar..."

"I know. Just give me a heading."

"…breaking up." The electrical activity in the storm wreaked havoc on their short-range communications. "Roughly twenty degrees west-northwest…your current position. Could be anywhere…approximately a square kilometer—"

Pike clicked off the transceiver and turned toward the island. No natural paths presented themselves. They were going to have to forge their own.

Walker shoved through the underbrush behind him.

"Where to now?" Walker asked.

Pike pressed his finger to his lips and scanned the forest. Other than the ruckus above him where the wind and the rain rattled the branches and rustled the leaves, there was only a preternatural silence marred by the occasional peal of thunder. The birds and animals must have bedded down to ride out the storm, but still, it was an uneasy quiet. The air felt electric, as though they stood under power lines.

He struck off through the jungle, weaving around the trunks, forging through waist-high shrubs, and swatting away vines. Tented roots and the lianas that constricted the gnarled ceiba trunks snatched at his feet. His body attuned itself to his surroundings with the practiced ease of the soldier he had once been. The training had been beaten into his very being. His heartbeat slowed and his breathing became silent. His tread lightened. He unconsciously reached for the firearm that wasn't there and had to settle for the hilt of the knife on his thigh. In his mind, he was the twenty-eight year-old sergeant leading his unit of the First Marine Division through the smoky streets of Kuwait City with the crackle of rifle fire in the distance beyond buildings still burning, with M1 Abrams tanks grinding ahead of them and Tomcats screaming overhead.

While the return of his skills pleased him, he couldn't help but wonder what had triggered them and why, when they were on an essentially uninhabited island stalked by nothing more intimidating than the crocodiles in the brackish river mouths and coastal lagoons.

Pike waved for Walker, who trundled through the foliage with all the grace of a charging rhinoceros, to fan out to the right. Twenty yards apart, they saw each other only as intermittent shadows through the trees. They had traveled perhaps half a kilometer when Walker shouted.

"Over here! I found something!"

Pike dashed toward the sound of Walker's voice, ducking and hurdling his way through the natural obstacle course until he found Walker kneeling at the edge of a furrow in the earth. The rain had eroded the edges, but the impression was still fairly well defined where the shrubs had been flattened. There were sloppy footprints to either side.

"Someone dragged a boat through here," Walker said.

Pike crouched and traced a pair of footprints with his fingertips. The rainfall had distorted their shape and puddled inside, yet he could still discern that they were made by different sized feet wearing different treads. They couldn't have been more than forty-eight hours old. He looked to his right and followed the trail through the trees in the direction of the beach with his eyes, then back and in the opposite direction to where the terrain grew rapidly steeper.

"They're still alive," Walker said.

"We would have seen smoke from a fire."

"It's been raining for nearly a week. Every piece of wood on this island must be saturated."

Pike shook his head, stood, and walked further inland. Walker called out for anyone within earshot. After a few minutes of hiking up the slope, a rugged crest of basalt pillars rose to his right like columns supporting the jungle, which cascaded down its face in flowering vines. Blue and white orchids bloomed from the moss that bearded the crevices. The workboat was partially concealed at its base under an umbrella formed by a stand of batai trees. The SART beacon, an orange canister that resembled a slender garbage disposal unit, was still attached to the frame. The housing of the outboard motor was cracked, the small screw bent. There were no personal effects, and other than the riot of footprints in the mud, there was no sign that anyone had been here recently.

Except for the smeared, bloody handprints on the rails.

Sixteen

"They must have headed for higher ground," Walker said.

Pike nodded and turned a complete circle. It made sense that whoever had survived would have instinctively sought the highest point nearby from which to gather their bearings in hopes of signaling for help. Of course, staying near the beach closest to the wreckage, knowing that it was only a matter of time before someone came looking for the *Mayr*, was probably more logical in the minds of civilians, unless they feared another tsunami. Or something else.

He crouched and inspected the footprints. Those closest to the small vessel were well preserved as the combination of the canopy and the pillared cliff saved them from the deluge. There were a good number of distinct sets of prints, which degenerated to vague sloppy impressions filled with standing water farther away from the enclave. Without a doubt, they were headed deeper inland and away from the eastern shore.

"They were in a hurry," Pike said, thinking aloud. "They didn't congregate here for very long to evaluate their situation, but instead struck off quickly and with little apparent indecision."

"You have to figure that wave could have washed nearly this high onto the island. If they feared a repeat performance, the last thing they would have wanted was to be caught down here on foot."

Pike pictured the eight men and women dragging their heavy craft through the mud, clothes thoroughly drenched, frozen to the bone, shivering, hearts pounding and hands trembling from their harrowing ordeal on the violent sea. The adrenaline would have been rapidly fleeing them, their core body temperatures steadily dropping. With the realization of relative safety and the understanding that the *Mayr* and all of their friends aboard it were now at the bottom of the ocean, shock would have descended upon them fairly rapidly.

He tried to put himself in their position. What would he have done? He would have ensured the preservation of the small vessel, just as they had. He would have recognized the need to conserve body heat once they were no longer moving and attempted to build a fire, which would have served the secondary purpose of functioning as a smoke signal. The ground here would have been protected well enough to shield a bonfire were they able to find enough dry kindling, but how would they have started it? He climbed into the boat and saw the empty brackets where the emergency kit had been mounted. The white plastic case itself lay overturned in the weeds against the face of the cliff in a mess of its contents. Pike performed a quick inventory of what remained. Missing were the First Aid kit, the waterproof matches, both of the hazard flares and the flare gun, and the emergency transceiver.

"Start scanning through the frequencies," Pike said. "Let's see if anyone's trying to broadcast a call for help."

"We would have picked it up on the tug when we neared the island."

Pike shot him a glance.

"Yes, sir." Walker stepped away from the boat and Pike heard the crackle of static.

In their shoes, he would have used the matches to start a fire on this very spot. A small stack of branches and crumbled leaves attested to the fact that they had at least started to do just that.

And then they had simply left without lighting it.

He walked back out into the sheeting rain. A gust of wind screamed through the wavering trees. The trail through the mud was now little more than an uneven trench that would be washed away altogether soon enough.

Pike was thankful he still wore the wetsuit, without which he would be beyond miserable like the poor souls whose path he now followed up the slope with Walker at his heels. The static provided a droning undertone to the clap of the rain and the sucking sounds of their footsteps.

After fifteen minutes of slipping and sliding uphill, using rocks and weeds to balance themselves, they reached a flat crest of land where the trees thinned. The elements had scoured the ground and erased the tracks. To the east, the Pacific stretched through the mist to the infinite horizon. The jungle grew denser to the north as it climbed up into the clouds that clung to the dormant caldera. To the west, the rolling hills would eventually give way to the kilometers of open sea that separated Ambitle from New Ireland and the chaos that had become of Papua New Guinea and Indonesia. A faint crimson glow stained the clouds, behind which the sun had begun to set.

"There's nothing on any of the bands." With a click, Walker silenced the buzz. "It's always possible their battery could be dead or they could have broken it or accidentally immersed it."

Or they could have grown wings and flown away, Pike refrained from adding. The hairs along his arms and neck rose uncomfortably beneath the skintight neoprene. It may have been years since he had last used his instincts in the field, but they had returned to him like a long lost friend.

Something was definitely not right here.

A dot appeared far off on the ocean to the east. With a wink of reflected lightning on the pilothouse windows, the *Huxley* announced her arrival.

"It's about time," Walker said. "We should be on the tug when she reaches the harbor. With a few more men and the proper equipment, we'll be able to form a proper search party."

The wind paused to draw another breath. In its absence, Pike smelled a familiar scent that both validated and churned his gut.

"Not just yet."

The wind blew into his face with a howl, chasing away the aroma, but he knew what he had smelled.

He struck off up the steep hillside toward the silent volcano. The trees clung to the harsh grade by sheer will alone, their exposed roots like the tentacles of great cephalopods. Using the trunks to haul himself higher, he reached a slanted obsidian outcropping that formed an overhang not quite large enough to qualify as a cave. Sprawled in its shallow mouth was exactly what Pike had expected to find.

Seventeen

Feni Islands
South Pacific Ocean
52 km East of New Ireland Island, Papua New Guinea
November 30th
5:42 p.m. PGT

Courtney awakened with a scream. She scrabbled backward, out from beneath the smothering weight on her body. She toppled from the bed and landed hard on her side. Her gaze darted around her unfamiliar surroundings in twitching movements as she screamed again and again until her parched throat felt as though it had been torn to ribbons. A man she had never seen threw himself to the floor beside her and gripped her shoulders. She planted her palms against his chest and shoved him with all of the strength she could muster. He landed on the wooden planks, flat on his back, a startled expression on his face. She took in his wetsuit, his damp brown hair and days' worth of stubble, his wide hazel eyes. He rose to his haunches. Courtney kicked at the slick deck until her back met with cold metal and she couldn't propel herself any farther away. In a panic, she searched the room with her eyes for anything she could use to hold the man at bay. All she saw were windows haphazardly boarded over with waterlogged plywood or spider-webbed with cracks, coils of frayed rope, a laptop computer on an iron drum, a bed to her left mounded with ratty blankets. A row of gaffes hung on the wall beside the lone entrance to the room, through which she could see only rain and the rolling brown sea. In order to reach them, she would have to fight through the man who now crawled warily toward her, open palms held up so she could clearly see them. His hands became those of the shadowed form on the other side of the isolation shield. She screamed and kicked at them.

It was only then, when her pale legs flailed in front of her, that she realized she was naked.

"Calm down," the man said. "I'm not going to hurt you."

Her heels connected with his hands and forearms and narrowly missed his face, which served to back him out of reach.

She gauged the distance to the gaffes. If she managed to land a solid kick to his face, she just might be able to—

A cold hand closed around her wrist, startling her to silence. Slowly, a man eased himself down from the bed and to the ground beside her.

"Shh." He folded his strong arms around her. She thrashed against him to no avail. "It's all right, Courtney. Everything's going to be okay now."

Her adrenaline spent, she collapsed into the man's arms. She buried her face in his bare chest and started to cry.

"We're safe now, Courtney." He stroked her auburn hair and whispered so close to her ear that she could feel his breath. "We made it."

She pulled away and looked up through tear-blurred eyes at John Bishop. His blonde hair was plastered back by blood from a laceration along his hairline. His face was so pallid that his blue eyes appeared recessed into bruises. He took her face in his hands and wiped away her tears with his thumbs.

"We survived," he whispered, and again drew her to him.

He dragged a blanket down from the bed and wrapped it around both of them. Her whole body shuddered as she sobbed. She pulled herself against him so tightly that her fingernails gouged into his back, but he only held her tighter.

The man in the wetsuit rose to his feet and cautiously eased closer to them. He just stood there, staring down at them as though uncertain how to proceed.

"Thank you," Bishop said.

The man nodded.

"Anytime."

With the realization of safety, the memories flooded back to Courtney, transporting her back aboard the *Mayr* in vivid detail.

She awakens to the sound of thunder and the wailing wind. She's too disoriented by her sudden arousal to make sense of her thoughts, a convolution of dream and reality. She struggles to open her eyes. Exhaustion had claimed her right there at her station under the hood in the lab. She must have just rested her head on her arms for just a second...

Courtney blinks away the sleep and raises her head. She peels a strand of hair from the corner of her mouth and wipes away the drool. The entire room is bathed in a scarlet glare, which only adds to the sense of displacement. She sits up and glances over her shoulder. All of the overhead fluorescents are off. The illumination is provided by the red light over the main door and another on the opposite side of the room near the batch reactor. The hum of machinery is subdued. It takes her a moment to realize that all of the non-essential equipment in the room has powered down. There is only the gurgle of fluid from her aquarium, the purr of the overhead fans, the continuous culture module, and the batch reactor, beyond which the contamination shield has been lifted and the recently sterilized steel walls reflect the red glow. Something must have happened to the main power for the backup generators to have kicked in.

Thunder rumbles overhead and the wind continues to shriek.

Even in her half-slumbering state, she recognizes there's something incongruous about the scene around her. The walls of the lab are reinforced by stainless steel and sound-damping insulation. She can't ever remember hearing a storm from inside the lab before.

Courtney stands and stomps the feeling back into her left foot. She yawns and stretches and gives her station a once-over to make sure she hasn't knocked over any of the test tubes of heme she'd isolated from the tube worm before heading toward the door. She looks at her watch. Almost midnight. She can't have been asleep for more than an hour. A good jolt of caffeine ought to clear her head. Maybe a sandwich if they still have the sliced turkey out. She'll swing by the mess, drop in on Ty, and come back to finish up before calling it a night. Her brother had been bedridden for the better part of the last two days following the incident with the ruptured seal, which had resulted in his confinement with his assistant Devin behind the biohazard shield for more than two hours and a lengthy and painful period of decontamination. The ship's doctor, a retired naval physician named Dr. Walter Partridge, had been treating him for what appeared to be a *dermatological reaction to the agents in the chemical shower and the burn to the left side of his face. His skin had first dried and cracked, and then begun to flake away, almost like in the aftermath of a sunburn. He'd spiked a high fever, had some pretty intense abdominal bloating and cramping, and bleeding from his nose and gums. During the rare occasions he'd been awake when she visited, however, he had remained in good spirits. She felt the pangs of guilt for how infrequent her visits had been due to her work, but he had assured her that he would be fine soon enough and was raring to rejoin her in the lab. Besides, Dr. Partridge seemed like he had things well in hand. The old doctor—who took these floating assignments twice a year to keep in touch with his nautical roots and to maintain his sanity with a wife he was quick to joke could peel the paint from the walls with the merest glance— had been incensed with both the manufacturers of the chemicals and the HazMat team for their obviously callous disregard of the safety protocols, which should never have led to such adverse reactions. If he had anything to say in the matter, Ty would be back on his feet in no time.*

She's peripherally aware that the rumbling sound has diminished and no longer originates from directly above her, but rather from somewhere near the port side. The wind sounds as though it's blowing unimpeded through the main corridor.

She presses the button to disengage the lock and the door slides back into the wall.

The world erupts in chaos.

Courtney cried out and clutched Bishop tighter. She shunted the memory before she was forced to relive another second of the horror.

Thumping sounds came from the stern and the boat rocked with transferred weight. She heard voices over the thrum of the rain. Three men appeared in the doorway.

"Dr. Martin. Mr. Bishop," one of the men said. He nodded to the man in the wetsuit. "I can't tell you how thrilled we all are that you survived. My name is James Van Horn. Let's get you aboard the *Huxley* so a doctor can have a good look at you."

He strode into the room and offered his hand to Courtney. The mention of the doctor suddenly reminded her of her brother.

"Where's Ty?" Courtney whispered.

"That's what we'd like to find out. We're all dying to learn exactly what happened here."

Courtney leapt up from the floor, shoved past the men, and ran out onto the deck. The rain pelted her naked body.

"Where's my brother?" she screamed across the raging sea.

Eighteen

Ambitle Island

Pike inspected the corpse and the rock ledge surrounding it from several feet away for fear of ruining any footprints. The body lay spread-eagle on a mat of gravel and decomposing leaves. He estimated the man was in his mid-twenties, although it was impossible to be certain with the way his facial architecture was distorted by fractures and the swelling from the absorbed seawater. Both of his legs were crooked from multiple fractures of his femora and tibiae, his black feet bare.

The wind screamed across the stone face, stirring the flies that crawled all over his skin and inside the gaping wound in his abdomen.

"This isn't one of the men from the lifeboat," Pike said.

"How can you be sure?" Walker's words were mumbled thanks to the hand he held over his mouth and nose.

"The edges of the lacerations to his gut. The level of decomposition makes it harder to tell, but you can see there's no bruising where the skin was torn. There's no blood either."

"There's no way the tsunami could have washed him all the way up here."

"Right. See those scuff marks on the ground over there? Someone dragged his body."

"You're suggesting some kind of animal hauled him up that steep hill and dragged him under this overhang so it could eat in peace out of the rain?"

Pike found a long stick and used it to brush aside the leaves that had accumulated on the remains, then peeled back the upper lip of the severed muscles and the layer of greasy fat. A vile stench billowed out on the wings of the disturbed flies. In the mess of rotting viscera, he made out the shapes of the liver and kidneys, the horn of the stomach cradling the pancreas, the thick black arteries and vena cava, and the musculature of the lumbar spine. Only the bowels had been removed. He let the flap close and turned a slow circle. No coils of intestine had been cast aside into the shrubs. Any animal that would have had the urge to consume a drowned man it had found washed up in the forest wouldn't have contented itself with the bowels alone. There should have been chunks ripped from the flesh, straps of muscle peeled away from the bones, and the prized internal organs sloppily consumed.

And it would have left tracks.

The bodies floating in the hold of the *Mayr* were nearly identical.

He could only remember one other time when he'd encountered corpses in this condition.

Pike brought the transceiver to his lips.

"Brazelton."

Static answered.

"Brazelton!"

Pike studied Walker, whose hand fell to the hilt of his knife as he stared down at the corpse, an expression of grim comprehension on his face.

"Brazelton!"

"I'm here. I'm here." His heavy breathing echoed under the stone lip. "The *Huxley* arrived. I...just helping them get...two survivors onto...Zodiac."

"Have they said anything yet?"

"The woman woke up screaming...before Van Horn boarded. I never had...chance to ask them—"

"They didn't say a word?"

"The guy thanked...and assured the woman they...safe now. She freaked...about not being able to find her brother."

"Nothing else?"

"What's going on...there, Pike?"

"Patch me through to Van Horn."

"What did you find?" Brazelton whispered.

"Get yourself changed and ready to head out. I need you on the ground over here. Now patch me through to Van Horn like I told you to!"

"Yes, si—" Brazelton cut himself off in his hurry to patch through the communication.

"Van Horn," came the crisp reply from the interim static.

"I need whatever men you can discreetly spare on Ambitle."

"What kind...men?"

"Our kind. Have them fully equipped and on the water in five minutes. They're to pick up Brazelton on their way. He knows where to go. You're on point over there. Get every available diver from the *Huxley* into the water to salvage anything that looks even remotely interesting. Every piece of equipment from every lab. I want those bodies down there brought to the surface and thoroughly evaluated. And get the data guy on that security footage now!"

"What aren't...telling me?"

"I want you personally to get everything they know out of the two we found in the *Mayr*, even if you have to beat it out of them."

"Someone else...handle things on this end. If you've got a...scent, let me—"

Pike terminated the transmission and stuffed the transceiver back into its holster.

"Think there's any chance the people who reached this island are still alive?" Walker asked. He finally broke his stare from the cadaver and looked at Pike. The sun had slipped from the sky, stranding them in darkness broken only by the sporadic strobes of lightning out over the open sea.

"That's what we're about to find out."

Nineteen

R/V Aldous Huxley

John Bishop gratefully cupped the hot mug of tea in his hands and allowed the steam to warm his chapped lips and nose. He felt as though he might never be warm again, especially not in these thin, baby blue scrubs and slippers that they insisted he wear. He still had no idea exactly how long he had been sealed inside the isolation chamber and tried his hardest not to even think about it. He focused on the speck of a tea leaf that swirled on the surface, on the cold sensation of the stethoscope against his back while the doctor listened to him breathe. Anything not to relive the confinement that nearly killed him. The eternal hours pacing back and forth behind that Plexiglas barrier, simultaneously praying for it to hold back the weight of the ocean on the other side and to break so they at least had a chance to swim to freedom, all the while able to see the release mechanism on the other side that he would never be able to reach. Listening to the metronomic *plip…plip…* of the water leaking through the seams and rivets, the accumulation inside their cage rising slowly, yet inevitably. The moaning and wailing of the research vessel as it tried to tear itself apart, blended with their own cries for help they feared would go unanswered. Wearing the oxygen masks long after the air had ceased to flow from the tanks in the wall, hoping that even a few molecules might leak out to keep them alive while they burned through their finite supply too quickly in their panic, and then more slowly as their bodies grew sluggish, their tired eyes wanting nothing more than to close for a few precious seconds. Resisting the urge while watching the silt accumulate on the other side, sealing them off from the laboratory with the finality of a tomb. Holding Courtney as long as he was able, trying to console her with his touch long after his words expired, until his arms simply fell from her shoulders into the rising water and the cold blackness claimed him, a part of him thankful for the release from the suffering. Most of all, he tried not to think about the fact that everyone else had died while he and Courtney still lived.

The hospital suite was nearly identical to the one on the *Mayr*. The same vinyl examination table with the same roll of paper to cover it. The same chair in the corner and the same black stool at the doctor's computer desk. The same cupboards and the same equipment mounted to the walls. Only the framed degrees were different, and where Dr. Partridge had tacked up the obligatory poster of a kitten clinging to a tree branch that read "Hang in there!", Dr. Stephen Kiley had mounted Christian Reise Lassen seascapes that made Bishop feel like he was drowning.

"Deep breath in," Dr. Kiley said. His head was shaved bald and so deeply tanned it looked like a catcher's mitt. His bulbous nose cast an omnipresent shadow over his black pencil-mustache. He was a cadaverous man with skeletal wrists and long, feminine fingers who appeared more than uncomfortable in his starched lab coat. "And again." At least the stethoscope had finally warmed to his skin. "There's a rattling sound in the lower lobes of both lungs called rales. It suggests there's fluid in there at the least, or quite possibly pneumonia. But considering what you've been through, if that's the worst of it, we'll call it a victory."

Bishop nodded and slurped the tea. The heat trickling down through his chest and into his belly was the most wonderful sensation he had ever experienced.

"We'll start you on a course of antibiotics..."

The physician's words faded into the background noise. Bishop looked through the open doorway into the observation room, where Courtney slept in the single hospital bed with the covers tucked up to her chin. A slim tube disappeared under the blankets from the IV bag hanging on the pole beside her. The bedside monitor tracked her heart rate, blood pressure, and pulse oxygen. Her slumber was artificially induced by the calming influence of the anti-anxiety medication and the mild sedatives, and he was grateful for it. After everything she had endured, learning that her brother had been lost to the sea was more than she could bear, like a butterfly emerging from its cocoon to find the world burning. In those long hours—days?—of imprisonment, of knowing with complete certainty that they were going to die, they had forged a bond that few people could ever comprehend. Not even he could fully rationalize the intense emotional connection they now shared. They were safely aboard the ship that would eventually take them home, among people who tended to their every need, and still he had to fight the urge to leap to his feet to pummel anyone who so much as approached her room.

He watched her breathe, as he had only wished he could in the darkness of the isolation room, rather than feeling her respirations slow through the arms wrapped around her to keep her from freezing to death even as he leeched her body heat from her. The nasal cannula filled her lungs with pure oxygen, giving strength to the rising of the blankets on her chest. The color was slowly returning to her face. Her freckles no longer stood out like blood spatters on snow. Perspiration beaded her forehead and dampened her slicked back auburn hair. After holding her so close for so long, his body felt her physical absence like an amputation.

He prayed her sleep was restorative, for when she awakened, he knew she would be forced to confront Tyler's death and the barrage of questions she would have to relive their nightmare to answer. As he was sure he would have to at any moment now, as well.

Kiley clapped him on the back.

"...a lucky man, Mr. Bishop."

Bishop could only nod.

The front door of the hospital suite opened inward. Unlike the laboratories on the level below them, there was no need for the pressurized stainless steel airlocks and the security codes.

A tall man Bishop recognized stepped into the room. He was one of the three men who had ushered him across the tumultuous ocean from the decrepit tug to the *Huxley*. Now that he was clothed and somewhat oriented to his surroundings, Bishop truly saw him for the first time. The man's rigid posture and bearing were pure military, and while he had a solid build and clearly defined musculature, he had the look of a man more accustomed to using his brains than his brawn. His dark hair shined with the pomade he used to smooth it back from his widow's peak. His perfectly tweezed eyebrows arched over blue eyes that sized up Bishop even as he scrutinized the man in return. The man offered a practiced smile filled with veneers.

"Our introduction was a little rushed earlier, and definitely not under the most ideal circumstances." The man strode across the room and proffered his hand. He casually wiped it on his pants after Bishop shook it. "I'm Dr. James Van Horn, a geneticist employed by our shared benefactor, GeNext Biosystems. To say we're all relieved to have you with us is an understatement." He smiled again and inclined his head toward Dr. Kiley. "This quack treating you well enough?"

Kiley chuckled as he returned his lab coat to its hanger and slung his stethoscope around his neck.

This whole disingenuous act was wearing on Bishop's already frayed nerves. And why had they sent a geneticist?

"I'd kill for a cheeseburger, but otherwise I'm fine." Bishop locked eyes with Van Horn. "So let's cut to the chase. What do you need me to do?"

The smile never left Van Horn's face. It was disconcerting, but not nearly as much as the almost predatory spark in the man's eyes.

"To be blunt, I need your help accounting for every second of the time between our last communication with the *Mayr* and her sinking. Are you up for it?"

Bishop hopped down from the examination table.

"I don't know how much help I'll be, but I'm more than ready to get this over with."

"Good." Van Horn gestured toward the open door. "Then if you'll come with me, perhaps we can get you that cheeseburger on our way."

Twenty

Ambitle Island

Pike stood at the edge of the forest, out of the rain, and watched his men haul the Zodiac past the debris and into the trees to his right. Storm clouds blotted out the stars and the moon. The only source of illumination in the otherwise pitch black night was the spectral lights on the *Huxley* that diffused through the mist rolling into the harbor from the east. Pike had hoped to smell wood-smoke on the wind after sundown, but wasn't surprised in the slightest that he didn't. If his suspicions were correct, there was no one left alive to start one. That wasn't exactly true. There was still someone on this island, whom he imagined would soon enough come looking for them.

He walked over to where his men were already equipping themselves from the padded cases on the small vessel. Each had already donned a pair of thermal infrared night vision fusion goggles, which allowed them to clearly see the forest around them and any variations in heat signatures. Anything below eighty-one degrees Fahrenheit appeared in shades of black and midnight blue, while above that the scale ascended through lighter blues and purples to reds and oranges, and finally to the brilliant yellow of human body temperature and blinding white above it. The men looked like sleek black insects. Under one arm, they each holstered military-issue Advanced Taser M26s with laser illumination and a thirty-five foot range, while beneath the other they packed Beretta M9A1 semiautomatic pistols with fifteen-round magazines of 9mm Parabellum jacketed hollow point rounds, and front-activated infrared laser sights. Walker tossed him a rucksack, the contents of which included a one-liter hydro bladder, an LED Maglite, a handful of nutrition bars and dry rations, matches, flares, heat packs, a chemical gas respirator mask, and a portable emergency scuba tank with a regulator. He slung it over his shoulder, exchanged his wet shoes for a pair of waterproof, steel-toed black combat boots, and donned the night vision gear. He switched on the apparatus and appraised his men. Their faces were yellow and orange below their goggles. Fuchsia coronae framed their heads. Their black scuba suits appeared purple and blue.

Van Horn had chosen well. In addition to Brazelton and Walker, the only one among them who hadn't been on the Zambian mission, Jericho Montgomery, a former biological warfare specialist with the Department of Homeland Security, and Roger Pearson, an experienced field surgeon, had made the crossing from the *Huxley*. Both men were broad-chested and stood over six feet tall. In their wetsuits and goggles, they could have passed for twins, save for Montgomery's thick blonde goatee.

Pike gave them all a quick once over, then struck off into the jungle. They weaved through trunks and snarls of vegetation, the rain on the leaves shimmering blue, until they reached the flattened trail and the abandoned lifeboat at the end of it. Pearson paused to study the blood smears on the gunwales.

"Nothing life threatening," he said. "The blood's superficial, not arterial."

Pike nodded and led them up to the crest of the slope where they'd found the disemboweled corpse on the rock ledge. The physician's assessment matched Pike's. The cause of death was drowning. The abdominal wounds had been inflicted postmortem, and only the intestines had been removed. A glance confirmed that Pearson had made the same leap of logic that Pike had. Montgomery drew his pistol and chambered a round.

Good. They were all on the same page.

"So what now?" Brazelton asked.

"Here's how I see it," Pike said. "Seven people reached the shore and dragged their boat high enough onto land that there was no way another tsunami could wash it away. They were drenched, shivering, and terrified. The first thing they did was crack open the First Aid kit to tend to whoever was bleeding while the others set about gathering whatever dry kindling and wood they could find. Then something startled them to flight. Possibly one of them discovered this gutted body while hunting for firewood…or maybe something else. Either way, they abandoned their craft in a hurry, taking only what was readily at hand."

"Then where did they go?" Montgomery asked.

"Their trail disappears at the top of this rise," Walker said. "There's no sign of them beyond that point. Whatever tracks they left were wiped out by the rain."

"There's always something," Montgomery said. "No one can pass through space without leaving a physical trace. We'll find their path."

"They had to have gone one of two directions," Pike said. "They either struck off toward higher ground, or chose the route of least resistance in order to travel faster, which means heading downhill toward the western shore. With the tidal waves coming from the east, they would have figured the bulk of the island would shield them."

"It would help if we knew for sure if we were dealing with civilians or crew."

"We have to assume both."

"Crew would have known someone would eventually track the activated SART on the lifeboat, and that's where they would start looking. Even under duress, they wouldn't have wanted to stray too far from it. A civilian's instinct would be to head for the nearest beach and try to signal an airplane or a passing ship."

"Then it's possible that in a panic they could have split up. We're going to have to do the same." Pike looked up the steep hillside toward the distant dormant volcano, then down to his left where the dense forest obscured the topography. "Montgomery and Pearson. You two head north toward higher ground. The rest of you, come with me. Keep your transceivers on. I want to know the moment you find anything. And I mean anything." He paused. "I know I don't have to tell you what we're potentially dealing with here. Take all necessary precautions, but use your tasers first. If at all possible, I want this thing alive."

He dismissed them with a nod and watched the multicolored spectral shapes of Montgomery and Pearson vanish into the blue and black forest without a sound.

"'I want this thing alive'?" Walker asked.

Pike brushed past him and started the treacherous westward descent through the slick mud, weeds, and brush.

"Saddle up, men," he said. "Let the hunt commence."

Twenty-one

R/V Aldous Huxley

Bishop followed Van Horn into one of the engineering rooms on the main deck. The worktables had been swept clean of the tools that had once covered them and replaced with a half-dozen computer terminals. Men he had never seen and who were given no introduction labored in front of the keyboards, their faces reflecting the changing colors on the monitors in front of them. None of them so much as acknowledged him with a glance.

Van Horn guided him to one of the stations and cleared his throat. The man at the terminal blinked his eyes and turned toward them.

"We're nearly done downloading the security footage from the *Mayr*," the man said. With his chestnut hair slicked back from his round face and black-rimmed glasses, he reminded Bishop of an owl. "Bear in mind, the storage unit wasn't designed to take such a beating, nor was it intended to be fully immersed for any length of time, so the quality is significantly degraded, but I think we should be able to clean it up well enough to at least make it viewable."

"Very good, Mr. Barnes." Van Horn drew a stool from beneath the table behind them and gestured for Bishop to sit. "While we wait, would you be so kind as to play the video from the dive earlier this afternoon for Mr. Bishop."

"Aye, sir."

Van Horn pulled up another stool and sat shoulder-to-shoulder with Bishop.

"What exactly do you need me to do?" Bishop asked.

"You're about to see the video feed from the divers who explored the wreckage and found you. I want you to tell me what we're looking at and everything you remember."

"The whole thing's still foggy. I can only clearly recall bits and pieces."

"Then perhaps this will refresh your memory."

The large monitor divided into four quadrants. The top two and the bottom left showed dim underwater images while the bottom right remained blank. Flashlight beams diffused into hazy water churning with small bubbles and microorganisms. Everything outside the beam's limited reach remained in absolute blackness until the diver swung the light in its direction. The reality that the *Mayr* had become a sunken ghost ship struck him like a hammer. It barely looked like the same vessel upon which he had set sail less than a month ago, as though it had been rotting on the ocean floor for decades. The walls were buckled, the doors warped. Sediment covered everything and schools of fish had laid claim to the ruins.

"As you know," Van Horn said, "three divers were sent down into the wreckage to divine the reason for her sinking and to salvage everything of importance. Their first pass was exploratory in nature, to help us gather topical information before searching for specific equipment and proprietary research."

Bishop's heart thudded in his chest. The images were startling. He felt himself holding his breath as though he were slowly suffocating all over again.

"Mr. Barnes, please enlarge the number one feed."

With a keystroke, the image from the top left filled the screen.

"What do you see, Mr. Bishop?"

"That's the stairwell leading from the main deck to the hold." He watched as the diver swam sideways and then upward into the corridor leading to the engine room. The ship had settled on its starboard side as he only vaguely recalled. A human shape materialized in the light and floated toward the camera. He recognized the pale, bloated face immediately. "Kim. Stanley, I think. She was one of the graduate research assistants."

Bishop realized that Van Horn was no longer watching the monitor. The man's eyes watched him instead, gauging his reactions.

"What do you remember about the hours preceding your time in the isolation chamber? Why did you and Dr. Martin seal yourselves in there?"

On the screen, the footage wound through a maze of pipes that cast long shadows through the murky water. In his mind, images flashed like bolts of lightning tearing the night sky. Waking from a deep sleep in his cabin to the sound of waves slamming against the hull and screams from the hallway. Stumbling into the corridor where bodies collided and raced past him toward the clogged stairwell. A spatter of blood on the wall. A black puddle on the floor from which sloppy smears and footprints originated. The crimson glare of the emergency lights. The ship rocking violently beneath him. Funneling into the crowd and down to the main deck where the screams intensified and he saw a man's body crumpled against the wall—

The same man's corpse floated into view on the monitor, pointing through the screen at Bishop from beyond the grave. Behind him, more bodies floated in cold storage, their limbs entangled.

"Jesus," he whispered. How had the body ended up all the way down there? He tried to look away, but couldn't tear his eyes from the corpses on the screen as the camera panned across their features one at a time.

"Talk to me, Bishop," Van Horn said. "We need to find out what happened here. Why were all of these people down in the hold when the ship was foundering? What made you and Dr. Martin decide to seal yourselves in the lab?" His voice rose with each question until it was nearly a shout. "What did you see?"

Bishop clenched his fists to stave off hyperventilation. He focused on his breathing, while on the screen the diver swam back through the engine room, down the stairwell, and into the main corridor. The doors to the labs passed at the edges of the light's aura, the stainless steel bowed, pitted, and deeply scratched.

"Tell me what you saw!"

The diver swam through the thin gap between the door and the frame leading into the clean lab. Two other divers hovered with their backs to him. Their headlamps diffused through the silt-blanketed biohazard shield. Closer and closer the camera came until he could see into the chamber. Two shapes were heaped in the corner in the standing water. With the way the video jerked, it was impossible to tell if either of them was alive.

"I'm running out of patience, Bishop. I need to know—"

Bishop leapt from the chair and staggered backward from the monitor. In his head, he was there again, his memories disjointed, flickering like a reel-to-reel projecting random frames. The shield dropping in front of his face, silencing the horrible cries. Courtney clasping his hand under the red glare. Smears of blood on the barrier, smudged handprints and arterial arches. A silhouette pacing on the other side, turning toward them, the emergency lights reflecting from its—

"Eyes," Bishop whispered. "I remember its eyes."

Twenty-Two

Ambitle Island

They picked up the trail under a section of canopy so thick it was impervious even to the rain about half a kilometer west-northwest from where they had split up on the rise. Clearly demarcated footprints led ever westward, not at a leisurely pace, but at a full-out sprint as evidenced by the spacing between them. There were four distinct sets: three adult males and a fourth, much smaller man, or, more likely, a woman. The spongy loam was frequently disturbed where one of them had fallen and hurriedly scrabbled back to his feet. Between the closely packed trunks, their snaking roots, and the vines that dangled from nearly every bough overhead, progress was slower than he would have liked. Pike could only imagine what could have scared the survivors badly enough that they had even attempted to navigate this forest at such a breakneck speed, blindly barreling through the shrubs and the thickets, branches tearing at their clothes and exposed skin, unable to see more than a few feet ahead of them at any given time.

Montgomery had radioed in twenty minutes ago with news that he and Pearson had found a similar path heading northward, confirming that the landing party had indeed split up. Their tracks had been spaced more evenly, their path less erratic. It was steeper going with portions of the eroded slope held together by the roots of the trees that clung perilously to the soil at sharp angles and the sheer stone escarpments that forced a more circuitous route.

Pike envisioned the circumstances that would have caused the group to divide in such a manner. Considering the speed with which they'd broken camp before it was even established, he couldn't fathom that there had been much debate. Perhaps it was possible they had willingly separated in order to increase their chances of finding rescue; however, he felt it more likely that something else, some external factor, had necessitated their sudden, chaotic flight.

And he had a pretty good idea what had done so.

Pike realized he was approaching the search from the wrong perspective. He needed to think less like the prey and more like the predator. If he were stalking a group of people, how would he do it? He would secure the high ground and run them like a herd of cattle until all of their energy was spent and they would provide the least resistance. He would hide his presence in the shadows and stay just far enough behind them that they could feel him there without being able to do anything about it, then wait until the right moment arrived to attack. Once he adapted his thinking, it didn't take long to find what he was looking for.

"I need more light."

Pike knelt on the soft mat of moss and decomposing leaves ten yards uphill from the trail, his night vision goggles pulled up onto his forehead like a unicorn's horn. He shined his flashlight onto the impression in the detritus, which bore the distinct, though poorly defined, shape of a human footprint. Walker directed his beam onto the print while Pike carefully extracted the vegetative matter to expose the black mud underneath.

"It looks like about a size twelve," Breazelton said. He held his own foot up beside the imprint. "Maybe thirteen."

"And it's bare," Walker said. "The edges aren't smooth, and there's no tread. The mud's more compressed where he bears his weight." He gestured to the print as he spoke. "This sideways L-shape here is where the ball of the foot was planted. No heel contact. You can see the gouges from the toes in front of it. Whoever left it was obviously running."

Pike traced his fingertip along the ridges left by the toes. They were teardrop-shaped rather than rounded. He glanced at Brazelton, who nodded that he had noticed the same thing. They had definitely seen tracks like this before.

There were two more footprints spaced approximately a meter apart before they lost the trail to the wilderness. Pike was about to suggest they fan out to follow both trails when his transceiver crackled.

"We found them," Pearson said.

Pike deciphered the nature of the discovery from the tone of Pearson's voice.

"Where are you?"

"Maybe half a kilometer…north from where we separated."

"What's their condition?"

"If it's confirmation…a theory you're looking for…consider it confirmed."

"Stay right there. Don't touch anything until I get there."

"Kind of hard not to," Pearson said.

"Keep following this trail," Pike said to Brazelton. He sheathed his transceiver. "Report in every fifteen minutes."

"There's one of them on this island," Walker said. "Those things we've been collecting for GeNext. That's what we're really hunting, isn't it?"

"If you encounter anything out of the ordinary, call me first," Pike said. "Do not attempt to engage this thing without waiting for backup. If confrontation is unavoidable, I expect you to do everything in your power to take it down alive."

Thunder rumbled across the sea from the west. Soft at first, it grew into a mechanical whooping sound as it approached.

"Don't screw this up," Pike said.

He whirled and sprinted back through the jungle as the pulsating sound of rotors swept overhead, shaking the canopy with hurricane force.

Twenty-Three

R/V Aldous Huxley

Courtney dreamed the dreams of the dead.

She was a child of seven or eight, wearing dirty shorts and a T-shirt decorated with the mud she'd wiped onto her chest from her hands, her red hair a wind-knotted mess, covered with freckles from head to toe. Her brother climbed over the rocky Jersey coast ahead of her, glancing occasionally back over his shoulder to make sure she wasn't about to fall. A frigid wind blew in across the Atlantic, driving the waves against the breakers with the sound of repeated freeway collisions and throwing foamy spray high above them to alight like rain on their backs. She struggled to keep up, knowing full well that Ty would always outpace her. When she eventually slid down the embankment, she found her brother crouching over a tide pool.

"They're stuck in here until the tide comes in to wash them away again," he said.

Courtney stared down into the water, where minnows darted restlessly, crabs fiddled in the sand, and snails mowed the green slime. At the very bottom, a creature with pale tendrils played host to a tiny, red-spotted yellowfin grouper that clung to the sanctuary it provided. It was an anemone, she was certain. She would have told Ty that she recognized it, if only she were able to make the word come out right. Anen...Amem...Amenome... But it wasn't like any anemone they had encountered in their explorations. This one was an almost translucent white with only five unevenly spaced tendrils that were tattered and falling apart where the scavengers had gnawed them. Weren't they supposed to be able to sting anything that bit them?

As she stared at it, the details became clear. The tentacles were fingers, the cup where the mouth should have been, a palm.

The stalk she assumed moored it to the rocks was instead a wrist that a crab used to crawl up to steal a morsel with its pincers.

Waves crashed harder and harder against the shore, a ceaseless thunder that made her want to clap her hands over her ears, but they wouldn't respond. She could only look down at the tide pool as her vision drifted in and out of focus until it settled upon the reflection on the water.

"Sometimes they're trapped in there for days at a time, until the animals on the land notice them and make a meal of them," Ty's reflection said. His skin took on the shimmering silver cast of a fish's scales and twin scarlet circles flashed in his corneas.

She awakened with the sound of waves still crashing inside her head. No, the pounding was too rhythmic, like a heart beating way too fast. It seemed to hover somewhere over her head.

"Feeling any better?" a man she didn't immediately recognize asked. He stood beside her bed, changing out the IV bag that tethered the tall metal pole to the point of discomfort on her right arm by a long tube.

She tried to speak, but only produced the clicking sound of her dry tongue peeling from the roof of her mouth. With the realization that she was in the shipboard infirmary, the memories flooded back, overwhelming her and rolling down her cheeks as tears. She remembered waiting to die in the isolation chamber while the ship was battered and driven to the bottom of the sea. Bishop holding her until the darkness without became the darkness within as her heartbeat slowed to the pace of the drops of seawater dripping into her tomb. The image of her brother's visage on the tide pool returned, only now as that of an adult, his face swollen and distorted, beneath the water instead of above it. A flash of red from his eyes and she was again inside her lab.

Screams assail her from the corridor. She hears what sounds like an air raid siren. Men and women formed of shadows by the scarlet glare streak past as they run aft. Her mind's unable to rationalize the bedlam.

She stands in the doorway, immobile as though in a dream, until someone veers in her direction and grabs her by the hand.

"What's happening?" she cries.

"I don't know!" a voice she recognizes as Bishop's shouts.

He pulls her into the hallway.

The floor heaves violently beneath her feet, throwing them both to the ground. Bodies topple onto them. Feet stampede past their heads. She reflexively throws her arms up in front of her face to ward them off and takes a heel to the gut. Bishop tugs on her hand and drags her to her feet. The tide has turned and those that had been running toward the stern now charge directly at them.

The ship lurches again, hurling them against the wall. The Mayr's turned her broad side into the waves. No longer cutting through them, she's at their mercy.

A rush of freezing water races down the corridor, rising over their ankles and threatening to sweep them off their feet.

The boat cants in the opposite direction. It's all she can do to stay upright amid the screaming figures streaming past.

Bishop pulls her again, this time back into the lab. Equipment falls from the worktables and shatters on the floor. Her elbow knocks a microscope from the counter. She trips over a stool, but manages to catch herself without dragging both of them down. They retreat from the doorway as the floor rocks and seawater floods across the threshold.

The klaxon continues to blare.

"What's going on?" she screams.

Bishop tightens his grip on her hand in response.

They retreat to the forward portion of the lab, away from the lone entrance.

The screams in the hallway reach a crescendo.

A rack of beakers plummets to the ground on the other side of the table with the machine gun-prattle of shattering glass. The real-time PCR machine wobbles and clatters against the mass spectrometer with a shriek and a crash.

Something hard presses into her back. She reaches behind her and feels stainless steel, smooth and rounded. It vibrates against her touch. Tubing coils around her wrist.

The batch reactor.

Metal groans as the ship heaves again. They stumble to the right. Courtney reaches out to brace herself. A round button gives way under her palm. Another klaxon joins the chorus.

"No!" Bishop shouts.

The Plexiglas isolation shield shoots down from the ceiling and embeds itself in the floor with enough force to drop her to her knees.

"Raise it!" Bishop yells.

He pounds his fists against the cordon. The floor tips on a steep incline.

"I can't! The mechanism to retract it is on the other side!"

A wave breaks against the hull like a torpedo, launching them from their feet. Her head strikes something hard and she tastes metal in her mouth. The entire world spins. She's vaguely aware of Bishop on top of her, blood pouring over his closed eyelids from a laceration across his hairline, and someone shouting over the tumult.

"Let us in! Please, God! You have to let us in!"

"Where's Bishop?" she whispered.

"He ought to be back shortly," Dr. Kiley said. "You should really rest in the meantime. Your pulse ox is still only—"

"No."

Courtney threw back the covers and attempted to lunge out of bed, but instead collapsed to the floor. The IV tube ripped out of her arm. A mixture of blood and saline ran down her forearm to drip from her fingertips. She struggled to her feet, and, swaying, staggered toward the door.

She had to find Bishop.

A swell of nausea washed over her and she had to lean against the door jamb to quell her dizziness.

"Please, Dr. Martin." Dr. Kiley stepped in front of her and took her gently by the shoulders. "You aren't in any kind of shape to—"

Courtney brushed him aside and crossed the exam room toward the door to the corridor.

The memory consumed her. In her mind, she was rising from the standing water inside the isolation chamber, unsteady from the blow to the head. Double-vision changed to single and then back again. The ship rocked wildly. She braced herself against the biohazard shield and peered out into the lab. Bishop grunted behind her in an effort to stand, but only ended up splashing back into the water. The crimson glare had bled onto the Plexiglas in smudges and arcs, from which glistening rivulets trickled. And through them, she watched the silhouette pace like a caged tiger. When its face turned toward her, twin circles reflected the emergency lights from its eyes.

Twenty-Four

Ambitle Island

Pike sprinted through the jungle. He pushed his body beyond its limits. He'd passed the point of exhaustion long ago and now functioned on pure adrenaline. His cheeks bled from the lacerations inflicted by the branches in his way. His palms and knees were skinned from repeatedly tripping and scrambling up the slick rock formations, but he was too focused on the task at hand to feel any of it.

Brazelton radioed in. He acknowledged the report with a double click of the transceiver. He had no breath to waste. He was nearly upon the location from which his men had called to announce their discovery. With a mixture of anticipation and apprehension, he burst through a wall of foliage into a small clearing filled with swatches of waist-high grasses and clusters of shrubs. Here the competing batai and rosewood trees formed a ring around a knoll that granted a glimpse of the storm clouds overhead, so low they seemed barely out of his reach. The slope dropped off to the east, affording a panoramic view over the treetops of the southern tip of Babase Island and the vast eternity of the Pacific. Mounds of dirt and clay stood from the earth like termite mounds beside foot-wide, circular holes where the ground had been cored, presumably by the mining firm out of Sydney that leased the mineral rights.

Montgomery turned from where he stood at the northern edge of the meadow and watched Pike approach.

A flash if lightning momentarily blinded Pike through his goggles. He jerked them up onto his forehead, grabbed his flashlight, and crossed the clearing.

"Took you long enough." Montgomery cupped a hand over his eyes to shield them from the rain and stepped out from beneath the canopy. "I was beginning to wonder if you stopped for a nap or something."

Pike wasn't in the mood.

"Where are they?"

"You're standing on the first one."

Pike stopped in his tracks and looked down into the swaying grass. He shoved aside clumps until he found the body. It was sprawled on its back, arms stretched out to either side. The man's face was gaunt and blackened by decomposition. His dark hair crawled with the insects that burrowed into his eyes and scurried through the gap between his parted lips. There was just enough left of his tattered shirt to reveal the stylized, DNA-helix X of the GeNext logo on his breast. His pectorals were slashed without evidence of healing. The lower anterior portion of his ribcage showed through an abdominal wound that looked like it had been inflicted by a shovel. Skin, muscle, and fat had been peeled away to either side where they were now greasy, desiccated straps of rawhide. Rain pooled on the remaining viscera in a vile puddle of rotting organs and squirming larvae. The smell was that of a stagnant marsh. At least the storm held the majority of the flies and mosquitoes at bay.

Pike crouched and sloshed the mealy water aside to better visualize the contents. Although deterioration was advancing at a rapid click, it was readily apparent that the bowels had been removed.

"What is it about the guts?" Montgomery asked. "If it were me, I'd be carving off ass steaks, not slurping down tubes full of shit."

"You didn't find the intestines anywhere around here?"

"Like I said, thing's probably kicking back somewhere squeezing crap out of them like toothpaste."

"Where's Pearson?"

"Just follow your nose."

Pike stomped through the weeds until they gave way to the forest and he ducked under the canopy. He found Pearson fifty yards into the overgrowth beside a scorched trunk, at the base of which a spent flare had been cast. The groundcover had managed to burn in a twenty foot swatch before the rain put it out. Amid the standing black water humming with mosquitoes, he saw two bodies. One lay on his face, his back opened to the left of his spine between his iliac crest and his lower ribs. Putrid viscera bloomed from the hole through which his bowels had been pulled out. The meat of his shoulders and upper back had been slashed repeatedly, his drenched shirt stained by blood. Another man was crumpled under the charcoaled branches of a senna tora shrub, his cooked legs alive with black flies. His hair was burnt to his blistered scalp. The flesh on his face was the consistency of barbecued pig skin. His mouth was frozen in a scream that exposed all of his teeth. The lacerations across his cheeks, neck, and chest had opened wider while he burned to weep a crust of blood and amber pustulates reminiscent of sap. His abdomen was seared crisp, but remained otherwise intact.

"It ambushed them in the clearing," Pike said. "It took down one of them and followed the other two into the jungle. They tried to fend it off with the flare."

"Somehow, they lost the flare, starting the groundcover on fire," Pearson said.

"Or else one of them caught himself on fire and it was his burning corpse that lit the forest."

"Either way, it ripped the hell out of that one's back in the process of disemboweling him, but made no attempt to gut the man lying in the bush, still burning."

"Why would it not finish off the one who was on fire?"

"Maybe it's scared of fire." Pearson shrugged. "Or maybe it just likes its food raw."

"There's more to it than that."

Pike walked a circuit around the remains. The drone of the insects made it difficult to concentrate. A riot of footprints was concealed by the black residua of the fire on the upper layer of soil. He shined his flashlight onto the trunks surrounding him. Several still bore dried blood spatters only partially washed away by the rain that channeled through the bark.

He tried to envision the aftermath. Burdened by a combined sixty feet of slick intestinal rope, it wouldn't have been able to move very fast. Nor was there any way it would have been able to consume that much mass, especially in a single sitting. The more he contemplated that quandary, the more he realized that they had to be missing something.

"Document everything you possibly can," Pike said. "Take pictures from every conceivable angle. Note everything you see or smell. Take samples of the soil and the blood spatters. Anything you can think of. Use your imagination. Then get these bodies back down to the beach for retrieval."

"You want us to lug these corpses all the way back down the mountain?"

Pike shot Pearson a glare that ended all debate. First and foremost, Pike was not about to leave these men to rot where they fell. Secondly, there was an entire team of scientists on the research vessel floating in the harbor that was surely raring to take a crack at them.

The ground shuddered underfoot. Pike looked at Pearson, who acknowledged the tremor with an uneasy shrug.

He turned his back on Pearson and donned his goggles once more. White flashes of lightning from behind him stretched the shadows of the trees leading to the west. He scanned the ground for footprints but came up empty. The only sign of passage was the occasional matted clump of grass or bent green limb. He wasn't exactly sure what he was searching for until he was more than a hundred yards downwind of the charnel smell. A faint buzzing sound drew him onward and downhill to the right. The buzzing grew louder until it separated from the patter of raindrops on the broad leaves overhead and he saw a deep purple cloud that at first looked like smoke swirling in the branches. As he neared, the smoke coalesced into individual dots that proved to be the source of the sound. He paused and surveyed the area. There were no heat signatures or any sign of movement beyond the blue outlines of the black trees. He again exchanged his goggles for his flashlight and directed the beam up into the massive kapok tree.

Flies swirled around what at first looked like a grayish python folded over a thick bough. Its coils shimmered with the reflected light. They were so swollen and engorged that Pike barely recognized them as one of the missing lengths of intestines.

He broke a branch from the trees, and, using the boulder beside the trunk for leverage, reached up to slide the bowels from the canopy. The tip of the stick pierced the mucosal lining and tore a long gash as the bowels uncoiled and fell to the ground. The foul aroma of rotten eggs and decomposition billowed from the tear as the tube sagged and deflated.

"Oh, for the love of…" Pike said. He had to cover his mouth and nose with his hand to combat the stench.

He studied it with his beam. The miniature vessels had turned black and it had lost its former elasticity. The colon was barely distinguishable from the jejunum by the bulging haustra. Digested contents seeped from the ragged laceration. The ends, where it had been severed from the stomach on one end and the rectum on the other, had been tied together. Pike stared at the sloppy knot for a long moment.

Why would anyone—anything—do something like that?

Twenty-Five

Feni Islands
South Pacific Ocean
52 km East of New Ireland Island, Papua New Guinea
November 30ᵗʰ
9:12 p.m. PGT

Bradley unfastened the harness, ducked against the wind from the rotors, and ran across the slippery deck toward the open doorway where two men in slickers awaited his arrival. They ushered him into the corridor and out of the sheeting rain while he waited for Reaves to be similarly lowered to the stern of the *Huxley*.

"How was your flight, sir?" one of the seamen asked. He had to shout to be heard over the thunder of the blades and the waves crashing against the hull.

"Seemingly interminable," Bradley said. The truth was that even the Lear jet had felt as though it was barely crawling across the Pacific, the Bell Iroquois that had been waiting for them on the tarmac in Rabaul on New Britain Island like a gnat at the mercy of a hurricane gale. Every second had been spent in communication with Van Horn and the technical crew on the research vessel as they detailed the status of the salvage operation, the condition of the survivors, and Pike's relayed communications from Ambitle Island. He watched every new video clip the moment it was downloaded. Even though he hadn't slept in nearly two days, he wasn't the slightest bit tired. He was wired, as though fueled by a mixture of caffeine and cocaine pumped straight into his bloodstream on an adrenaline infusion. The more he heard and saw, the more he became convinced that his quest had finally come to an end. At last, the truth of his obsession was about to be revealed to him. He tried to temper his enthusiasm with the fact that so many had died here, but even such a sobering thought did little to dampen his excitement. A part of him knew that was morally reprehensible, but the majority of him simply didn't care.

The tugboat a hundred yards off stern was bristling with activity. Spotlights had been mounted to its decrepit wheelhouse to light its bow, where men in wetsuits hauled equipment from the bottom of the sea with the winch, unloaded them, and prepared them for transport to the *Huxley*. As he watched, the steel cable raised a large batch reactor from the rough waves. Its smooth housing glinted indigo with a strobe of lightning.

Reaves slipped out of the rope seat and ran to join them. The Huey rose into the storm clouds and banked westward back toward Papua New Guinea.

"Shall we?" Reaves asked. He squeegeed the rain from his hair and gestured toward the dimly-lit corridor.

"If you'll follow us then, sirs, we'll see you to your cabins—"

"Take us to the command center," Bradley said, more sharply than he had intended.

The man held up the bags he clutched in either hand as though asking what he should do with them. Their personal effects had been lowered to the deck before them.

"Would you be so kind as to drop those off in our cabins after you take us to see Mr. Van Horn?" Reaves asked far more tactfully.

"Aye, sir."

The first man led them into the ship, while the second trailed with their bags. Bradley had studied the *Mayr*'s deck plans so many times since her sinking that he knew exactly where they were going on her twin. The flickering lights through the open doorway to the engineering room welcomed them into the impromptu command center. Van Horn glanced toward the door when they entered and strode to meet them with a smile.

"Dr. Bradley. Dr. Reaves," he said, proffering his hand to each in turn. "Glad you made it safely."

Bradley surveyed the room. There were four faceless men working at as many computer terminals. Two more darted around the room from one piece of hardware to the next, then back again. One man stood apart from the rest. He was bundled in blankets and propped on a stool. His blonde hair was wild, his face pale. Eyes

MICHAEL McBRIDE

recessed in shadow, the man merely watched them with an unreadable expression. Bradley recognized him immediately from the personnel file he'd read so many times he could probably recite it by heart.

"Mr. Bishop." Bradley disengaged himself from Van Horn and Reaves and offered his hand to the submersible pilot. "I can't tell you how sorry I am for your harrowing ordeal and how thankful I am that you survived it."

Bishop merely stared at him. Despite Van Horn's reports to the contrary, Bradley wondered if the man was still in shock.

"Forgive me if I come across as overbearing, Mr. Bishop. My name is Graham Bradley. I'm the founder and COO of GeNext Biosystems. The man who arrived with me is Dr. Brendan Reaves. We flew straight here from Seattle the moment we learned what happened to the *Mayr*, or, more precisely, the moment that we learned that you and Dr. Martin miraculously managed to stay alive." This time when he offered his hand, Bishop took it in a cold but firm grasp. His bland affect never wavered. "We came all this way in hopes of determining the cause of the *Mayr*'s sinking and to make sure that everything was handled the right way. So, first things first, is there anything *I* can do for you?"

Bishop eyed him curiously for several seconds before he finally spoke.

"I could use another cup of coffee."

He held out the empty mug from beneath his blanket.

Bradley laughed and accepted the cup.

"Of course, Mr. Bishop. A refill's the very least I can do."

He headed back to the entryway where Van Horn and Reaves conversed quietly. A member of the crew took the mug from him and disappeared into the hallway.

"Has he said anything useful yet?" Bradley whispered.

"Other than the thing about the eyes?" Van Horn said. "No. But we've downloaded a good number of files from the *Mayr*'s security system and were just about to find out what's on them."

"Excellent." Bradley's heart was racing. He shared a look of anticipation with Reaves. Together, they'd worked so hard for so long that even the prospect of the payoff was exhilarating. "No time like the present."

"Mr. Barnes," Van Horn said. "Are the files ready for viewing?"

"Yes, sir," a man who looked uncannily like an owl said. "But again, I should caution you that the potential level of digital degradation—"

"We trust your skills, Mr. Barnes," Bradley said. "I'm sure they will be of the best possible quality under the circumstances. Now. If you wouldn't mind…"

Barnes nodded and repositioned his monitor so they could see it. Van Horn, Reaves, and Bradley crowded around him. Bishop scooted his stool with a screech in order to see between them.

"About that coffee…" Bishop said, but Bradley was too focused on the list of files on the monitor to even acknowledge that the submersible pilot had spoken.

"As I'm sure you know," Barnes said, "the security cameras in the access-controlled laboratories are motion-triggered to record from the time the first person enters until the last person leaves. The remainder of the ship—minus the individual cabins, the heads, and the hold—could be set to record manually. In the event of an emergency, they were programmed to automatically kick on."

Bradley was out of patience. He wanted to take the man by the throat and shake him. He hadn't traveled all this way to hear about the security protocols he'd helped implement.

"Are the files time-stamped?" Reaves asked.

"Yes, sir. They're also indexed by camera number and location. You can see here that the number of feeds collected spikes at 1:52 a.m. on November 28th, which implies that this was the point at which the emergency backup systems were engaged and all of the cameras began to record simultaneously. You can also see the time at which they all stopped, the theoretical termination of their power source. 3:36 a.m.. We're looking at a peak period of activity of approximately one hour and forty-four minutes." He turned to face them. "Where would you like to start?"

"My records indicate that there was a potential Level 3 Biohazard incident, reported as the release of unknown airborne microorganisms, in the Biology/Analytical Clean Room that required Hazmat intervention at 4:56 p.m. on November 26th, roughly thirty-three hours prior to the *Mayr*'s foundering," Bradley said. He shared a conspiratorial glance with Reaves. "I'd like to start there."

Twenty-Six

Ambitle Island

Jericho Montgomery strained against the weight of his cargo. He and Pearson had stripped the forest of vines and used them to lash the three corpses together, face-to-face, in a bundle, leaving several long lengths they could use to drag them down the steep hillside. The vines had snapped repeatedly, once freeing all three of the cadavers to tumble down the muddy slope. When they reached the lifeboat, they used the solar blanket from the emergency kit these very men had left behind to haul them down the path flattened by the shallow hull to the beach. While it was comforting to be out of the oppressive jungle, especially knowing what potentially lurked somewhere up there in its dark embrace, the deluge wasn't much of an improvement.

The lights from the salvage vessel and the *Huxley* were a diffuse aura through the mist across the bay. The monsoon winds alternately whipped the rain into their faces and then away from them. They'd found the tarp right where Pike had said it would be, clearly visible from the shoreline but far enough under the canopy to protect it from the worst of the torrent, with two bodies already beneath it, weighted down by stones on the corners.

"We've reached our destination," Montgomery said into the transceiver. "We're now depositing our payload."

Pearson pulled back the tarp to find the remains covered in crabs. Dozens scuttled away across the sand, but the majority brazenly continued to nip at the rotting flesh. One man's nose had already been plucked to a skeletal nub.

"Christ almighty," Pearson said. He kicked one away from a man's eyes.

"When you're finished," Pike's voice said through the speaker, "call...retrieval and hurry your asses up. You should be able to follow our trail...easily. Radio in once you reach the stream...crosses our path about a kilometer west of where we originally split up so we...arrange a rendezvous."

"Copy," Montgomery said.

"You sure you want to put these bodies under there with the others?" Pearson asked. "There'll be nothing left of them by the time anyone arrives from the ship to collect them." He stomped on the ambitious crabs that advanced toward his boots. "Where the hell did all of these things come from?"

"You have a better idea? I'm not about to drag that dead weight any farther."

"All I'm saying is they'd have been better off where we found them. I'd hate to think we nearly killed ourselves dragging them all the way down here just to feed the bloody crabs."

Montgomery switched the channel on the transceiver and brought it again to his lips.

"Come in *Huxley*."

"*Huxley*, copy."

Pearson spread out the silver blanket and arranged the carcasses side by side. They were muddy and disheveled and it looked like one of them had dislocated its shoulder in the tumble.

"Hell if I'm putting them over there with the others," he said.

"We need pick-up service for five on Ambitle," Montgomery said.

"Tell them to bring a net and have the cook start melting the butter."

"Would you shut up about the damn crabs already?"

"Copy that, Ambitle. Leave...light on, would you? We can't see...noses on our faces out here in this fog."

"They're like the ocean's version of spiders," Pearson said.

"Copy, *Huxley*. Out." Montgomery shoved the communication device back into its holster. "You going to cover them up or what?"

"What's the point? Fat lot of good it did the others."

Montgomery shed his backpack and rummaged through the contents until he found a flare. He took off the cap and, with a flick of the wrist, summoned a blinding pink flame that chased a gout of black smoke into the air. After waving it over his head for good measure, he cast it down onto the sand and headed back into the jungle. The wind whistled past them through the trees, bringing with it an assault of raindrops and the scent of the rotting meat left behind.

Both men lowered their goggles again to transform the night into digitally enhanced twilight. Best Montgomery could figure, they had about two and a half kilometers to make up, and Pike's patience will have exhausted itself before they even halved that distance. The last thing any of them wanted was to incur his wrath tonight, which promised to be more than long enough as it was.

Montgomery broke into a jog, balancing his pace against the weight on his back and the way the goggles bounced over his eyes. Any faster and his vision through the scope was like shaking his head rapidly back and forth and up and down; any slower and he feared Pike would have his head. He still wasn't convinced that whatever was out here in the jungle was the same kind of thing they had found in Zambia. Granted, the similarities between the gutted remains were remarkable, but, really, what were the odds? Lord only knew what kind of creatures stalked this island already without throwing their mythical Chaco Man into the mix.

Pearson's tread slapped behind him in the mud. Bushes swished against his thighs. Both men had fallen into the metered breathing of the long-distance runner, their breath pluming violet from their mouths.

The occasional gold and orange creature darted through the canopy above them with a screech or a hoot. Flashes of lightning stabbed through the dense leaves and branches, striking the ground in almost palpable white columns. Vipers hung from branches, distinguishable from the vines they tried to imitate by subtle shades of blue and the sporadic flicking of forked tongues. While disorienting, the odd color schemes were vastly preferable to charging blindly through the pitch-black forest.

At the crest of the first hill, they paused to survey the vast expanse of jungle stretching across the deep lowlands and up the sharp mountainous outcroppings in hopes of catching a glimpse of movement or the heat signatures of their group in the distance. They had to settle for the nearly indistinguishable break in the trees at the bottom of the next valley, where presumably the stream flowed just wide enough to halt the advance of the forest, if only for a few meters.

Without a word, Montgomery jumped from the crest and slid down the rapidly eroding slope, using his hand for balance. At the bottom, the trees and bushes closed around him once more. It was difficult to fathom that in this day and age of global overpopulation that a place like this could still exist. The jungle was positively primeval. He knew there was a small village with a Catholic mission on the other side of the island, but outside of the holes drilled higher on the volcanic slope, he had seen no sign of man's trespass. It awakened something primal inside of him. Instincts honed in the heat of conflagration resurfaced. His senses sharpened. He heard every distant bird call, every howl of a monkey, every crinkle of the detritus—

He stopped dead in his tracks.

The only sound of footsteps had been his own.

Montgomery turned around and stared back down what passed for a path, through screens of leaves and looping vines, toward the muddy hill, where thin brown streams channeled through the soft earth.

"Pearson?" he called.

The only response was the clamor of raindrops on the canopy above him.

Slowly, he walked back in the direction from which he had come, carefully brushing aside branches and placing each step so as not to make a sound.

A flash of lightning glimmered on the wet leaves.

Where the forest faded at the foot of the slope, he saw a poorly defined orange and purple shape on the ground through the rustling bushes.

His footsteps made a slurping sound in the muck, forcing him to slow his pace even more to compensate. The shape became clearer as he passed through the shrubs and rounded a tree trunk the size of an overpass pillar. A human form was sprawled prone in the mud and standing water, an amoeboid fuchsia glow diffusing around it. Even as he watched, the concentration of yellow in the head and chest softened to a reddish-orange.

He silently withdrew his Taser from its holster and eased to the edge of the cover.

Pearson's face was invisible below the level of the runoff. Only the base of his head, his shoulders, and his buttocks breached the surface. His backpack lay a dozen paces uphill where the mud was disturbed by more than footprints. It looked like Pearson had lost his footing and tumbled down to where he now rested.

Pearson made no effort to rise from the mire.

Montgomery's instincts channeled an electrical current through his veins, sensitizing him to even the most subtle change in the air around him. He moved his head slowly from side to side to compensate for his narrowed field of view. Leading with his weapon, he pressed through the foliage and stepped out into the rain.

A strobe of lightning preceded the sound of thunder, which rumbled down from the caldera like an avalanche. Momentarily blinded, he held his breath and waited for his enhanced vision to clear.

Something struck his back, driving him forward.

His feet left the ground.

He tried to reach out to brace himself, but his face struck the water first.

The horn of his goggles embedded itself in the mud, snapping his head sharply backward.

A heavy weight landed on top of him. Claws carved into his neck.

He drew a breath to scream and filled his lungs with fluid.

Twenty-Seven

R/V Aldous Huxley

Courtney stood trembling in the doorway, unnoticed by the men gathered around the computer monitor in front of them. She watched the screen through the gap between their heads. The footage was warped at the edges and horizontal bands of static traveled up and down the image in shivering bursts. Even in black and white and with the electrical distortion, she could still tell exactly what was playing out before her. She recognized her lab from the vantage point of the camera mounted discreetly under a black globe in the corner above her aquarium. She watched herself pounding against the isolation shield, beyond which the gray mist had begun to dissipate. Fortunately, the recording lacked sound so she didn't have to hear herself scream. Her brother materialized from the cloud and pressed his palm against the barrier. Helplessly, her smaller self matched the gesture, before the storm troopers in white charged into the room and hauled her out of the camera's range.

Tears streamed down her cheeks.

On the monitor, Ty retreated from the advancing men until his back met the rear wall. He slid down to the floor and buried his face in his hands.

She stifled a sob and all eyes in the room turned in her direction. Bishop rose from his stool and hurried to her side.

"Dr. Martin…" She recognized Dr. Graham Bradley right away. "I'm terribly sorry. That must have been very difficult to watch." He stood and gestured to his chair. "Please. Have a seat."

Courtney could only shake her head. The video playback ended and froze in a black rectangle scarred by lines of static like a bar code, but still she couldn't make herself look away.

Bishop wrapped his arm around her shoulders and attempted to delicately guide her back into the hallway.

"We should get you back—"

"No," she said with such force that Bishop stopped in his tracks. Their stares met for a long moment. He acquiesced with a nod and stepped out of her way so she could enter the room.

"Can you tell us what we just witnessed, Dr. Martin?" Van Horn asked.

"Have you found my brother yet?"

"No. Not yet. But that's a good thing. Since he wasn't among those found in the wreckage, there's a chance he's still alive." Van Horn glanced at Bradley, who gave a hardly perceptible nod. "We found one of the work boats on Ambitle Island. Our men are tracking the survivors as we speak."

Courtney felt such a swell of relief that her legs nearly gave out underneath her. If there was even the slightest hope that Ty had managed to survive, then nothing on this earth would keep her from finding him.

She wiped away her tears and steeled her resolve.

"What can I do to help?"

"We expect to hear from our team on the island anytime now, Dr. Martin," Bradley said. "You'll be the first to know when we do. In the meantime, it would help us tremendously if you could assist us in piecing together the timeframe leading up to the sinking of the *Mayr*."

She slid past him and sat in his vacated chair. One of the other men hopped out of his so Bradley could sit beside her.

"Would you replay the recording, Mr. Barnes," Van Horn said.

Courtney described the scene for them in painstaking detail. The others listened silently until the video ended.

"After my brother was finally released from the isolation chamber, he spent the next four hours undergoing a painful period of decontamination that left his skin red and abraded. The doctor took all kinds of samples and treated him for the erythema and the burn on the side of his face. Ty started feeling nauseous the next morning. The headaches and the skin condition developed shortly after that."

"What about his assistant, Devin Wallace?" Van Horn asked.

"I don't know. I was preoccupied with everything that was happening to Ty. I saw him a couple of times right afterward, but I don't remember seeing him after that."

"Where was your brother when the *Mayr* started to founder?"

"Under observation in the infirmary."

She caught a shared glance between Bradley and Van Horn.

"You found bodies in the hospital suite."

"Just one," Bradley said. "Dr. Walter Partridge."

"Then where's my brother?"

"That's what we're trying to figure out," Van Horn said. "His wasn't among the bodies recovered on the *Mayr*."

"I should have been with him." Courtney bit her lip to keep from crying and smeared the tears from her eyes with the backs of her hands. Now was not the time to fall apart. Ty was out there somewhere, and right now he needed her more than ever. She shook her head and laughed. "Instead, I was holed up in the lab isolating heme that's now at the bottom of the ocean. Time well spent, wouldn't you say?"

Bishop rested a hand on her shoulder. She unconsciously leaned her head against it.

"Dr. Martin," Bradley said softly. His eyes met hers. In them she saw a measure of compassion, but also something else. A twinkle of excitement, maybe? "What was in your brother's bioreactor?"

"Hydrothermal precipitates from the Medusa vent, but no one had a chance to analyze them. He was in the process of transferring them to the batch reactor and the continuous culture module when the accident happened."

Bradley turned to the man on his right, whose leathery skin and sun-streaked hair made him look out of place in his expensive suit.

"Dr. Reaves, would you mind checking with the diving team to see if we could get Dr. Partridge's hard drive from the hospital suite? And see what you can do about procuring samples from the batch reactor."

Reaves nodded and headed directly out into the hallway, where he collared one of the waiting seamen and ducked out of sight.

"You really just came here to make sure that all of your research remained intact, didn't you?" Bishop said. His face flushed and his grip tightened on her shoulder. "All of those people dead, and you're worried about some goddamned black smoke. Where are your priorities? You want more? I'll go down and get it for you myself. For now, maybe you could spare a thought for those who lost their lives in your service."

"Mr. Bishop—" Van Horn started, but Bradley silenced him with a wave of his hand. After taking a moment to compose his thoughts, he answered for himself.

"Regardless of what you may think, Mr. Bishop, right now my only concern is for the crew of the *Mayr*. You're right. These men and women died because I sent them here, which makes me ultimately responsible." He sighed. "And part of that responsibility is determining exactly what happened. Their families—the entire world for that matter—will demand that someone be held accountable, and I willingly accept my role, but more importantly, they're going to want to know why. When I tell them, I need to be able to look them in the eye and explain why their husbands and wives, siblings and children will never be coming home again. Anything less would be unacceptable. Not just for them, but for myself, as well."

Bradley shook his head and rubbed his red eyes.

"Here's how I see the situation. Roughly a day and a half before the *Mayr* ended up strewn across the reef nearly a hundred kilometers from her last charted location, there was a Level 3 biohazard emergency involving exposure to as-of-yet unclassified biologic agents that left a man in the infirmary. We have a lifeboat that reached the island, its passengers somewhere in more than a hundred and fifty square kilometers of steep, heavily wooded tropical forest that ascends right up to the rim of the volcano. And other than the security footage we have yet to watch, all we have to go on is the information we can glean from the wreckage and what two people we found on the verge of death seem unable to clearly remember. If we're going to assemble this puzzle, we need all of the pieces."

"What aren't you telling us?" Bishop asked. "Something else happened on that ship, didn't it?"

"That's exactly what I intend to find out, Mr. Bishop." Bradley turned to the man at the computer. "Mr. Barnes, would you kindly show us the files recorded when the *Mayr*'s emergency systems came online?"

Twenty-Eight

Ambitle Island

Pike had caught up with Brazelton and Walker at the edge of a basalt cliff that overlooked the entire southwestern slope of the island. The ocean was barely visible beyond the trees and through the fog and sheeting rain. He imagined the survivors standing on this very precipice, gathering their bearings and plotting their course. Their pace had slowed dramatically, as evidenced by their tracks, where they could find them. They were much closer together, and deeper and more clearly defined to suggest an advancing level of fatigue. The rain was already erasing their path. What had they been thinking as they stared down upon acres of untamed and uninhabited jungle and the vast expanse of the tumultuous sea, bereft of any craft they could hail for help? Had their hopes been dashed when they saw not a single vessel in the aftermath of the tsunami? Had they despaired, or had they bolstered their resolve and forged ahead? Upon determining that this high ground held no advantage, they would have definitely headed for the western beach, where they could have built a bonfire both for warmth and to signal seagoing ships and any airplanes that might fly over. Not that anything other than Bradley's chopper had since he and his men had first chugged into the harbor in the tug so many hours ago. It was imperative that he take into account their state of mind. If they had seen what he suspected they had, it added an element of unpredictability to their flight. A smart man with a level head would leave false trails and choose the least likely path to throw off his pursuit. With the rate at which their tracks were deteriorating, such a maneuver could cost Pike and his men valuable time trying to find the real trail, which might no longer exist. If they were instead spurred by panic, however, they'd make a bee-line directly toward the most accessible beach and pray to be rescued before whatever stalked them caught up.

Pike favored the latter theory, but there was no room for assumption. They needed to decipher the clues left behind in a hurry before they were washed away forever.

The wind shifted and he smelled rotten eggs.

"Interesting," he said.

"What?" Walker asked.

"You smell that?"

"Wasn't me," Brazelton said.

"Yeah," Walker said, turning his face into the breeze. "Sulfur dioxide. Either a warm-water slough, or, more likely with the level of geothermal activity on the island, a hot spring."

"Hot springs?" Pike said.

"Ambitle's riddled with them," Walker said. "There are even shallow-water hydrothermal vents off the northwestern coast in Tutum Bay. They spew one and a half kilograms of arsenic into the coral reef ecosystem every day. In its concentrated form, that's more than enough arsenic to kill ten thousand adult humans each and every single day."

"Full of trivia, aren't you?" Brazelton said.

"I'm a geologist. What can I say?"

Pike could barely discern a cloud of steam clinging to the canopy about half a kilometer downhill where the ground leveled off. The wind rose again and the cloud dissipated into the rain. Without a word, he started down the slick path. The tracks they'd been following were all but obliterated now. Were it not for sections of forest where the branches were so intertwined they blocked out even the sporadic flares of lightning, he might have thought they'd lost their quarry. Here and there, amid tangles of roots, the moldering detritus was compressed into a jumble of tracks, one overlapping the next. Add to it the snapped branches and the occasional tatter of fabric, and he knew they were still moving in the right direction.

The ground trembled with a faint rumbling sound. All eyes turned to Walker.

"Rock and roll," the geologist said through a smirk.

Saved from the worst of the monsoon winds here, moss flourished on the limbs and bearded the boughs. The humidity seemed to be trapped in an oppressive mist that made sweat bloom from Pike's pores. Mosquitoes hummed in swirling swarms around stagnant puddles that reeked of flatus. His attempts to swat them away from his face were met with stingers to the back of his neck. Bats swooped across the path, picking off the insects with such speed that they appeared as little more than orange blurs in his peripheral vision. Pygmy parrots squawked from enclaves saved from the tumult. Deafened to the complaints of the men at his heels, he picked his way through the overgrowth and around basalt pillars draped with vines from the steep jungle above them, which felt as though it could come cascading down upon them at any moment in the muddy streams that carved through the slope.

The smell of rotten eggs intensified. Wisps of steam curled through the ceiba trees ahead of them. Through the goggles, it was a churning miasma of pinks and purples. The tracks in the mud grew closer together to such a degree that they canceled each other out. He imagined the survivors slowing to appraise the steam, whispering as they debated forging ahead or circling around it. Their decision evident by the continuation of the trail, Pike pressed forward through the trampled undergrowth and stepped out into a small clearing. The steam was so thick, the colors so vibrant, that he could see nothing else. He shed the goggles in favor of his flashlight and his own two eyes.

An oblong pool roughly the size of a koi pond filled the majority of the gap. The rain had raised the water level so that it spilled over its banks and flooded a marsh of barren trees, their trunks stunted and deformed. Nearest the edges, there were concentric rings of lemon yellow and flame orange, while closer to the center where the superheated fluid was forced up from the mantle the water was a deep blue. The microorganisms aggregated in the various temperature zones that radiated outward from the hydrothermal vent. There were no grasses or weeds along the banks, just bare limestone thriving with chemosynthetic and photosynthetic bacteria alike.

There was a body lying across the edge with its torso in the shallows.

"And then there were three."

Pike followed a pair of Reeboks to filthy, ripped jeans and an untucked, red and green flannel shirt. He knelt over the remains and directed his beam down into water the temperature of a spa. The hands were swollen and the flesh had begun to slip away from the exposed bones in wavering strips. Cellular dissolution and adipose tissue clouded the water. The gold ring around the fourth digit on the left hand was unadorned and too large to belong to a female. He guided the light along the length of the arms to the shoulders and the neck, through which the ridges of the spinous processes of the cervical spine jutted like the spikes on an iguana's back. Most of the man's hair had already boiled away. The few clumps that remained were short and black. Sections of the skull showed through the skin, and what little he could see of the face was devoid of flesh. The bared teeth grinned at him from underwater.

"Drag him out of there," Pike said.

He stepped back and watched his men each take an ankle and haul the man up into the steaming overflow. Pike slid the toe of his right boot under the man's chest and rolled him over. Hollow orbits stared up into the heavens as raindrops beat on his skeletal features.

Brazelton shined his beam onto the man's forehead.

"Depressed fracture of the frontal bone," he said, "which suggests blunt-force trauma."

"He hit his head on the rocks in the shallows."

"It would have taken significant force above and beyond a simple fall."

"I think whatever carved up his chest should have been able to supply it." Pike shined his light across the man's shirt, which had been torn to ribbons. While the majority of his pectorals had rotted away in the water to reveal the horizontal slats of his ribs, the lower chest and abdomen were gouged by parallel lacerations so deep they had peeled apart to allow the yellow fat to bloom out.

"This one isn't disemboweled."

Pike nodded. It wasn't as though this was the first body they'd found with its abdomen intact. The one thrown high into the treetops by the tsunami and the one that had been burned alive had been spared that fate. And now this one, whose head had been smashed down against the bank and his body left to decompose in the scalding water and swirling steam.

"Over here," Walker said.

Pike walked away from the corpse and joined Walker on a small knoll that stood above the water level. A dead sapling twisted through the steam at an impossible angle. The geologist directed his flashlight down at the mud, highlighting a single, bare footprint.

"I don't think that's normal," Walker said.

"Get a shot of this," Pike said to Brazelton, who removed the digital camera from his vest and snapped several pictures from various angles. The imprint was identical to those Pike had found paralleling the survivors' path through the jungle, only this one was more clearly delineated where the long toenails cut through the muck. "I'll radio Montgomery and Pearson to let them know they have another pickup. You two start scouting the area. Either find me the rest of their bodies or where their trail leads away from here. We've already wasted too much time as it is."

He removed the transceiver from its holster and watched his men fan out into the mist, holding their flashlights against the sides of their Tasers.

"Montgomery," Pike said into the communication device. "Montgomery. Do you copy?"

The static fizzled and hissed through the primordial mist like some primitive creature skulking through the shadows.

"Montgomery!"

The crackle droned on.

Twenty-Nine

R/V Aldous Huxley

Bishop couldn't shake the feeling that there was more going on here than these men let on. Maybe five years had passed since he left the Navy to find his own way in the world, but his training was still intact. They didn't let just anyone into Uncle Sam's fleet. Well, maybe they did. Like every other branch, they needed fodder for the cannons, but were it not for what he had seen in a war that had never been his to fight, he'd undoubtedly still be among its ranks. He had never truly believed in the ideals of the imperial government that had rushed him through Boot Camp in Great Lakes, Illinois to get him on a carrier bound for the Persian Gulf where he'd been sent to protect people who didn't want his kind of protection and wage war against an enemy his side had armed and taught to kill in the first place. All he'd wanted was to escape a situation at home where his father beat him for no other reason than he could, while his mother looked the other way in a vodka-induced fugue. Sure, a part of him had wanted a little adventure on the high seas, but never had he thought that he would be confronting the enemy from closer than the distance of a Tomahawk strike, nor had he contemplated the prospect of wading through the bodies of the women and children who'd been the recipients of its fiery vengeance. Two tours and he'd called it quits. But even after the years spent on these private research vessels and in training for the submersible dives to the bottom of the world, it was startling how quickly the distrust that had been beaten into him returned. He wanted to know what was really going on here, and he wanted to know right now.

There was no reason that the helicopter that had ferried Bradley and his associate from the mainland hadn't picked up Courtney and him while it was here and flown them back to

Rabaul where they could receive proper medical attention, at least more attention than could be provided by a single company physician in an infirmary ill-equipped to handle anything more traumatic than the common cold. He understood their need to find answers. They were potentially dealing with a massive amount of lawsuits despite the waivers all personnel had signed before boarding, especially if something had gone wrong on the *Mayr* before the tsunami swamped it. A part of him almost felt as though he and Courtney were being kept here for more than their ability to help figure out the events prior to the sinking, even though he personally doubted their capacity to do so. It felt like they were being held hostage to a certain degree to *prevent* them from sharing their experience with the rest of the world.

He watched Bradley from the corner of his eye. The man's expression was indecipherable. While his tone and his words reflected a measure of compassion, the way he masked the physical manifestation of his emotions convinced Bishop that Bradley was hiding something. And the sooner he figured it out the better. He could positively feel a storm brewing on the horizon, and every instinct insisted that he didn't want to be here when it arrived.

Courtney's hand found his. Her cold fingers laced between his. He glanced at her face. It appeared to have been an unconscious gesture on her part. She had put on a brave front for her brother's benefit, which did little to mask the fear she tried to hide behind it. If they even thought about using her brother against her, he would make sure they regretted it. That was a large part of his uneasiness. The way they talked about Ty, their fascination with the nature of his accident in the lab, suggested they suspected something they weren't prepared to divulge.

So far, none of the security footage they had watched betrayed any of the details Bradley and his men were obviously seeking. They had watched men and women stampeding each other in the hallways under the crimson glare of the emergency lights, which appeared gray in the black and white scale. Bradley had grown impatient with viewing the videos in the order in which they'd been downloaded and made the executive decision to go right to the first file from the pilothouse.

While they waited for Barnes to find a file that was more than a screen filled with jumping static, Van Horn, who had been called away perhaps fifteen minutes ago, returned.

"We're bringing the ship as close to the shore of Ambitle Island as we can without riding her up onto dry land in order to expedite the process of ferrying the salvage aboard." Something unspoken passed between Van Horn and Bradley. "The sooner we can have our team evaluate what we've collected from the island, the sooner we can compare it to the findings in our database."

"The Zambian database?"

"Yes, sir."

"Has our forward team on Ambitle reported in?"

"Yes, sir. Pike is still following the trail toward the western shore." Van Horn leaned down and whispered into Bradley's ear. Bishop witnessed a quick widening of Bradley's eyes before he suppressed his surprise. His tone took on a sharp edge when he spoke.

"Then once everything from the beach has been loaded, that's where I want this ship. We're wasting time over here if there are survivors looking for rescue over there."

"You didn't see anything when you flew over, and we had the chopper pilot scan the shoreline before he returned to the mainland."

"At least eighty percent of that coast is nearly vertical and covered with jungle. Just because we didn't see them doesn't mean they aren't there."

Barnes opened a file that appeared to be of more than just shivering horizontal bars and turned to Bradley for permission to let it roll.

"I expect this ship to be headed around the island in under thirty minutes. And I want updates from the lab by the time we're moving." His fingertips tapped a tuneless beat on the table in front of him, and for a moment he appeared lost in thought. He finally spoke in little more than a whisper. "We've been given a second chance. We can't afford to mess this one up. We might never get another."

A second chance? Bishop thought. *A second chance for what?*

"What about the tugboat?" Van Horn asked.

"Thank the captain for his service on such short notice and let him know that he is free to return to the mainland, with the standard non-disclosure contract and fee, of course."

"Yes, sir." Van Horn hurried out of the command center and into the hallway, where Bishop heard the sound of the man's footsteps break into a sprint.

"Please play the file, Mr. Barnes." Bradley's voice was taut, his thin lips white. "Dr. Martin, please tell me about this skin condition that you mentioned Tyler developed."

The monitor displayed an image Bishop immediately recognized as the pilothouse from a vantage point on the ceiling that showed the bridge against the backdrop of the slanted wall of glass, which looked out over the bow and the sea beyond. Lightning reflected from the rivulets of water on the windows, through which the distant storm clouds flashed with gray electrical arcs. A skeletal crew manned the helm for the third shift. Even through the bars that traveled up and down the screen, Bishop identified Second Mate Ellis Rivers standing in front of the ocean view. The horizon tipped from side to side as waves hammered the *Mayr* broadside. Shipboard technician Jeremy Erskine darted from one console to the next in an effort to do the job of three men. Both glanced up at the emergency light housed in the Plexiglas and wire cage on the wall. They must have just heard the first klaxon blare.

"Dr. Partridge called it a 'systemic outbreak of psoriatic plaques'," Courtney said. "He said he'd never seen such an aggressive form of psoriasis."

The video skipped and static reigned. When it cleared, Erskine was nowhere to be seen, but Rivers was looking across the room toward the door to the chart room and shouting something they would never hear. Erskine stepped onscreen a heartbeat later with the fire extinguisher he must have liberated from its glass housing in the hallway and tossed it to the Second Mate. Erskine turned back in the direction from which he'd entered, then appeared to throw himself to the ground and slide out of the picture with his arms trailing across the floor behind him. Rivers stiffened and held up the nozzle of the fire extinguisher.

Bishop glanced at the ocean on the digital horizon, which continued to rock to the same fierce rhythm.

"Did Tyler have a preexisting condition of psoriasis or was it possibly caused by an adverse reaction to whatever was inside the bioreactor?" Bradley asked.

"That was the first time Ty had developed any kind of skin condition, as far as I know."

"You said systemic, not local, correct? Describe it to me."

Rivers shouted something and stumbled backward toward the windows without noticing the flashing warning lights on the bridge, which was lit up like a Christmas tree. He raised the nozzle of the red canister and fired a burst of chemical smoke toward the door just below and to the left of the camera. The chalky pall hung over the room like fog, through which Rivers appeared as a silhouette against the windows, which burned a brilliant white with lightning before fading and forcing the aperture of the lens of rationalize the sudden shift to darkness.

"It started as erythema, just little red patches of dry skin that itched to no end on his forearms and legs, but soon enough he was scratching at similar outbreaks on his chest, neck, and cheeks. His skin took on a silver cast and his epidermis started to flake away. The patches looked like a trout's scales."

"And eventually they covered his entire body?"

"More or less."

"You said he had headaches, too?" Bradley's voice grew more animated. The other computer technicians looked up at him from their workstations. The constant clatter of keystrokes ceased. "What else?"

"They were migraines. He became hypersensitive to light and felt nauseous all the time. And he said his bones hurt, deep down, like something was trying to burrow out."

Bishop was growing increasingly uncomfortable with the situation. Bradley's excitement was not only inappropriate, it was a tell. Proof positive that he knew what had happened to Courtney's brother. He wanted to shake Bradley and demand answers, slap him around a little if he had to. His temper rose like a coiled rattlesnake and he was about to round on Bradley when Rivers blasted two more clouds of ammonium phosphate across the bridge and pressed himself back against the flashing bank of windows.

Another dark form streaked through the settling haze directly toward the Second Mate.

"What else?" Bradley asked.

"That isn't enough?" Courtney snapped. "He was in nearly constant pain. Were it not for whatever happened to the ship, Dr. Partridge was planning to call you and convince you to have Ty airlifted to the nearest hospital."

The shadow vanished momentarily in the white cloud before reappearing on top of the console and hurtling toward Rivers. The shape struck the Second Mate, who fired several more bursts up into the ceiling, causing the entire screen to go white.

"I'm sorry." The fervor had drained from Bradley's voice. "I didn't mean to push as hard as I obviously did. It just felt like we were onto something there for a moment. You have my apologies. You have to understand that I was an honest-to-God physician before I ever became...this." He gestured to his fancy, rumpled suit. Or perhaps toward the aging man inside of it.

Courtney nodded.

On the screen, the white cloud settled like falling snow.

"There was one other thing..." Courtney said. She paused as she too joined the others in what seemed to be an interminable wait for the cloud from the fire extinguisher to clear. Bishop realized he was holding his breath. He couldn't see any sign of movement through the mist. "His gums had started to bleed."

Bradley turned quickly to face her. Whatever he had planned to say was forgotten, as on the screen it was now painfully apparent what had happened to Second Mate Ellis Rivers.

"Christ almighty," Bishop whispered.

Arcs of black fluid crisscrossed the windows before which Rivers had just been standing. Even in grayscale, he could see tiny streams of blood rolling downward from the long spatters. The console was smeared where Rivers's body had been dragged over it. The warning lights were blinking like crazy now. The horizon yawed dramatically through the blood-streaked glass, thrown into stark relief by a strobe of lightning. Another bloody trail marred the white floor, leading to the doorway and the stairs beyond.

Thirty

Dr. Brendan Reaves leaned over Dr. Angela Whitted's shoulder, hoping to catch a glimpse of the bacteria on the scanning electron microscope's monitor beside her. They were in the Biology/Analytical Clean Lab on the *Huxley*, where the batch reactor had been relocated following its retrieval from the *Mayr*'s carcass. The loss of power on the *Mayr* had killed the systems that regulated the heat, pressure, and agitation. All of the microorganisms that had been transferred into it from the bioreactor had died shortly thereafter and aggregated into a microbial sludge on the bottom. From that sludge, the microbiologist had extracted several representative samples that were now stained and matted on a series of microscope slides she was finally ready to analyze. Angie worked on retainer for GeNext as part of Reaves's discreet team of scientists dedicated to cracking the riddle of the mutated skeletons they'd discovered through the years. By day, she was Deputy Director of the National Institute of Biomedical Imaging and Bioengineering, a division of the U.S. Department of Health & Human Services, and co-chaired the Presidential Council on Emerging Infectious Diseases. While her pedigree lent to formality and aloofness, Angie was one of the most down-to-earth women Reaves had ever met. Her enthusiasm and love for her job were contagious. They had even shared a few passion-filled nights back in the subterranean labs of the GeNext complex that he was certain not only challenged his flexibility, but the laws of gravity as well.

Angie crinkled her freckled nose like she always did when she squinted her aquamarine eyes into the eyepiece lenses of the microscope. She slowly licked her lips and tucked her blonde bangs behind her ears.

"Looks like a lineup of the usual suspects." She drew her eyes from the lenses and gestured toward the microbes on the screen. "This bacterium here that looks like a turnip with a bunch of hairy roots is *Thermococcales hydrothermalis*. These things that look kind of like fluke worms are *ectothiorhodospira*. Those over there that resemble halved pomegranates with worms coming out of them are *Methanococcus valcanius*. See those that look like lily pads with a bunch of tadpoles under them? That's *Methanococcus jannaschii*. And that circular prokaryote with all of the long flagellates is our good friend *Thermococcus litoralis*."

"That's what you'd expect to find in a hydrothermal vent?"

"In the South Pacific anyway. The types of bacteria vary by location. Most of these are endemic to this area, but you could expect to find *ectothirhodospira* and various species of *archaea* in pretty much any geothermal vent as far north as the Solfataric Fields in Iceland."

"You have every microscopic organism memorized, don't you?"

"Not every *single* one of them." She winked at him and his stomach tingled. "Look at it this way. Until recently, we didn't even know these things existed. And we're still finding new ones all the time. No one really knows what all they're capable of. They could prove to be the greatest boon to mankind the world has ever known, or they could end up producing pathogens capable of destroying all life on earth. There's no way of knowing until we discover and identify them, and then crack them open to see what they can do.

"Take this little bugger here, *Thermococcus litoralis*. It produces an enzyme called DNA polymerase that serves as a catalyst for DNA replication. It's able to not only copy existing strands and synthesize new ones, it can also repair damaged DNA. And this is an organism that by all means should never have come into physical contact with man based upon its natural habitat, and here it is capable of manipulating our genetic code."

"Makes you wonder why we haven't found a way to weaponize it yet."

"Who says we haven't tried." She winked again. His mind flashed back to a cluster of four small moles at the base of her spine that reminded him of an arrow. As if she could read his mind, her elbow nuzzled his lap. "Wait...a...second...What do we have here?" She zoomed in until she focused on a single bacterium that looked almost like an acorn with dozens of wispy antennae.

Inside its bulk were several spiked balls that could have passed for microscopic sea urchins. Reaves at least knew enough to recognize them as viruses. "Well, hello there, handsome."

"What are we looking at here?"

"Your guess is as good as mine. This one's new to me. All of a sudden, things just got interesting." She smiled and pressed her eyes back against the microscope. "Oh, how I love a good challenge."

"Tell me what you see." Reaves's heart was beating hard and fast and his hands trembled with excitement. "Is it possible that this—?"

"You'll know as soon as I do. Now scoot. Scoot. I have about a million tests to run. And I need to dice up those viruses and map their proteins…"

Her words trailed into an unintelligible mumble. He'd seen her this way plenty of times. She'd gone into that special place in her head where she simply ceased to exist as a physical entity. She was now a being of pure thought, to whom the rest of the world, including him, no longer existed.

"Tell me this is our culprit and I'll get down on one knee—"

"Sounds kinky," she said. "Now go bother someone who isn't trying to unlock the secrets of the universe."

Reaves smirked and left her to her business. As he was crossing the corridor and preparing to enter the main laboratory, a thought struck him from out of the blue. Until that moment, it had been an abstraction. If they really had found the microorganism responsible for the mutations in Chaco Man, then they needed to seriously consider the fact that someone aboard the *Mayr* could truly have been altered. Sure, they were fairly confident working under that assumption, but the reality of the situation was something different entirely. All of the evidence—from the disemboweled corpses on both the ship and the island to the footprints Pike had photographed—pointed to that fact. However, in his excitement, he hadn't stopped to think about the implications. The gnawed bones in the cave under Casa Rinconada and piled at the foot of the altar beneath the *sivalinga*. The gutted corpses scattered around the village in Zambia. The nearly identical bodies stashed down in the hold of the *Mayr*. If a living and breathing Chaco Man had butchered the entire crew and somehow managed to follow those who escaped onto the island, it could be out there at this very moment. Until now, he had never considered the possibility of being forced to confront it in the flesh. What would they do when they came face-to-face with something capable of tearing them apart with its bare hands without a second thought?

It struck him exactly how poorly prepared there were. They had the advantage of knowledge and firepower, but how much good would either do against an entity that had managed to survive in one incarnation or another through the eons with the kind of predatory instincts that caused it to immediately begin killing everyone around it?

A shiver rippled up his spine. For the first time, he questioned what they were doing, his whole life's work. If Chaco Man had indeed been spawned by bacteria exhumed from deep under the Kilinailau Trench, then his creation was directly their fault. His fault. He had arranged for the collection of thermophilic organisms from the active vents under the auspices of bioengineering research. He had put these men's and women's lives at risk. He was responsible for their deaths. And who knew how many more to come.

It took him some time to compose himself before he typed in the code and entered the main laboratory.

Dr. Henri Renault, a trust fund child who had attended medical school with Bradley at Cambridge so many years ago, and whose initial infusion of capital into GeNext entitled him to a minority share of the company, sat at a laptop with a wet computer tower still rife with algae dripping saltwater onto the floor beside him. His position, and Bradley's lone indiscretion with a man he considered a friend, had allowed Renault to insinuate himself into their inner circle of scientists as their resident physician. After all of this time, it was something of a relief to finally be able to put his only useful skill to work. Renault glanced up from reading Dr. Partridge's electronic medical files, which had been transferred by the technical staff on the *Huxley* to his personal laptop. His bushy brows looked like charcoal flames burning over brown eyes magnified by glasses that could have been cut from storm windows. He had raked his hair into odd parts with his fingers and his mouth was set into a perpetual O of surprise.

"What does the chart say?" Reaves asked. While medical management wasn't his forte, he'd learned enough over the course of the last dozen years via his anemia research and the massive Chaco Man undertaking to at least have a yeoman's grasp of it.

"Let us just say that Dr. Partridge's notes are spartan, to be kind," Renault said in a thick French accent. "This is a physician whom modern medicine passed by long ago. His patients were fortunate he did not have access to leeches or attempt to 'candle' them."

"All judgment aside, have you found anything useful?"

Reaves had tired of the pompous windbag years ago. His ego was like a yapping terrier sitting on his shoulder.

"Let me walk you through it." Renault rose from his chair and paced behind the deck with his hands clasped behind his back. Reaves rolled his eyes. "The patient, a thirty-four year-old Caucasian male, presents with a second-degree burn on his left cheek, shortness of breath, and a cough. A topical anesthetic, lidocaine and prilocaine cream, is used to treat the pain from the burn, while the remaining symptoms are addressed with an albuterol bronchodilator."

"A nebulizer."

"Correct." Renault waggled his fingers behind his lower back. "Four hours status-post initial examination, the patient returns to the infirmary, complaining of pruritus and accompanying erythema." Could the pretentious blowhard not just say an itchy rash, for crying out loud? "The physician addresses this with a topical antihistamine, and during the course of which determines the patient to be febrile."

"He had a fever."

"Would you like an actual medical case history or would you prefer I rap it in the vernacular to which you're obviously more accustomed?" He sighed. "Americans…"

"I know all of this so far. Shortly thereafter, the rash becomes a silver plaque of flaking skin Partridge diagnoses as a systemic form of psoriasis, which spreads all over his body."

"You have to understand that psoriasis is a largely heredity inflammatory immunoresponse. One does not simply acquire it."

"Regardless, he has it. From there, the migraines begin: acute frontal headaches with hypersensitivity to light. The fever becomes harder to manage. The psoriasis covers nearly every inch of his body."

"Dr. Partridge, in his infinite professionalism, described the patient in his chart as looking like a sockeye salmon. Twenty-four hours post-exposure, the patient is admitted for observation, during the course of which hourly updates are entered into his chart."

"Only a single patient is in the infirmary at this point, correct? Dr. Tyler Martin? Is there any further mention of his graduate assistant, Devin Wallace?"

"There were no additions to Mr. Wallace's chart following his initial treatment. Dr. Partridge recommended short-term follow-up, but apparently neither man had the inclination to see it through."

"Is there anything in there that's even remotely helpful?" Reaves was exhausted from the cock-of-the-walk routine. There was still so much he had to do. In addition to coordinating the research in the lab, tracking the progress of Pike's team on the island, and his overwhelming desire to watch the security recordings in hopes of catching the merest glimpse of what he knew would be there somewhere, he needed to rush this old blowhard through his recitation so he could begin to examine the corpses that had been brought over from Ambitle and would soon enough be stinking up the submersible hanger. "Check that. Let me streamline this process. I'll ask a question, and you answer as directly as possible."

It was Renault's turn to roll his eyes.

"Bloodwork?"

"Elevated RBCs and WBCs."

"Platelets?"

"Normal."

"Anything else abnormal in the blood?"

"No."

"Toxicology?"

"Negative."

"Serology?"

"Not performed."

"CSF?"

"I doubt the good doctor even considered a puncture."

"Physical observation?"

"Yellowing and accelerated growth of the finger- and toenails. Scleral icterus, yellowing of the whites of the eyes."

"Jaundice?"

"The liver was enlarged upon palpation. No function tests or enzyme assays were performed."

"Assessment?"

"Dr. Partridge's conclusion was that he was unable to properly manage the patient's deteriorating condition and planned to call for air retrieval the following morning, November 28th."

"But something happened and the ship sank first."

"Would you care for my personal impressions of this case?"

Oh, for the love of God.

Reaves made a show of checking his watch, then glanced at the door.

"The variety and progression of symptomatology is what concerns me. In regard to the classical model of escalation, this disease shares a good number of traits with an immunodeficiency disease like AIDS. In my professional opinion, this is the work of a retrovirus."

Reaves's thoughts shifted back to the bacterium on the slide filled with spiny viruses.

His theory about the relationship between the geothermal events and exposure had been correct. The earth had thrust a pathogen that had been patiently waiting under the crust to the surface, one that had been biding its time until it could perform its sole biological imperative.

And there was something he'd never considered: Was it possible that this virus was contagious?

They needed answers, and they needed them right now. There were men on the island, presumably tracking not only the survivors, but one of the infected, as well. And there was the matter of the second man, Devin Wallace, whom everyone had apparently lost track of after his initial treatment following his exposure to the contents of the bioreactor.

What the hell had happened to him?

Thirty-One

Ambitle Island

Pike had known exactly what Montgomery's radio silence meant. He had called the *Huxley* and had them triangulate the GPS beacon in Montgomery's transceiver. While the signal could only be pinpointed to within a square half-kilometer on this remote island, which was of precious little geographical use to him, the satellite had been able to confirm that the beacon was static. In more than forty minutes now, the transceiver hadn't moved at all. He didn't need to discuss the implications with Brazelton and Walker. Neither of them was by any means stupid, which was why they didn't suggest that they turn around to investigate. Montgomery and Pearson weren't the kind of men to be lying in the mud, wounded, waiting for the cavalry to arrive and rescue them.

At least now Pike knew they had roughly a two kilometer lead on the hunter, although that fact was only slightly comforting considering that the twin trails they had picked up on the far side of the spring continued to head due northwest without any sign of doubling back upon themselves. If whatever had followed the survivors had re-crossed the island and was now behind them, then he had no doubt that there were only corpses ahead of them on this path.

They traversed the steep topography through trees that eclipsed even the storm, around the bases of sheer limestone escarpments, and through flooded gullies, their water levels deceptive, their banks beyond treacherous. Far downhill, he could hear the repeated crashing sound of waves breaking against the rocky shoreline. There were no white sprawls of sandy beaches, only sharp stone teeth waiting to crush a boat's hull, groves so dense they grew right down into the ocean, and cliffs to shame those of Acapulco. This was by far the least hospitable stretch of coast he'd encountered north of Antarctica. Maybe this side of the island provided safety from the tsunamis, but it offered precious little hope of rescue. In their shoes, with death nipping at his heels, he never would have considered the option of heading back east, which left either slowing their pace and attempting to scale the steepening, heavily forested slope up to the caldera, or continuing to skirt the western shore in a northward progression until they reached anything that resembled a beach or the Tolai village on the northwestern-most point of the island. He wondered if they had suspected what he already knew. Their pursuit would eventually overtake them. It wasn't a matter of if, only of when and where.

Pike lost their trail for hundreds of yards at a time, but now that he had assumed their mindset, picking it back up again had become second-nature. He could read their exhaustion in their footprints, in the occasional drop of blood on a leaf or smeared handprint on a trunk saved from the rain, where one of them had paused to catch his breath. Were he the predator, these signs would have spurred him into a frenzy. Unless, of course, he was the kind of ghoul that reveled in the hunt more than the kill.

The former was a monster; the latter terrifying in its unpredictability.

All three men carried their Tasers, leaving their other hands free for a quick grab at the Baretta M9A1s holstered under their opposite arms. The Taser delivered enough voltage to drop an enraged steroid-head on angel dust at twenty feet, but there was no point in taking any chances. A couple bullets through a pair of shattered patellae would definitely end an engagement. And Lord only knew exactly what they were dealing with here. For all any of them knew, with the extra time on the island to familiarize itself with the jungle, their pursuit could be silently closing in at this very moment.

"You realize they're all already dead," Walker said from behind him.

"Yes," Pike said after a moment's deliberation.

"What does that mean we're walking into? Why don't we just get the hell out of here now, while we still can?"

"Because we have a job to do, soldier."

"Soldier?" Walker chuckled. "I haven't been a soldier since I was discharged a decade ago. I only signed on for this job because of the money, and, let's face it, the fact that we maybe work six months out of the year and never really see any action."

"All we're doing now is hiking through the forest on a tropical island." Pike's patience was wearing thin. "I wouldn't classify this as action."

"What are you talking about? How many corpses have we come across? And most of them have been gutted like fish! You know as well as I do that eventually we're going to run into whatever was capable of doing that. And then what?"

"We light it up like the Fourth of July," Brazelton said.

"What do you propose we do with it then? Drag it across the island to the ship? Am I the only one that remembers what those things are capable of, what their skeletons look like? Their freaking teeth?"

"If a bunch of primitives and natives could take them down with sticks and stones, imagine how we'll fare with Lightning and Thunder," Brazelton said, lifting each weapon in turn.

"Fat lot of good either did Montgomery and—"

Pike rounded on him and got into his face, so close that when he spoke, spittle struck Walker's lips.

"Then tuck tail right now. Head back the way we came. I dare you. When you come across Montgomery and Pearson, pass along my regards."

Walker drew a breath to protest, but said nothing. He averted his eyes. Pike waited for several beats while the red drained from his cheeks before whirling and striking off down the trail toward where their path crossed a thin stream at the bottom of a fifty-foot waterfall that materialized from the ceiling of mist. He sloshed through the runoff and scrabbled up a steep rise of scree. At the crest of the hill, he stopped and tilted his nose to the breeze.

The scent wasn't fresh, but it was recent enough to linger.

He broke into a jog and slalomed through the trees, crashing through the wet shrubs and leaping over tented and buttressed roots. When another smell joined the first, he slowed and picked his way silently through the foliage until he reached a small clearing at the foot of a sheer carbonate embankment, at the base of which was a lip that shielded a small cave. In its mouth were the charcoaled remnants of a fire only partially consumed. The burnt flare beside it meant that the survivors were down to just the flare gun with two cartridges at the most. While the residua of campfire on the wind had been what initially caught his attention, it was the other smell that drew his eye to the rear, smoke-blackened wall where the buzzing flies voiced their displeasure at the interruption of their meal.

The body was propped against the rocks like a carelessly discarded doll. Bloated black flies crawled through her bangs, which were crusted into dreadlocks by her blood. They concealed her face, where the buzzing of the hidden insects made a sound like snoring, as though they had caught the woman mid-siesta. Her shirt was torn to reveal her black bra, beneath which the open maw of her abdomen seethed with green-eyed flies. Pike waved them away and found what he expected. The bowels had been excised, leaving the rotting viscera to settle into the void. Her ripped khakis were crisp with dried mud and smears from where her intestines had been uncoiled onto her lap.

Pike grabbed a fistful of her bangs and raised her head.

"Get a picture."

Brazelton crouched in front of her and snapped a digital image to forward to the *Huxley* for identification purposes, if one could even be made. Her lips were swollen and split, he front teeth chipped, her nose broken, and both closed eyes black from bruising. It looked like her face had been repeatedly slammed into the rock wall before she was hurled down to the ground.

"It's just playing with them," Walker said. He kicked ashes from the fire, stepped back out into the rain, and leaned his head back to allow it to wash over his face.

Brazelton lifted the woman's left arm and shook it. The joints in her elbow and wrist were stiff. He glanced back over his shoulder at Walker before he turned back and spoke to Pike in a whisper.

"We still have solid rigor."

"I noticed as soon as I tilted her head back."

"You know what that means."

Pike nodded. "She can't have been dead for more than twelve hours."

"Which means that if it stalked the remaining two survivors for any significant length of time—"

"It has to know a shortcut across the island to have been able to sneak around behind us to pick off Montgomery and Pearson."

"And if it does, it could be moving to intercept us on the path *ahead* of us right now while we're skirting the coastline."

"Or if it didn't go after the other two survivors right away, they could still be alive somewhere down the path."

"Using them as bait? That implies a tremendous amount of intelligence and cunning. If that were the case, it would have had to know that eventually rescuers would be dispatched to the site of the shipwreck and that we would find and follow the tracks from the beach."

"Exactly."

"That scenario suggests that it herded the survivors to the far side of the island—"

"It's toying with them."

"—in order to lure us as far away from the ship as possible." Brazelton paused. "But why? To isolate us? It did manage to split up our group so it could take down Montgomery and Pearson."

"Maybe." Pike walked back out into the night. The trail left by the two remaining was clearly evident; that of their stalker, much less so. "Or perhaps, if it's as smart as we suspect, it had another motive in mind."

"What's that?"

Pike pictured the bodies floating in the hold of the *Mayr*.

"Maybe it wants to lure the rescue vessel and all aboard to this side of the island."

From this vantage point, they could barely see the ocean through the fog and the trees. And the lights on the deck of the *Huxley* as it cruised around the southwestern fringe of the island.

Thirty-Two

R/V Aldous Huxley

Courtney watched the videos from the *Mayr*'s digital security system in abject horror. None of them spoke as Barnes played one corrupted file after another. There were scenes of bedlam in the hallways, men and women she knew colliding as they fought their way out of their rooms, into the throngs, and toward the stairwells. Shoving, stomping, and trampling one another in their panic. Fighting against the tilting decks that threw them alternately against one wall and then back across the corridor against the other. Friends crumpled on the floor, screaming in pain and terror as they grasped visibly broken ankles and wrists. Spatters of blood on the walls as though the entire ship had been converted into an impromptu Jackson Pollock gallery with the entirety of the *Mayr* as his canvas. And in each and every file, a shadowed figure darted at the periphery, never clearly visible, always just at the edge of sight with eyes that reflected the dim glare like those of a dog caught briefly in headlights. As though it knew where the cameras were mounted and deftly avoided them. All the while the horizontal bars jumped and shivered up and down the screen in a pathetic effort to hide the chaos.

Tears streamed down her cheeks. While watching each file, she strained her eyes to pick out her brother's face, to recognize his silhouette or gait, to find him in the midst of a nightmare. Never once did she see him. Not on the limited salvageable footage from the 02 Deck where the infirmary was located. Not on the 01 Deck where both of their cabins were. Not on the main level where the people flocked toward the stern and then back like so many mice unable to escape a maze.

They watched until there was no longer action to watch. The only movement was the bodies sprawled on the floor or piled in the stairwells and exits as the rising water flooded over the deck and carried them in whichever direction it chose, as though these men and women with whom she'd worked shoulder-to-shoulder, with whom she'd dined and watched movies in the lounge, were little more than driftwood.

Until at last, when they reached the final dozen rescued files, the shadow partially revealed itself.

"My God," Bradley whispered next to her. His face had blanched. Maybe the spark in his eyes had waned, but it never left. The flickering static flashed on his features. "It's absolutely beautiful."

Bishop's hand found hers. She squeezed it tightly, as if to let go would send her plummeting into the surreal world on the screen before her.

"What the hell is that?" Barnes asked.

On the monitor, the bodies continued to slide up and down the corridor at the mercy of the floodwaters that sloshed from one side of the hall to the other, splashing up the walls as though trying to lap at the blood spatters. An inhuman vision stalked in their midst, like Charon wading through a shin-deep River Styx to find the dead souls to ferry to Hades. It clung to the walls under the cameras, a mere shadow stretched across the water, until it had no choice other than to expose itself. It ducked out into the frame, each time keeping its back to the recording as it grabbed the bodies one by one, by an arm, a leg, or by their clothing, and dragged them toward the stairwell, where it threw them down the first flight to the landing. Its silhouette was limned with a shimmering glow like molten silver that almost made it appear entirely separate from the carnage around it. Never completely in focus, it moved with serpentine grace, an entity composed of muscle and sinew that seemed to flow more like the water around it than like a man. Movements so fast and fluid that each time the footage jumped, it was nowhere near where it had been a second prior. She caught fleeting glimpses of smooth, reflective skin, of the spikes that poked through its back from the base of its skull down to between its shoulder blades, of its hunched posture that was almost reptilian in the way its legs stayed flexed, its torso lowered to the ground, its center of gravity transferred forward along with arms that were held almost defensively in front of its face. Not with fists, but with splayed fingers curled into claws. All of this was revealed in rapid bursts of activity that never displayed every detail at once, but rather forced her mind to assemble the whole from the pieces.

They were the same eyes with the same hollow, predatory stare that had watched her through the lowered biohazard shield. Eyes that had scoured her body as though she were a slab of meat, that had left her feeling tainted by the hunger behind them. Eyes she would never forget as long as she lived.

"The next one, if you please," Bradley said, his voice the whisper of a man recovering from a punch to the gut.

"I think…" Barnes started. "I think I've seen enough."

"Please."

Barnes double-clicked the next file, then turned away from the screen.

Through the worst static yet, Courtney saw the biohazard insignia on the blood-smeared Plexiglas divider, and beyond it a single human outline she knew to be her own. Another shape stood on the near side with its back to the camera, moving laterally in motions made twitchy by the horizontal distortion. Two bodies were crumpled at its feet against the barrier.

A flash of memory.

"Let us in!" a man shouts. His eyes are all whites, his dark hair matted to the right where a wound drips blood down his forehead and temple. She recognizes him now. Shaun Wrightson, the Chief Steward. "Hurry! For the love of God!"

"I can't!" She unconsciously recedes from the barrier toward where Bishop still struggles to regain consciousness. "It only opens from the outside!"

"Please!" There's another man with him, little more than a boy. He pounds the glass with both fists, leaving bloody smears. She's only met this Able Seaman nicknamed Walleye for his bulging orbits in passing. A laceration bisects his pale face from his left eyebrow, across his nose, and to his chin. "You can't leave us out—!"

A third shadow rises behind them.

An arc of fluid spatters the Plexiglas.

She steps backward so quickly that her heel snags on something and she topples to the floor.

More and more blood splashes against the barrier. Hands paw at the slick surface seeking purchase they'll never find. Bodies are slammed against it, smearing the blood until she can barely see through it. Their shrill cries, infused with so much pain, are abruptly silenced. First one, then the other.

She sobs and kicks at the floor to push herself all the way up against the rear wall. Tucking her legs to her chest, she tries not to look at the dark form on the other side of the streaked barricade. It paces back and forth as if seeking a weakness by which to smash its way in, before eventually fading out of sight into the crimson fog.

Shaking and trembling, she screams for help at the top of her lungs. Screams her throat raw. Screams until there's nothing left of her voice.

She watches as the red glare darkens the drying blood. Her mind becomes sluggish and her body grows cold and numb from the onset of shock.

Courtney's shoulders shook as she started to cry.

On the screen, the shadowed man whirled and sprinted out of sight, leaving her digital doppelganger curled into a ball and sobbing on the floor, where Bishop was only now struggling to rise from the standing water.

Bradley turned and looked past her to where Van Horn hovered. She hadn't heard him return after being called out to attend to radio communications from the island. Something passed between the two men. Van Horn nodded.

"Mr. Barnes," Van Horn said. "You're dismissed."

Barnes nodded, stood, and was out of the room like a shot without making eye contact with any of them. Bradley assumed his place at the controls and began clicking through the remaining files. Each showed an empty hallway on the main deck, filling with rising water, or one of the upper decks, the floor smeared with so much blood it looked like crude oil sloppily spread by a mop. All except for one recording, which captured the stairwell leading down to the hold, where body upon body were piled. Before their eyes, the mound grew smaller. The corpses disappeared down into the hold where the lens couldn't follow.

Courtney had no idea what she was supposed to say or do. Her world no longer made any kind of sense. Was any of this real, or was she still trapped in the lab on the *Mayr*, waiting for her final breaths to still in her chest?

"You need to call the authorities," Bishop said. "This wasn't just a shipwreck."

"Every emergency agency in Oceania from China to Australia is already occupied by the aftermath of the tsunami. They already have tens of thousands of bodies of their own to sift through."

"This is different," Courtney said. "This wasn't a natural disaster. The people on our ship were murdered."

"Call the Coast Guard. They have jurisdiction even in international waters—"

"Mr. Van Horn," Bradley interrupted. "Would you please see Mr. Bishop and Dr. Martin to their accommodations and make sure they are properly attended."

"Yes, sir," Van Horn said. He rested a hand on each of their shoulders.

"Wait a minute," Courtney snapped. "You can't force us to do anything."

"You knew about whatever that is on the ship all along, didn't you?" Bishop said. "You aren't surprised in the slightest."

"Mr. Bishop," Van Horn said. "If you would kindly come with us..."

Three seamen appeared in the doorway. In a matter of seconds, they took up position to either side of Courtney and Bishop.

"What was that thing?" Bishop asked. "You're responsible for it, aren't you? That's why you were so interested in the accident in the lab. You knew exactly what it was. There was something in that chimney, something we brought on board in the bioreactor. That wasn't just *something* in that footage, was it? It was someone."

"Let go of me!" Courtney shouted. Two of the men grasped her beneath her armpits and lifted her from her chair. Her heels dragged the floor as she was manhandled into the corridor. Bishop's words echoed in her mind.

That wasn't just something *in that footage, was it? It was someone.*

Oh, God.

She felt like she was falling into a deep well. Her legs gave out, and her hearing became tinny. The world around her darkened. From a great distance, she heard Bishop shouting.

"Please, God," she whispered. "Not Ty…"

Thirty-Three

Reaves heard commotion in the hallway, but by the time he ducked his head out of the lab, there was no one in sight. He walked down the corridor and entered the makeshift command center to find Bradley alone in the room, staring at the monitor with his fingers steepled beneath his chin.

"What was all the ruckus?"

Bradley waved off his question and continued to be mesmerized by the screen in front of him. It was paused on an image with a thick bar of static frozen in the center, above which Reaves saw a stairwell that looked identical to the one he had just passed on his way in. He eased into the room and was nearly at Bradley's side when he saw what held his longtime employer and friend enrapt. There were bodies mounded in the threshold like sandbags heaped along the banks of a flooding river. They were mostly obscured by the crackling black bands, but just on the other side, a pair of eyes glowed gray with reflected light, twin circles of eyeshine. The black silhouette to which they belonged was outlined with the same gray.

"That's it, isn't it?" Reaves said. "We were right."

Bradley nodded, but said nothing.

Reaves took the seat beside him and stared at the vaguely human shape on the screen for a long moment before finally turning to engage Bradley. He forgot what he was going to say when he saw the tears glistening on Bradley's cheeks and the pained expression on his face.

"How long have we waited for this moment?" Bradley asked. "How many years have we been searching? How much time and effort have we expended to bring us to this very moment?"

Reaves waited silently. Bradley was obviously building up to something.

"Did you ever think this would happen? I mean really happen?" He broke his stare from the screen and turned to face

Reaves. "I don't know if I actually ever did. All of these years of imagining what it would be like, and now we're actually going to have the opportunity to study a living example of Chaco Man."

"We don't have him yet."

"It's only a matter of time."

"You have to remember that somewhere inside of that mutated body is a living, breathing human being. It's not like the remains back in The Crypt. This is someone's child, someone's—"

"Brother," Bradley said.

"You're sure?"

Bradley nodded and looked back at the screen.

"Do you think she knows?" Reaves asked.

"I don't think so. At least not yet."

"Eventually, she will. And then what?"

Bradley smiled wistfully.

"What's the value of the information we could learn from studying him? We're looking at the next step in the evolution of humanity. We're apes confronted with Neanderthal Man."

Reaves leaned forward and tapped the screen where the corpses were piled.

"This isn't the future. This is an aberration. We're not dealing with the progression of mankind, but rather something set upon the earth to prey upon it. This is the spontaneous emergence of a predator as deadly as any that has ever stalked the earth. And on this monitor is proof-positive why we should never coexist." He bumped his chair against Bradley's and gave a single chuckle. "Do you remember how this whole quest of ours started? You should have seen the look on your face when you saw the bodies for the first time. I thought you were going to piss that fancy suit of yours."

"I nearly did." Bradley snorted a laugh and shook his head. "I'll never forget that moment. It changed the course of my life. It gave me purpose."

"And what was that purpose?"

"I wanted to understand them. I wanted to know how such fantastic mutations could arise. I wanted to study every facet of their existence. Why had they been entombed under the ruins? Why had they been buried with live animals? Why were there human bones all around them? Were they the reason for the evidence of cannibalism? And most importantly, I needed to know how they came into being."

"And that's the revelation we're on the brink of right now." He rested his hand on Bradley's shoulder. "Possessing Chaco Man has never been our goal. We will be the first to study him, and we'll be the first to understand him, even if we end up having to share him with the world."

"I'm more worried we'll be forced to destroy him. Just like so many other times in the past."

"Brendan," a voice interrupted from behind them. He turned to find Angie leaning around the doorway. Her face was positively aglow with excitement. "You have to see this."

Reaves met Bradley's stare, and together they leapt from their chairs and hustled out into the hallway. Angie was already a good five paces ahead of them, her hips swishing like a speed walker's.

"That microorganism you saw? The one with the viruses inside of it?" she said without looking back. "It's an unclassified species of thermophile similar to *thermococcus litoralis*. At least physically, anyway. I've barely begun to examine it, but I've already been able to isolate one of the viruses. You have to see this thing to believe it."

Angie ducked into the main lab and both men followed. She sat in front of the scanning electron microscope and gestured toward the screen.

"This is at 26,400x magnification." The virus looked like a fuzzy sac containing twin budding willow branches, each of which were long and filamentous.

"It's dead," Reaves said.

She spun in her chair to face them, her eyes wild.

"It's a retrovirus."

When neither immediately said anything, her face flushed with frustration.

"Don't you get it? This is a super-aggressive form of virus. I haven't had the opportunity to break down its protein structure yet, but I can tell you right now that this is one scary bug.""A retrovirus," Bradley said. "Like AIDS?"

"Exactly. Think of it as a little dictator that infects the body and imposes its will over every cell. It copies its proteins directly into the host's DNA and forces the body to make changes more conducive to its proliferation. Consider the human immunodeficiency virus. Through the process of reverse transcription, it inserts a copy of its RNA into the host's DNA, so that every time a cell divides and replicates, it reproduces the virus' genetic code as a part of its own. In the case of HIV, it depletes the number of T cells in the body, which weakens the immune system and essentially creates its own ideal environment that allows for the development of full-blown AIDS.

"Based on the symptoms the doctor on the *Mayr* documented—the sudden onset and rapid advancement of inflammatory skin plaques, and the accelerated growth of the nails—I think we're dealing with a virus that attacks the cells with the most rapid reproduction rate. The subsequent immune reaction caused the patient to spike a fever. I can only speculate from there, but here's my theory. The initial infection serves as a form of distraction. While the lymphocytes are waging a losing battle against the psoriatic condition, the virus attacks the remainder of the body. It triggers rapid proliferation of ordinarily slow-dividing cells like the bones of the maxilla, which causes those sharp protuberances that mimic teeth, and the tissues of the retina, to cause the development of a low light-enhancing film similar to the *tapetum lucidum* in nocturnal animals. It'll take years of playing with this little devil before I can conclusively demonstrate this, though."

She looked at each of them in turn, a mischievous smile on her face.

"Want to see the coolest part?"

She leaned across her desk to the microarray workstation where several test tubes filled with cloudy fluid were balanced in the warmer. She used a micropipette to draw a sample from one of them.

"This is a concentrated solution of aqueous hydrogen sulfide and saline," she said, waving the tip under her crinkled nose. "Just like you'd find in one of the hydrothermal vents where the bacterium was collected."

It smelled like she passed gas.

"You won't believe this." She lowered the pipette to the stained slide they now viewed. A tiny drop shivered from the tip before snapping free. It spread across the monitor, making the entire virus buck to the left. She had to track it down and center over it once more. "Check it out."

"Hold the slide still," Reaves said.

"I'm not touching it."

"I can't get a good look at it with you moving it around like that."

"Like I said, I'm not doing it."

The hairy filaments on the screen flipped back and forth in twitching movements, the clear, bud-like balls along their lengths colliding.

Angie raised her hands palm-up to show that she wasn't manipulating what they were witnessing.

"It's alive," Bradley said.

"I've never seen anything like it," Angie said. "It's as though they can exist for extended periods of time in a dormant state that imitates death. It's chemosynthetic. Apparently, it requires a high level of hydrogen sulfide to survive."

"Even inside a host?"

"Especially inside of a host. It's natural environment is rife with hydrogen sulfide."

"Is there enough naturally occurring in the atmosphere to sustain it?" Reaves asked.

"It wouldn't have been dead on the slide when you walked in if there were."

"Then how in the world does it survive?"

Angie smiled. A devious expression Reaves had seen before, although in a dramatically different context, crossed her face. Again, his stomach fluttered.

"I have a theory about that…"

She made them wait her out.

"What does hydrogen sulfide smell like?" she finally asked.

"Like a great big fart," Reaves said.

She waved her hands as though trying to coax the obvious answer out of them.

"And where do 'great big farts' come from?"

"Son of a bitch," Bradley whispered.

Thirty-Four

James Van Horn opened the door to the submersible hanger, which now served as a temporary morgue until the bodies were properly studied and transferred to more permanent accommodations in cold storage belowdecks. There was no way to perform formal autopsies on corpses that eventually had to be returned to the families of the deceased. His footsteps echoed in the large garage as he walked to the center of the bay. The control room up the flight of stairs to the left was dark, the submersible *Trident* to his right in dry dock. Ahead, the garage door to the launch on the stern was closed. Twenty feet overhead, the stadium lights mounted to the exposed girders shined down on the smooth floor, spotlighting the lumpy tarps and the five cadavers they covered. The two divers who had dropped what they were doing on the ocean floor to collect them from the island stood as far away from the remains as possible, their backs against the wall beside the door through which he'd entered. Neither spoke as they stared around the room at anything other than the source of the putrid stench.

Several crabs made clacking sounds as they scuttled across the ground. Van Horn swept aside the nearest with his boot and approached the remains.

"What kind of condition are they in?" he asked. He watched small lumps move under the amassed tarps like the heels of a baby through an expectant mother's belly. It was going to be a long time before he ordered crab legs again.

"You think either of us looked at them?" one of the men said. "We just hauled them to the Zodiak and dragged them in here like you told us to. No one said anything about having to look at them."

Van Horn couldn't blame them. He didn't relish the prospect much himself. After days rotting in the elements and with the obvious attention from the scavengers, he could only imagine their condition.

"You're dismissed," he said.

With a shared sigh of relief, both men ducked out the doorway and into the corridor. The door closed behind them with a loud *thud* that reverberated through the hollow chamber.

The transceiver clipped to his belt squawked.

"What...you doing?" Pike's voice snapped through the fuzz.

"Just making sure we retrieved all of the stiffs before turning them over to scientific." He stood before the tarps, wishing he had some sort of mask to pull over his mouth and nose. All smells were particulate. The thought of rotten flesh dripping from his nostrils onto his tongue and down the back of his throat was enough to churn his gut. "Believe me, it's not a task I anticipate enjoying. At all."

"No. What...ship doing on...west side of the island?"

"Bradley's orders. If there's the possibility that the survivors reached the shore, he figures that's where we should be." He chuckled. "It was either that or start raising the dead from the *Mayr*, and I'm in no hurry to have any more stinking corpses on board."

"Turn around," Pike said. "Right now, for the love..." His words dissolved into the static. "Just...around."

"The electrical interference is getting worse. I can barely understand what you're trying to say." He slipped on the pair of nitrile examination gloves he had pilfered from one of the labs on his way to the hanger and lifted the corner of one of the tarps. Another crab snapped at his fingers before dancing away. "Nasty little critters."

"...exactly   what   it   wants...herding you...already...Montgomery and Pearson...response..."

"I'm not following. Your transmission's cutting in and out."

Van Horn drew a deep breath, steadied his resolve, and threw back the first tarp. Three men lay supine on a solar blanket, their remains crawling with the blasted crabs. One of the men was scorched black, the other two gutted, staring blankly up at him through filmy eyes. Insect larvae burrowed through their wounds and under their skin.

"Ugh." Van Horn groaned and turned away to choke down his gorge. He had known what to expect, but still hadn't been prepared. The next bundle only held two corpses, he knew, fortunately only one of which had been disemboweled. It was a miserable day indeed when that was the reason to consider himself lucky. He walked around to the other side and prepared to raise the tarp. Now that some of the bodies were exposed, the smell had intensified tenfold. The last thing he wanted to do was add to it.

"...hear me, damn it! I...don't...I repeat, don't..."

"You're breaking up on me. All I caught was 'don't'."

"...within a mile of the island...keep...distance...If it...someone like...Montgomery..."

"What about a mile from the island? Can you see something from where you are?"

Van Horn crouched, grabbed the corner of the tarp, and, in one quick motion, threw it back. It fluttered like a magician's cape and crumpled to the ground.

"Don't moor the ship...mile of the island!" Pike shouted. "Do...copy? It's...trap. The goddamned thing...luring the *Huxley*..."

The two recently exposed bodies rested on the floor beside the others. The one nearest to him had been savaged, its belly opened to cradle standing water and decomposing viscera.

"Repeat, Pike. It sounded like you said something about a trap."

The body next to it was still clothed and intact. Its entire body appeared bloated and swollen, its abdomen massively distended.

Its chest rose ever so slightly.

"What the hell?"

"Do not...that ship within a mile..."

He looked from the man's chest to his bruised neck, beside which he caught a flash of silver as something slid out from under the corpse—

A pair of eyes snapped open. The bright halogens overhead reflected as twin golden circles. It shoved the drowned man's body off of it and sprung to its feet. Scaled lips peeled back from a mouth filled with multiple rows of sharp teeth in a horrible mockery of a smile.

Van Horn screamed and flung himself backward, but the creature was already upon him. He reached for his gun and came away with only his transceiver. It clattered from his hand and slid away from his fingers.

"Just listen…me…Horn. Do not…that damn ship within a mother-loving mile…"

Another scream passed from his lacerated trachea as a gurgle of fluid.

A puddle of dark blood spread beneath him, seeping away from him to where the transceiver rested, pooling against its side.

"…copy, Van Horn? I said, do…copy?"

Pike's words drifted away into the hanger over the soft slapping of wet, bare feet and the sound of tearing flesh.

Thirty-Five

Ambitle Island

Pike roared in frustration and hurled the transceiver against the trunk of a kapok. Broken plastic and fractured electrical components cascaded into the underbrush.

Lightning crackled across the sky in a ceaseless display.

"Give me your transceiver," he said to Walker.

"So you can break it, too?"

"Just give me your goddamned transceiver!" Pike shouted, his voice echoing through the valley.

"All right, all right," Walker said. "Keep it together, man."

Pike's stare bored holes into Walker, who turned away to look upon the sea, where the *Huxley* sailed out of sight through the canopy to their right.

"Ambitle to *Huxley*," Pike said into the transceiver. "Come in, *Huxley*."

The only reply was the crackle of static.

"There's too much electrical interference," Brazelton said. "We're just going to have to wait it out. Besides, I doubt there's anywhere on this island equipped to dock a vessel the size of the *Huxley*. They won't have any other choice but to moor far off the coast." He turned to address Walker's back. "You said the western shore is shallow, right?"

"I said there are shallow-water hydrothermal vents. The shelf drops slowly, but Tutum Bay is still several hundred feet deep within shouting distance of the coast."

"The ship's draft is too deep to even attempt it. They'd tear the hull out on the reef."

"But they'll still dispatch a landing party," Pike said.

"Not if we get there first," Brazelton said. "Right?"

Pike took a deep breath of the crisp night air and forced down his rage. The cold rain helped him focus. Brazelton was right. Surely they'd be able to contact the ship before any forward party was launched, or, failing it at that, if they really kicked it in gear, there was still the slimmest of chances that they could reach the most accessible beach before the *Huxley* settled in and deployed a landing party.

That plan still left one glaring problem. If he was right about whatever stalked the island trying to lure the ship to shore, they would be sprinting headlong into the teeth of its trap, as well. And if this thing was smart enough to concoct such a cunning plan, then surely it knew the *Huxley* could only come so close to land.

Pike didn't care if he had to stand on the beach and fire shots at the vessel himself to drive it away. This was going to come down to him against their pursuit, and he wouldn't have it any other way.

The fact still remained that if it had taken out Montgomery and Pearson as he suspected, they still had a huge head start on it. There was no way it could cut across the steep forest of the volcanic interior and beat them there.

If nothing else, at least he was certain of that.

He memorized the view and committed the spot to memory for when it came time to collect the woman's remains. There was no time for anything more.

"Forget the Tasers," he said. "No more screwing around. If you get a shot, take it. Aim to incapacitate. Kill only if absolutely necessary. We still want this thing living, but not if it means our lives. Are we all on the same page?"

The other men nodded.

"Good. Then from here on out, we go on the aggressive. We know exactly where we're headed, and so does this thing. We need to get there first."

Pike drew his Beretta, chambered the first parabellum, and reveled in the snick of the slide snapping home.

He sprinted into the jungle without a backward glance, barreling northward through the dense foliage, one eye on the western horizon in hopes of catching the *Huxley*'s running lights, the other on the tangles of trees and shrubs, praying to see the whites of the monster's eyes.

Thirty-Six

R/V Aldous Huxley

Bishop opened the door to the hallway. The guard posted outside of the stateroom shook his head, smiled, and patted the sidearm holstered to his hip. Bishop was confident that the man wouldn't use it on them. It was a display of control more than anything else, but Bishop still wasn't prepared for the confrontation. His body was at the mercy of exhaustion and his brush with death. And besides, he still needed time to figure out what they were going to do before he made any kind of move. At least they hadn't separated him from Courtney. The last thing he would have wanted was to have his focus divided by worry for her while he tried to plan some sort of escape.

"What are we going to do?" Courtney asked. She sat on the edge of the bed, tears rolling down her cheeks. Behind her green eyes, Bishop saw neither the fear nor the resignation he would have expected.

He stopped pacing and plopped down next to her on the bed. The honest truth was that he simply didn't know. Everything was happening too quickly and he was still struggling to rationalize it himself. He sighed and squeezed her hand. His stare wandered the room. There was a private head in the corner, military clean and freshly stocked with towels. A desk and a bureau, both of which were bolted to the floor, lined the wall opposite the bed. They were effectively cut off from the world they could see speeding past through the twin porthole windows.

"We'll get out of here soon enough," he said. "It's what happens afterward that concerns me."

"Why?"

"Think about it. Why didn't they immediately have us airlifted to the nearest emergency facility when they rescued us? And why haven't we had the chance to communicate with anyone off of this boat? There's the armed guard outside our door, of course, and the fact that no one seems willing to tell us what's going on when they obviously know more than we do. Yet still they're keeping us here in hopes of extracting information I don't think either of us has."

"They can't hold us prisoner. If we wanted to, we could walk out of here right now."

"After the bum rush we got earlier, do you really think there's any chance of that?"

"Watch me."

Courtney rose in a huff, stormed across the cabin, and threw open the door. The guard whirled smoothly from his post against the wall to bar her passage.

"Out of my way. I need to speak with whoever's in charge."

"Sorry, princess. I have orders to keep you in there until I'm told otherwise."

"What are you going to do? Shoot me? I'm a citizen of the United States of America, and, last I knew, that entitled me to the right not to be confined like a criminal."

"You're a world away from the good old US of A out here." The badge on his chest read: S. Aronson. While the crew cut, granite-jawed man wore the uniform of a civilian mate, his posture and physique spoke to his naval training. "Look at it this way: They'll be fishing bodies out of the South Pacific for the next five years. Who's to say yours couldn't be among them? Now be a good girl. Close the door, lie back and relax, and soon enough all of this will be over."

Bishop saw Courtney tense. While he believed the man wouldn't shoot her, he wasn't about to take that chance. He'd been out here on the open sea long enough to know that a different set of rules applied. If she made a move, she was going to get hurt. And there was no way in hell he was going to allow that.

"Step aside," Courtney said. The tremor in her voice confirmed that she was about to do something she'd regret. "I'm going to go talk to Dr. Bradley right now, and neither you nor anyone else on this godforsaken vessel can keep me from doing so."

Bishop leaned back and pulled the pillow out from beneath the covers. Silently, he pulled off the pillowcase, twisted it tight, and gripped it in his fists.

"Lady, you really don't want to do this. Trust me."

Courtney glanced back over her shoulder at Bishop.

"I'm leaving now. Are you coming with me or not?"

The moment she returned her attention to the hallway and took the first step forward, Bishop sprung from the bed and lunged toward her. The guard grabbed for his pistol. Whether he intended to use it or just to brandish it, Bishop needed to make sure it never cleared the holster. He shoved Courtney aside, wrapped the pillowcase around the man's wrist, and gave it a solid twist, pinning it behind his back and up between his shoulder blades. The man grunted and Bishop heard the clatter of the gun hitting the floor. He used his momentum to swing the man around and drive him forward toward the opposite wall. Transferring his grip on the ends of the pillowcase to his right hand, he used his left to palm the back of the man's head and ram his face into the trim around the doorway at the moment of impact. There was a crunching sound and the man dropped like a sack of grain.

Bishop released the pillowcase, which fluttered down onto the crumpled body, and stumbled back toward the room. His eyes found the starburst of blood on the wall where the man's nose had broken. A familiar sensation of numbness flooded his veins. He grew lightheaded as he knelt over the man's crimson-spattered face and felt for the carotid pulse at the side of his neck. Fortunately, there was a slow but steady tapping of the vessel against his fingertips. He breathed a sigh of relief. For the briefest of moments, he feared he might have killed the man. As it was, they were already in deep enough trouble.

Everything had happened so fast that he hadn't thought his actions through. What were they supposed to do now? They couldn't walk back into the command room and pretend like nothing happened, nor could they just sit back down on the bed and wait for the man to wake up. And since no one was willing to evacuate them from the ship, it stood to reason that they probably had a pretty good reason for it, even if he couldn't fathom what it was. There was always the distinct possibility that their leaving this ship had never been part of the plans, which left only one safe option.

They needed to get off this boat, and they needed to do so right now.

He grabbed Courtney by the hand and sprinted toward the stairwell.

Thirty-Seven

Dr. Henri Renault stood on the starboard bow, saved from the worst of the torrent by a gaudy yellow slicker and the overhanging lip of the deck above him. Waves blasted up over the gunwales in flumes and washed back down into the ocean through the scuppers in a choreographed nautical dance that had been performed since man had first set out to conquer the seas. The island passed before him through the fog, which granted intermittent glimpses of steep, sharp slopes so densely forested it looked as though it would be impossible to find the space to even walk between the trunks. Lightning flashed in the clouds, framing the outline of the dormant caldera he had yet to clearly see. Thunder boomed as though the electrical siege were tearing the island apart. It was a view he would have ordinarily enjoyed, were it not for the fact that his Dramamine had worn off while he was absorbed by Dr. Walter Partridge's files. At least it helped to some degree to see the horizon, sporadic though the glimpses might be. Coupled with the calming influence of the rich smoke from his pipe, he would be fine until the dimenhydrinate worked its magic again.

It was a blessing to be out here on his own, besides. He knew the men inside loathed him for his position, and while inconvenient, he frankly didn't care. He had invested capital into a fledgling biotech corporation in order for it to get off the ground, just like any of the rest of them would have done had they the means. And he had earned his just rewards. Granted, the risk had been minimal thanks to the enormity of the fortune from which he'd drawn the funds, but that didn't mean he didn't deserve everything that had come to him. What he didn't deserve was the overt contempt with which even the inner circle of the scientific team treated him, as though his presence were merely tolerated, like he didn't have the requisite medical skills to have rightfully claimed his spot on this vessel.

He set aside his frustration and focused on the task at hand. He was stalling and he knew it. The prospect of inspecting the rotting remains of the men they had recovered from the island was daunting. There wasn't the time for proper study, least of all with the dozens more to come from the sunken research vessel once they returned to the eastern bay. He would simply have to give each a relatively topical once-over, establish cause and approximate time of death, and move on to the next.

Two more solid pulls from his pipe and he tapped it out on the railing. The island continued to roll past through the mist to the east. It truly was a beautiful sight, an untamed vista like Magellan and de León must have seen once upon a time when all of the world was a discovery.

He headed back into the ship and hung the heavy slicker on the rack by the doorway. His wet shoes squeaked on the slick floor. The sound echoed hollowly away from him. He glanced through the open door into the makeshift command center, where Bradley and various members of his entourage were still gathered around a monitor shivering with static, as he passed. The submersible hanger was at the end of the corridor, but he could have found it by smell alone. They would all be better off once he was done with the cadavers and they were moved down into cold storage, where, if nothing else, at least the fragrance would be contained.

They had better have properly equipped him, he thought as he opened the door and stepped into the vast space beyond.

The brilliant lights overhead required a moment to adapt. His eyes found the deep sea vehicle first, seated on its trolley in front of an iron staircase that ascended to a platform nearly hidden by myriad couplings and cables. The office at the top of the room to the left was dark. In the center of the hanger, the bodies rested on a series of tarps as if they'd just been thrown there with a despicable level of disregard. He grunted his displeasure as he scanned the vicinity for a rack of proper tools. Not even a bloody box of examination gloves.

This was entirely unacceptable. He was going to have to talk to Mr. Van Horn, who had assured him that—

He stopped halfway to the spread of bodies.

The light reflected from a puddle just past the remains. His mind fought to rationalize what he saw. There were five bodies side by side, and a sixth several paces away, its face a shimmering mask of blood. The gaping wound in its neck glistened. No. This wasn't right at all. There had been no mention of the sixth. This was not proper protocol at all. And where had this additional one come from? It was obviously far too—

He held his breath when he heard the clacking noises behind him, sounds not dissimilar to those of his prized Pomeranians on the marble tiles in his foyer.

Everything was out of context. Renault was a man of science, a man whose life was defined by organization. He struggled to return some semblance of order to his surroundings.

Brow furrowed, he turned toward the tapping sounds.

A flash of silver.

The whistle of something sharp cleaving the air.

A sudden sensation of pain in his throat.

Damp heat on his hands when he clutched at it.

Twin circular reflections of light.

Rows of sharp teeth that curled under like those of a great white shark.

A scream that would never pass his lips.

The cold anesthetic of darkness.

Thirty-Eight

Courtney clung to Bishop's hand as he bounded down the staircase ahead of her. He stopped when he reached the stairwell on the main deck and pressed her back against the wall beside him. Beyond him, she could see only a small section of the deserted corridor. She closed her mouth to quiet her breathing, and over the jackhammer of her pulse, listened for the sound of footsteps. When she heard none, she spoke in a whisper.

"Where are we going?"

She could see the indecision in his eyes when he turned to face her.

"We have to get off this ship."

"What?"

He took her by the shoulders and brought her face close to his.

"Don't you see? They have no intention of ever letting us go."

"That's absurd. Why would they—?"

"Didn't you see the security tapes? That thing we saw on them, that thing that was dragging all of the bodies down into the hold… That's what they're after. Surely you saw the excitement in their eyes. They don't care that everyone on the *Mayr* is dead. They want whatever killed everyone before it sank. And they think it's still out there somewhere."

"We didn't have anything to do with that. You and I were locked in the isolation chamber while all of that was going on."

"But it started before that. With the accident in the lab. That's why they were desperate to salvage the batch reactor, why they needed the doctor's notes on your brother."

"They think…" They were so painful that she choked on the words. She had struggled against the revelation as hard as she could. "They think that creature is my brother."

"Listen, Courtney. Whether it is or not is irrelevant. What matters is that these people are bioengineers who think they've stumbled upon the find of a lifetime and they don't want anyone else to know about it. Why else wouldn't they have called for help searching for the survivors on the island? For us? They want this thing all to themselves."

"So what are they planning to do with us? Keep us on this boat forever?"

"I don't know, but I sure as hell don't want to stick around to find out." His eyes locked on hers. "Do you?"

She remembered the shine of the crimson eyes through the Plexiglas shield, the hours of slow asphyxiation, being rescued only to find herself studying security tapes of the violent deaths of her colleagues, describing Ty's rapidly deteriorating condition to men who couldn't get enough of it before being imprisoned in a cabin with an armed guard stationed outside the door. She thought about what would happen to them, what would be done to them, when those that controlled this ship learned that they had incapacitated the guard. No one else even knew they had survived. As far as the rest of the world was concerned, she and Bishop could easily have gone down with the *Mayr*, even if their bodies were never found.

Surely these men weren't capable of something like that...were they?

She made a split-second decision.

"No," she whispered.

Bishop nodded and took her by the hand again. He craned his neck around the threshold and peered out into the corridor.

Besides, if there was a chance that her brother was still alive, she needed to find him first. Whatever his condition. And it was readily apparent that the only way to do so was to get off of this vessel.

"Come on," Bishop whispered, and tugged her out into the hallway.

They ran toward the stern, then ducked into the short hallway that led to the starboard rail. At the hatch, they paused long enough for Bishop to crack it just wide enough to scan the deck. The bow was clearly visible from the pilothouse, and last she knew the stern was a hotbed of activity as the men loaded and stowed the salvage from the *Mayr*. The inset door in front of them was recessed below the 01 Deck. They would be invisible until they approached the rail.

Bishop threw the door all the way open and dragged her out into the storm. Raindrops pummeled her from a sky that was a battlefield of lightning. Spray from the thundering waves added to the torrent, through which she could barely see a wooded island in the distance.

"Can you swim?" Bishop shouted into her ear.

"I'm a marine biologist. Of course, I can—"

He jerked her by the hand and sprinted toward the rail. The moment they reached it, he helped boost her up on top of it. Her wet hair slapped her face. Her hands slipped on the slick rail.

"We should take one of the lifeboats," she shouted down to him. She could barely keep her eyes open with all of the water in the air. "Or at least life jackets."

"They'd be big orange bull's eyes." He strained to help her maintain her balance of the slippery rail, which plunged beneath her as the *Huxley* cut through the chop. "Can you make it or not?"

She glanced across the rolling black waves toward the island. She knew that distances like this were always deceptive. It looked like the rugged shore was only a quarter mile away, which meant that it could easily be three times as much. And with the tempestuous sea, the currents, and the undertow, the exertion would be tremendous. Her body was still exhausted from their ordeal. She was already freezing and soaked to the bone. Just balancing on the rail seemed to tax every muscle in her body, but what choice did she have?

"I can make it," she said.

"Then I'll meet you there."

He tried to smile for her benefit.

She grabbed him by the back of the head and pulled his face to hers. Before she even knew she was going to do it, she kissed him on the mouth. Hard. His eyes widened in surprise. She didn't give him the opportunity to say anything as she dove from the rail toward the roiling black ocean.

The almost comical expression on his face was the image in her mind when the sensation of weightlessness rose inside of her and she struck the frigid water as though breaking through the ice on a frozen lake. Her momentum and the ship's wake turned her head over heels until she could no longer tell which way was up. The pressure tried to compress her lungs. The cold bit into her skin and made her appendages leaden. She kicked with all her strength toward what she hoped was the surface, struggling through water that seemed intent on shoving her back down.

Her breath staled in her chest.

She opened her burning eyes and saw only blackness.

Only blackness.

She prayed that somewhere above her were the waves and the sky.

If not, she would never see them again.

Thirty-Nine

"You did what?" Reaves snapped, louder than he had
intended. All eyes in the room were drawn to him. He offered a
placating smile, and again lowered his voice. "Are you out of your
mind?"

"I don't see where I was left with any other option," Bradley
said.

"No other option than confining them to your stateroom? How
was *that* even an option?" He bit his lip to keep from raising his
voice again. When he heard it rumored that Bradley had locked up
Bishop and Martin, he hadn't believed it for second. He could
scarcely believe it now, even coming from the horse's mouth.
"What do you think is going to happen to us when we return to
Seattle, huh? They'll cry civil rights violations so fast it'll make
your head spin. And you know what? They'll have every right to
do so. You can't just go locking people up whenever you damn
well feel like it."

"What would you rather I do?" Bradley gestured to the paused
image on the screen before him. He had skimmed through every
one of the security files until he had found the one best
representation of what they had come all of this way to find. It was
little more than a black silhouette limned with gray, a lithe outline
propelling itself up into a darkened stairwell, using its hands on the
stairs for leverage. Its face was frozen in time, turned so briefly
toward the camera that the gray reflections from its eyes were
blurred. There was a glimmer of light on a mouthful of bared teeth.
Had Reaves not spent so many years poring over the skeletal
remains in The Crypt, he might never have recognized it for what
it truly was. "If we had allowed them to contact the outside world,
they would have run their mouths off in a second. And then what?"

"Do you think anyone out there would believe them?"

"Let's say someone did. Or even if they didn't, we'd have the
military crawling all over these ships trying to figure out what

happened. How long would it take them to figure it out? Next thing you know, our discovery—*our Chaco Man*—and everything we've worked so hard for would be stolen right from our grasp and wind up in some top-secret bunker in the middle of the desert being vivisected to find out if there's some way to turn its truly amazing mutations into some kind of biological weapon."

"And what do you propose *we* do with it? Say we somehow manage to capture this creature that has already killed dozens of people…what then? Do we take it back to corporate headquarters with us so we can vivisect it and determine if there are ways to capitalize on its 'truly amazing mutations' for our own purposes?" Reaves tapped his finger on the image on the screen. "We created this thing, whether deliberately or not, which makes it our responsibility. Its life is our responsibility. All of the deaths are our responsibility. This thing here…" Tap-tap-tap. "This thing was once a living, breathing human being whose life as he knows it no longer exists. Lord only knows what thoughts he thinks now, or if he even thinks at all. And the woman you imprisoned is up there is his goddamned sister. Would you destroy that entire family?"

"You can drop the self-righteous act. How did you think this was going to play out? Did you think this transformation would just magically happen? That Chaco Man would simply materialize out of thin air? You and I both understood that it needed a human host, that all of our research was designed to isolate whatever organism caused the changes, and bring the two together. From the very start, this project required a sacrifice. And purely by accident, we got exactly what we wanted. Now we need to track this man down and bring him in alive so we can thoroughly study everything about him, or that sacrifice will have been in vain. And who knows? Maybe in the process we'll find a way to change him back."

"This isn't some stray dog we're talking about here. This is nature's perfect killing machine. This is an aberration created solely to prey upon members of its own species. It caused the Anasazi to flee Chaco Canyon. It chased the Champa out of central Vietnam and the Maya out of Guatemala. It drove the early Polynesians from Easter Island and terrorized coastal Japan. And who knows what all else. Do you really believe we're going to be able to throw a collar on it and take it home?"

"Listen to yourself, Brendan. We're so close to realizing our shared dream. Just think, in a matter of hours we'll be able to see this creation in the flesh, to touch its skin, to look it in the eye and find out what looks back. Pike is on its trail as we speak. Soon enough, he'll call in with the news we've waited our whole lives to hear. Tell me you aren't every bit as excited as I am."

It hurt Reaves to admit to himself that he was. He had just never thought through the logistics. Bradley was right. There was never any other way it could have played out.

"I want you to release Bishop and Martin," he whispered. "They've already lived through enough. If she doesn't know already, it's only a matter of time before she figures out that her brother is dead to her, if not his body. Will you do that for me?"

Bradley sighed and met his stare with genuine compassion and a kind smile.

"Give me twenty-four hours to see how things unfold. When all is said and done, we'll find the right price to buy their silence. I guarantee they'll walk away from this rich beyond their wildest dreams."

"And what if they can't be bought? We're talking about a girl's brother here. Do you really think that if she understands what happened to him, she can be paid off with any amount of money?"

"Everyone has a price."

"What if she doesn't? What if Bishop doesn't? What will happen to our research, to us, if word of what happened here leaks out?"

"That will never happen."

"How can you be so sure?"

"Because I won't let it." Bradley's voice rose, again summoning the attention of the computer techs who had resumed their tasks. "I refuse to allow anything to derail our project. I will not allow anyone to ruin everything we've done."

"How can you stop them?"

"I'm willing to do whatever it takes."

"What are you saying?" Reaves asked.

Bradley leaned back in his chair and looked him directly in his eyes. What Reaves saw behind that stare was something he'd never seen there before, something beyond fervor, something cold and insidious.

Reaves turned away from his old friend and exited the room now occupied by a stranger.

Forty

South Pacific Ocean
48 km East of New Ireland Island, Papua New Guinea
December 1st
12:00 a.m. PGT

Bishop had lost sight of Courtney the moment she struck the water. There hadn't been time to wait to make sure she surfaced. Not only was he too exposed standing out on the deck by the rail, but the longer he waited to dive in himself, the farther he would be from her when he made it to land. He could only pray that she was a strong enough swimmer to reach the island on her own, a prayer he said for himself, as well.

The violent waves rose and fell so dramatically that it was impossible to tell how far he had come. He could barely see over the next crest before it fell out from beneath him. The island was a black wall that never seemed to grow any closer, while the lights from the *Huxley* had faded behind him into the fog without the sound of shouting or spotlights crisscrossing the ocean. His arms had passed beyond mere aching and into a realm of pain beyond anything he had ever experienced. The cold water leeched through his skin and into his bones, where it threatened to lock his joints and shut him down from the inside out. Every wave attempted to pull him under. His chest burned. Even on his best days, this swim would have been a nightmare. Physically depleted as he was, it was suicide. Only the exertion kept him going through sheer force of will and the lone image that spurred him on.

Courtney.

Her auburn hair. Her stunning green eyes. When he had thought they were dying inside the wreckage of the *Mayr*, he had been scared, the only time in his life that he could honestly say that. But it hadn't been fear for himself. He defied death every day inside the submersible and had long ago accepted the fact that one day it would claim him. He'd been frightened for Courtney. Watching the dwindling oxygen slowly killing her, ushering her into her final sleep, had been like witnessing a star fading from the night sky into oblivion.

Over the roar of the waves, he heard the bass drum-thumping of the breakers. Lightning turned night to momentary day. At the top of a swell, he glimpsed the island, now close enough he could make out the individual trees ascending the sheer, rocky slope. He reached down deep for whatever reserves he could find and stroked for everything he was worth. He gritted his teeth and pinched his eyes shut against the pain of icicles being driven through his shoulders, of the flames that were stoked in his lungs with every breath, of the coldness he was certain meant the amputation of his fingers and toes.

When he opened his eyes again, he was upon the rocky crags that thrust upward from the ocean floor like fangs from a lower jaw. Whitened by eons of crusted bird feces, they stood out against the black boulders of the shoreline, now close enough that with each stroke he expected for his hand to brush them. A jagged rock slashed through the meat of his thigh, another through the skin on his belly. Foam crashed around him before exploding up into the air, where the lightning froze it in time. The next swell raised him above the rocks and hurled him against the breakers, knocking the wind out of him. He desperately wrapped his arms around a massive stone that felt like it was coated with glass shards. The thunder of the waves deafening his ears as they tried to beat him against the boulders and wrench him back out to sea, he clung to his salvation until he was able to breathe once more and cautiously began to ascend toward dry land.

Saturated and shredded, the scrubs they had given him on the *Huxley* hung from him in tatters. They provided about as much protection from the wind as if he were wearing nothing at all. He barely had enough sensation in his fingertips to comprehend that they were lacerated and bleeding, and barely gripped the ragged edges of the stones he used to pull himself upward. His entire body shook from the combination of exhaustion and from shivering against the wicked cold. Now that he was well above the waves, which voiced their rage at his escape by booming against the shore, he wanted nothing more than to rest for a little while, just long enough to catch his breath and wait for the feeling to return to his appendages, but he knew that if he stopped he would never be able to start again, and forced himself to continue climbing.

When he finally crested the rise, he collapsed to his chest and vomited seawater onto the spongy, moss-covered ground. The canopy overhead shielded him from the majority of the wind and rain. He looked back out across the ocean and saw only an infinity of angry troughs disappearing into the mist. There was no sign of the *Huxley*, nor did he see the figure he had hoped to find already at the top of the rock shelf.

The frozen hand of panic clenched his heart.

"Courtney?" he called, his voice little more than a croak. He fought to all fours and somehow managed to stagger to his feet. "Courtney!"

Using the tree trunks for leverage, he shoved through the vines and broad-leaved shrubs, following the shoreline to the south. The crags below him were nearly invisible in the darkness until lightning tore the sky and he stole brief glimpses of the glistening wet rocks and the tempestuous ocean.

"Courtney!" His voice was swallowed by the storm and the sea. "Courtney!"

He fell repeatedly, only to drag himself back to his feet and press on. His eyes scoured the coast faster than his mind could keep up. What had once been panic now progressed to sheer terror. He tried to run and only managed to collapse into a thorny desmodium bush.

"Courtney!"

He heard something. It sounded like the wail of the wind, yet at the same time distinctly separate from it. He lunged back into motion.

"Courtney!"

There was the sound again. He threw himself forward, through the foliage and moss-bearded boughs, through tangles of vines, until he heard the sound clearly. Down and to his right, he saw Courtney clinging to the escarpment. Her face was so pale that when she looked up at him, her lips blue, he feared it had taken too long to find her. He dropped to his stomach and reached down the slick rocks until he was able to grab her right wrist with both hands. She shook as she sobbed. Tears shone on her cheeks, and he saw the combination of desperation and hope in her eyes. Below her, the waves pounded the rocks like sledge hammers. She wouldn't survive the fall if his grasp slipped.

"Hold on," he said. His knees dug into the earth and he hooked his feet onto tree trunks that bit into his skin. He looked directly into her eyes the whole time. "Don't you dare let go."

He strained against her weight as he pulled with all the strength he had left. When he finally dragged her over the ledge, she collapsed into his arms.

Neither said a word as he cradled her shivering form to his chest and held her as tightly as he could.

Forty-One

R/V Aldous Huxley

Bradley's eyes widened in astonishment at the words whispered into his ear. He whirled to face the man who stood before him, face sticky with clotting blood from his eyebrows to his collar, nose askew to the left. The entire front of the man's uniform shirt was streaked and spattered. His eyes kept trying to roll upward into his skull, but he repeatedly blinked them back down. He swayed back and forth and bared teeth rimmed with scarlet as he fought to maintain his balance.

Bradley had never been so furious with one person in his entire life.

"What do you mean 'they escaped'?" he blurted. He rose from his chair and pulled Aronson out into the hallway by his upper arm. "How in the world did they get past you? Where's Van Horn?"

"I tried radioing him first." Aronson's words were slurred and his lips glimmered with a fresh sheen of blood. "When I didn't get an answer, I came directly to find you."

"No answer? I want you to raise him on that radio right now."

Three other seamen stood back from the first. None of them made eye contact with Bradley.

"Sir, I repeatedly tried to hail him on the transceiver to no avail, sir."

"I'll find Van horn. You four. Find Bishop and Martin. They have to be on this ship somewhere. They can't have gotten far. I want a door-to-door search and every nook and cranny explored. Since the *Huxley* and the *Mayr* are identical on the inside, you have to assume they know this vessel every bit as well as you do. Now go find them. If they're not in your charge again in the next half hour, the lot of you will be swimming back home. Now go!"

The men turned on their heels and hurried down the hallway with the clamor of footsteps. Aronson signaled a plan to the others, who split up at the stairwell.

Bradley massaged his throbbing temples. Everything was spiraling out of control. He hadn't come this far only to fail in the twelfth hour.

He shoved aside the thought of that fool Aronson being suckered by a man who was barely able to stand and a woman who only hours earlier had been nearly catatonic with an IV in her arm. His anger rose, but he choked it back down. This was no time to panic. They had to be hiding around here somewhere and it shouldn't take too long to find them. Once they did, he could breathe easier and focus on the mission again. He'd be damned if he was going to let anyone ruin this for him. This was his life's work and no one—*no one*—was going to ruin it for him, not now that they were so close.

His hands clenched into fists and he had to force them to relax. Nothing irreversible had happened. This was only a minor inconvenience that would be easily enough rectified. He needed to find Van Horn, who was paid specifically for contingencies like this, and make sure that the situation was quickly handled.

Last he knew, Van Horn had gone to the submersible hanger to make sure that all of the remains from the island had arrived intact. If he wasn't still there, then surely he'd told Henri, who must have been elbow-deep in the corpses by now, where he was going. It was always possible that Van Horn was supervising the transport of the bodies they'd already studied to cold storage where he simply couldn't hear his transceiver over the deafening roar of the engines.

Bradley stormed down the corridor toward the hanger and threw the door inward.

The smell struck him in the face like an uppercut.

He recoiled and eased into the room more slowly. There were corpses scattered all across the floor. Five were lined up like matchsticks on tarps in the center, while two more lay at angles to them.

There were standing pools of blood everywhere, connected by arterial arcs and smears where the bodies had either crawled or been dragged through their own rapidly fleeing lives. A pair of tentative steps deeper into the room and he could clearly discern Henri's hair and suit jacket on the corpse closest to him. He was facedown, his arms splayed above his head. Van Horn was on his back a dozen yards away, his throat opened into a startled crimson gasp.

Bradley momentarily froze as the scene played out in his head. His first thought was that Bishop must have attacked them in his desperation to escape the ship, but the level of carnage was staggering, inhuman. And the bottom line was that Bishop had merely broken Aronson's nose and left him unconscious. He hadn't slit the man's throat, for Christ's sake.

So if it hadn't been Bishop, then who...?

Bloody footprints led away from the corpses. They grew fainter and less distinct as he followed them with his eyes to the ground right in front of him. He leaned over to better see the question mark-shape of a bare human footprint. The five toes left ovals, above which tiny dots marked where toenails had barely tapped, like those of a dog.

He quickly straightened and spun toward the doorway. The tracks faded with each step as they crossed the threshold into the hallway. He followed them out the door and to the right, where they disappeared into a puddle of rainwater at the foot of the door that led to the stern.

Bradley cracked open the door and rain immediately filled the gap. A peal of thunder greeted him.

His heart thudded so hard that the edges of his vision throbbed. What the hell was going on here? Van Horn and Renault...both dead? A feeling of dread washed over him with the deluge as he shoved the door wide open with trembling hands. Lightning flared, illuminating the raging black ocean, which appeared to boil with the impact of raindrops. Another clap of thunder boomed.

It hadn't been Bishop who had slain his men. No, it had been something else entirely, something that had preceded him out this exact same doorway, something that had somehow found its way onto their ship and even now roamed it, out of sight.

Whatever footprints had been transferred to the deck had been washed away by the rain. Waves pounded against the hull and washed over the gunwales, sweeping across the stern, ankle-deep.

Bradley battled through the fear. Maybe he was wrong in his assessment. Bishop had been in the Navy after all, and it certainly didn't train its men to be teddy bears.

He walked farther onto the deck and had to shield his eyes from air that seemed to have been transformed into water. The stern was empty. Through the submersible's A-frame launch he saw only an eternity of chaotic waves. He scoured the ground for any sign of passage, then turned back toward the ship, the bulk of which rose above him like a four-story building capped with a massive satellite assembly that the wind threatened to tear right off. The porthole lights inside the cabins were attenuated by the fog. The external stairs to the 01 Deck were empty in front of him.

Bradley held his arms out to the sides for balance as the ship rocked, sending the floodwaters first one way, then back the other, trying to rip him off his feet. The vessel slowed and banked eastward toward the island, where the mouth of a marginally calmer bay yawned wide for them.

Another fork of lightning split the sky. The water on the ship's siding reflected it with a ghostly luminescence.

Movement.

He thought for a second he saw something moving up there.

A dark shape.

Here one moment, gone the next.

Clear up near the bridge. Its banks of windows stained the clouds like a forlorn lighthouse.

The resultant clap of thunder made his heart skip a beat.

His breathing grew fast, shallow.

He tried to pinpoint where he had seen the motion, but only saw the swirling fog and sheeting rain.

This was idiocy. If what he feared were true and their prey had somehow boarded the *Huxley*, the last thing he should be doing was standing out on the deck alone. Images flashed through his mind. The bodies trapped underwater in the hull of the *Mayr*, the recorded bedlam in its corridors, the specter hauling the corpses down the stairwell, the Second Mate taking his last stand against an intruder with only a fire extinguisher—

A burst of lightning and Bradley saw it. A human form bathed in quicksilver, scaling the side of the ship from the third deck to the fourth. In one swift motion, it scurried up over the top of the pilothouse and disappeared into the forest of antennae and parabolic dishes.

"No," he whispered, his voice obliterated by the thunder.

He could no longer see movement. What could it possibly be doing up—?

A steel guy-wire snapped like a cracking whip. The radio tower wobbled. Another line flailed into the air. A heartbeat later, the entire assembly toppled away from him and vanished over the opposite side of the vessel.

"No!" Bradley shouted.

His feet were rooted to the canting deck. He couldn't look away from the roof of the pilothouse for fear that he would lose sight of what he knew was up there. As long as he could see it, he was—

The grim realization struck him as the inside of the pilothouse windows were painted with black spatters that cast eerie shadows into the mist.

A hatch led from the roof to the chart room to grant the engineers access to the communications array.

He glanced toward the island. They were cruising at an angle directly into a bay surrounded by a horseshoe of rugged crags and endless trees.

His heart clenched in his chest.

He stole his stare back from the pilothouse and its blood-spattered windows, and ran back through the door into the main corridor.

"Abandon ship!" he shouted as loud as he could.

Just like the *Mayr*, the *Huxley* was doomed.

What in God's name had they done?

"Abandon ship!"

Forty-Two

Ambitle Island

"We have to keep moving," Bishop said. His teeth no longer chattered, but his arms still shivered around her.

Courtney didn't want to get up. For the first time in as long as she could remember, she felt safe, if only for this one moment in time. She was drenched, freezing, and long past the point of exhaustion. She wasn't even sure if she had the strength to stand, let alone walk barefoot across this harsh terrain toward God only knew what. It was only a matter of time before those on the boat figured out their deception and dispatched men to hunt them, if they hadn't already. There was already a team on the island, tromping through the forest in search of the survivors from the work boat, and whatever else stalked the jungle. She thought of Ty, and what those on the ship were convinced he had become. The tears flowed once more. She remembered her brother, lying on the bed in the infirmary, his skin covered with scaly silver growths. Heat had positively radiated from him. He had taken her hand in his and given her a smile meant to reassure her, but the blood shimmering on his gums and lining his teeth had produced the exact opposite effect. She recalled catching golden reflections from his eyes before they drifted back up into his head as she stood from his bedside and walked away from him for the last time. She'd been unable to even tell him that she loved him for fear that her voice would betray her. That was now her cross to bear. Rather than stay by Ty's side, she had used her work as an excuse to distance herself from him, to protect herself when he was the one in need of protection. He had needed her and she had abandoned him.

She wiped away her tears and concentrated her will. If Ty had somehow managed to survive and reach the island, regardless of his condition, she was going to find him. And nothing—not the fear, the cold, the exhaustion, or the prospect of what he had become—was going to stop her.

Using the trunk of a ceiba tree for leverage, she struggled to her feet and truly looked around her for the first time. A high rock shelf separated her from the furious Pacific fifty feet down and to the west. To the east, the impossibly forested slope ascended into the mist where the dormant volcano slumbered. The path to both the north and to the south was little more than a happenstance pattern of jungle growth influenced by the sandpaper wind, thick with brine. She knew only that somewhere across the sea to her left was New Ireland Island, and beyond it, Papua New Guinea and Indonesia, just not their current location on this godforsaken rock.

"I say we head north," Bishop said. "If I remember correctly, there's only one formal settlement on this island, a Tolai village with a Catholic mission. Surely they'll have some way for us to contact the mainland and arrange for transport—"

"I can't leave," Courtney whispered. "Not yet."

"What are you talking about? If they find us again, they're going to kill us. You realize that, don't you?"

Courtney started walking to the north. The underbrush groped for her torn scrubs.

"Wait a second." Bishop grabbed her by the arm and spun her around. "You can't just go wandering off on your own."

"Watch me." She shrugged out of his grasp and shoved through the branches and vines.

Lightning stabbed white spears down through the canopy. The wind screamed along the rocky coast. The trailing thunder made the ground shake. Or at least she hoped it was the thunder.

"Wait up," Bishop called. He crashed through the shrubs behind her until he caught up and took her more gently by the wrist. When she turned around to yank her hand from his grasp, he pulled her to him and kissed her. Caught by surprise, it took her a moment to ward off the shock. When she did, she brought him closer and kissed him even harder. She poured all of her conflicting emotions, all of her fear, into a desperate passion, and from him drew courage and strength. Her hands traced the hard muscles of his back, so firm under her touch, even as his surprisingly delicate palms caressed the gentle slope of her lower back and the upper curve of her buttocks. She pressed her hips against his and found him willing. A part of her needed him right now, needed to exert a measure of control over an untenable situation, to banish the horrors of the world around her, if only for a few precious minutes. Recognizing as much, he withdrew his mouth and leaned his forehead against hers. His breath was warm on her lips.

"Wherever you go," he whispered, "I go."

"Thank you," she said through the ghost of a smile.

"We just have to be careful." He caressed her cheek as he spoke. "We can't charge headlong into the unknown, not when our lives are at stake."

She could only nod.

"I think that if your brother was among the survivors, he would have tried to reach the village. Don't you?"

Again, she nodded.

"Then that's where we need to go, but I'm sure we aren't the only ones who've made that assumption. That's where the others will be going, too, and we need to make sure that we stay as far away from them as possible. They aren't going to let us go a second time."

She leaned away from him and looked up into his eyes.

"I know," she whispered.

Courtney released him and stepped back. She held his hand a moment longer as if to squeeze every last drop of reassurance from it. When she turned away from him, he spoke to her back in a soft voice.

"And if they're right about your brother...are you prepared to find out that there's nothing left of him?" He paused. "Are you ready for the fact that he—whatever he may have become—might be beyond saving?"

"Yes," she whispered. Tears once again welled in her eyes.

She remembered the predatory crimson eyes of the man on the other side of the isolation shield as he paced back and forth, seeking a weakness in the barrier he could exploit to reach her.

"Are you prepared to find out that he might want nothing more than to kill you like he did all of the others?"

In response, she shouldered her way through the trees toward the answer she couldn't find the voice to vocalize.

Forty-Three

R/V Aldous Huxley

Scott Aronson reached the end of the corridor on the 03 Deck. He had already awakened the Master of the Ship and his First Mate, as well as a handful of grumpy chief scientists whose annoyance was as thinly disguised as their contempt for his station. Under different circumstances, he would have happily broken their noses and left them crying on the floor. He tried not to think about the fact that that was exactly what had happened to him, but the pain and the watering eyes made it impossible to forget. When he got his shot at Bishop again—and he *would* get another crack at him—he fully intended to return the favor. And then some. The merciless throbbing in the center of his face and the taste of his own blood in his mouth was bad enough, but the embarrassment…well, that was far worse than the injury itself. And it had been a cheap shot to boot. When his turn arrived, he was going to make sure that Bishop saw it coming. He wanted to see that flash of recognition in the man's eyes when he understood what was about to happen and that there was absolutely nothing he could do to stop it.

He smiled to himself and paused at the foot of the stairs leading upward to the 04 Deck. His radio crackled at his hip.

"Oh-Two Deck clear," a static-addled voice said.

"Oh-One Deck, as well," another added. "Although there's some sort of commotion coming from the Main Deck under me."

Aronson unclipped his transceiver and brought it to his lips.

"Oh-Three Deck all clear. Moving on to the Oh-Four. Hold…I want an update."

"With all these pipes and crates, they could be hiding anywhere," a fourth voice said.

"Keep looking. We rendezvous on the Main Deck in five minutes. If they aren't in the pilothouse, they have to be either outside or holed up in one of the labs," Aronson said. "And give me an update on that ruckus."

He clicked off and returned his walkie-talkie to his hip.

This door-to-door nonsense was getting them nowhere. It was a waste of time and they all knew it. If he were the one trying to hide on this vessel, there was no way anyone would ever find him. There were gaps beneath every floor where pipes flowed and service access panels that led to hollow compartments and ladders granting easy access to hidden nooks on every level. But eventually, his quarry would have to come out, and when they did, he would be ready.

He ascended the stairs toward the chart room for formality's sake. If Bishop and Martin had made a break for the communications network or the wheelhouse, the third shift duty officers would have blown the whistle on them in a nanosecond.

A cool breeze caressed his face. Even through the clotting blood in his nostrils and sinuses, he could smell brine and ozone. For the briefest of moments, it soothed the ache in his nose and behind his eyes.

At the top of the staircase, he turned left into the chart room. The shelves at the rear had collapsed, scattering large books of maps all over the wide table and floor, where puddles had formed.

Bang!

Aronson nearly jumped at the sound. He looked up at the ceiling, toward the source of the sudden noise. The wind threw the roof-access hatch open again. Raindrops and runoff poured through the gap. Lightning burst in the clouds above, highlighting the wet rungs of the ladder leading up to the empty space where the radio tower should have been.

This was all wrong.

There was no reason for Bishop to try to reach the roof, and disabling their communications was contrary to his best interests. It was theoretically possible that the ferocity of the storm could have torn the tower from its moorings, but they were constructed to withstand far harsher conditions than this.

Pages of maps riffled on the cold wind that blew down from above. He studied the pools on the floor and noticed a series of indistinct wet footprints leading back out of the chart room and toward the pilothouse, where they petered out in front of the reinforced steel door of the bridge, which stood wide open.

Warm fluid trickled down the back of his throat from his sinuses. For a second there, the organic smell of blood overpowered even the scents of the ocean and the rain.

Monitors beeped beyond the threshold, through which he could see straight out into the indigo-flashing belly of the storm, thanks to the slanted wall of windows.

As he passed through the doorway, an alarm sounded to his left. He turned toward the sound to find a man draped over the console. Warning lights blinked all around him, where the screens and housings were spattered with copious amounts of blood.

"Jesus Christ!" he gasped, and fumbled with the transceiver hooked to his belt.

From somewhere below him, he thought he heard people shouting before a voice erupted from his unit.

"I'm on the Main Deck now. Someone's hollering to abandon ship. It's chaos down here."

"We've got an even bigger problem up here," Aronson said. With his free hand, he drew his sidearm. He turned away from the shipboard technician and saw the Second Mate crumpled on the floor between the bridge and the windows, which were crisscrossed with black arterial spurts. Beads trickled from them in thin rivulets. The man's face was a shimmering scarlet mask, his throat a tattered mess of macerated flesh and severed tendons and vessels. His uniform shirt was saturated with his lifeblood.

Lightning flashed through the windows above the corpse, illuminating the sheer forested slopes of Ambitle Island directly off the bow, looming up into the clouds.

There was a clamoring sound on the far side of the bridge. A monitor toppled from its perch and hit the ground with a shower of sparks. A shadow crossed the wall.

More lights blinked into being on the console.

He heard faint clicking noises, stealthily approaching.

The hell if he was sticking around to find out what was making them.

"They're dead!" he shouted into the transceiver. He whirled and bolted toward the stairs. "There's no one manning the helm! We're headed straight for—!"

Something struck him from behind and sent him careening into the air over the stairwell. He hit the steel steps on his chest with the weight on his back. Both the transceiver and his pistol clattered away from him. He tried to brace himself, to slow his momentum, but his legs flipped up over his head. Cartwheeling, he felt something sharp tearing through his clothes and into his skin even as the repeated impact with the stairs snapped ribs and dislocated his shoulder. He struck the deck below with such force that it knocked the wind out of him. A scream came out as little more than a gasp.

He looked up from the floor, spattered with droplets and arcs of glistening crimson, to see several faces peek out through the gaps of their stateroom doors. His fate was reflected in the widening terror in their eyes.

The weight scrabbled and clawed on top of him.

Pressure on his neck.

Cold pain.

The sensation of fingers moving under his skin, between the muscles.

A rush of warmth.

His hands slipped in his own blood and his face struck the floor.

He was peripherally aware of the screams.

And then of nothing at all.

Forty-Four

"Just look at that proliferation rate," Angie said. "It's beyond anything I've ever seen."

Reaves watched in awe as the odd-shaped organisms multiplied before his very eyes. They were being cultured on a gelatinous agar upon which Angie had dripped human blood. Every time one of the unclassified thermophiles came into contact with a lymphocyte, it appeared to pierce it, then emerge on the other side, only there were now two of them every time it did. Half of its virus load was left behind in the cell to colonize it, lending it an almost blurry appearance where once the edges of the sphere had been relatively smooth.

"Now watch this." She removed the culture and exposed it to a stream of concentrated oxygen for a full thirty seconds. When she replaced it under the microscope, all movement had ceased. The altered surface of the white blood cells resumed their normal spherical shape. In a matter of seconds, the cellular membranes ruptured. Their contents oozed out like filling the from a donut. "They can't survive without an environment rich in hydrogen sulfide. The only problem is that neither can the cells they've already infected. The epithelial tissues I've experimented with are even more sensitive."

"So there's no way of reversing the process?"

"Given enough time, we might be able to find some way. Maybe a slower exchange of hydrogen sulfide for oxygen wouldn't trigger such dramatic effects, or perhaps—"

Voices rose in the corridor outside the lab. More shouting joined the fevered chorus.

"What the hell's going on out there?" Reaves asked.

They both slowly stood from their stools and walked toward the door. It sounded like pure bedlam on the other side.

Yelling.

The rumble of running footsteps.

Angie pressed the button to disengage the lock and the door slid back into the wall.

The shouts became a roar. Men sprinted past the threshold, barreling through the hallway, bellowing in a tumult of voices. Reaves isolated Bradley's from the din.

"Abandon ship!"

The moment he saw Bradley's white head of hair, he lunged out into the corridor, grabbed him by the upper arm, and whirled him around.

"What's going on?" Reaves shouted.

"It's on the ship." Bradley's eyes were wide with panic. Spittle flew from his lips when he spoke. "I saw it. Up there. I saw it go into the pilothouse through the roof. And the men in there. The men. They—"

"Saw what? Slow down and—"

"There's no time! We have to get—"

Screams erupted from somewhere above them, horrible screams, men and women alike, filled with such pain and raw anguish they chilled his blood.

The overhead lights flickered once, then again. A heartbeat later they died with *thud* that shook the floor. Crimson lights bloomed from their glass and wire casings on the walls.

A klaxon blared.

Shadowed people thundered down the stairway and met with those already in the hallway in a collision that sent bodies to the floor amid tangles of limbs and frantic cries.

"What's happening?" Angie screamed.

The floor bucked beneath them. They stumbled and grabbed each other to maintain their balance.

"We have to abandon ship!" Tears streamed down Bradley's cheeks. "We don't have time to debate this!"

Bradley grabbed Reaves and hauled him into the chaos. He barely had a chance to grab Angie's hand before they were swept into the stampede. His thoughts were jumbled. Nothing made sense. It was as though they had stepped out of the cold and rational world of the lab and into a nightmare.

The screams on the higher decks intensified over the thunder of footsteps.

They were being channeled back toward the stern, past the doorways of various laboratories where terrified faces peered out before being shoved aside by men and women seeking sanctuary. He pictured the isolation barrier in the lab he and Angie had just abandoned and the fates of those on the *Mayr* who hadn't sealed themselves behind it.

How had everything fallen apart so quickly?

The deck lurched again and threw them toward the port side wall. Angie's hand was torn from his. He heard her scream and strike the threshold as he was tossed into the converted engineering room. He slid into a forest of chair legs and tried to pull himself back to his feet before the ship canted again. The entire room was scarlet, save for the computer monitor on the table he used to right himself. It must have been plugged into one of the outlets serviced by the emergency generator. On the screen, the security tape from the *Mayr* continued to play. No. It wasn't from the *Mayr*. The picture was too clear. There was no static. The time stamp in the bottom right corner rolled past with today's date. The screen was divided into four quadrants. The upper left showed a still-life of the wheelhouse. Lights blinked on the console, over which a man was draped, unmoving. Another body was crumpled in a heap under the bank of windows. Lightning flashed. The upper right picture displayed the third level hallway, now abandoned, except for the two figures sprawled prone on the floor in a wide pool of black. The bottom two quadrants featured men and women fighting through each other to get to the stairwells. In the bottom left corner image, he caught a brief glimpse of a shadow at the periphery, right before a man in a button-down shirt and chinos was hauled from the melee.

Christ. Bradley was right. How in the world had it gotten aboard the ship?

The frightening truth hit him.

It was only two decks above him, a mere twenty vertical feet.

Something grabbed his arm and he screamed. He spun around to find Angie tugging at his elbow, urging him toward the hallway.

The floor tilted and hurled them both through the doorway.

"Come on!" she screamed.

They merged into the crowd and were funneled past the submersible hanger and through the door into the sheeting rain.

People slipped and fell on the slick deck. They grabbed onto those around them in an effort to pull themselves back to their feet, only to drag the others down with them.

"Over here!" Bradley shouted.

He was near the starboard rail, leaning over a white canister that looked like an industrial-size propane tank. When he broke the seal and threw back the upper half, the life raft inside of it leapt into the air and began to self-inflate. It dropped over the gunwale and splashed into the ocean. Beyond him, Reaves saw the island rapidly drawing nearer. A wide bay opened before them like a great mouth preparing to swallow them whole.

Lightning flared and he saw two of the round orange boats already riding the rough waves. Neither had more than two silhouettes in them. The shadows struggled to distance themselves from the *Huxley*. Since they were launching at less than full capacity, there wouldn't be nearly enough space for those still trying to abandon the research vessel.

He and Angie were barely halfway to the life raft when someone shoved Bradley aside to clamber over the rail. Bradley hit the gunwale and dropped like a stone. By the time Reaves reached his side, a small group had already cut the tether that moored the craft to the ship and were drifting away toward the others.

Reaves knelt beside Bradley, who looked up at him through distant, unfocused eyes. A gash across his forehead dripped blood through his brows.

"Get up!" Reaves shouted. He wrapped his arms around Bradley's chest and lifted him up, but he wouldn't be able to bear his weight for long.

"Hurry!" Angie yelled.

The screaming from the boat grew louder as more and more people herded out onto the stern. Reaves looked through the jostling bodies for any sign of what to do. He couldn't see any more of the life raft canisters and battling against the flow toward where the creature worked its way in their direction in order to reach the rafts on the bow wasn't an option. To his right, several people were already leaping down into the sea from under the A-frame winch.

He glanced again toward the island, which a moment earlier had appeared to be rushing toward them, but now seemed so far away.

Maybe if they could swim just far enough to reach one of the nearly empty life rafts...

More screams behind him. He turned to see a shimmer of silver and twin reflections from a pair of eyes, and then a man was jerked back through the open doorway even as he ran.

They were out of time.

"Go!" Reaves shoved Angie toward the rear of the ship. "I'll be right behind you."

He saw the terror in her eyes. She said something, but her words were drowned out by the awful cries.

"We're going to have to swim for it," he said directly into Bradley's ear. "I can't do it for both of us."

"My fault," was Bradley's only reply.

When they reached the edge, Reaves stared down into the violent waves fifteen feet down in the vessel's wake. The moment they hit the water, they were going to be pulled under and swept away from each other.

He suddenly thought of the souls on the *Mayr* whose corpses they had yet to find. They were somewhere on the ocean floor, weren't they? They had attempted this exact same flight and never reached the shore. Was he now preparing to join the ranks of bloated, waterlogged remains now buried in the reef, feeding the scavengers?

"Swim as hard as you can!" he shouted.

With one final glance back over her shoulder, Angie leapt out into the air. She vanished as soon as she hit the waves.

Reaves looked into Bradley's eyes.

"I'll see you on the other side," his old friend said.

"Not if I see you first," Reaves said through a weak attempt at a smile.

He drew a deep breath and stepped off the precipice and into the swirling wind that preceded the impact and the bitter cold.

Forty-Five

Ambitle Island

There was no way Pike was going to make it in time. He had underestimated the distance to the nearest navigable harbor and the going had become increasingly treacherous despite his complete disregard for his safety as he hurtled through the forest. His cheeks and hands were lacerated from the branches that seemed to bar his every move and he had given up on the thermal vision goggles that were constantly swatted against his forehead. Running little more than blind, he had forsaken looking for the tracks of the survivors and barreled ahead along the route of least resistance. He was barely conscious of the sounds of his men crashing through the underbrush behind him. The wicked displays of lightning in the clouds overhead made the ground leap and the tree trunks buck with a disorienting strobe effect. His lungs had long since passed the point of burning and his legs had crossed over from aching to a form of numbness. The topography routed him higher, into jungle that housed only mist and shadows. The metronomic thumping of the breakers to his left was his only means of geographical navigation. Occasional gaps in the canopy afforded spotted glimpses of the ocean. By the time he recognized them and the lack of lights from any visible vessels that may have been sailing past, they were behind him.

The trees abruptly fell away to either side. Pike barely had time to stop before charging right off a limestone cliff and plummeting down into the treetops thirty yards below him. From here he could see the calmer waters of a deep bay and the first stretches of open sand since the one upon which they had initially beached. The land rose steeply from it on three sides to where the impenetrable fog claimed it. If he were one of the people who managed to reach the island in the work boat, that was exactly where he would go. And if he were piloting the *Huxley*, that was the kind of harbor he would seek.

As if to prove his point, he saw lights through the trees downhill to his left, moving northeastward at a decent click directly toward the relatively sheltered cove.

"There she is," Brazelton managed to gasp as he struggled to catch his breath.

Pike raised the transceiver and shouted into the microphone.

"Ambitle to *Huxley*. Acknowledge, *Huxley*." He released the transmit button and listened to the reply of dead air. "Damn it, *Huxley*! Acknowledge!"

He quickly scanned through the channels, trying repeatedly to hail the vessel, which cleared the trees and headed straight for the beach.

"Something's wrong," Walker said.

"*Huxley*! This is Ambitle to *Huxley*! Acknowledge for Christ's sake!"

"They're coming in too fast."

"Take this." Pike thrust the transceiver against Walker's chest. "Keep trying to raise them."

He raised his pistol and aimed at the research vessel. It was too far away to hit, but that wasn't his intention. He wanted them to see the flash of muzzle flare, to hear the clap of the report. Anything to get their attention and persuade them to turn around. He fired off six rounds in rapid succession. With his ears still ringing, he watched for any sign of reaction from the *Huxley*.

It continued to steam into the bay at an angle.

Pike bellowed up into the sky and fired another half dozen shots.

Behind him, Walker cursed and yelled into the transceiver.

"Why aren't they responding?" Brazelton asked. "It can't just be because of the electrical interference. We're in direct line-of-sight."

"They aren't slowing down," Walker said.

"I can see that!" Pike snapped. He knew damn well that something was wrong on the ship and he was helpless to do anything about it.

He kicked a rock over the precipice as lightning seared the sky.

There was no more time to waste.

"We have to get down there before it's too late," Pike said, but he understood on a primal level that it already was.

He sprinted to his right, where the rock ledge abutted the sheer slope and leapt down into the runoff. The mud was slick enough to carry him downhill in a controlled slide, past exposed roots that reached for him like tentacles and around piles of debris that clogged the thin stream.

The screaming sound of shearing metal echoed up from below him.

The *Huxley*'s lights flickered through the branches. Its engine roared. The bow tipped downward and the stern rose high up on the water.

"No, no, no!" he shouted.

She was tearing herself apart on the reef.

The lights flickered once more and then extinguished, leaving the black silhouette of the vessel careening toward the shore, sinking lower and lower toward the waterline.

The sound of ripping metal metamorphosed into the dull wrenching sound of the hull being completely disemboweled. There was a *whump* as the air was forced from the hold by a massive rush of seawater flooding in and the resultant change in pressure.

She was sinking quickly now and there wasn't a damn thing he could do to stop it.

Pike heard the screams in the distance, a choir of torment at the gates of hell.

Through the interlaced branches, he watched the sea rise up over the gunwales and onto the main deck. Metal buckled. Windows shattered. A skin of oil spread out across the waves, reflecting the lightning with rainbow colors.

He'd never stood a chance.

A shout of pure anguish exploded past his lips.

It wasn't until he saw the life rafts and the people struggling to swim in the dark waters that he realized it could only get worse.

Forty-Six

Bradley barely clung to consciousness. His head throbbed and his vision wavered. He felt disconnected from his appendages, which grew colder and more sluggish with each passing second. The only warmth was from the blood trickling down his forehead and into his eyes, which drifted in and out of focus. He wanted nothing more than to close them, if only to ease the sting of the saltwater...

"Wake up!" Reaves shouted. He slapped Bradley on the cheek, splashing water into his face in the process. Bradley sputtered and coughed, and raised his chin up out of the water again.

He was disoriented. Everything that had happened blended into an oddly shifting, disorganized mess of images in his mind. The screams still resonated in his ears. He saw the rail rushing toward his face. He remembered the chaos on the boat as blurs of people fighting past him and through him, standing on the deck with the rain pelting him, held upright by Reaves. He recalled stepping from the stern into a world defined by a cold blackness and then fists hauling him up onto the vicious waves by his shirt and dragging him into a lesser darkness. There was barely enough illumination coming through around the waves to see the faces of Reaves and Dr. Whitted, both of whom clung to the straps overhead, just as he did. The black rubber ring around them was perhaps eight feet in diameter. Orange fabric was stretched over it and lashed to the inflatable ring. They were underneath one of the life rafts, in the small pocket of air between its body and the ocean. He vaguely recalled Reaves paddling both of them toward the craft in hopes of hauling them aboard. The men already on it had shouted for them to let go before they capsized the raft and beaten them back down into the water with their fists. Rather than give up, Reaves had dived underwater and brought him up into this insignificant gap where at least they could hang on to the boat and breathe without being bludgeoned by the men who had not only refused to save them, but had been eager to consign them to their deaths.

He thought of the men and women shoving each other, trampling their own ranks in their rush to abandon ship. He remembered the pitiful howls of the injured on the floor as they were stampeded without a single soul stopping to help them to their feet. His head still pounded from being shoved out of the way so that the men who would later try to drown them could have a life raft that should have held ten all to themselves. He thought of the creature on the boat, a random aberration of evolution, the same demon that had caused the end of so many once flourishing societies, and wondered if its genesis had been less an accident than the will of a God whose children had lost their way.

The men shifted overhead, nearly shoving them back underwater. Over the rumble of the storm and the clapping of waves against the small craft, Bradley could still hear the screams and cries for help, only now they sounded much more distant, haunting.

He tried not to look at the others for fear he would see the blame he felt reflected back at him.

There was a sudden shift in the current beside him, as though something large swam just past his legs, not quite close enough to touch. He knew full well that the South Pacific was home to some of the largest and most aggressive sharks in the entire would, and all of the bodies flailing around in the water, bleeding like he was now, must have been calling them from far and wide.

The raft suddenly dipped. This time, he was driven beneath the waves.

He struggled back to the surface, spitting seawater and gasping for air.

Above him, the boat rocked dramatically. The taut polyurethane-coated fabric bucked up and down as the men moved quickly from one side to the other and back again. He heard first their startled shouts, then their screams. Something tore through the fabric, opening a seam to the sky. Then again. And again. The slashes were barely wide enough to see bursts of frenetic activity. Shadowed forms darting past so quickly that they could have been specters, momentarily frozen in time by a strobe of lightning.

One scream abruptly ceased, while the other seemed to linger, painfully, infinitely.

"What the hell—?"

"Shh!" Reaves hissed. He clapped his hand over Bradley's mouth.

The ragged tears allowed just enough light to pass through for Bradley to see Reaves's wide eyes looking up through the slits. Dark fluid poured over the edges. Whitted held out her palm and placed it in the stream. She immediately flung the fluid from her hand and wiped it on her blouse. The expression of terror on her face confirmed his suspicions.

Blood.

The remaining cries waned, then stopped altogether.

The fabric bowed above them, one section at a time, as though under first one foot, then the other.

There was a loud splash to his left, and he felt the same change in the current he had mere moments prior.

They all held their breath as the blood continued to trickle down into the ocean between them.

He looked from Reaves to Whitted and then through the ripped bottom of the liferaft at the flickering storm clouds.

The silence overhead was painful. He kept waiting for some sign of movement, a dip in the fabric, a rocking of the boat, but nothing happened.

When he could bear it no more, he reached up, grabbed hold of the nearest slit, and pulled himself up just far enough to clearly see through it. The rapidly cooling blood ran down his forearms and dripped onto his face. His already narrowed field of vision canted with the craft. At first he saw only the rim of the inflatable tube and the straps wrapped around it. When they hit the next chop, a body flopped into view. He saw a limp arm and a face covered with so much blood that he hardly recognized it as belonging to one of the men that had battered him back into the sea.

Bradley dropped back down so quickly that he lost his grip and Reaves had to help fish him back out of the water before he was swept away.

"Dead," he sputtered.

"It's in the water with us," Whitted said. Her voice rose an octave when she spoke. "It climbed up onto the raft right above us and killed them both, didn't it? Mere inches away from us!"

"Shh," Reaves whispered. "We don't want to draw attention to ourselves if it doesn't already know we're here."

Bradley attuned his hearing to even the faintest sound as they communicated silently with their eyes. He listened to the screams of his fellow survivors fighting for their lives against the violent sea, and realized how few voices actually remained.

In his mind, he pictured a silver-skinned creature only part man knifing through the water like a Great White, grabbing the helpless swimmers and dragging them underwater where it could tear them apart.

Forty-Seven

Pike lost sight of the beach as he charged through the forest, but he could still hear the screams. They guided him through the dense groves and over rock formations and channels of runoff. The grumble of the ship's engines had faded to a cough and then to nothing at all. The sound of shearing metal had been swallowed by the waves. The klaxons had been smothered underwater. No longer could he see any manmade lights through the canopy, only the random electrical discharge from the storm clouds and the occasional blue sparks from the ship as it took on water. But the screams...the screams grew louder and more terrified by the second.

He had to trust that his men were following him. The slope was too treacherous to glance away from his footing, and even if they did fall behind, their ears would lead them to the beach. Assuming all of the screams hadn't been silenced by then.

He should have diagnosed the trap sooner. It was his job, for Christ's sake. But he had underestimated his adversary, the most critical of all mistakes. And the cost of his failure would be the lives of all those aboard the *Huxley* and their only means of escaping the island. With the research vessel torn to ribbons and sinking into the black depths, they had effectively been cut off from the outside world. Their radio and satellite communications networks were ruined. Their weapons cache was now submerged under hundreds of feet of seawater. Their only functional boats were the inflatable Zodiacs and the life rafts that would essentially leave them at the mercy of the storm and the unpredictable waves.

There was still the outside chance that they would be able to find a functional radio in the village that they could use to hail the mainland, but his adversary had already proven its cunning. If it was smart enough to lure an entire vessel to its demise, then surely it had considered every possible contingency, especially one so easily remedied.

For the first time in his life, he felt the stirrings of despair. He bared his teeth and stuffed them down. Now was not the time to allow fear to take root, not while he still had blood pumping through his veins and a Beretta in his fist.

The cove had been out of sight for maybe fifteen minutes as he plunged through the dark jungle. He had to be getting close to the beach by now. The screams were minion, and so awful they pierced his very soul. He recognized the difference between terror and pain. He had heard both so many times passing the lips of the wounded and the dying. These were the heartbreaking cries of people desperately entreating the ear of a deaf God, channeling their life forces into their voices knowing that their physical vessels were already lost to them.

They were the screams of a slaughter.

He burst from the jungle and found himself upon the top of a limestone crag, where he again came under siege by the rain and the ferocious wind that propelled it into his face. Ten yards below him was the beach he had seen from above. The waves dragged wreckage onto the shore, bringing with them the lifeless bodies already partially covered with sand and seaweed. Rafts still bobbed a hundred yards from the shore, while those who braved the ocean without them flailed toward the shallows.

There wasn't a single living soul on the beach. He had expected to find something inhuman attacking the survivors the moment they crawled from the sea, but instead encountered only sand so choppy and rutted by the rain that it was impossible to tell if there were footprints of any kind.

The stern of the *Huxley* was still visible far out where it was lodged on the reef, the tall A-frame a dramatic arch through which the cresting waves spilled onto the deck. Her back was broken. The entire bow and everything forward of the partially collapsed submersible hanger was now underwater. Only the very crown of the wheelhouse with a single misshapen satellite dish breached the surface.

And between there and where he stood, dozens of people fought for their lives against the sea.

He scrambled down a series of staggered rock ledges until he dropped into the wet sand and sprinted toward the shoreline. Amid the mess of sheared metal and debris, there were at least a half-dozen unmoving bodies. When he reached the nearest, he paused to survey the area around him down the sightline of his pistol. Behind him, there was no sign of movement in the jungle, only the branches that swayed on the monsoon winds. Regardless, it took all of his strength to turn his back on the forest with a mere twenty yards of sand separating him from it. Across the sea, the life rafts drifted inexorably toward him on the roiling waves, while flailing arms alternately appeared on the distant crests before vanishing into the troughs. Their cries and pleas for help were already diminishing. He knelt over the corpse and rolled it onto its back. A man's face stared up at him, his mouth and eyes packed with sand, his skin coated with it. His uniform was that of a crew member, although his nametag was undoubtedly somewhere on the ocean floor. Pike didn't recognize the man, but the gash across his neck left no doubt as to his cause of death. The horizontal gash was so deep that Pike could clearly see the exposed musculature and severed trachea, from which saltwater trickled to fill the wound.

He hadn't seen anyone on the beach. However the man's throat had been ripped open, it had happened somewhere out there before his remains reached the shore.

Pike leapt up, scanned his surroundings again, and ran to the next body.

Brazelton and Walker scurried down the escarpment from the south and approached his position, weapons covering the tree line.

At least now there was someone to watch his back while he inspected a woman who lay supine in the surf. Her clothes were ripped, revealing a belly and chest transected by deep scratches that showed no indication of healing. Her neck was intact, but there was standing water behind her parted lips. He felt for a pulse at the side of her cold throat.

Nothing.

The voices from the sea grew steadily louder. A glance confirmed they were maybe fifty yards out. As he watched, one struggling shadow rose up a wave, then quickly disappeared beneath it, arms raised over its head, grasping only empty air. Pike scrutinized that same point for several long seconds, but the swimmer never reappeared.

"We have to get them to shore," Walker said. He shed his backpack, dropped it to the sand, and waded out until he the water reached his waist. He held his pistol high in one hand.

"Where is it?" Brazelton asked. He kept his back to Pike while he swept his Beretta back and forth across the trees. "It has to be around here somewhere."

Pike had been wondering the exact same thing. There was something wrong with this scenario. He hurried to the next corpse, and the one after that. Both of them had been cut deeply across their stomachs, chests, necks, and faces. One's wounds appeared to have been capable of causing a fatal amount of blood loss, while the other's looked fairly superficial. For them to have reached the beach first, they had to have either been in the water well before the others or physically dragged ashore. Yet there were no distinct footprints, at least not that he could tell. And how had the pilot driven the *Huxley* into the reef with all of the navigational systems at his disposal. There should have been warning lights and alarms going off everywhere.

His blood ran cold.

"Jesus," he whispered. "It was already on the ship."

He leapt to his feet and stood at the edge of the sea, which threw brine up over his ankles and tried to drag him out to his death. How had he not seen it? All along, he had thought that after killing Montgomery and Pearson, the creature was cutting across the island overland to spring its trap when the men from the vessel attempted to land, but it had simply doubled back to the eastern bay and somehow boarded the *Huxley*. Just as it had done on the *Mayr*, it must have dispatched the captain, leaving the ship helpless as it sped into the harbor and struck the reef. The people out there in the ocean...they weren't merely fleeing the sinking boat, but whatever had been on it as well, which meant that—

"It's out there in the water," he shouted.

"What?" Brazelton said. He eased back until his shoulder brushed Pike's.

"That goddamned thing is out there with them!"

The corpses that had washed to shore...they'd been attacked while trying to swim to the island.

A pair of life rafts rode the waves toward them, a mere thirty yards out. The paddling arms of a dozen swimmers slapped at the water just beyond the breakers. All of them dark silhouettes. He couldn't decipher a single detail, even with the blinding flashes of lightning. No faces, no eyes. Nothing.

For all he knew, any one of them could be the creature.

Forty-Eight

They had heard the commotion from perhaps a kilometer away. Distance was impossible to gauge in the dense jungle through which they blindly forged their way, through bushes nearly as tall as they were and around trunks so poorly spaced it was like trying to shoulder through a crowd on a busy city street. Bishop had recognized the noises, for he had heard them all far too recently. The forlorn wail of an emergency klaxon. The muffled screams. The shriek of shearing metal. And the resounding thud of the sinking vessel suddenly taking on water. By the time they managed to get close enough to see the bay, it was already too late.

From where they had climbed ashore after fleeing the ship that now lay in ruins, he had chosen a slowly ascending route that would still lead them to the north, but into the steeper hills where they could maintain the high ground and have a better chance of spotting their pursuit, which would undoubtedly favor the lowlands where the forest was slightly thinner and the passage easier. If they identified trouble before it found them, they could easily disappear into the seemingly impregnable interior of the volcanic island where no one could ever find them.

Now they stood at a crossroads.

Far below them, through the sparse gaps in the canopy, they watched a sliver of beach and the nightmare out on the ocean. The mist drifted past, concealing and then revealing the horror. The *Huxley*'s stern stood from the reef at an angle, while the ocean around it bubbled and boiled as the fore section of the vessel settled into the silt. Life rafts that looked like Cheerios from this height rolled toward the shore while specks that could only be swimmers dotted the whitecaps. He may not have been able to clearly see them well enough for a head count, but it was obvious that he was looking at a fraction of those that had been aboard.

"How could this have happened?" Courtney whispered.

Bishop shook his head. He hadn't the slightest clue. All he knew was that with all of the computer navigation equipment on the bridge, there should have been no way they could have bottomed out the vessel on the reef. The only scenario he could imagine was if there had been no one on the bridge to see the console come to life with warning lights or to react to the blare of the emergency klaxon. He thought of the *Mayr* and stifled a shiver.

"We should help them," Courtney said. She crouched beside him behind a broad-leaved shrub covered with what looked like string beans.

"There's nothing we can do for them now."

"We can't just let them die."

"By the time we're able to reach the beach, their fates will have already been decided."

"That doesn't mean we shouldn't try."

"Tell me you haven't forgotten what happened to us on that very ship. We were prisoners, Courtney."

"What do you propose then? That we just sit here and watch them drown?"

"No." The wind rose with a howl, eclipsing the screams for a blessed moment. "We need to take advantage of this opportunity to get ahead of them so we can reach the village first. It's our only chance."

"But what kind of people would that make us?"

"The living kind," Bishop said.

Courtney shook her head. Tears glistened in the corners of her eyes before she wiped them away. Bishop's heart went out to her, but nothing could change his mind. His only priority right now was keeping them both alive. Besides, these were the same men who would have undoubtedly killed them to protect their secret. The fewer of them left the better.

He took Courtney by the hand and pulled her out from behind the bush. They needed to make every second count. It was only a matter of time before those on the beach regrouped and came to the same realization that he and Courtney already had. Their only chance of calling for rescue meant gambling that there was a functional communications system in the village. The *Huxley*'s emergency beacon would eventually summon help, but as Bishop could attest, with the aftermath of the destructive tsunami, days could pass in the interim. He and Courtney needed to take matters into their own hands.

His plan was simple. They contact help and set up a rendezvous on the far side of the island. Once they were safely off this godforsaken rock, he'd send back assistance for the others. Beyond that, all he cared about was that they weren't killed first.

He envisioned the island in his head and tried to plot a course in his mind. The Tolai Village was on the north end of Tutum Bay, which, if he was correct, should be approximately six kilometers from where they were now. If they forged ahead as quickly as they could through the remainder of the night and the better part of the day, they should reach it by sometime in the early afternoon. Maybe they would even get lucky and hail a passing freighter that could get them off of this infernal island by sundown.

The plan hinged upon them finding the village well ahead of the others while traversing the steeper and more perilous terrain to hide their tracks, in little more than their tattered clothing and bare feet.

"Come on," he whispered. He tugged her by the hand toward the invisible path that meandered deeper into the jungle. Only the cries from the beach followed them, but eventually they were drowned out by the rain on the canopy.

Forty-Nine

Pike fought through the hip-deep waves to help Walker pull the first life raft to shore. A man in uniform and a woman in a pantsuit cringed away from them like drenched, beaten dogs. Their wide eyes and pallor told the tale of what they had endured. Once they'd dragged the inflatable craft onto the sand, they headed back out without a backward glance. Two more swimmers reached the beach and now crawled toward where Brazelton still covered the tree line, bringing the grand total to five, including the man who lay on his side, vomiting seawater. Five of the dozens of bodies they had seen paddling away from the sinking ship. While they landed the second life raft, in which a solitary able seaman huddled against the storm, the final swimmer, a young woman Pike recognized as the seismologist they had hired at the last second, finally crawled to shore, sobbing as she collapsed face-first into the sand. The lone remaining liferaft drifted slowly toward them.

"Start a fire," Pike shouted to one of the stunned men from the first craft. "We need to warm these people up in a hurry."

He and Walker sloshed back into the ocean toward the last vessel. Including the three of them who had been on Ambitle prior to the *Huxley*'s foundering, that brought the grand total of survivors to ten, plus however many were on the raft that was almost within reach. Ten of sixty-two souls. The rest had been lost to the sea and whatever hunted it. Their ship was a part of the reef, their communications fried by the water. At least the EPIRB distress beacon would have been activated the moment the waves flooded the main deck. Someone would be able to find them, eventually, when there were finally enough spare hands in tsunami-ravaged Oceania to break away from the mainland to search for them. In the meantime, he needed to keep these people alive long enough to welcome a rescue party. After witnessing what had happened to the survivors from the *Mayr*, he knew that would be no small feat.

Once the raft was close enough to grab, he and Walker both started pulling it landward. At first, Pike couldn't see anyone over the tall rubber ring and feared it might have been launched empty, but then he smelled it...the faintly metallic scent of freshly butchered meat. He pulled himself up to get a better look and saw the carcasses sprawled on the slashed fabric. Two men had been cut to ribbons, their clothes so bloody it was hard to tell their uniforms apart from their lacerated skin. They'd been attacked with such ferocity that they were unrecognizable. Every inch of exposed skin was sliced as though they'd been dragged behind a car over a road paved with broken bottles.

"God damn," Walker said.

"Out of the water," Pike said.

"What in the name of God did this to—?"

"Get out of the water! Now!"

Pike was about to shove away and splash toward the shallows when something brushed his leg. He yelled and kicked at it, connecting with something soft and forgiving. It grabbed him around the thigh. He pointed his pistol at the water and tightened his finger on the trigger—

A face breached the surface in front of him with a gasp and he nearly put a bullet right between Bradley's eyes. His employer sputtered and threw his arms around him.

"Thank God," Bradley said, over and over.

Pike extricated himself from the embrace and shoved the older man toward where the others congregated on the beach. He turned back in time to see Reaves and Whitted pop up from beneath the life craft.

"What happened out there?" Pike asked Reaves as he dragged the man quickly away from the orange raft.

"It was in the ocean with us...It-it...just climbed up onto the raft and slaughtered them...with us right underneath...the whole time...listening to them scream...the blood—"

"On the *Huxley*," Pike snapped."What happened aboard the *Huxley*?"

"It got onto the boat. Somehow. There was no warning. I just heard Bradley shouting. And the next thing I know, the halls were packed...people trying to abandon ship. I saw...on the monitor...in the pilothouse...the captain...We just...like the others...just jumped overboard and tried...tried..."

"See if you can help start a fire," Pike said. Between the man's incoherence and the chattering of his teeth, Pike could barely follow what Reaves was trying to say, but he got a clear enough picture. As he had surmised, the same thing that had happened on the *Mayr* had transpired on the *Huxley*, and right now that creature was out there at this very moment. Somewhere. And if it didn't fear attacking a large vessel filled with more than sixty able-bodied men and women, then it would have no qualms about coming after their disorganized lot on this isolated beach.

"Hurry up with that fire!" he shouted.

More than the heat, right now they needed the light. The beach was too open, indefensible. Their hunter had already demonstrated that it had no aversion to water, and the forest to the west was so dense that if it approached from that direction, it would be upon them before they even knew it was coming. They had three pistols and three Tasers between them, a pathetic arsenal against something so obviously capable, and not nearly enough to guard against an assault that could come from any of the three hundred and sixty degrees. The majority of them were half-drowned and settling into shock. A part of him thought the rest be damned; he was saving himself. But like a herd of gazelles, keeping the stragglers around was the best defense against predation. At least then the strong among them would have some warning.

With a flash of pinkish light, a flare burned into being. Two silhouetted men raided the emergency kit from one of the life rafts in the glow. Another brilliant glare joined the first. Despite the storm's wrath, the chemical fire stained the night fuchsia, casting a weak pall of light over their small section of the beach. A pathetic pile of damp wood smoldered over one of the flares between two of the crafts, producing more black smoke than flame.

Pike grabbed the mewling seismologist and yanked her to her feet.

"Get up and find some dry wood," he shouted into her face, then turned to the others. "All of you. Gather as many dry logs as you can find. We need more light!"

If only the infernal rain would cease. There was no point in trying to start a fire under the protective canopy. They needed to be able to create a perimeter, without which they'd never see that thing coming from the concealing jungle. The way Pike saw it, they had to make it until dawn. After the sun rose, assuming it more than diffused into the omnipresent cloud cover, they could strike off for the village to the north. As it stood now, a dozen civilians stumbling blindly through the black forest behind them would be like leading lambs to the slaughter.

He turned away from the flare and lowered his goggles over his eyes once more. Across the ocean, all was deep blue and black, save for the distant golden smoke billowing from the *Huxley*'s stern. No color beckoned from the horseshoe-shaped beach in the distance, nor from the forest rising up the steep slopes away from it.

The deluge diminished, if only by degree.

Other than the sound of movement and voices behind him, he heard only the growl of the breakers and the whispering waves washing up onto the sand.

He again raised his goggles when the aura of the growing fire behind him skewed his vision.

The hunter was out there somewhere. He could sense its stealthy advance from all around him at once.

It was close now.

Watching them.

"Get that fire going! We need some goddamned light!"

He felt its eyes upon him.

It was coming.

And it was coming soon.

Fifty

Ambitle Island

Reaves had to keep moving. If he sat down for even a moment, he knew the shock would claim him. His legs grew increasingly numb and warmth coursed through his veins despite the fact that he couldn't seem to stop shivering. He tasted blood in his mouth from his nipped tongue and had to suppress the image of the fluid pouring down on them through the torn fabric of the life raft. This was all his fault. He was the one who insisted they try to collect the thermophiles from the hydrothermal vents. What had he expected to happen? There could be no success without everything playing out exactly as it had, but he had never imagined...this. It had all been abstract, a theoretical, almost mythical quest, and now how many lives had been lost because of his lack of foresight?

He dropped an armful of damp kindling and lianas onto the fire, which miraculously stayed alight even as the rain tried to quench it. When he turned back toward the forest for the return trip, he froze in his tracks. The trees seemed somehow malevolent. The darkness beneath them, now crawling with smoke, was ominous. He couldn't go back in there, despite the two men who guarded them from the tree line with automatic pistols.

Not only was this all his fault, but he was a coward who couldn't bring himself to face his own creation.

He wished he had never found the cavern beneath the kiva in Chaco Canyon, that this was somehow a dream from which he would awaken to find himself ten years younger and again an idealistic anthropologist with his entire future ahead of him.

For the hundredth time, he glanced at his bare wrist where his watch had been. He had no idea when or where he had lost it. Not that it mattered. Like all the rest, he now just waited for the sun to rise and prayed for it to hurry. The sooner they set off for the village, which in their minds had become some mystical Shangri La filled with radios that were powerful enough to tug on God's ear, the sooner they would be on a boat headed far away from here. He just couldn't bring himself to think about what would happen back in the real world when they returned and had to somehow answer for the deaths of more than a hundred men and women who had sailed under the GeNext corporate flag on an errand primarily of his design.

But before he could fathom the future, he had to reckon with the present manifestation of his past, of his species' collective past.

Brazelton and Walker never diverted their attention from the jungle. The fire at their backs made their shadows flag on the sand, stretching them to the wall of batai and rosewood trees, from which a trio of silhouetted forms emerged, burdened by stacks of wood. None of them made eye contact as they passed him, as though they feared they would see their ultimate fates mirrored in his stare. Frightened though he was, the idea of the fire dying for his inaction was every bit as mortifying as again venturing into the darkness.

Lightning crackled across the sky. The thunder followed, only the gap between them had lengthened noticeably. Whether or not it was only wishful thinking, he was convinced the rain was slowing.

When he finally summoned the courage to move, Angie fell in beside him. As much as he wanted to hold her, the last thing he needed right now was to be reminded of his feelings for her while knowing that he had nearly been responsible for her death, and still might be before the night was through.

"I've been thinking," she said so softly that only he could hear her. She clammed up as they walked between the sentries until they reached the edge of the jungle. "What do we know about this thing?"

Reaves began sifting through the detritus, feeling for dry patches under the wet leaves and moss. Angie knelt beside him and continued. Both of them looked up from their task every few seconds to make sure there was nothing sneaking up on them from the darkness.

"It needs a constant supply of hydrogen sulfide to fuel the bacteria inside of it, without which we've demonstrated they will die, correct?" She waited for him to nod before plowing on. "I don't think human bowels produce enough of the gas to tide them over for very long, at least not in the requisite concentrations. So what does that mean? That somewhere nearby there has to be a sustainable source of the gas, something capable of continuous production, something like the hydrothermal vent the bacteria originally came from. Maybe a hot spring or something along those lines. That's where it has to have set up some kind of home base."

"So what are you suggesting? After it consumes the gas from the intestines of those it kills, it returns to some sort of geothermal formation to wait for the opportunity to hunt again?"

"Think about the historical precedent that originally led us to study the hydrothermal vents in the first place. Each of the previous instances revolved around a massive seismic upheaval capable of generating significant amounts of hydrogen sulfide. The eruption of the volcanoes in Arizona and Japan, and the lava fields in Vietnam and on Rapa Nui, would have filled the air with it. And even the hot springs in Zambia would have produced copious amounts under the right conditions. For this thing to have survived here as long as it has, there has to be some naturally occurring source that it returns to in order to refuel, for lack of a better term, the organisms responsible for its transformation. Otherwise, it would surely be dead by now."

"Not when there are so many of us on the island producing the gas for it."

"But there's more. What did you notice about it in all of the security footage?"

"There was never really a clear shot of it. The whole time, it barely ever entered the camera's range."

"But when it did, what did you see?"

"Hardly more than a blurry shadow."

"Come on, Brendan."

"Its eyes, Angie. I saw its eyes."

"Exactly. Because of the eyeshine. So what does that tell us?"

"That its night vision is a hell of a lot better than ours." A shiver rippled up his spine. Suddenly he realized that by the time he saw the creature approaching—if he even did at all—it would already be too late for both of them. They had to get out of the jungle this very second. He crawled away from her and started grabbing as much wood as he could find, regardless of whether it was dry or not.

"Right," Angie said from behind him. "Its *night* vision. Bright light, especially sunlight, would overstimulate its retinas and effectively render it blind."

He finally saw where she was going with this line of thought.

"So you think that before sunrise it will need to return to whatever geothermal formation sustains it?"

"Maybe not before sunrise, per se. The jungle is so thick that it blocks out the majority of the sun's light. But shortly thereafter, for sure."

"Then all we need to do is make it to the coming day."

"And get off of this island by nightfall."

"You're brilliant."

"I could still be wrong. In which case, it will relentlessly hunt us down until we're all dead and then eventually die itself."

After a momentary surge of hope, that sobering thought made his stomach clench. Even if she was right, there still wasn't even a hint of down on the horizon, but hurrying back to that big, bright bonfire sounded good right about now.

The back of his hand brushed what felt like a log protruding from under a rain-beaded shrub. One more good-sized piece and he could call it quits and get out of the darkness. He transferred the bundle of sticks awkwardly to his left arm and grabbed the log. The bark had an odd, almost leathery texture, and something tangled around it. He traced its length toward—

"Jesus," he gasped and threw himself backward. The wood clattered beside him as he scrambled away.

It wasn't a log. Not with laces and rubber tread. It was a boot. Attached to a leg. Hairs. A pant cuff.

Angie looked over his shoulder and screamed.

He grabbed her by the hand and sprinted toward the wan glow of the flames through the branches.

Fifty-One

Pike whirled at the sound of the first scream. Until that very moment, he had expected the assault to come from the sea. There was no way in hell that thing could have flanked them, not with the way he'd been carefully monitoring the waves as they pounded the desolate shore. He sprinted away from the waterline toward where the fire now burned several feet high in the lee of the two life rafts. A dozen shadowed bodies huddled together as though hiding in the suffocating black smoke, which made it impossible to see the tree line from his vantage point. As if it were contagious, the screaming spread to the group around the flames. He shoved through them and saw Brazelton and Walker silhouetted against the wall of trees, the wet leaves of which reflected the golden light. His men's shadows snapped across the sand like windblown sheets on a clothesline.

Two figures burst from the foliage and Pike nearly squeezed off a round before he recognized Reaves and Whitted at the last second. The woman continued to scream as Reaves led her between Brazelton and Walker, who scanned the jungle down the sightlines of their pistols.

Pike grabbed Reaves by the arm, nearly cleaving him from his feet.

"What did you see?"

"It's in the jungle! We found a body, and it...it..." Reaves tried to jerk his arm from Pike's grasp to no avail. "Let me go, for Christ's sake! It's right behind us!"

Pike released his grip and continued toward the forest in a two-handed shooter's stance.

"Any sign of movement?"

"No," Walker said, "but I can't see a blasted thing."

"Fall back and cover the civilians. I want to know exactly what Reaves saw if you have to beat it out of him."

"Yes, sir," Walker said, and backed toward the fire without taking his eyes from the trees.

Pike was tired of being hunted. It was time to go on the offensive.

"We're going in there, aren't we?" Brazelton said.

"Unless you have a better idea. We could always just sit around and wait for it to pick us off one by one."

"Today's as good a day to die as any."

Pike smiled and donned his thermal vision goggles. Together they advanced to the edge of the forest. The flickering firelight made the liana-coiled trunks of the trees dance. Wet branches brushed his thighs and chest and grabbed at his face. He didn't so much as blink as he forced his way through the leaves and vines until the fire was but a memory behind him. Silently, he placed one foot, and then the next, all the while swiveling his narrowed vision from side to side, his finger pressed into the sweet spot on the trigger, prepared for the orangish glow of body heat to materialize at any second when the attack commenced. Twenty paces in, he saw the first deep blue spatter on the ground through a cluster of saplings.

Thunder grumbled overhead as the rain continued to clap on the canopy. The occasional stream drained through the upper reaches and pattered the sloppy ground.

He crept straight through the vegetation toward the source of the color. The body was already rapidly cooling from its vaguely purple core outward to its blue extremities. The side of the man's neck looked like it had been gnawed by a pack of wolves. Spatters and droplets of blood glowed blue on the leaves and detritus. Based on the coloration and the rate of cooling, he'd been dead for roughly thirty minutes, which was before he had initially even reached the beach.

"Shit," Pike whispered. He'd been outmaneuvered again. By the time he turned around, it was already too late.

Gunfire erupted amid a chaos of screams behind him.

"Go!" Pike shouted and barreled past Brazelton. He had to shove his goggles out of the way before the firelight blinded him.

Pike counted three shots in rapid succession before all he could hear were the cries and shouts over the echo of the final report. He bellowed in rage as he burst from the jungle onto the beach. A man nearly knocked him down in his hurry to flee the site where their fire was now scattered. Embers billowed in an expulsion of ash as a man flopped around on the dwindling blaze. People were running everywhere with no apparent direction.

"How did it get behind us?" Brazelton shouted.

"It was never in the forest! The whole thing was a ruse!"

In the waning firelight, it was impossible to tell who was who amid the panic. Pike aligned his pistol with first one panicked face and then another. The body that smothered the flames twitched and then stilled, leaving the unrecognizable man's clothes smoldering, his charred flesh beginning to cook. He counted two more bodies sprawled on the sand. Someone trampled the nearest in his hurry to sprint for cover behind one of the life rafts. Beside the black neoprene-clad body lay Walker's weapon. Pike ran over and spared a quick glance at the man before again returning his attention to the bedlam. The back of Walker's neck had been savagely attacked. Skin and muscle alike had been ripped away from the exposed knobs of his cervical column. The gaping wound was filled with blood and rainwater. He had never seen his assailant coming.

"Where is it?" Brazelton yelled.

"Everyone! Calm down!"

The other body closer to the surf belonged to a young crew member Pike had helped out of one of the life rafts. A section of his trachea had been torn away. Based on the lacerations surrounding the wound, it appeared as though it had been inflicted by a large clawed hand.

He spun in a circle, but only saw the dark shapes running through the night.

The screams tapered as more and more of the survivors reached hiding places beside or beneath the twin orange crafts.

Pike raised his pistol to the sky and fired into the air. The thunder-clap of the report silenced the cries.

"Can anyone see it?" he bellowed.

The only response was whimpering out of his direct line of sight.

"It's not on the beach," Brazelton said.

Pike stormed around to the far side of the nearest life raft, grabbed one of the cowering men, and hauled him to his feet.

"What happened?" Pike shouted into his face.

The man blubbered something unintelligible. Pike shoved him back down.

"Over here!" Brazelton called.

Pike ran to where his comrade stood near the shoreline, staring at the crashing waves.

"What?" Pike snapped.

"You tell me," Brazelton said, and turned away without explanation. "Everyone come out from where you're hiding! We need to do a quick headcount!"

It only took a moment for Pike to figure out what Brazleton had noticed. When he did, he roared his frustration across the sea.

The corpses no longer littered the shallows.

They were gone.

Fifty-Two

Courtney felt sick to her stomach. With all of those people swimming in the open ocean, trying desperately to reach the shore, she and Bishop had simply walked away. A part of her knew that Bishop was right. By the time they reached the distant beach, they wouldn't have been able to affect the outcome. Life and death would have already been decided. The only thing they would have accomplished was delivering themselves into the hands of the enemy. But that justification didn't make it easier to live with the decision. Still, she continued to listen for the cries for help that had long ago faded and watch the sky for flares. The fact that she neither saw nor heard a thing only compounded her guilt.

Every tree was identical to the last, every grove a twin to the one before. The world became a seamless tangle of vegetation interwoven by vines that attempted to ensnare her like the invisible strands of a spider's web. Her bare feet were nearly numb from the cold mud that squished between her toes. What little strength she held in reserve was failing with her resolve. Even if they did manage to find Ty, what then? If he was infected as the others suspected and truly had been responsible for the deaths of those aboard the *Mayr*...

She envisioned the eyes on the other side of the biohazard shield. The hunger. The relentlessness. She wrapped her arms around her torso to combat a violent shiver.

They ran the serious risk of freezing to death unless the rain stopped and the sun heated them up in a hurry.

She crinkled her nose at the smell of rotten eggs. Her first thought was again of her brother as the ruptured seal of the bioreactor fired scalding steam into his face. As the stink intensified, the forest thinned. No longer were the trees one indistinct conglomeration of trunks and branches and vines. There was enough room to clearly pick their way between them. Despite the increased exposure to the elements and the standing water, the ground grew firmer. The faster pace helped to warm her, if only by degree.

Steam swirled through the forest ahead of them. The trees fell away, and the few that dared grow near the source of the sulfurous stench were stripped of all leaves and bark. Their gray, skeletal forms stood sentry around a hydrothermal spring that hid behind the steam. The rain had tapered during their time under the canopy, but she could still hear it pattering on the standing water and felt the merciless cold tapping on her head and shoulders.

Bishop walked in front of her through the mist like an apparition. He held out a hand to signal her to stop and ducked behind the hollowed carcass of a dead tree. She knelt behind him and whispered into his ear.

"Why are we stopping?"

He turned around, pressed his index finger to his lips, and then pointed up into the steam. There were two human silhouettes, mere shadows appearing and then disappearing into the billowing whiteness as though suspended in midair.

"Stay here," Bishop whispered. "Don't follow me until I signal that everything's clear. And if anything happens to me, you run." He squeezed her hand for emphasis and looked her in the eyes. "Understand?"

Courtney nodded. She watched as he crawled out from behind the trunk and scampered quietly behind another dead tree. He ducked his head out and then quickly back, then again more slowly. In a crouch, he darted into the steam and out of sight.

"Jesus," he whispered.

Lightning crackled through the clouds overhead. Was it her imagination, or were the storm heads paling in anticipation of dawn's arrival?

Bishop materialized from the steam, still moving at a crouch. Whatever sound he might have made was swallowed by the distant grumble of thunder.

"We're going to have to go around to the west," he said.

"What did you see?"

"We can't get past through there—"

"What did you see?" she interrupted.

"Courtney—"

"Damn it, Bishop. Tell me what you saw!"

He took her by the hand and eased her to standing.

"Trust me. You don't want to—"

Courtney broke free and ran into the mist. She focused on the bodies suspended above her as she approached. An unvoiced prayer filled her head as the shadows drew contrast.

Please, Lord. Don't let it be Ty.

The detritus gave way to bare limestone, flat and slick with algal proliferation and condensation. She had to slow down to keep from slipping and cracking her head open, and paid more attention to her footing than the bodies hanging above and in front of her, from which a droning buzz emanated. Bright yellow and orange rings encircled a small body of water that reminded her of the Grand Prismatic Spring she had seen on a visit to Yellowstone as a child. The topaz-blue water sizzled and popped with rainwater as steam swirled across the surface and rose to where two men had been hung from the dead trees by vines lashed around their necks and chests. They'd been stripped and gutted, their gaping abdominal cavities alive with swarming flies. All of the muscle had been peeled from their buttocks, thighs, and calves, leaving the exposed bones to blacken and the tendons to peel away from their points of insertion. She feared that if she looked closer she would see teeth marks lining what little flesh remained. The skin on their faces was mottled black and more of the insufferable insects lay siege to their eyes and buzzed into their nostrils and open mouths. One man's scalp was stubbled with gray, the other's thick with curly black hair. While she couldn't distinguish their facial features, she was able to identify them as two of the seamen she had seen on the deck of the *Mayr* prior to the *Corellian*'s launch. They must have been on deck already to have reached the work boat and eventually the island when no one else had.

She felt terrible for the swell of relief that surged through her that neither was her brother's corpse.

There was still a chance that his was among those lost to the sea, sinking into the silt even as the crabs and fish gnawed them to bones, but deep down, she could sense that he was still alive. Maybe it was just wishful thinking, but she was certain that her brother was out there somewhere at this very moment, possibly in desperate need of her help. She wondered if he experienced the same kind of connection to her. Was he hunting her even as she searched for him?

An icy finger traced her spine and she had to look away from the remains. Whoever said there was beauty in death had been wrong. All that was left of these men were eviscerated carcasses that would continue to rot until either their flesh decomposed or the vines snapped and dropped them into the—

"Come on," Bishop whispered. He tried to gently guide her away from the spring. "We need to keep moving."

"Wait."

Something shimmered where the blazing orange bacterial ring met with the limestone.

Courtney knelt at the pool's edge, careful to stay clear of the torrid water. She looked around until she found a stick and used its slender end to scrape out a sample of the snot-like thermophilic sludge. At first she had thought the silver hue at the waterline was a mere reflection, but now, as she studied the sloppy gob on the stick, the source of the shiny coloration was obvious. She held it out for Bishop to see. Smooth silver flecks dotted the fluorescent orange slime. She tilted them to reflect the light.

"What are they?" he asked.

Courtney closed her eyes and pictured Ty, drifting in and out of consciousness on the examination table in the hospital suite while what the doctor called "inflammatory plaques" colonized his skin, but what they had really looked like were—

"Scales," Courtney whispered, and dropped the stick into the spring.

Fifty-Three

When the dust settled, four of them were dead, and another two were missing, leaving seven of them standing on the beach around a pile of blackened sticks and charcoal. Shock had settled over the group like a wet blanket. Bradley recognized how fortunate they were, but that was of little solace. The grim truth with which they all needed to come to grips was that it was only a matter of time before they were all dead. None of them had so much as sensed the attack coming. Even now, looking back, it had all happened so quickly that Bradley couldn't think of any way they could have stopped it. One moment he was staring up into the sky, thanking his maker for allowing them to survive the sinking and begging for forgiveness for his role in the deaths of so many, and the next, he had been surrounded by gunfire and screaming. He remembered turning around in time to watch Walker fire his pistol into the sand while a sinuous form composed of what looked like quicksilver clung to his back, tearing at his neck as though trying to rip his whole head off from behind. Golden circles of eyeshine had flashed in his direction, snapping him out of his momentary paralysis. He recalled diving to the ground behind a life raft and burrowing into the sand so he could wriggle underneath it. After that, all he could remember was being alone in the darkness, assaulted by the horrible cries of pain and terror, until the craft was lifted off of him and he crawled trembling back out onto a beach dotted with fresh corpses.

When Pike had pulled him aside and demanded to know what he had seen, all he could say was that it had happened so fast that he honestly couldn't be sure. No, he hadn't seen where the creature had appeared from or where it had gone. No, he hadn't gotten a good look at it, other than the fact that it moved as though made of fluid. No, he hadn't noticed how the other men had been killed or what happened to the remains that had washed ashore. None of them had. It was as though the creature had simply materialized out of thin air between them and then disappeared every bit as suddenly. All Reaves had seen was a man hurled into the fire, choking and coughing up a flume of blood. One of the others had heard a man cry out in agony behind her, but hadn't been able to find the courage to turn around. Between the eight of them, they couldn't piece together a single useful account. Whatever demon they had unleashed was as incorporeal as the wind.

Pike held the blinding pink flare at the center of their circle. There would be no new fire, for as little good as it had done them. Pike's unilateral decision was to head out, and to do so quickly before the creature decided to come back and finish them off.

Bradley stared from one expressionless face to the next. Reaves held Angie in his arms as she shuddered against his chest. In his old friend's blank stare, he saw the same guilt that must have been radiating from his with the intensity of the sun. Libby Parsons, the seismologist, shivered beside them, arms drawn to her breast, looking out from beneath the tangled clumps of her bangs at something apparently only she could see. Brazelton stood beside her, his eyes flicking nervously across the beach, his finger white on the trigger of his pistol. Barnes stayed close to him, or, more accurately, to the man with the weapon. The Taser he had commandeered shook in his fist, forcing him to constantly readjust his sweaty grip.

"We need to move out," Pike said. His eyes roamed from them to the beach as he turned in slow circles. "This thing has been dictating the situation from the start and we've played right into its hands. It wanted us here so it could do exactly what it just did. It's time to see if we can assert a measure of control, or at least see if we can throw a wrench into its plans."

"So you want to strike out into the jungle where it could be hiding anywhere?" Libby snapped. "You think that doesn't fit into *its plans*? And what happens when the rescuers arrive and we aren't here? They aren't going to know to hike inland to try to find what's left of us!" Her voice grew shrill with hysterics. "Does it really matter anyway? Wherever we go, it will find us! And what then? You saw how quickly it snuck up on us. None of us really even saw it. Staying here is our best chance. We can rebuild the fire and signal—"

"You want to stay here?" Pike's expression was unreadable. "Fine. Stay here. We'll tell them where to find your body when we get off this island. And as far as your imminent rescue theory? Think about this...The *Mayr*'s emergency beacon began broadcasting more than four days ago now. In that time, how many people have come looking for it? We're stranded in the middle of nowhere while all available aid workers are on the mainland sifting through countless tons of debris to disinter tens of thousands of waterlogged corpses. This close to the epicenter of the quake that produced the tsunami in the first place? They've already written us off. It'll be several more days before they even think about broadening their search from the major population centers to canvass the sea for what they already assume are sunken vessels."

"I don't want to die," she sobbed.

Barnes squeezed her elbow in a sad gesture of support.

"Then do exactly what I tell you to do and there's a chance you'll live through this."

"A chance?" Bradley nearly laughed. "What chance do any of us have?"

Pike snarled, grabbed him by the bicep, and dragged him out of earshot.

"Get a hold of yourself. This has always been the road we were headed down. There was never any other way this could happen. So suck it up and let me do the job you pay me to do." He leaned closer so that their noses nearly touched. Spittle struck Bradley's chin when Pike spoke. "And if you ever contradict me in front of these people again, I'll put you down myself. So grow a set in a hurry. We all need to be at the top of our game right now."

Bradley could still feel the pressure of Pike's grip even after he let go and walked back toward the others.

"Grab only what you can carry," Pike said. "We're leaving now."

"What about...them?" Bradley gestured toward the life raft in which they had heaped the bodies of Walker and the two seamen. Even with the rain, the flies had found them and a conspicuous number of crabs scuttled between pools in the sand.

"I've got a hunch this thing will be coming back for them. Don't you think?"

Not with all of this fresh meat wandering into another of its traps. Bradley didn't vocalize his thoughts, and instead offered Pike a single nod.

Far off to the east, beyond where the ocean merged with the sky, the horizon was stained pink. Soon enough, the rising sun would burn off the mist and hopefully the storm clouds as well. He prayed they were right about the creature's vision and that they would make it safely off the island before darkness fell.

There was no way they would be able to survive another night.

Fifty-Four

Pike led them through the dense forest, conscious of every minuscule detail around him. The rain had slowed to a patter from a sky that must have significantly cleared to allow the occasional slivers of the rising sun's amber rays to pass through the nearly impenetrable canopy. Droplets and rivulets still fell from where the water had collected in the upper reaches, as though the trees themselves now rained. Monkeys screeched and birds called from out of sight through the mist that crawled through the branches and across the wet loam. As he had hoped, it was finally beginning to dissipate with the coming of day, but as it burned off, the humidity increased tenfold, which made it impossible for their clothes and hair to dry. Even with the increased visibility, the trees and shrubs were packed so tightly together that what few gaps they afforded were strung with vines. None of the others spoke, yet still the sounds of them crashing through the underbrush like a herd of cattle masked the more stealthy noises of the jungle, and the whine of the mosquitoes in his ears threatened to drive him mad.

For not the first time, he debated just ducking off the path and leaving them to fend for themselves. They were his responsibility, but considering their adversary, they were probably dead men walking regardless.

They weren't even half a kilometer to the northeast of the beach when he heard something that made him hold up his fist to signal them all to stop. Even without the ruckus of their passage, he had to concentrate to clearly decipher the sound over their labored breathing. He peered around the six civilians behind him to see Brazelton, who brought up the rear. The expression on his face confirmed that he had heard the sound and understood the implications as well. Pike signaled his intent and ducked off the path. He carefully picked his way through the untamed proliferation, cautious even of the crinkle of wet leaves underfoot. The noise ahead of him grew louder with each slow step. Down the barrel of his pistol, he could see the swarming black dots through the leaves. He tightened his finger on the trigger as he advanced. The buzzing sound of flies called to him from beyond a screen of willows. He breathed shallowly through his mouth to combat the stench of death. Before he even eased through the bushes, he knew exactly what he would find.

There had to be half a dozen corpses, all stacked like corded wood. Despite the branches that had been broken from the trees to cover them, he could still see portions of their bloated bodies. Swollen faces teeming with flies and ants. Bruised and discolored chests and legs. Their abdomens were distended with intestinal gasses. Livid wounds marred their flesh.

Pike slowly scoured the surrounding forest along the length of his pistol, expecting something to lunge at him at any moment. Several green birds knifed through the canopy with a startled cry. If this was where the creature had brought the bodies, then how far away could it possibly be?

One silent step at a time, he crept into the small clearing. The sheer amount of insects crawling on the remains made them appear to move. He glanced down at the sloppy earth and was rewarded with the sight of more footprints like those he had followed from the other side of the island. Burdened by the extra weight of the bodies, they were deeper and more clearly defined. Without taking his eyes from the forest, he knelt and traced their contours with his fingertips. They were bare, size twelve or thirteen. The toes left teardrop impressions like those of the wolves and mountain lions he had tracked on hunting trips with his father growing up. The prints formed a trampled circle around the corpses that Pike followed until he reached a point that he could see the beach, maybe fifty yards down a ravine. He was on the northern end of the heavily wooded horseshoe bay, where the forest grew nearly all the way into the ocean. It would definitely have been possible for someone to emerge from the ocean and slip into the trees without being seen by the naked eye from where they'd built their fire on the beach, but he still should have been able to see a heat signature through the thermal goggles. The tracks led directly to the stones lining the ravine. He walked a complete circle around the festering remains. No other tracks led away into the forest. After hauling the bodies up here, the creature must have returned to the beach, but why?

Pike tried to construct a mental timeframe. How had this thing had the time to attack them on the beach, abscond with the dead, and then drag them all up here? The only possible way was if it had swum from one side of the beach to the other at a high rate of speed and been strong enough to carry the corpses over its shoulders while it ran up the gulley.

The prospect of that kind of physical prowess was terrifying. It would have easily taken two highly skilled men to accomplish that task so quickly.

None of them would be leaving this island alive.

If the thing had doubled back to the beach, it could be sneaking up behind his party at this very moment while he was distracted by the bodies. He hurried back in the direction from which he had come without any of his previous caution, certain that the screams and gunshots would erupt at any second. He was surprised when he burst through the foliage to find the group still standing right where he had left them.

Their stalker could easily have crept up behind them by now and butchered them all as efficiently as it had demonstrated it could mere minutes ago on the beach.

So why hadn't it?

Was it possible that Tyler Martin's eyesight had been altered so dramatically that he could only see well enough to hunt at night like the scientists believed? Pike hadn't been prepared to buy that explanation without proof, for such speculation could cost them their lives if they were wrong, but was that exactly what they had now? Proof that as long as the sun was up they would be safe from attack? If this was really the case, then they needed to take full advantage of every second of daylight to distance themselves from the creature, despite the fact that he didn't know where it was.

He thought about the tracks leading back to the ocean's edge.

Where could it possibly have gone?

Pike caught Brazelton's attention and confirmed what he had found with a nod. Brazelton lowered his brows in confusion as he followed the same line of logic that Pike had.

"What's out there?" Bradley asked.

"Nothing," Pike said. He turned back to the north and the trek ahead. "Nothing at all."

If they were going to capitalize on this opportunity, then he was going to have to drive them as hard and as fast as he could, regardless of the noise and their condition and the terrain.

"Move out!" he called back over his shoulder. "We're wasting daylight."

Fifty-Five

Bishop looked back over his shoulder at Courtney. She hadn't said a word since they left the spring where they'd found the partially-consumed bodies of the men from their ship. And the scales. He knew what she was thinking. He'd seen the skin condition growing on her brother's face and chest as well, but he couldn't begin to fathom how she felt. Bishop had never been close to his parent and he didn't have any siblings. He had seen plenty of men die during his years in the Navy, some of them in gruesome and horrible ways, but he'd never really been more than superficial friends with any of them. Their passing had affected him, just not in the soul-deep kind of way that Courtney must have been feeling. He wanted to reach out to her and yet give her the privacy that she needed to grieve at the same time. There was still the chance that they'd misinterpreted what they'd seen and that her brother was still out there somewhere. Surely there was something supportive he could say, but if she was barely clinging to a thread of hope, he could easily sever it with even the best of intentions. So he continued to forge their path through the wilderness, watching the trees for any sign of pursuit, while he could think about nothing other than the pain and sorrow on her face.

He heard the trickling sound of running water ahead and shoved through the bushes to find a small creek. Its narrow banks overflowed with runoff from the steep slope of the caldera. From somewhere uphill and through the trees came the sound of a series of waterfalls. There was a slim gap between the branches overhead, granting him his first true glimpse of the sun in as long as he could remember. He almost wept at the sight. After days trapped in darkness and the horrors of the previous night, he had thought he might never see it again. Tiny raindrops fell as little more than a damp mist. He stepped down into the shallow stream, spread his arms out to either side, and leaned his head back to feel the warmth caress his skin. The frigid water soothed his aching feet and the seemingly millions of small cuts on his soles.

Courtney splashed into the creek beside him and moaned in relief. Her feet were so badly lacerated that when he looked down he could see the blood diffusing into the water. As much as they needed to hurry, thirty more seconds in the blessed water wouldn't kill them.

He held out his hand to her. She took it as she stared up into the sky.

"Are you going to be all right?" he asked.

She nodded and a tear slid down her cheek.

"You know it's possible those scales could have come from some kind of fish or lizard."

"In a geothermal spring with a temperature of more than a hundred degrees?"

"It doesn't mean they came from your brother. For all we know—"

"It's okay." She squeezed his hand. A green parrot with a red face squawked and took to wing through the canopy. "I love my brother. If he's still alive, and if there's any way he can be saved, I'll find it."

Bishop turned and looked into her eyes. In them he saw not hopelessness, but resolve. He pulled her closer and kissed her, softly, tentatively. She leaned into him with such urgency that they both nearly slipped on the smooth rocks.

He was not going to allow anything to happen to her. They were going to get off of this godforsaken island and—

The ground shuddered. From somewhere above him, he heard the loud crack of a boulder breaking free and crashing into the forest.

He pulled her out of the water as the earth once again stilled and the rumbling sound ceased. The stream flowed momentarily higher before resuming its former level. Leaves fluttered down from the trees like green butterflies.

"Aftershock?" he said.

"Not this long after the fact." She pointed up through the trees toward where wisps of smoke drifted into the sky over the forested rim of the caldera. "We're in the Pacific Ring of Fire, the most notoriously unstable geological region on the planet. If the tectonic plates in the Kilinailau Ridge are still shifting like they were when we were there, anything could happen."

"One more reason to get the hell off this rock."

She pulled him to her this time and kissed him. When she finally broke away, she leaned her forehead on his chin.

"I can't leave," she whispered. "Not while there's a chance Ty might still be out here."

He nodded and kissed her hairline.

"I understand," he said. "I'm not leaving without you."

Of course, when the opportunity finally arrived, he'd drag her off this island kicking and screaming if he had to.

She smiled and held him for a moment longer before she turned back toward the forest and the journey ahead. Bishop took her by the hand and reluctantly guided her out of the sun and into the shadows again.

Fifty-Six

Reaves had no idea how long they'd been walking or how far they had traveled. The fugue that had settled over him had finally begun to lift, leaving in its stead a deep-seated desperation that made him feel like crawling out of his own skin. He needed to get off this island. The urge was so overwhelming that it was all he could do to keep from shoving the others aside and sprinting through the jungle. He kept imaging the cavern under Casa Rinconada and the buried temple in Vietnam, and all of the bones scattered on the floor. Was there already such a place in this hell and would some anthropologist in the distant future be poring over his gnawed skeletal remains? What had happened to Tyler Martin now felt real in a way that it never had before. He had undergone the same metamorphosis that had transformed the creatures that had driven entire societies from their homes and to migrations that had ultimately led to their demise. Entire societies! And the Anasazi, Champa, and Maya weren't peace-loving agricultural societies ill-prepared to defend themselves against such a threat. They were warring, often merciless, tribes whose ferocity should have all but guaranteed their survival. If they had fallen, what hope was there for the seven of them stumbling through the jungle?

As an evolutionary anthropologist, he had to find the objective balance between science and God to explain the changes that caused the rise and fall of civilizations, that led to the physiological and sociological alterations, and the physical differences that mere geographical origin couldn't explain. He now had to wonder if both conspired against them. There were plenty of examples of relatively sudden evolutionary shifts, of random mutations that had altered the future of entire species. Birds had evolved from their extinct dinosaur forebears thanks to the rise of feathers from scales. *Homo sapiens* branched from *homo erectus*, which had died off shortly thereafter. Were they now standing at the precipice of another dramatic evolutionary leap? Was this the event that would spell humanity's extinction and spawn a new species to take its place, or was this simply a random event without cosmic design, set into motion by two separate organisms that were never meant to come into contact with one another? Or was this a punishment unleashed by God to cleanse the planet of the scourge of mankind like the tsunami that killed so many in Oceania and the earthquake that decimated Haiti? Was the reign of *homo sapiens* finally coming to an end?

Had he played an integral role in the extinction of his own species?

Maybe for now this was an isolated event confined to this island, but if he didn't return to Seattle, someone else would find his research and pick up right where he left off. It was too enticing for anyone who understood the significance to pass up.

Worse still, if someone could crack the genetic code of the bacterium that caused the changes, what monstrous aberrations could they create?

He glanced over at Bradley.

What had *he* intended to do with the knowledge once that power was his to wield?

This had all been one giant mistake. The focus of his *entire life* had been a mistake. There were just some things that man was simply never meant to learn.

At least their theory about the creature's nocturnal habits had thus far been correct. Or had it? Maybe their stalker had set another trap somewhere ahead of them and even now they were walking obliviously into it. Best case scenario, all they were doing was distancing themselves from it, but would that be enough? Their only hope was to evacuate the island before nightfall. With the sheer number of geothermal formations on the island continuously producing hydrogen sulfide, this was the ideal habitat for the creature to survive indefinitely. Again he had to wonder if such a coincidence wasn't the work of some omnipotent hand.

They could only pray that there was a radio at the mission they could use to call for evacuation. If not, then it was only a matter of time before the monster that was Tyler Martin found them. With every hard-earned yard forged through the jungle, they were merely creating a path that would lead it straight to them.

A gap opened in the forest to the west. The tranquil Pacific stretched clear to the horizon. Golden sunlight sparkled like diamonds on the aquamarine waves. Cotton ball-clouds drifted through the seamless blue sky. He wished the sun's ascent would stall, stranding it above them for as long as possible.

The ground rumbled beneath his feet again. He leaned against the nearest tree for balance and turned to the east. High above the rim of the volcano, smoke merged into a bank of storm clouds that seemed to be building in height, rising into the stratosphere like a great fist preparing to smite them.

"Just ride it out," Pike said.

Birds shrieked from swirling flocks overhead before dropping back to their roosts in the canopy, from which they'd been unceremoniously rousted by the quake.

The waves to the west grew choppy and boomed against the rocky shore like cannon fire.

"That one was bigger than the last," Libby Parsons whispered. "They're growing in frequency and intensity. Every time the tectonic plates shift, they create massive amounts of energy. All of these little discharges..."

Her words trailed off as a sudden gust of wind swept a mist of brine from the sea.

"What?" Bradley asked. "What about them?"

"They could be nothing...or they could be building up to something. The earth can only store so much energy before..."

"Before what?" Reaves asked.

Libby turned to face him, her eyes wide, her face stark white.

"Before it has to release it."

Reaves raised his stare again to the east, where more dark smoke furled into the sky above the tops of the trees that ringed the mouth of the caldera.

Fifty-Seven

Courtney winced with every step. With all of the cuts on the soles of her feet, even the spongy moss felt like beds of nails. She was starting to wonder how much farther she was going to be able to go. At least the pain served to focus her mind on something other than the realization of what her brother had become. The biologist in her had run around and around in her mind, trying to figure out a solution to his problem, but she always came back to the scarlet tube worm. When the chemosynthetic organisms in its gut died, so did the worm. She wished she knew more about the bacteria themselves. Ty was the expert on thermophiles, but he was currently in no position to help them. She again forced her brother from her mind in an effort to concentrate on the here and now. If there was a way to save him, she would find it. First, however, they needed to put more distance between themselves and those from the beach, who were surely trudging toward the same destination that they were. Bishop was right. They needed to ensure their own safety from the human element before they could even think about helping her brother.

Over the course of the last several hours, they had been slowly creeping downhill to the west as they continued north. Every now and then she caught a glimpse of the distant shimmering waves through the canopy and prayed to see a ship heading toward the island. At least the rain had stopped for the time being, but with the way the clouds were darkening to the east, she knew it was only a matter of time before another storm commenced. With any luck, they'd be indoors in the village long before then.

Another mini-quake shook the ground and she had to grab Bishop to keep from stumbling.

"There's more smoke this time," he said.

With each of the increasingly frequent quakes, they had taken to looking toward the caldera. Where initially there had been a few twirls of smoke nearly indistinguishable from the clouds, it now looked like a wildfire raged somewhere inside the mountain. They smelled burning wood, and beneath it, a faintly sulfurous scent. The volcano had been dormant for thousands of years, despite the constant tectonic activity all around it. What were the odds that it would come to life after all of this time?

The sun slipped behind the leading edge of the storm clouds before emerging once again. In that fleeting moment, she thought she saw the bellies of the clouds closest to the cone glow faintly orange.

"We need to keep moving," Bishop said. "I want to try to reach the village before the storm hits. If the people from the boat are following us, it'll slow them down." He attempted a smile. "Besides, now that I'm finally dry, I really don't feel like getting drenched again."

They started forward again through a grove of ceibas that grew just far enough apart that they could nearly walk side-by-side.

"There's something we haven't considered," Bishop said. He reached back and took her by the hand to hurry her along. "If there's a radio at the mission, then it's possible that someone on the *Huxley* could have called ahead, and Lord only knows what they might have said. We could find that they won't exactly roll out the red carpet for us."

"What do you propose then? It's our only option."

"It's not our *only* option, but it's by far the best we've got right now. I'm not suggesting we avoid it. I'm just saying that we need to be really careful how we approach it."

"And what if it does play out that way? What if they think we're some sort of criminals?"

"I don't even want to contemplate our backup plan yet."

Courtney had to nearly jog to keep pace. To her left, the waves booming against the rocks became quieter, and she could have sworn she almost heard the shushing sound of waves spilling onto sand. Seagulls called from ahead of them, a riot of squawks and squalls. The ground gently descended to the north. Bishop's grip grew tighter on her hand and he slowed his pace.

"Wha—?" she started, but he silenced her by pressing his index finger to his lips.

A path cut through the groundcover directly ahead of them, a line of choppy mud where the detritus had been packed into the earth. He led her slowly toward it and stopped several paces away. She couldn't clearly discern any footprints between the puddles, but it was readily apparent that it was a frequently used trail. It wound down through the forest toward the origin of the gull racket before vanishing into the trees.

"We're close," he whispered into her ear. "I want you to stay right behind me and do exactly what I do."

He looked her in the eyes and waited for her to nod her understanding.

She followed him across the path and to the east, where they worked their way into denser forestation. They eased cautiously from behind one tree trunk to the next, all the while descending toward the rising sounds of the surf and the shrieking gulls. She was reminded of the Jersey shore of her youth in the evenings when the fishing boats were returning to the docks with their day's catch, where clouds of the birds whirled around the schooners in anticipation of feeding on guts and leftover chum.

Bishop lingered longer and longer behind each trunk. He peeked around them several times before guiding her quickly downhill and behind the next. Through the branches, she caught an occasional glimpse of wooden constructs, gray with age and exposure to the elements, but never a clear look. Above them, hundreds of gulls wheeled against the sky.

A new scent reached to them on the breeze. She crinkled her nose. Bishop's posture stiffened and he stopped dead in his tracks in front of her.

The infernal racket grew louder, and through the branches, she saw a riot of white feathered bodies nearly colliding and beating each other back down to the ground.

Bishop lowered himself to his haunches and advanced in a crouch. Mimicking his movements, she clung to the cover of the shrubs as she trailed him. The seagulls were so loud it felt like they were inside her head. Onward they crept until Bishop finally stopped behind the buttress roots of a monster kapok tree. Through the gaps between the slanted roots and the bushes on the other side, she saw a pair of wooden huts with thatch roofs, built on stilts.

Every inch of air space between them was packed with squabbling gulls, which made it nearly impossible to see the ground—

Courtney gasped and closed her eyes, but there were some things that once seen could never be erased from memory.

Fifty-Eight

Pike had been driving the survivors as fast as he possibly could. None of them wanted to fall behind for fear of becoming lost and alone in the jungle. The civilian cattle whined and complained and whimpered behind him, but he didn't care how tired they were or how much their feet hurt or how frightened they were. He would sooner abandon them than lose any more time, which he could feel flying past as the shadows and columns of light continued to shift around him. The occasional glimpses of the sun through the canopy made it appear to lurch across the sky in jerky stop-motion animation. The hell if he was going to still be on this island when it sank into the ocean to the west.

He attuned his body to the jungle until he felt every noise as much as heard it and became a living extension of the soft earth underfoot. Birds startled then silenced at the sound of their approach and unseen animals darted away from them through the branches. Condensation on the broad, leathery leaves high above them dripped to the ground. The ocean pounded the shoreline in time with his metered breathing.

His best guess was that they were within a kilometer of the village, so he wasn't surprised when he found the first hint of a trail.

He signaled for the others to stop behind him and surveyed the area with his pistol before finally shoving through the bushes toward a hardly visible line through the ferns and shrubs. Anyone else would have missed it, but not Pike. To him, the faint path might as well have been paved. The bent branches and broken stems showed the direction of travel, and while the spongy loam and ferns had begun to spring back up, he could still tell exactly where each footfall had been placed. Someone had passed through here, and recently. Not more than half an hour ahead of them.

Had the creature somehow swung around and outflanked them from the steeper jungle to the east?

He turned, locked eyes with Brazelton, and communicated what he had found without words. Brazleton nodded and pushed through the others so he could cover Pike with his weapon.

"What's going on?" Bradley asked.

Pike silenced him with a glare and knelt down in the bushes. He carefully brushed aside the leaves and groundcover until he found a decent print.

Behind him, Brazleton hushed the nervous whispering of the civilians.

The footprint was human, presumably from a male, approximately size twelve. The same as the other tracks they had found, but this one was distinctly different. The heel was wider and the impressions left by the toes were ovular rather than teardrop-shaped. Where the ball of the foot touched, the imprint was clearly defined by either excessive weight or fatigue. He leaned closer and something caught his eye. Carefully, he excised a blade of grass from where it had been squashed into the mud and raised it to his face.

Blood.

The tip of the broad blade was smeared with blood.

He turned to his right in the direction from which the trail led. The slope of the volcano rose up into the miasma of clouds and smoke. The angle of the trail was shallow, as though whoever had made it was working slowly westward toward the sea.

Again, he looked down and isolated a second set of prints. They were much smaller, perhaps size six or seven, and while he couldn't be completely certain, he was comfortable working under the assumption that they belonged to a woman. Just like the first, they were bare and it only took him a moment to find the blood now that he knew to look for it.

Pike rocked back on his heels and scoured the area. The tracks were definitely different than those he was convinced had been made by the creature, but why were they bare? And what was the source of the blood? Had they happened upon a path left by natives returning to their village or had they been left by someone else? The fact that the path had been recently forged through the foliage suggested that someone other than the natives had made it. After countless generations on the island, surely the villagers had well-worn paths leading everywhere they needed to go. But if not them, then who? There were still two survivors from the liferaft on the *Mayr* for whom they had yet to account. Was it possible that they had finally caught up with them? And if so, what happened to their shoes?

He followed the line of prints with his eyes. The small spots of blood were in the same locations. The wounds had to be on the soles of feet unaccustomed to traversing such terrain barefoot. Either the last of the survivors from the *Mayr* had miraculously made it this far or he supposed it wasn't entirely impossible that two of those who had vanished in the chaos on the beach when the creature attacked had managed to navigate the jungle on their own. He cursed himself for not taking the time to properly inspect the remains he had found hidden under the branches, but he undoubtedly wouldn't have been able to recognize all of their faces considering he had never really gotten a good look at them in the first place.

"What did you find?" Bradley asked.

Pike stood and walked back toward the group.

"Two sets of tracks," he said. "Whoever left them can't be very far ahead of us."

"They aren't—?"

"No. These show no signs of physical…malformation."

"Who do you think…?" Bradley started, but Pike had already turned his back on him. He was weary of talking and tired of all of the questions, especially those he couldn't answer.

But not for much longer.

The trail they now followed was still fresh and those who had left it were surely slowed by their wounds. If he set a fast pace, it wouldn't be long before they overtook them somewhere in the vicinity of the village.

The ground trembled again and he glanced to the east. He could no longer see the caldera through the smoke, although there was a reddish flicker where it should have been. The storm clouds had eclipsed it on their westward journey. Beneath them, the air above the highest trees was hazy with rain.

There was a loud rumbling sound as boulders broke away from the slope and cascaded down into the forest.

He returned his focus to the path and the thinning forest, and started forward at a jog.

Fifty-Nine

Bishop had known what they would find the moment he smelled the comingling aromas of blood and decomposition, but he still couldn't believe his eyes. He had seen the bodies strewn in the debris surrounding car bombs, in markets where men had strapped explosives to their chests before detonating themselves in the crowd, and lying in courtyards below an impromptu sniper's nest, but this...this was a massacre without reason. He had anticipated problems gaining entry to the village from suspicious natives or difficulty negotiating the use of the radio with some foreign priest. Never once had he considered the possibility that they would arrive at the village to find everyone dead.

He glanced over at Courtney. Her pale face was drawn into an expression of horror.

When he looked back into the village, it almost appeared as though the bodies had multiplied. They were everywhere, cast aside on the ground like refuse. He was thankful that the ghastly details were hidden by all of the gulls that hopped on the remains, skewering the rotting flesh with their beaks before tossing back their heads to choke the morsels down into their gullets. The formerly bare dirt was nearly white with the staggering amount of bird feces and feathers. Whenever one of the scavengers took to flight, another dropped from the churning flock to take its place. They lined the thatch roofs of the lashed wooden huts and flew in and out of the open doorways. In all of his years at sea, he had never seen so many of the vile birds in one place, even as the commercial trawlers docked near the processing plants with their decks piled high with several months' worth of fish.

He wished he had a gun, if only to fire it into the air to scatter the seagulls and salvage what little dignity remained for the dead. The fact that they were left to rot on the ground without even a halfhearted attempt at burial told him everything he needed to know.

There was no one left alive to bury them.

Who could have done something like this?

His first thought was of the men on the *Huxley* who had been prepared to kill them to protect the secret of their terrible discovery, but even they couldn't be this cruel. And unless they had done this prior to extracting them from the *Mayr*'s sunken carcass, they wouldn't have had the time. These people had been dead for quite a while now. This level of carnage was beyond the devices of man. It was savage…inhuman…

Goosebumps rippled up the backs of his arms and prickled his neck.

He remembered the screams in the confusion on the *Mayr* and the video from the diver's helmet that showed all of the bodies trapped underwater in the hold.

There was no longer any doubt in his mind. Whatever had slaughtered everyone aboard their ship was on this island, and it had been in this very spot not long ago.

For all he knew, it could still be here now.

"Stay here," he whispered as he ducked out from behind the tree.

Courtney grabbed him by the wrist and jerked him back.

"Where are you going?"

"I need to find the radio."

"I'm not staying here alone."

"You can't come with me, Courtney. Just look down there. What if whoever did this is still here?"

"That's precisely why I'm going with you."

"Damn it, Courtney. We can't take the chance—"

She lunged forward and stepped out from behind the cover of the trunk and the bushes before he could stop her. He hurried to take her by the hand and tried to pull her behind him so he could at least shield her with his body if he had to.

She was going to be the death of him.

Most of the seagulls leapt up when they entered the clearing and joined the frenzied flock swirling over the rooftops, shrieking so loud he could barely hear himself think. Other brazen individuals held their ground, webbed feet balanced on the corpses as they continued to spear strips of muscle like worms. Bishop wanted to shout to scare them away, but he feared betraying their presence, if by some slim chance all of the squawking hadn't done so already. In their absence, he could see all of the flies crawling on the bodies. What little clothing was still draped over the remains was shredded. Some wore shirts and shorts surely donated to the mission, while others wore skirts of woven reeds.

All of the bodies had dark skin, most of which was black and livid with putrefaction. Not that there was much flesh left. The majority had already been plucked away to expose knots of tendon and connective tissue covered with feathers. The occasional tattoo of odd geometric shapes and puffy scars that appeared to have been deliberately inflicted for aesthetic reasons stood out from random sections of body parts. Their abdomens were hollowed out to reveal broken rib cages like the mouths of so many Venus flytraps that held puddles of rainwater and bodily dissolution. Their eyes and cheeks were gone. The black holes in their orbits and their bared teeth made them appear enraged.

Bishop tried not to look at them as he picked his way across the clearing. There had to be at least twenty of them sprawled on their backs and sides inside the ring of huts. Men. Women. Children. All gutted, decomposing, and partially consumed. Instead, he focused on the open doorways of the wooden domiciles, through which he could see little more than shadows. Anything could have been hiding at the back of the single rooms, staring right at them, and he wouldn't have been able to see it until it leapt into the light mere feet away. Between those to the west, he could see the ocean over the treetops farther down the slope near the beach.

The first raindrops slapped his shoulder and the top of his head.

He studied the rooftops past the curious gulls in search of a cross, a radio antenna, anything that might identify the mission, careful not to pay too much attention to the blood spatters on the sides of the huts that had been saved from the torrent by the overhangs.

Every time a branch bowed or leaves fluttered or the grass skirts of the corpses riffled at the behest of the wind, he had to fight the urge to grab Courtney and sprint for cover.

They continued to the north on a path between huts that led into a grove of mango trees. The cloud of seagulls behind them dropped to the ground with a whistle of wings so loud it could have been a scream. Several more bodies were crumpled in the bushes along the trail, hidden from the bulk of the birds where the flies could have them all to themselves. Bishop had to swat the bloated insects away from his face. The trees gave way to another cluster of huts, at the back of which was undoubtedly the mission they had traveled all this way to find. Rather than rows of lashed sticks, it had been built with native stones and adobe, and poorly patched by mismatched mud through the years. It reminded Bishop of the missions scattered throughout the countryside in California. A cross stood from the top of the stunted *campanile*, in which a single rusted bell hung. The slanted roof of the crumbling, single-story domicile was composed of broken clay tiles that had been replaced by clumps of thatch. The whitewashed adobe had been scoured away by the wind and replaced with a chalky crust of brine. The shutters over the windows appeared to be nailed closed, and whatever door had once protected the narthex had been replaced by a clapboard construct of ill-fitting boards.

And behind the building and the crumbling quadrangle walls was exactly what he had prayed to find. A tall metal antenna with all sorts of horizontal branches loomed over the sloped roof. Slanted guy-wires tethered it to the trunks of the surrounding palm and date trees.

There were no bodies on this side of the village, only hard-packed dirt with standing puddles surrounding a fountain that overflowed with green sludge and a fire pit of stepped gray stones, most of which had cracked and turned to pebbles. He could see the amassed ash and burnt wood inside, and what could have been the charred bones of a boar or a pig.

He caught a glimpse of the ocean again. The wind was whipping up the waves. The glimmer of sunlight had been replaced by whitecaps.

Raindrops pattered the ground around them as the clouds overtook the sun, which lost the race across the sky to the west.

Bishop led Courtney up the stone steps to the mission's front door.

He gave the handle a solid tug, but the door didn't budge. After several more futile attempts, he gave up. Had it been nailed shut from the inside?

They were going to have to find another way in.

He looked at Courtney, at the brave front she tried to project, and gave her hand a reassuring squeeze. Together they descended the stairs and started around the side of the building, behind the quadrangle wall.

Sixty

The waves beat against the cliffs faster and louder, like the tolling of some great bell as they marched to the gallows. They had run to keep up with Pike for as long as possible, until one by one they had fallen back with Brazelton, who grew increasingly frustrated at their slowing pace. Pike had long since vanished into the jungle ahead of them. Every now and then, Bradley caught a glimpse of him through the trees before he vanished once more. Barnes had found several partially edible mangoes on the ground that they shared, stealing bites around mealy black bruises and insect holes.

The raindrops grew larger with each step and the thinned canopy no longer protected them like it once had. His hair was already wet, and cold ribbons trickled down his spine into the waistband of his slacks. His entire body ached and he would have paid a king's ransom to rest his legs and feet, if only for a few minutes. Had he known what lay ahead when he left Seattle, he would have at least brought more comfortable walking shoes.

He chuckled aloud at the thought, which drew nervous glances from his companions, who undoubtedly feared he had snapped. Maybe he had. This entire nightmare was surreal, as though they had crossed over into some other world where none of the normal rules applied, but Bradley knew better. After all, whether he had envisioned it or not, like Pike said, this was surely what he had hoped would happen all along. There had never been a way to unleash such evolutionary power without fulfilling its awesome potential and producing the very monster it had been biologically designed to create. It had been such an all-consuming passion that he had never paused to consider the ramifications. And all to satisfy his own curiosity, when common sense should have intervened to stop this madness before it had even begun.

The blood of more than a hundred men and women was on his hands. What did he have to show for their unwitting sacrifice?

Those of them that remained would be lucky if they even survived long enough to escape this infernal island with their lives.

He saw the way the others looked at him, the blame in their eyes. None of them had signed on for this. He had deceived them, but worse, he had fooled himself into thinking he was capable of wielding the power of a god when there was some knowledge that nature had gone to great lengths to hide where no one should have ever found it.

The ground shook again, dropping him to his knees in the mud. He wasn't sure if he had the strength left to stand, or even if he wanted to. The burning smell was growing worse. The entire volcano was shrouded by smoke, wisps of which now filtered down into the branches overhead. He heard a loud cracking sound like thunder. It was as though the entire island were breaking apart with them on it.

Gulls squalled from directly ahead.

He struggled back to his feet and staggered onward with the others. None of them spoke. After all, what was left to say? Either they would be able to use the radio in the village to call for help or they were going to die this very night.

Pike emerged from the forest and walked back toward them. As always, his expression gave nothing away, but he still walked with his pistol firmly in a two-handed grip. Whatever he had found down the path certainly hadn't set him at ease. Pike walked right past him and collared Brazelton. The two of them stepped off to the side and conversed out of earshot.

"What's going on?" Reaves whispered.

"I have no idea." Bradley rubbed the scab on his swollen forehead where he had struck the rail. The headache had burrowed behind his eyes. "But it doesn't look like he's too happy about it."

"This isn't your fault alone. We all share the responsibility for what happened. If I had never instigated that dig under that kiva..."

Bradley rested his hand on his old friend's shoulder.

"Eventually someone else would have. Or we would have still learned about the remains in Vietnam from your student. Regardless, we would have eventually found ourselves doing precisely what we're doing now."

Reaves nodded and looked away through the forest toward the ocean. Bradley knew how Reaves felt. Saying the words out loud didn't make him feel any better either.

Pike broke away from Brazelton and addressed them all in little more than a whisper.

"Form a single-file line. Stay close together and right behind me. I don't want to hear a sound from any of you."

Before Bradley could ask if he'd found the village, Pike struck off to the northeast, away from the path. Bradley hurried to keep up with him. A twig snapped under his foot and earned him a fiery backward glance.

They worked through the densest shrubs and groves, staying close to whatever cover they could find. Downhill to the left, the squawking of seagulls grew louder. He occasionally glimpsed a white flock circling through the treetops and wondered what could have attracted so many of them.

Pike's head and weapon swiveled in unison, from left to right. They continued on their current course until they eventually veered westward once more. The smell of smoke continued to worsen. Bradley had to swallow hard to stifle a cough for fear of incurring Pike's wrath. A new scent reached him, and suddenly he understood the reason for Pike's detour. The shrieking gulls...the smell...

If something had happened in the village, then all was lost.

The darkening sky flashed with lightning. The distant reply of the thunder eventually grumbled toward them from the east. As if on cue, the storm commenced in earnest with the sound of clapping on the leaves overhead.

They passed the concentration of seagulls until, despite their ceaseless racket, he could faintly hear the ocean. Pike led them due west now. When he lowered to a crouch, Bradley did the same. They advanced another dozen paces before Pike finally stopped. Bradley followed Pike's line of sight through the gaps between the branches and almost moaned in relief.

There was a bell tower with a wooden cross perched on top of it. And farther to the right, something metallic glinted. He leaned to the side to get a better look at the radio tower.

"We made it," he whispered.

There was a hint of movement near the base of the tower, mere silhouettes passing through shadows.

"Not quite yet," Pike said. He raised his pistol and eased through the bushes toward the source of the motion.

Sixty-One

They entered a small enclosure around the back of the building that had once served as the priest's garden. Flowering hedges grew up against a rear wall draped with vines. Weeds and ferns surrounded the base of the radio tower, the tethers of which formed the framework of a teepee over the trapezoidal space. A smaller rear door was in the same state of disrepair as the front, and fit so poorly that Courtney could nearly see into the room behind it through the wide, uneven seams. Just to its right, a bundle of black cords passed through the adobe wall and ran straight into the ground. As she neared, she saw small mounds of earth, and then the hole from which they'd been excavated.

Her heart dropped into her stomach.

"No," Bishop whispered.

Courtney stared into the hole and started to cry. Both ends of the severed wires poked out of the standing water and mud, frayed and unraveling. She couldn't believe her eyes. The rain poured down on her, but she could no longer feel it. How could this have happened? Such cruelty…This couldn't have been Ty…He was the most generous, gentle soul she had ever known.

"The antenna's for long-range communication," Bishop said. "We still may have enough juice to reach the mainland or the nearest passing ship without it."

There was a crack of splintering wood behind her. She turned in time to see the boards that had been fashioned into the refectory door clatter to the dirt, leaving Bishop standing there with the makeshift knob in his hand. He cast it aside and stepped into the shadows. Courtney walked to the threshold and peered inside. The small chamber housed little more than an unmade bed, an open trunk brimming with clothes, and a faded leather-bound bible on a crate in the corner. The manila walls were spider-webbed with cracks. There were sections where the plaster had crumbled away to reveal the chicken wire framework and the rotting timber behind it. A slender doorway led to the dark patio at the heart of the mission. There was a pitted antique desk under the window where the cords from the antenna entered the room. Bishop stood in the center of the priest's quarters, staring down at the broken casing of the radio and the components strewn across the wood-plank floor in a mess of wires. He reached down and picked up the desktop microphone. Its cut cord dangled uselessly. He studied it for a long moment before he whirled and spiked it against the wall. When he turned around again, his face was drawn with anguish. He kicked the pile of fractured circuit boards across the room and raised his stare to meet hers.

"I'm so sorry," he whispered.

"You said you had a backup plan."

He shook his head.

"I was hoping not to have to even think about it. It's not an especially good one."

"If you have one at all, it's far better than anything I can come up with."

"There are a ton of glaring problems with it. Most notably, we'd have to turn around and head back in the direction we came from. If anyone's following us, we'd be walking right back at—"

He stopped abruptly and cocked his head.

"We could try to go around—"

He closed his hand over her mouth and pulled her against him.

"Shh," he whispered into her ear and slowly withdrew his hand.

All she could hear was the sound of the raindrops tapping on the clay tiles on the mission's roof. A low rumble of thunder rolled down the mountain from the west. The settling smoke clung to the treetops as it slowly filtered to the ground, a dark mist nearly indistinguishable from the storm clouds. There was only a sliver of blue sky left over the eastern wall of the garden.

Bishop guided her toward the eight-foot-tall rear quandrangle wall, never once taking his eyes from the western wall and the tall trees that encircled the adjacent hut beyond it.

"If I boost you up," he whispered, "can you climb over?"

"What's going on?"

"Can you do it?"

"I think so."

"Once you hit the ground, I want you to run as fast as you can toward the beach." The way he looked past her, unblinking, was unnerving. She risked a glance in that direction, but saw only the wall and the forest leading up into the clouds. "I'll be right behind you. If I don't make it—"

"What's happening? What do you see?"

She heard a faint splash and the slurp of a boot rising from the mud.

"Go!" he whispered. He grabbed her around the waist and hoisted her up until she could reach over the edge.

She climbed up, swung her legs over the other side, and was just about to drop down to the ground when she caught movement from the corner of her eye. Bishop had already leapt up beside her and had one leg over the top of the wall when a shadowed figure darted around the corner of the mission and into the garden.

With a squeal of surprise, she let go and fell down into the mud. Her feet slipped out from beneath her and she splashed onto her rear end in a puddle. A split-second later, Bishop grabbed her by the hand and yanked her up again. They were already sprinting past the decrepit hut and into the tall weeds behind it before she found her balance. The leathery leaves of fruit trees slapped at their faces. She could barely keep her eyes open long enough to make sure she didn't barrel headlong into a trunk.

There was a shout from behind them, which only served to make Bishop run faster.

The ocean called to them from downhill. She saw sporadic swatches of white sand and blue sea through the branches. Her lungs burned from the smoke.

In her mind, she saw the non-descript figure, a mere blur of motion ducking into the garden, its body a seamless, shimmering black. Had she seen a horn on its forehead? White-blonde hair? Everything was happening too quickly.

They burst from the jungle onto the beach, their bare feet slapping the wet sand. Jagged rocks stood from the surf like massive snaggled teeth. The waves pounded them, throwing spray high into the air before racing across the shore toward their feet. A wide bay spread out before them through the smoke. The angry waves were dimpled with raindrops, and reflected the lightning that streaked past through the clouds overhead. The wind chased tatters of brown leaves and detritus past their legs.

The crack of gunfire stopped them dead in their tracks.

Bishop nervously looked her in the eyes as the report echoed away into oblivion.

"Lace your fingers behind your heads!" a voice shouted.

Bishop nodded to her, released her hand, and slowly raised his arms. Courtney's heart pounded in her chest as she did the same.

"Now turn around. Slowly."

They turned their backs to the ocean and again faced the jungle. And the scuba-clad man who had rescued them from the submerged isolation chamber on the *Mayr*. He narrowed his eyes.

"How the hell did you two get here?"

Sixty-Two

Pike had seen the severed wires poking out of the hole the moment he turned the corner into the garden. A glance through the doorway had shown him his worst nightmare. The radio transmitter lay in ruins. That must have been what had made the loud crash he had heard as he approached the mission. They were effectively cut off from rescue now. And the two people standing before him now, the very same ones he had saved from their tomb at the bottom of the sea, had destroyed their only hope of leaving this island alive. The rage boiled inside of him to that point that it threatened to explode in a fusillade of bullets.

How had he allowed this to happen? While he cursed himself for his mistake, it was one he looked forward to rectifying.

Tufts of smoke rolled past him like tumbleweeds from where they crept out of the jungle at his back. His eyes stung and his chest burned, but neither would affect his aim.

He scrutinized Bishop and Martin down the barrel of his pistol. They hadn't been among the survivors of the *Huxley*'s sinking. He would have recognized their faces among those swimming or floating to shore. They were still wearing the same scrubs as when he had last seen them on the ship. Their sagging posture and the dark rings around their eyes reflected sheer exhaustion. One glance at their feet confirmed that it was their bloody trail he'd been following, a trail that had intersected theirs from an overland course. Unless they'd abandoned ship on the opposite side of the island before the *Huxley* set sail, their path should have kept them near the coast. He could only conclude that they had been deliberately trying to avoid those of them who had managed to escape from the foundering vessel, which left him with the glaring question of why. Had they somehow contributed to running the ship onto the reef?

Then it hit him.

Courtney Martin's brother was Tyler Martin, the creature that had somehow sneaked aboard the vessel and caused its demise. What was she willing to do to protect him? Sabotage their only means of calling for evacuation, even if it meant taking the chance that they would all be killed by that very same monster? Was she so convinced that he could still be saved that she was willing to risk all of their lives?

The fearful expressions on their faces spoke volumes. They knew they had signed all of their death warrants and that's why they had run when they saw him coming.

He knew what he had to do, and he had to do it quickly before the others caught up with him and he gained an audience.

"Get down on your knees!" he shouted.

"Don't do this," Bishop said.

"You destroyed our only chance of getting off this island!"

"What are you talking about? We didn't—"

A deafening rumble drowned out his words. The ground felt as though it dropped several feet below him. He staggered to maintain his balance. The roaring, whooshing sound of high-velocity wind filled his ears. He looked back in time to be struck in the face with a roiling wall of smoke. Cinders and ash flew around him like fireflies.

The damn seismologist had been right. All of those little quakes had been building up to something, all right.

When he turned again, all he could see was a haze of smoke and the hint of the shoreline. He barked a cough and scanned the beach. He couldn't see Bishop or Martin anywhere.

He arched his back and bellowed his fury into the sky. Ash darkened the raindrops that spattered his face.

It was time to end this.

Now.

He removed his chemical gas respirator from his backpack, slipped the strap over the back of his head, and fitted the mask over his mouth and nose. The activated carbon filtered the smoke from the air. Now he had the advantage. He would be able to silently track them by the sound of their coughing, while he would remain entirely unaffected.

They couldn't have gone far. Surely they were hiding among the rock formations lining the shore. He would have seen them if they'd tried to get past him.

The ground continued to tremble as he started forward, pistol held out before him. His eyes watered, yet through the tears he could clearly see the growing waves racing in from the sea to spread across the sand at his feet, where their tracks were obvious. They led to the south, toward where the rocky shoreline reared up and became the massive stone cliffs they had been skirting all day.

With a smile, he lowered his goggles and struck off in that direction. The smoke hampered his visibility, throwing a shifting blanket of bluish-black over everything, but now there was nowhere they'd be able to hide. He would see their heat signatures long before they were able to pick his silhouette out of the smoke. Cinders fluttered across his field of view like golden snowflakes. The black tide crashed to his right. The waves were growing rougher and louder by the minute. Far up the slope to his left, a starburst of white-yellow drew his eye. Flumes and spatters and geysers fired into the air above the caldera. Magma overflowed the cone, weeping down into the forest and burning swaths through the trees.

He needed to wrap up this hunt in a hurry so he could focus on more pressing matters, like the fact that the island was self-destructing while something capable of killing them all was waiting for its opportunity to do just that. There was nothing he could do about their saboteurs other than to make sure they paid for what they had done.

A deep purple and midnight blue human shape knifed past twenty yards ahead, streaking from behind a cluster of rocks shaped like a Volkswagen Beetle toward the village.

Pike swung his pistol after it and managed only a single shot before it ducked out of sight into the forest. He was certain he had hit it, but it didn't even slow.

He wasn't falling for that ruse.

Judging by the size of the heat signature and the way it moved, he was certain that it was a male. Bishop was trying to lead him away from Martin, and in making such a desperate play had revealed his Achilles heel. All Pike had to do was take the girl, and Bishop would come to him. Quick and easy.

Two shots.

Point blank.

Done.

He walked toward the boulders, mindful of the rasping sound of his breathing through the emergency respirator. The smoke billowed around him. He could hear the others coughing all the way from the village. Surely by now Brazelton was packing them into the mission, out of the worst of the smoke, at least for the time being.

As he neared the rocks, he placed each footstep carefully so as not to make a single splash in the water. He listened for any sound to betray Martin's presence, but couldn't hear a thing over the grumble of the volcano churning smoke and magma.

A cinder stung his cheek. Suddenly he was thankful for the rain, without which the entire jungle would surely be on fire.

He eased forward to the edge of the formation, took a deep breath, and swung around to his right.

The black waves provided the only source of movement. There was no color. No body heat.

Pike raised his goggles and looked down at the sand. The waves had turned the footprints into mere water-filled impressions, which grew more defined farther inland. He followed them until he found the first clear print. There was only one set. It was large and bare, as he had expected, but there was no blood around the edges. Minimal heel contact. Deeper scoops where the ball had struck while moving at a sprint, the toes carving into the ground with teardrop—

"No," he whispered.

He looked deeper into the jungle. The branches of the shrubs still swayed in the creature's wake.

It was headed straight toward the village.

Sixty-Three

Bishop pressed Courtney back against the rock to keep her out of the direct line of fire and listened for any sound to give away Pike's location over the wind tunnel-sound of the erupting volcano, the thunder of the breakers, and the slapping of the rain. The ocean was deep enough here that they could stay mostly submerged as they clung to the crevices in the otherwise smooth formation and rode the merciless waves up and down. They were about ten yards from shore, just close enough that he could barely see the silhouettes of the tall rocks on the beach through the smoke. High above them, the fiery glow of the magma propelled a mushroom cloud of ash and debris miles into the atmosphere, while the initial front that had rushed down the slope like an avalanche was slowly beginning to dissipate. He had torn the sleeves from his shirt and soaked them in the brine. They each now held one to their mouths and noses to filter out the smoke. The fabric was already starting to blacken and lose its effectiveness.

The moment Pike had turned around as the wall of smoke struck him, Bishop had grabbed Courtney by the hand and seized the opportunity. They had sprinted south along the shore for as long as he could bear before ducking out of sight behind the first stone formation large enough to hide their intent and swam for a bird-crap encrusted rock with three sharp points like tip of a lancet. When he heard the gunshot, he had thought their ruse had failed, but the yelling that followed had become more distant with each passing second.

They couldn't afford to wait much longer. If those indecipherable shouts had been Pike calling for backup, then it was only a matter of time before the entire beach was staked out and there would be nowhere to sneak ashore. With the way the waves continued to grow, he didn't like their chances of swimming for it. Besides, where could they possibly go?

Courtney retched behind her makeshift mask.

"Dip it in the water and ring it out again," he said directly into her ear. "Be ready to swim for the shore when I tell you."

A foaming wave nearly submerged her as she nodded her understanding. They both cleaned the tatters of fabric and replaced them over the lower halves of their faces.

Bishop peeled apart every sound as well as he could. He couldn't hear a blasted thing over nature's wrath.

"The moment we reach dry ground, run south as fast as you can. If we get separated for any reason, head straight for the *Huxley*. I'll meet you there."

"Why do you want to go back there? There's nothing left."

"It's our only hope of escape."

"The ship's destroyed. What could we possibly—?"

He took her gently by the upper arm and looked her directly in the eyes.

"Do you trust me, Courtney?"

Her eyes searched his for a long moment before she finally nodded.

He pulled the mask away from his face and leaned close enough that he could whisper into her ear.

"I'm not going to let anything happen to you." He kissed her neck. "I promise."

A wave nearly tore them both off of the rock.

"Are you ready?"

She nodded.

"Then swim for it!"

Bishop released her and stroked for the shore. The moment his feet struck sand, he struggled to stand and staggered out of the sea. All he could see through the smoke were the hazy outlines of the rocks around them and the trees at the edge of the jungle. There was no sudden movement, no gunfire. He whirled, took Courtney by the hand, and sprinted down the shoreline as fast as his aching feet and the wet sand would allow.

He tried not to think about the odds of his plan working. It was a long shot at best, but it was their only chance.

There was no doubt in his mind that if his idea failed, they were going to die on this island.

Sixty-Four

"There has to be a way!" Reaves's voice rose to an unmanly shriek. Who would have done this to the radio? Whoever did might as well have murdered them himself. And if the creature had done this...if it was smart enough to recognize and disable their sole means of contacting help, then they were already as good as dead. "You're supposed to be the electronics expert! Fix it, for Christ's sake!"

"I'm telling you, it's beyond repair!" Barnes snapped back. "This thing is older than I am! I'm not even sure I'd be able to fix it if all of the parts weren't broken to pieces."

"You have to try! This is our only hope!"

Bradley rested a hand on Reaves's shoulder in an effort to calm him before his fear gave way to panic. Reaves knew there was nothing that could be done. The components spread across the ground looked like they'd been smashed by a hammer.

"Mr. Barnes," Bradley said in a maddeningly composed voice. "Is there anything here you could use to amplify the signal from our transceivers?"

"Maybe if given enough time, but even then I couldn't hope to broaden the range by more than a couple of kilometers. We're still talking line-of-sight. We'd have to be able to see a ship on the horizon to have any chance of reaching it."

"Do you think we could salvage enough parts from the *Huxley* to repair the radio?"

"As soon as the electrical system submerged, everything undoubtedly fried. Even if we could dive through the wreckage and find what we need, it would be useless."

"The majority of the stern had yet to sink when we left. If it's still above water, then surely we could find something you could use to repair this. Aren't the majority of the electrical and engineering rooms aft near the submersible hanger?"

"Maybe, I..." Barnes paused and appeared lost in thought. Reaves coughed and readjusted his shirt over his nose and mouth. The smoke lingered in the garden behind the refectory as though held captive by the quadrangle walls. He glanced nervously up into the clouds for the hundredth time. The entire rim of the cone was now on fire where the magma rolled through the forest like molten cake batter. He didn't know a blasted thing about volcanoes or how long it would continue to erupt, but he did know that he sure as hell didn't want to still be here if the lava flows reached the beach. "What would you suggest? That we swim out there? It has to be easily half a kilometer and you saw what happened to all of those people. How many actually made it to shore?"

"I just want to know if it's possible, Mr. Barnes."

Reaves held his breath while he waited for the answer. Over the wall, flames took root in the smoldering thatch roof of the neighboring hut. When Barnes finally spoke, it was in little more than a whisper.

"Yes. It's possible. But if the stern's underwater by the time we reach it, we're screwed."

"That's all I needed to know, Mr. Barnes," Bradley said. Reaves recognized the faraway look in his old friend's eyes, the very same look he had seen when they first returned to the surface from under the kiva in Chaco Canyon. It was that same expression of determination that had initially launched this lifelong quest. Maybe there was still hope after all.

Banging sounds from inside the mission drew his attention. He glanced through the doorway into the priest's quarters. Through the opening to the interior courtyard, he could see shadows cast by flashlights dancing on the walls and the floor. Brazelton had gathered the others to begin barricading the windows and doors from the inside. While that tactic might save them from whatever hunted them and the threat of suffocating in the smoke, if the lava and fires continued their relentless advance, the ancient building would burn like kindling soaked in gasoline. The old mission positively breathed desiccated straw and timber particles.

"How long do we have before sunset?" Bradley asked.

"You want to make a run for the *Huxley* now?" Reaves asked.

"With all of this smoke, would we even be able to tell the difference?" Barnes said.

The words struck Reaves hard enough to knock the wind out of him. With all of the smoke, visibility was nearly nonexistent. Add the cloud cover from the storm and the sun might as well have already set for all the good it did them.

The creature didn't need for it to be night.

It only needed darkness.

"Oh, God," Reaves whispered. He felt the truth of the words before he even spoke them. "It's already here."

Sixty-Five

Without a doubt, Pike had definitely hit it. At the edge of the forest, the ground and the leaves of a shrub were spattered with fuchsia, which slowly darkened to a deep blue before his eyes. It was no insignificant wound, for the same midnight blue droplets and smears guided him through the dense foliage. The creature was losing blood fairly rapidly, but not at the life-threatening pace Pike would have preferred. He had to carefully monitor the speed with which he tracked it. If he went too slowly, the drops would cool to the same temperature as the ground and become invisible; too fast and he could end up stumbling upon the creature where it lay in wait. From everything he had learned about this monster so far, he couldn't rule out the possibility that it was using its own blood to lure him to his death.

He knew he should call ahead and inform the others of what was headed in their direction, but he feared that even the sound of his whispered warning into the transceiver would tip off his prey, if it wasn't already aware that he was following it. If it was as smart as he thought it was, then it would recognize him as its most immediate threat and attempt to isolate and eliminate him first before engaging the group as a whole.

Right now, it was just the two of them. Him against the beast. He had the weapon and the skills to use it. It was a wounded animal, which made it even more deadly.

One of them was going to die within the next few minutes, and he sure as hell didn't intend for it to be him.

Pike emerged from the jungle into the southernmost ring of huts. He covered the clearing with his pistol, expecting the creature to come streaking at him from behind any one of the stilted dwellings, yet all he saw were the bodies strewn across the ground and the diminishing pattern of blue splotches heading due north toward the mission. He glimpsed a momentary flash of magenta through the trees and broke into a sprint. When he reached the section of the jungle that separated the halves of the village, he again slowed and proceeded more cautiously.

The forest faded away to either side as he stepped out into the open. Ahead of him, the bell tower rose into the smoke. He heard the muffled sound of voices from behind the building.

There was no sign of movement other than the ash that swirled in the air and accumulated in drifts against the tree trunks like snow, which made the droplets of blood coagulate into beads. They led him not directly toward the mission as he had expected, but in the direction of the adjacent hut to the west. He crouched first to make sure that it wasn't hiding under the raised floor, then focused on the dark entryway. Only shadows waited inside. He was nearly upon the hut when he noticed a blue-black smear, not on the ground, but on the reeds that formed the roof. Why would it—?

And then he saw the matching smudge on top of the quadrangle wall beside it and the thin ribbons running down the side. It must have climbed the wooden construct and leapt onto the wall. There were blue handprints on the steep, tiled roof of the mission. He caught a flash of fuchsia over the roofline, a mere blurred silhouette, before it plummeted out of sight into the enclosed courtyard.

Sixty-Six

Bradley was walking through the priest's quarters toward the inner patio, where he was prepared to tell Brazelton that he was headed back to the *Huxley* to salvage the parts they needed to fix the radio and that no one would be able to dissuade him, when he heard the first scream. A silver comet streaked toward the ground at the edge of his peripheral vision. By the time he turned in that direction, arcs of blood filled the air. He saw the startled expression on Libby's face contort into a cry of fear and pain before she was hurled to the ground. The blood splashed down on her back and rapidly expanded in a pool beneath her.

There was a flash of eyeshine from the shadows near the ground, where a figure crouched momentarily before springing to its feet and hurtling across the courtyard.

Brazelton shouted and gunfire echoed in the confines. Chips of tile and marble exploded from the tiered fountain in the center of the sanctum as the silver blur passed. Brazelton was still firing off round after round when it struck him. His war cry metamorphosed into a horrible scream as he hit the ground with the creature on his chest. It buried its face into his neck and Brazelton fell abruptly silent. An arc of blood patterned the adobe wall above his head.

Everything was happening too quickly. The creature moved like lightning, a flash of liquid mercury and it was a dozen paces away from Brazelton's crumpled body. Bradley uprooted his feet and turned to flee.

There was a banging sound from the front door, as though something large were being repeatedly slammed against it.

Angie's screams reverberated from the walls. From the corner of his eye, he saw her dart out of the doorway to the sacristy and make a break for the front door.

Bradley passed through the short corridor into the refectory and barreled into Barnes and Reaves in their hurry to see what was happening. He lost his balance and sent all three of them tumbling to the floor.

Behind him, Angie's screams grew even louder.

"No!" Reaves shouted and tried to crawl out from beneath him.

Bradley glanced back in time to see Angie lunge for the door, but the creature was faster. It closed the distance and launched itself at her with the speed and ferocity of a striking adder. Its body eclipsed hers as they slammed against the wooden construct. Her hair flared in a golden corona as the creature's mouth latched onto the side of her throat. The expression on her face was the most awful thing Bradley had ever seen; a mixture of terror, agony, and the comprehension that her life was at an end.

Blood spurted from her neck like the first bite from an overripe orange.

And she screamed no more.

Angie's body slid down the bloodstained door as someone continued to beat against it from the other side. A solid impact split the wood and toppled her forward onto her face.

The creature turned toward them. Its entire face shimmered with crimson, save for the twin reflective disks of its eyes. Slowly, it lowered to its haunches in a sinewy movement reminiscent of a serpent coiling, and bared a nest of hooked teeth that curled under in interlocking fashion. Some poked through its lips like piercings.

"It's magnificent," Bradley whispered.

It sprung toward them like a panther, leading with its outstretched arms, which it used to push off from the ground and propel itself into the air long enough to get its legs underneath it.

The door burst inward behind it, sending broken chunks of wood flying in all directions.

The silver blur crossed the courtyard so quickly that Bradley barely had time to throw his arms up in front of his face.

He heard the resounding crack of gunfire and felt warmth on his hands and face before the weight of the creature slammed down on him. The crown of his head struck the wall. He cried out and threw himself away from the creature. He expected to feel talons slashing through his skin or those hideous teeth sinking into his neck.

When he finally slid out from underneath it, his torso was sloppy with blood. The creature was facedown on top of Reaves and Barnes, who punched at it to get it off of them. Its long silver legs spasmed and its toenails carved at the planks with a screeching sound, but it made no effort to rise.

Across the room, he saw Pike climbing through what was left of the front door, his unwavering pistol pointed directly at the body at Bradley's feet. Pike didn't even look down at Angie as he stepped over her body, or at Brazelton or Libby, whose corpses were on opposite sides of the fountain. He strode directly toward Bradley and stood over the creature.

"Stand back." Pike directed the barrel of his pistol at the back of the creature's head. "We can't afford to take any chances."

Sixty-Seven

The final gunshot echoed from the face of the volcano, where a steady stream of lava and flames advanced downhill toward them.

Courtney waited for another shot to come, but was rewarded with only silence. From where they knelt in a blind of shrubs and wild grasses, they could barely see the silhouetted huts and the mission though the smoke that clung to the treetops and drifted through the clearing.

"What's happening down there?" she whispered.

"I don't know," Bishop said. "I can't see a thing."

The moment she heard the first screams, Courtney had stopped and turned toward the source, knowing full well where they had originated.

"We have to keep moving," Bishop had said, but she'd been frozen in place.

If there was screaming, then undoubtedly her brother couldn't be far away. She needed to see him with her own eyes, needed irrefutable proof as to whether or not it was really him. Even if they managed to escape the island, she couldn't possibly spend the rest of her life wondering if it truly was him. And she wouldn't be able to live with the thought that she had abandoned him when he had needed her the most. While Bishop had been less than thrilled about the prospect of giving up a single second of their head start, he had reluctantly agreed to seek a better vantage point from which to view the village from afar.

They crawled forward into a blind of shrubs until they could see the roofs of the huts beside the *campanile*.

She tried to decipher any sound over the rumbling ground and the pounding surf. Were those barely audible voices in the distance or just the roar of the fire consuming the island? A flicker of lightning, a mere gray discoloration through the ceiling of smoke, preceded a peal of thunder.

What if they were all dead down there and whatever killed them was now silently stalking Bishop and her through the jungle? Or what if Pike and the others had survived and the monster they assumed to be her brother hadn't?

"I need to know," she whispered.

She could feel the weight of Bishop's stare, but she couldn't bring herself to look at him.

"Courtney..."

"If Tyler's down there...If there's any way I could have helped him and didn't..."

"Those people had guns. If they didn't make it, what chance do we have?"

"I know my brother. There's no way he would ever hurt me. Regardless of the situation...or what he might have become."

"You're willing to take that risk?"

"What other choice do I have?"

"You know he would have wanted you to be safe at all costs. He never would have allowed you to put yourself in danger. Even for him."

"But he would have done just that for me. What kind of person would I be if I weren't willing to do the same?"

"You'd be alive, Courtney." He placed his hand on top of hers. "That's the most important thing. *I* need you to stay alive. I'm not letting go of you this easily."

"What if they got him? What if he's lying down there bleeding to death? What if there's something I can do to help him?" She paused for a long moment before resuming in a voice so quiet even she could hardly hear it. "What if this is my only opportunity to say goodbye?"

The rain continued to beat down on them, clearing the sludge of ash and tears from her cheeks. She wrung out her essentially useless mask in a puddle more mud than water and covered her face again.

"Whoever survived down there will be coming for us soon anyway," she whispered. "At least if we can get close enough to see, we'll know what we're up against."

"If we can see them, they can see us."

"Better to look death in the eye than to listen for his footsteps."

"You're not going to let this go, are you?"

The corners of her lips curled upward into the ghost of a smile and she finally turned to look at him.

"Okay," he said. "We're only getting close enough to figure out what happened. No closer. And as soon as we can tell what's going on down there, we're out of here. Do we have a deal?"

It didn't matter if she agreed out loud or not. He was only saying the words for his own benefit. Surely by now he knew that if her brother was down there, nothing on this planet would be able to keep her away.

"What made you change your mind?" she whispered as they started down through the forest.

"I don't see where I ever had a choice."

Sixty-Eight

"God...hurts..." Angie sputtered through a mouthful of blood. It flowed over her chin and down her neck, where it merged with the rest. The glistening wound in her throat revealed the tattered musculature, tendons, and trachea, despite Reaves's best efforts to hold it closed. Blood sluiced out from between his fingers onto her drenched chest, which hitched with every futile breath. Her eyes were already glassy, a look Pike had seen hundreds of times before. She was a goner, and there was absolutely nothing any of them could do about it. The humane thing to do would be to end her suffering, but he knew damn well how the others would react if he suggested a bullet to the temple, so he didn't waste his breath.

"You're going to be all right," Reaves whispered over and over. He stroked the side of her face with his free hand, which only served to smear crimson across her cheek. She didn't even blink her eyes when he grazed her lashes.

Pike brushed past them and stepped through the remains of the front door. With a groan, he flopped Libby's carcass off of his shoulder and onto the ground. Her wide eyes stared past him into the heavens. Brazelton's body lay beside hers, his throat opened to such a degree that Pike had barely been able to keep the head attached when he carried it out here. Bradley handed him the blankets they had stripped from the priest's bed and he wrapped each of them in turn, bundling them like so many pupae. The blood soaked through in Rorschach patterns. If a stray cinder were to ignite the decrepit mission, no one wanted the bodies to be incinerated inside. They only needed to be saved from the scavengers long enough to be retrieved and shipped back home for burial. Or at least that was Bradley's plan. Pike had other plans for their permanent disposal, assuming the lava didn't claim them first, which was starting to look like a distinct, and welcomed, possibility. It was his job to protect GeNext and make sure that no one ever learned what had happened on this island.

He set aside the remaining sheet, knowing it would only be a matter of minutes before Dr. Whitted needed it. Once she was similarly prepared, they could cover all three with the plastic tarps they had found in the sacristy, where they were draped over the shelves of supposedly holy relics to shield them from the holes in the rotting roof.

Pike turned at the sound of footsteps to see Reaves framed in the demolished door. His face was a deathly shade of pale. He somehow stared both beyond them and through them when he spoke.

"She's gone," he said, then disappeared back inside.

"Would you mind...?" Bradley asked.

Pike walked through the door to collect her remains and nearly ran into Reaves as the anthropologist carried her body across the threshold. He laid her down almost lovingly on the ground beside the others and carefully bound her in the sheet.

"She's getting wet," Reaves said. He tilted his face to the sky, but made no effort to block the rain. "I don't want her to get wet."

Bradley clapped him softly on the back and glanced at Pike, who agreed to the unvoiced request with a nod. He went back inside, collected the tarps, and covered the three bodies. He weighted the edges down with stones. The raindrops tap-danced on the plastic.

Now came the part he'd been waiting for. Since all of the human needs had been formally met, it was time to tend to the inhuman.

He headed back into the building, gathered the last tarp, and crossed the courtyard toward the refectory. The body was sprawled exactly where he had left it. Spatters of blood and gray matter painted the floor around its head. The pool of blood from the exit wound in its forehead was already becoming sticky. The crater at the back of its head was framed by fragments of bone. Pike hoped the rain had cleansed him of the blowback, but with how tight the skin around the corners of his mouth felt, he wasn't counting on it.

It had proven itself a worthy adversary, but in the end, it was just another animal.

He rolled the corpse onto its back and maneuvered it onto the spread tarp. Clenching the plastic in his fists, he dragged it toward the door. He knew it was already too late, but he wanted to minimize the amount of the creature's blood he got on his skin. Lord only knew what kind of viruses and bacteria wriggled through it, none of which he particularly wanted to infect him.

As he neared the front door, he heard Reaves softly crying.

"Suck it up, for God's sake," he whispered. He dragged the body out into the rain and across the clearing toward the tree line, where Barnes continued to dig in the muddy ground at the base of a kapok tree with an old, rusted shovel. The site was exactly one hundred paces due south of the mission's keystone at the southwest corner. Even if the entire village and the surrounding forest burned, they would still be able to find this spot.

He heard sloshing footsteps behind him as Bradley and Reaves followed him across the clearing.

Barnes had made less progress than Pike would have liked, but the hole was probably large enough to serve their purposes. He didn't want to waste any more time here than they absolutely had to. The important thing was to get it buried in such a way that when they returned to the island they could find it and exhume it as quickly and easily as possible.

"I still don't understand why we don't just torch the bastard." Barnes cast aside the shovel and looked at anything other than the cargo on the tarp. "I'd be happy to do the honors."

Pike didn't feel like expending the energy to reply. It didn't matter what Barnes thought. After all, he wouldn't be around after he fixed the radio with the parts they needed to gather from the *Huxley*. Like the others, his would just be another of the bodies decomposing in the silt at the bottom of the reef.

But at least now that the creature was no longer a threat, he had the freedom to implement his plan on his own timeframe and as he saw fit, beginning with the interment of their ultimate prize.

"Can I borrow your flashlight?" Bradley asked.

Pike studied him for a long moment before removing the Maglite from his backpack and handing it to him.

"Thank you." Bradley knelt beside the creature's corpse and directed the beam down at it. "I just wanted to...look at it...one last time."

"We'll be coming back for it soon enough," Pike said.

Bradley offered a wistful smile.

"One never knows."

He shined the light onto its face. The beam reflected dimly from behind the creature's clouded eyes.

Sixty-Nine

Courtney closed her eyes and stifled a startled gasp. Tears streamed down her cheeks. Her lips quivered. The entire world seemed to simultaneously drop out from beneath her and spin on a titling fulcrum. Bishop tensed beside her and squeezed her hand even tighter. She thought she had been prepared for what she would see, but nothing could have been further from the truth. When they had crept close enough to the mission to see Pike and Bradley in the clearing and the expressions on their faces, she had known the outcome of the firefight. She had felt it as a cold knot in her gut. If her brother really had become the monster, then his fate was decided. Whatever misguided hope she had held that she might be able to save him was now every bit as dead as he was.

But there was still the possibility that the others were wrong, that Tyler hadn't become what they thought he had. Of course, that undoubtedly meant that he hadn't survived the sinking of the *Mayr*. If that were the case, she would still never be able to see him again, never be able to say all of the things she wished she had said while he was alive, but at least she still had the opportunity to honor his memory by proving that he wasn't responsible for all of the death, if only to herself. It was the least she could do for the man who had always been there to protect and encourage her, even when she didn't believe in herself.

She and Bishop were maybe five yards away, crouching inside a broad-leaved bush spotted with white blossoms. The sound of their approach had been muffled by the crunching noises of the computer technician she recognized from the *Huxley* digging what she now realized was a grave. They had dared encroach no closer for fear of discovery, and had watched in horror as Pike carried body after body out of the ruined mission door. When none of them had been moved to the single grave, she had recognized precisely whom it was for, and shifted so that she could clearly see it, if nothing else.

And now that she'd seen the condition of the body, she wished she hadn't.

She forced herself to open her eyes. Bradley knelt to the corpse's right, the beam of his flashlight reflecting from the grayish skin...no, scales...that covered every inch of the naked form. She recognized the texture and coloration, although now subdued by death, as that of the skin condition that had afflicted her brother the last time she had seen him. An exit wound bloomed from its forehead, a strange flower composed of white chips of bone, furled gray matter, and congealed blood. She couldn't clearly see its eyes in their recesses. It slender nose tapered to a blunt point above teeth that protruded from its bulging mouth and even through its lips.

Pike used a stick to prod what could have been another exit wound just below its left clavicle.

"Through and through," he said. "Son of a bitch should have been in some serious pain."

Courtney flinched at the comment and had to suppress the urge to storm out of hiding and punch him squarely in the jaw. Bishop must have sensed her thoughts. He again squeezed her hand, or perhaps tightened his grip to keep her from charging.

"Look at its hands," Reaves whispered barely loud enough for her to hear. He raised the left arm and fanned he blood-crusted fingers apart. The fingernails had grown into claws that more closely resembled those of a lizard than the talons of a bird, but she realized that wasn't what he was referring to. A thin membrane stretched between the first knuckles of each finger. "They're webbed."

Lightning flickered overhead. The subsequent thunder was indistinguishable from the rumbling sounds of the island.

Bradley lowered the flashlight from the hand back down to the head. A puzzled expression crinkled his face. He turned the face away from him and shined the beam at the side of its neck, just below the base of its jaw. He reached out, withdrew his hand, and then tentatively touched it with his trembling fingers. When he stroked the skin from back to front, fringes peeled apart like the pages of a book. He glanced up at Reaves and then at Pike before looking back down. Carefully, he parted two of the folds and stuck his thumb and index finger inside the creature's neck. When he pulled them out, they pinched pinkish-gray flaps of tissue with edges like a dulled circular saw blade.

As a marine biologist, Courtney immediately recognized what they were.

Gills.

A cloud of smoke passed between them, momentarily obscuring her view.

"We need to get moving," Bishop whispered directly into her ear, "while they're still distracted."

She knew he was right, but she couldn't bring herself to leave. Not yet. Not until she was certain one way or the other. The problem was that there was still so little of his former humanity left that she couldn't discern a single specific characteristic. She couldn't see the birthmark on his left shoulder of the scar on his chest for the scales. She couldn't see his eyes or his smile or any of the facial expressions she probably knew better than her own. She couldn't hear his voice or see the way he walked. If this really was her brother, then there was absolutely nothing left of him in that lifeless vessel with the crater in its forehead. All she had to go on was her gut reaction, and whether rational or not, it was insistent.

Courtney wiped away her tears and crawled quietly out of the bushes behind Bishop. They stayed low to the ground as they wended a circuitous route up the hillside, clinging to the deepest cover they could find. All the while, she rehearsed the images in her mind. The scaled skin. The clawed and webbed hands like a frog's. The gills. The teeth. The long legs with the severe toenails. Her instinctive reaction gave way to certainty. She didn't know how she knew for sure. She just did.

She waited until they crested the first ridge to finally put voice to the words.

"That wasn't my brother."

Seventy

Reaves watched Pike wrap the body in the tarp and pack the dirt back over the impromptu grave. Pike kicked the detritus back into place and covered it with a mat of branches. Reaves wondered why he even bothered, considering the whole island was going to burn. He prayed none of them would return to this accursed spot to exhume the remains. Nothing good could ever come from the knowledge contained within its genetic code. The world was not now, nor would it ever be, ready for its secrets to be revealed. Within this one specimen was enough ammunition to drive humanity to extinction a hundred times over, enough to remake mankind not in God's image, but in myriad ways unbounded even by the wildest imagination.

Mere feet under the ground lay temptation greater even than Eve tasted. This corpse was the new forbidden fruit, one metaphorical bite from which would insure not a mere fall from grace, but an abrupt evolutionary end.

This was God's wrath, His ultimate failsafe.

This was the ticking bomb at the Earth's core.

This was how the slate would be cleaned.

Reaves shivered, wrapped his arms around his chest, and watched the rain puddle on the gravesite. He couldn't bear to turn around and see the filthy tarp covering Angie's body. Her final breath still rattled in his ears on a continuous loop over which even the sound of the volcano spewing their demise was a blessing. The rain absolved him of her blood, which had covered the entirety of the left side of his face and his shirt. He cursed himself for how casual they had kept their relationship. There had always been a tomorrow for two people so invested in their careers, that mythical day when their stars would align and they would be together. Now there were no more tomorrows. Not for them. The thing that had brought them together had irrevocably torn them apart. He had invited her into their inner circle, and, as such, he was responsible for her death. For all of their deaths. And if anyone ever came back to claim this body, he would be responsible for the extinction of his species.

You're being melodramatic, he could hear Bradley saying, which was why he couldn't share his feelings with his longtime friend. Bradley would never understand the evolutionary ramifications should man begin to experiment with things like this, with which he was never meant to coexist. All along that had been Bradley's intent, and for the longest time it had been his, as well. Finding this creature—or, to be brutally honest, *creating* this creature—had been their shared obsession. And now what did they have to show for it? More than a hundred dead and a former human being whose life had been usurped by the bacterium that would be the destroyer of mankind.

He pictured the hollow eyes and the mouth full of hooked teeth like those of a shark.

If mankind had been made in God's image, then whose visage was this?

He feared nothing more than finding out in the eternity of damnation ahead.

"Time to get moving," Pike said. "I want the radio fixed and running before nightfall. We're getting off this rock."

"The sooner the better," Barnes said. "I don't want to stick around long enough to find out how far that lava's going to flow."

"At least we don't have to worry about what's sneaking up behind us anymore," Bradley said through the mask he had commandeered from Brazelton's supplies. Reaves wasn't jealous in the slightest. He had appropriated something of his own.

"That doesn't mean this is going to be a leisurely stroll," Pike said. "We can't afford to waste any time."

Pike whirled and struck off to the south at a rapid click without bothering to glance back to make sure that the rest of them were coming.

Reaves stood his ground. He turned around to see the rain-beaded tarp by the front door of the mission. One of the corners had peeled free and flapped on the breeze. He could see Angie's slender lower legs and feet.

"We're not just leaving them…like this…are we?" he asked.

"You can stay and keep them company, if you want," Pike called back. There was an almost mocking tone in his voice. "Although I imagine you'll have to carry the conversation."

Reaves felt sick to his stomach. This was the road he had chosen, the one he had sacrificed his career, his entire world, to travel. How had he not seen that this had always been his ultimate destination?

In his mind, he saw Angie smiling at him, giving him that devilish wink of hers.

This was his mess to clean up, and he intended to do just that.

He started forward slowly, one step at a time, then jogged to catch up with the others, but he had to slow his pace when the object he'd tucked under his waistband nearly bounced out. He readjusted the Beretta he had found by Brazelton's body and made sure that his shirt concealed it.

No one could ever return to this island to claim the knowledge that body contained.

Pandora's Box had to remain closed.

Regardless of the cost.

Seventy-One

Bishop was silent for a long moment as he contemplated his words carefully. If there was a right thing to say, it eluded him. Courtney's suffering was written all over her face, and while he wanted nothing more than to make her feel better, he feared the emotional ramifications of fueling a potential fantasy. If she were to find out that the body the men at the mission had been in such a hurry to bury was her brother's, it would crush her, yet at the same time, hope was worth its weight in gold. In order to elude the men who undoubtedly were already coming after them, they needed to stay sharp. Both of them. He wouldn't be able to pull off what he had in mind alone.

"How can you be sure?" he finally asked.

The tower of ash expanded overhead to the point that it nearly reached the far horizon to the west, where the Pacific met the sky. The lightning display no longer even penetrated the roiling cloud, and the raindrops fell dark and heavy. Ash had finally begun to descend from the heavens like snowflakes, decorating the leaves overhead and carpeting swatches of the ground, which they avoided to prevent leaving pristine footprints. Smoke wafted around them like a fog rolling out to sea, where the waves pounding against the breakers and the sheer limestone escarpments alternately appeared and disappeared. From uphill to his left, the flames heralding the advance of the lava were an orangish smear through the smothering smoke. He had already been forced to shed his shirt and tear it into straps in order to provide fresh fabric to cover their mouths. The ash in the air could accumulate in their lungs and asphyxiate them in no time flat.

"You don't believe me," she whispered barely loud enough to be heard over the grumble of the eruption.

"Of course I believe you. I just want to know.... Was it something you saw? A physical trait? Something you recognized? Some small detail? Anything?"

"There was just something that wasn't quite…right. I can't put my finger on it, exactly, but I know beyond any shadow of doubt that what we just saw was not my brother."

Bishop nodded and helped her across a thin stream. His feet were killing him, but he wasn't about to stick them in the water, which had been heated uphill to the point that steam rose from it.

They needed to pick up their pace if they wanted to keep from losing their head start. Once they reached the *Huxley*, he figured they would need at least half an hour to execute his plan, and that was the best case scenario. If they reached the ship and found that everything wasn't set up like he hoped, then they were in big trouble.

"If that wasn't your brother, then who could it possibly be?" Bishop asked.

They walked in silence for several minutes before Courtney finally spoke.

"You don't have any siblings, do you?"

"No."

"Then you wouldn't understand. There's a bond…I don't know how to describe it. When you see someone nearly every day of your life…When you watch them grow and change in subtle ways, you come to see them as a combination of who they were, who they are, and who'll they'll become at the same time. It's not a psychic connection or anything metaphysical like that. It's more like…" She paused as a flock of startled parrots shot through the canopy above them and continued out over the ocean. "It's like there's a person inside the body that only you can see, a person that's been revealed to you in ways that make it so that you can recognize them despite their outward appearance, not because of it."

Bishop debated whether or not he should even attempt to vocalize his thoughts. He decided the question was crucial to determining her state of mind. If he wasn't going to be able to count on her, he needed to know now.

"Then you know what that means?"

"That Tyler's probably dead?" She stated it so bluntly that it surprised him. "Yeah. I understand the implications. But you'll have to forgive me if I'm not willing to give up on him just yet. We managed to survive. Who's to say he didn't?"

Bishop smiled. That was precisely what he needed to hear.

"Once we get off this island and find help, I promise we'll come back and tear every inch of this jungle and the reef apart until we find him."

"We?"

"You aren't planning on ditching me just yet, are you?"

She squeezed his hand.

"You're that confident you're going to be able to get us out of here?"

"Not a doubt in my mind." He hoped he sounded more convincing than he felt.

"You're a rotten liar."

"I prefer to call it optimism."

"And if you're wrong?"

He offered a crooked smile.

"How far do you think you can swim?"

Seventy-Two

Pike had picked up the trail before they were even out of sight of the village. For as discreet as Bishop and Martin were being, they might as well have been leaving behind bread crumbs. The broken branches, the trampled shrubs, the bare footprints in the ash. They had doubled back toward the mission instead of fleeing while they had the chance. Had they taken off when Pike was distracted by the creature and the pending siege, they could have been miles ahead by now. So why had they taken the risk to come back?

Martin.

She needed to see with her own eyes if the creature was truly her brother. He hoped she liked what she saw, because her curiosity was about to get her killed. The fact that their tracks had yet to be covered by the settling ash and the bushes they'd stomped still hadn't sprung back into place meant that they couldn't be more than half an hour ahead of them on the path.

And it was obvious where they were headed.

There was something they needed aboard the *Huxley*. Otherwise they would have fled in any number of directions. If they had been the ones who disabled the radio in the village, as he had begun to seriously doubt, then were they planning on destroying any components that could possibly be used to fix it? No, they hadn't broken the radio. The creature must have crippled it to prevent someone in the village from calling for help before the slaughter commenced. At the sound of the first screams, surely someone would have gone straight for their sole means of signaling the outside world. Bishop and Martin had gone to the village for the exact same reason that his group had. They wanted to get off this island. They knew that even if they survived the creature, there was no way they would be allowed to tell the world about what they had seen. Making a run for the *Huxley* was a desperate ploy. What did they hope to accomplish?

Surely they didn't think they could round up the necessary electronics, sneak back past them, and fix the radio without getting caught. And destroying the components was a fool's proposition. They had to know that if Pike's party wasn't able to leave the island, he would spend every waking moment hunting them down like dogs. The satellite tower had been ripped from the roof of the wheelhouse. There was no power, no functional computers. The EPIRB beacon was only designed to broadcast an emergency distress signal, not any kind of outgoing message. Diving for the weapons cache would be a waste of time. The magnetic lock would have shorted in the locked position, and even were they able to open it, whatever was inside would be all but useless after prolonged immersion in the brine. With the way the waves were rolling in, there was no way they would be able to paddle the massive life rafts past the breakers by themselves, not without some form out outboard motor, and he couldn't think of any craft on the research vessel equipped with—

Pike laughed out loud.

"Well, what do you know," he said.

This changed everything.

How had he not seen it right from the start?

He amended his plan on the fly. Not only were they getting off this rock, they were doing so tonight. By this time tomorrow, they'd return with a new ship to collect their prize and erase any sign that they'd ever been on the island. He couldn't have asked for things to work out any better.

Pike glanced back over his shoulder at the others. They'd fallen so far behind that he could barely see them through the maze of vegetation. They trudged with their heads down, dead on their feet. He debated simply leaving them, or perhaps putting each of them down right now, but the time wasn't right. Not yet. He still needed their help.

And while he would like to get Bradley safely back to the mainland in order to cash in on all of his hard work and capitalize on the leverage he suddenly had on his employer, he realized that he now held all of the cards.

If he was the only one to survive this ordeal, then he would have sole possession of the corpse and the secrets it contained. He could write his own ticket. How much would any of GeNext's competitors be willing to pay for the knowledge they could glean from one of its legs? A foot? A single toe? How much would someone like Amgen be willing to pay for its brain? He could auction off the parts to the highest bidders and make more money than any human being had ever amassed, not just the paltry bonus Bradley would pay him for saving his pathetic life.

He smiled.

If none of the others survived, no one would ever know.

"Hurry up back there!" he called.

He had a long journey ahead of him.

But first, they all had a date with destiny.

Seventy-Three

Courtney barely had the strength to keep going. Her feet were badly cut and she had passed the point of exhaustion long ago. And now she had to fight against her failing body with sheer will alone, the will to persevere, the will to survive. Wherever Ty was now, she knew that was what he would have wanted, what he would have expected from her. While it was a relief that he hadn't become what everyone believed he had, she understood that his remains might never be recovered, that she would never learn what had happened to him. With that realization came a marrow-deep sorrow that threatened to rob her of her fading resolve.

In her mind, she saw the scaled, gray carcass spread out on the tarp beside the shallow grave. The structure of the facial bones was all wrong, even with the mutations. And the legs were too long. The corpse was too tall to be her brother's.

She had suspected where Bishop was leading her the entire time, but it wasn't until the sound of the waves thundering against the cliffs softened to the roar of the ocean raging against the beach that she knew for sure. Through the trees, she saw the whitecaps rolling into the bay and sweeping all the way up across the sand and into the forest. The smoke hung above the water like a fog, so dense she could hardly see the life rafts floating fifty yards from shore as though trying to battle their way past the breakers, which were now little more than crests of rock that disappeared beneath every tall wave. She pondered the prospect of trying to paddle one of the inflatable orange crafts out to sea, but with the way the sea roiled, they would never escape the bay. And even if they did, where could they possibly go? They'd be adrift in the midst of a storm on the furious Pacific and possibly swept away from Papua New Guinea rather than toward it. By the time anyone happened to come across them, they could be long dead from exposure or dehydration or any number of things. She felt suddenly deflated.

All of the hardship, everything they had endured, had been for naught.

Her legs gave out and she fell to all fours at the edge of the jungle. Water raced through the detritus and over her wrists and knees. She started to cry when the saltwater found her wounds.

"Come on, Courtney." Bishop eased her back to her feet and helped steady her. "We still have our work cut out for us."

"We'll never make it," she whispered. "Without motors, those rafts will never clear the bay."

"Who said anything about rafts?" The corner of his mouth lilted into a crooked grin. "Are you ready to get wet?"

"I'm already drenched." She held her arms out to her sides to showcase her saturated scrubs, from which rivulets of water already drained. Her auburn hair hung in clumps that partially obscured her face. "How much wetter could I possibly get?"

"We're going to have to swim for it."

She looked him in the eyes in an effort to gauge if he was making a poor excuse for a joke. In them, she saw only determination.

"You're out of your mind." She turned away and let her arms fall to her sides in exasperation. "We're nearly sixty kilometers from the nearest landmass."

"We don't have to go nearly that far." He pointed to the southwest, where the wreckage of the *Huxley* drifted in and out of the smoke. The stern stood from the reef at roughly a twenty-degree angle, and the ocean had risen halfway to the submersible hanger. It wouldn't be long before the reef gave way and it settled to the ocean floor with the bow. "We just have to make it to the ship."

Courtney started to laugh, but stopped when she saw that he was serious.

"And then what? Sail away? Hide and wait for it to sink? We did that once before, remember? How well did that work out?"

"You're going to have to trust me, Courtney." The smirk returned. "Can you make it that far?"

"What's on the ship?"

"If I'm right, our ticket off of this island."

"And if you're wrong?"

"Do you think you can swim that far or not?"

"What if I can't?"

"I'm going to need your help, Courtney. Either we both make it or neither of us does. And to be blunt, as much as I've enjoyed spending time with you, I don't want to spend another second on this island." He took her by the hands and stared deeply into her eyes. "You can do this."

She held his gaze for a long moment, then finally nodded. She'd heard that drowning was the most peaceful way to die. If she couldn't pull this off, they could dredge her body out of the reef with her brother's.

Bishop smiled, released her left hand, and guided her out into the ocean. The waves reached up her shins and over her knees, nearly knocking her onto her rear end. She leaned into them as her feet sank into the eroding sand. The wind whipped the raindrops through the churning smoke and into their faces. The *Huxley* appeared to move farther away as she watched.

It was now or never.

"I'll be right behind you the whole way." Bishop released her hand and waded deeper. "Don't even think about drowning on me."

Courtney staggered forward. The waves punched her in the chest nearly hard enough to knock the wind out of her and lifted her from her feet. She spit out a mouthful of saltwater, drew a deep breath, and plunged under the next wave. When she broke through on the other side, she barely had time to steal another breath before the next wave washed over her. She could no longer feel the sand underfoot. All she could do was stroke against the surf and try not to let it slam her against the rocks. Every crest she survived nearly robbed her of her forward progress. She was already swallowing brine and the soles of her feet hurt so badly she could hardly kick. Every glimpse of the wrecked research vessel confirmed that it was still far off on the horizon.

She'd been wrong. She wasn't going to make it.

Courtney mustered what little strength remained and swam for her life.

Seventy-Four

Bradley walked in a daze, as though his mind had detached from the body that trudged through the endless jungle. He imagined himself traveling though time, an invisible specter walking among men and women long since decomposed in the earth.

He stands in the red desert as brick-skinned warriors painted for battle wall in the sacred chamber under the kiva, while livestock shriek and squeal from the other side of the stacked stones. The braves glance toward the setting sun, a blood-red stain through the ash- and smoke-filled sky. Chanting voices echo from the canyon walls. He blinks and finds himself in a jungle markedly different from the one through which his corporeal form travels. A group of men is gathered on top of the knoll where a linga to the auspicious one, Shiva, will soon be erected. There are bodies sprawled in the earthen orifice. One man raises a wicked blade and swings it at the silver body pinned at his feet. A head bounces down the slope to where a holy man waits to collect it. Already people are arriving with carts filled with bricks. Onward Bradley travels, to yet another tropical forest, this one sparser and more arid. He can feel the coldness radiating from the hole in the ground. Someone screams, no...something...as it flails against the chains that ensnare it. Shadows emerge from the trees and throw their shoulders into the boulder, similarly bound in chains, perched at the precipice. The creature opens its horrible mouth and cries its indignation as chains snake through the weeds and rip it from its feet. Its screams become hollow as it slides over the edge and plummets into the cenote, where it's abruptly silenced by a splash. On and on he travels, through steep Japanese mountains and sheer volcanic cliffs, until he again finds himself tangled in a doorway with Reaves and Barnes, a silver-skinned demon bearing down on them, mouth open wide like a shark breaching the waves.

Bradley ducked from the path and vomited into a shrub.

All of this death...and for what?

Bradley wiped the strands of saliva from his chin and returned to the path. The others were already a good dozen paces ahead of him. No one had even bothered to wait, let alone stay behind to make sure that he was all right. He hurried to catch up before they abandoned him altogether.

He tried to think of all the good they could do with the knowledge contained in that one buried carcass, which so many lives had been sacrificed to obtain. The bacterium obviously held the key to unlock the human genetic code and the ability to seamlessly insert modified genes capable of immediate physical manifestation. With the right combinations, they could cure Down's syndrome and all kinds of hereditary diseases *in utero*. They could stimulate malfunctioning systems to eradicate functional disorders of all kinds. The cure for cancer was so close he could positively taste it. But what if they couldn't control the mutations, or, God forbid, this remarkable biotechnology fell into the wrong hands? Mankind could be remade into something it was never meant to be. There were factions out there that would undoubtedly like to create more creatures like the one that had nearly killed them all. Imagine an army of soldiers with this kind of destructive potential slipping across a hostile border under the cover of night. It would be an absolute slaughter. Whichever nation held this power would rule the world in whatever manner it saw fit. Maybe this knowledge would remain the proprietary property of GeNext for a while, but how long would it be before it leaked or whatever patents it held expired? It would be a biotechnological free-for-all. And then the race to Armageddon would officially commence. Every company would rush to develop and market products and solutions that could only lead to one possible outcome.

Genocide.

Bradley thought back to that day at the Pueblo Bonito ruins when he had first laid eyes on the original Chaco Man. His had been a noble pursuit, or so he told himself. Perhaps he had only been on a quest to solve a riddle for which there was no answer and had never really expected to find such a miraculous specimen in the flesh. The notion had been abstract, as he supposed the idea of giant reptilian killing machines must have been to the first man to exhume the fossils of a dinosaur. And he knew damn well what would happen if scientists found a way to tinker with their genetic code. He'd read *Jurassic Park*. How was this any different? They had figured out how to unleash nature's perfect killing machine, and once they opened that door to the world, they would never be able to close it. And all of the lives lost here wouldn't be a tragedy…they would be a prelude.

Forget his competitors and those who would abuse this knowledge. Was he alone responsible enough to wield the awesome might of evolution? Were the millions of cancer deaths he could potentially prevent worth the risk of creating even a handful more of these monsters?

They would eventually be evacuated from this island, and when that moment arrived, he was going to have to make a decision. All he could do now was pray that he made the right one.

By the time he caught up with the group, he was splashing through ankle-deep water. The others stood facing the southwest. Beyond them, the violent sea wreaked havoc on the bay. The beach from the night before was gone, and the vicious waves had already knocked down scores of trees at the verge of the jungle on their way to meet their opposite number, the lava flows that burned their way down through the forest.

The waves had to be easily ten feet tall past the breakers and rolled in one after the other from where what was left of the *Huxley* prepared to disappear forever. It was tilted in such a way that he could see into the darkened rooms exposed when the ship's back broke. Unless he was mistaken, the one on the right had been the very same engineering room in which he had spent the majority of the previous night. If he had known then what he knew now, how much would he have done differently? It had been upon his orders that they sailed to their deaths on the reef, but the creature had already been aboard. Would rethinking that choice have made any difference in the long run? At least with the bulk of the computer room saved from flooding like the engine room below it, they ought to be able to scavenge whatever supplies Barnes needed to fix the radio. But the ship was so far away, and the waves seemed to be growing larger by the second.

"How do you propose we get all the way out there?" Bradley had to shout to be heard over the rising wind. "Trying to swim all that way would be suicide!"

"We should just wait for the storm to die down," Reaves said. "It's not like we have to worry about the creature anymore."

"Maybe not," Barnes said, "but the whole damn island's about to come down on our heads."

"You'd risk drowning instead of waiting to see how things play…"

Bradley tuned out the arguing and watched Pike, who stood stock-still, staring out across the sea. His face was blank. He barely even blinked as the raindrops peppered it. Whatever thoughts raced through his mind, he betrayed nothing. Even during all of the years in his employ, Bradley had never quite figured out how to read him, which had, until this point, served him well. Whatever messes Pike had cleaned up for him, it was always best that he never learn the details. There had undoubtedly been scores of problems Pike had rectified that he had never even known about. That was the whole reason he employed an entire security contingent. Such was the nature of the job, and the reason that Pike and his men were paid so handsomely for it, but right now, Bradley would have killed to know what was going on inside of his head.

"…never make it that far," Reaves said.

"If you want to stick around to prove me wrong, be my guest. I'll bet there were a bunch of Romans who felt the exact same way when Mt. Vesuvius started to blow."

"They were Pompeiians, not—"

"Enough," Pike said. He didn't even need to raise his voice to silence them both. His cold blue eyes bored through each of them in turn. "We're all going, and we're not coming back. If you want to take one last look at this island, now's your chance to do it."

"There's no way I can swim that far," Reaves said. "How do you suggest—?"

"Leave that to me," Pike said.

He shed his backpack and hung it from a branch. He unzipped the bag, removed a small portable oxygen tank and regulator from the main pouch, and exchanged his night vision apparatus for a pair of diving goggles with a small headlamp. Without another word, Pike waded out into the ocean and dove beneath the waves.

Bradley stared at the spot where he had disappeared and couldn't help but wonder if Pike was ever coming back for them.

Seventy-Five

Bishop breached the water with a gasp and grabbed onto the rung of the ladder as tightly as he could. The waves tried to wrench it from his gasp with nearly enough force to dislocate his shoulder. He braced his feet against the hull and frantically scanned the sea for any sign of Courtney. He'd glimpsed her cresting a wave ahead of him not so long ago, but with the ferocity of the ocean, she could have been dragged down in the blink of an eye. He'd never been this physically exhausted in his entire life and could only imagine how she must have felt.

"Courtney!" he shouted, but the screaming wind stole her name from his lips.

He looked in every direction at once, watching each wave rise and fold over itself, praying not to see her body being tossed around like driftwood.

"Courtney!"

She should have beaten him here. Had she climbed up onto one of the other ladders along the side while he was swimming around toward the stern? Had the waves bludgeoned her against the ship? He could think of a thousand ways she could have died.

"Courtney!"

"I may have water in my ears, but I'm certainly not deaf."

Bishop turned and looked up the column of rungs to see Courtney crouching at the edge of the starboard rail mere feet above him. She held onto the handrails lining the walkway that serviced the control console for the A-frame winch, an elevated platform ten feet above the deck, which was now mostly below the water level. A shiver of relief rippled through him as he quickly ascended the slanted rungs and hauled himself up onto the metal platform.

Courtney smirked down at him.

"Took you long enough."

Bishop crawled over, wrapped her in his arms, and kissed her. She positively trembled. Her skin was ice-cold, her breath lukewarm. He couldn't imagine he was much better off. They needed to warm up in a hurry and get to work before the reef crumbled and this metallic oasis plunged under the sea with them trapped inside. Reluctantly, he pulled away and helped her to her feet.

The formerly horizontal walkway ascended toward the 01 Deck at an angle steep enough to necessitate the use of the railings. Ahead, the staircase leading downward to the stern terminated in the waves that lapped up the smooth deck nearly all the way to the garage door of the submersible hanger. Only the steel arch of the upper quarter of the twenty-five-foot A-frame and its winch assembly reared from the ocean to his left. It had been much higher the last time he had seen it from the shore. The vessel was definitely going down. All that remained was to see if he could get them safely on their way before it did.

He glanced to the east, toward where an impossible cloud of ash gushed from the invisible cone and the orange glow that appeared close to engulfing the entire volcano. Never in his life had he seen such destructive force. That gray mushroom cloud must have been clearly visible from space as it eclipsed the entire sky overhead.

He and Courtney navigated the canted stairs and stood knee-deep in the frigid water once more. The deck was every bit as slick as he had anticipated. If they couldn't secure traction, they were going to have to crawl and hope for the best. He didn't know if he had the strength to swim back aboard if he slipped and slid back into the ocean.

"Where are we going?" Courtney asked.

"To the hanger."

With those three words, he eased away from the handrail and out into the water. He kept his center of gravity low and forward as he ascended. The interior door was maybe fifteen feet away, but it might as well have been a mile. He slipped and fell to all fours. He was barely able to halt his rapid descent with his palms and knees before starting forward once again, his heart pounding.

He looked sheepishly toward Courtney, who was only now stepping onto the deck. She was far more graceful than he was.

Like a tightrope walker, she advanced carefully toward the door until she was forced to lower her hands to the ground for balance, her rear end held high in the air.

Bishop nearly slipped again as he watched it move, that perfect apple shape to which the scrubs clung like a second skin. He had to lower his stare to focus on what he was doing. By the time he was halfway there, he heard the squeal of hinges and then the thud of the door slamming against the wall. He peeked up to see Courtney leaning in the open doorway, clinging to the trim. The expression on her face was one of amusement.

"Need a hand?" she called.

"I'm fine," he grumbled, even as he slipped once more. "Just give me a second."

When he finally crossed the threshold and pulled himself upright, Courtney was a silhouette ahead of him against the rectangle of gray sky where the hallway now abruptly ended in tattered metal. A steady stream of rainwater ran past their feet. The stench of death was nauseating. He pressed his palm against the wall, yanked it away wet, and cringed at the thought of what he might have gotten on his hand. Surely it was only the elements leaking down through the crumpled roof. He did his best to ignore the rust-colored spatters on the ceiling and walls, and prayed that whoever had left them hadn't suffered for very long.

"What are we looking for in the hanger?" Courtney asked.

"You'll see soon enough."

She twisted the handle and shoved the hanger door inward. With gravity added to the weight of the door, she had to lean her shoulder into it in order to squeeze through. Bishop caught it before it could close and followed her into complete darkness that smelled even worse than the corridor. Wherever the bodies were, he was thankful that he couldn't see them. There were no exterior windows, and without power, there was no hope of turning on the banks of spotlights mounted up in the exposed rafters. He flicked the switch beside the door up and down a couple of times to be sure. Fortunately, he'd spent so much time in this hanger and its twin on the *Mayr* that he could navigate it blindfolded, a skill that until now he had never thought would come in handy.

"Stay right there," he said.

"Where would I possibly go?"

Bishop shoved away from the wall in a straight line toward the center of the industrial garage. The floor here was wet with condensation and might just be slick enough for what he had in mind. He faced the downward slant, took two quick steps forward for momentum, and slid like a batter into third base. Objects flew past to either side of him, close enough to sense but not quite feel. The garage door had to be coming up fast now. If he'd planned this right, he should strike the base of the two-story door dead-center. He maneuvered both feet in front of him and flexed his knees to absorb the impact. Instead of colliding with the lowest horizontal panel, his soles slammed into something soft and forgiving.

"Jesus," he groaned.

His kingdom for a pair of shoes.

He distinctly felt the torn fabric and the cool, distended skin that sucked in his feet like a garbage bag filled with oatmeal. Whatever part of the body his right foot had sunken into had renewed the stench with a vengeance. He struggled to stand, but only ended up slipping in the vile sludge and flopping back down.

"Are you okay?" Courtney called. Her voice echoed in the confines.

"Oh, yeah." He scooted to his right until there were no corpses between him and the garage door, and finally rose to his feet. "Absolutely wonderful."

He followed the door to where it met with the roller track that raised it. Just to his left, at waist level, was the locking mechanism. He cranked it until the lock disengaged with a clang. When he finally found the handles, he raised the door as high as he could. He caught movement from the corner of his eye and nearly shouted a warning to Courtney, but it was just the bodies that had been wedged against the garage door continuing the journey that gravity had started. They rolled and slithered and tumbled down into the waiting ocean in a tangle of appendages. He caught glimpses of the gray cast to their skin, the gaping wounds, and the bloodstained clothing before the waves pulled them under and carried them away.

Bishop was grateful he hadn't seen any of their faces well enough to recognize them or for long enough that he'd been able to count how many of them there were.

He located the pulley-and-chain system on the wall and used it to raise the door all the way up to the ceiling. The smell of smoke rushed in to at least temper the reek of decomposition.

Straight down the stern deck, he could see the very top of the A-frame like the mouth of a flooded tunnel. The submersible's rails ran straight toward it before vanishing underwater. The setup couldn't have been more perfect. He turned to face Courtney with a smile so broad it hurt his chapped cheeks.

"Well?" he said. "What do you think?"

"Of what?"

He gestured toward the port-side wall and gave a slight bow.

"Your chariot, m'lady."

Seventy-Six

Pike cruised against the current over the sharp reef. The coral formations were like a forest of dead trees coated with broken beer bottles on a mountainous landscape. He could hardly see the skeletal shapes through the cloud of silt that clung to them like a dirty mist. Fish darted from one enclave to the next, mere flashes of silver and then they were gone. Sporadic columns of bubbles flooded upward from the invisible holes in the ocean floor where the hydrothermal vents forced copious amounts of superheated hydrogen sulfide and cyanide, among other toxins, up from the mantle. A larger silver shape knifed through the reef below him too quickly for him to clearly see. His passage must have disturbed a shark riding out the storm in the coral cliffs, or scavenging the bodies with the crabs. He stayed as close to the surface as he could to keep from eviscerating himself on the coral, but far enough below it that he wouldn't be battling the waves. His emergency oxygen tank only held two hours of oxygen, which was still far more than he would need to do what he had to do.

He encountered the pilothouse of the *Huxley* first, where the ruined reef had crumbled down the steep ledge like an avalanche. The bulk of the vessel was shrouded in silt to such a degree that he couldn't see the lower decks or the hull. Or the debris and remains scattered across the seabed. Not that he particularly cared, but those were distractions that he simply didn't need right now. He was of singular focus. He needed to rig a setup to get Bradley, Reaves, and Barnes onto the boat before Bishop and Martin left. It made the most sense to deal with them all at once, in a location where he could control every variable, where there was no way they could escape. With any luck, Bishop would have everything set up perfectly for him when he arrived.

He loved it when a plan came together.

The roof of the pilothouse was already brown with settled dirt. Through the bank of windows he could see several bodies floating in the flooded bridge, where schools of fish had already found them. He didn't even slow as he passed over the naked roofline and the bent metal posts that marked where the satellite communications array had once been mounted. The windows of the 02 and the 03 Decks had shattered. He caught the occasional twinkle of broken glass below him under the rubble and sediment. It looked almost like a normal ship sunken nose down until he reached the point where the ship had been torn in two. From behind, it reminded him of an apartment building with one of its exterior walls removed. He could see into each of the rooms and the corridor between them. Bed linens fluttered from where they were still tucked into the mattresses. Drawers and bureau drawers stood ajar, their former contents hovering in the clouds of silt. An oily sludge that refracted the wan light in rainbow colors burbled toward the surface from whatever was leaking in the engine room, which hid below the fog of sand.

He followed the trail of metallic debris up a cliff of purple and blue algae-coated live rock, from which ledges flourishing with coral of all shapes and sizes protruded. The rear third of the *Huxley* was perched precariously on top of it, canting in the opposite direction as it threatened to slide down the opposite side of the reef. The razor-honed, sheared metal of a bulkhead framed the open orifice of the hold. Globs of glistening oil and sewage trickled upward from the severed network of pipes. A steady stream of bubbles raced along the ceiling in search of the sky from the sealed storage holds still slowly taking on water. That was probably the only thing stalling the sinking of the stern. Once that air was replaced by water, the remainder of the vessel was lost.

He swam all the way into the hold before turning on his headlamp, for all the good it did him. The light barely diffused into the murk, lengthening the shadows and creating more where there had been none previously. He knew exactly what he was looking for and where to find it. He just needed to make sure that his presence wasn't detected. The problem was going to be getting everything he needed back to the beach fast enough to arrange their transportion and make the return trip before Bishop and Martin split. If they were allowed to reach the open sea, there would be no hope of catching them.

Veering to his left, he finally saw the ladder bolted to the wall behind a mess of wires and broken pipes. He shoved them aside and ascended the rungs to the service hatch, which led into the oxygen tank recharge station off of the divers locker room, across the hallway from the submersible hanger. The wheel of the airlock screeched when he turned it. With the pressure differential, it took all of his strength to open it and shove it upward. He climbed up into the slanted room and the water followed him, spreading across the floor and pooling under the massive reserve oxygen tanks.

The ship groaned and shuddered.

Silently, he crossed the chamber to the door, opened it, and entered the locker room. To his left, banks of lockers framed the door to the hallway. The impact had jarred their doors open and emptied their contents onto the ground around the benches bolted in the middle. The floor was covered with a thick rubber mat riddled with holes to allow water to pass through and into the floor drains. Directly ahead of him was a bank of shower heads, on the other side of which were the remnants of the main laboratory and the open air beyond. To his right were storage closets that contained all sorts of miscellaneous diving gear. He opened the door of the closet on the right and swept his headlamp through the darkness until it alighted on bundles of nylon rope looped over hooks. He took two ten-yard bundles, slung one over his head and left arm, and the other around his neck and right shoulder so that they crisscrossed on his chest and back in matching Xs.

He turned a slow circle. When at first he didn't see the most crucial component of his plan, he nearly punched the wall. After several slow, calming breaths, he saw its smooth yellow plastic shell, like the carapace of some alien insect, on the floor under a jumble of supplies thrown from the shelves. He shoved aside the clutter and there it was. The SeaBob RaveJet was like a miniature submersible jet ski. It was maybe half his height and as broad as his shoulders, and weighed just over a hundred pounds, but underwater that 3.3 horsepower impeller jet-propulsion motor would fire him like a torpedo at nearly fifteen kilometers per hour. Fully charged, the battery could only provide sixty minutes of use at depths to forty meters below the surface, but with the purpose he had in mind, he'd be lucky to get half that amount. Everything hinged upon the unit being fully charged.

Pike hefted it to his chest and carried it back to the open hatch in the floor. He closed his eyes and listened for the sound of what he assumed was transpiring in the hanger across the hallway, but heard only another moan of the settling ship. He couldn't take the risk of trying to get visual confirmation. Not yet. Not until everything else was in place.

He lowered the RaveJet through the hole and let it fall into the water, then dropped down right behind it. Its nose had barely touched the ground when he took it by the handles, directed it into the main aisle, and thumbed the accelerator sensor. He weaved through the slalom of pipes until he was aligned with the ocean, tucked himself behind its hydrodynamic body, and launched himself toward the shore.

Seventy-Seven

Reaves stared out across the ocean toward where the life raft bobbed on the waves. Pike had appeared beside it as if by magic, clambered aboard, and then hauled a large yellow personal submersible unit of some kind up into the raft. As he watched, Pike shed two bundles of rope from around his shoulders, tied one end of each to the inflatable ring, and the other ends to the self-propelled motor craft. In less than three minutes, Pike lowered the unit back into the water and dove in after it. The raft gave a sharp jerk, spun sideways, and darted toward the beach to his left, where an exhausted Barnes huddled against the trunk of a rosewood tree, as far out of the rain as he could get. With the way he rested his forehead against his knees, Reaves couldn't tell if he was sleeping or not.

He looked away and to the sky. Raindrops assailed his face and ran down the skin beneath his already saturated clothes, but he felt none of it. All he could feel was the cold steel of the pistol against his belly and the weight of the decision he would soon be forced to make. He'd never fired an automatic pistol, let alone pointed one at another human being. Drawing a gun wasn't like raising a fist to strike a man. It was a choice that couldn't be taken back. If he were to pull the Beretta on Pike, he knew he had better be prepared to pull the trigger, because Pike wouldn't hesitate. Was this really the path he wanted to take anyway? Perhaps the other men would listen to reason. He'd barely even tried, after all. But how could he explain the evolutionary and anthropological ramifications of their discovery to men for whom history began at their birth and the future only extended until their deaths? In the grand scheme of the universe, mankind was but a mayfly on the earth. Like his predecessors *homo habilis* and *homo erectus*. Like the dinosaurs. Surely the Maya, Champa, and Anasazi had expected their bloodlines to flow forever, even lacking the arrogance of modern Americans, who expected to rule the world indefinitely as the Roman Caesars must have. How could he convince the others to see that the decision the four of them made right here on this island would impact the fate of their entire species?

He realized that Bradley was talking to him and turned to face his old friend.

"Welcome back," Bradley said. "You were somewhere else for a few minutes there. I was just about to go looking for a sharp stick to prod you with."

"Sorry." Reaves offered a meek smile of apology. "Just thinking is all."

Bradley turned his attention to the sea, where the life raft raced toward them across the waves, firing spray in its wake.

"I know what you're thinking," Bradley said, still facing the oncoming craft.

"Then you know we don't really have much of a choice in the matter."

"There's always a choice, Brendan. It's just a matter of making the right one."

"And what is the right choice?"

Bradley sighed and shook his head. When he turned to face Reaves, Bradley appeared to age before his very eyes.

"There are shades of gray between the black and white, old friend. I'm confident that the two of us, together, could find the right one."

"The road to hell is paved with good intentions."

The faint hum of the submersible's motor reached their ears. The orange raft was only twenty yards from the shore now, and closing fast.

"We could improve the lives of millions."

"Or eradicate billions."

"Don't you think I recognize the potential for that?"

"Then stop this before it's too late."

"If I do, then all of these people will have died for nothing."

"Not for nothing. Don't you see? Their deaths have shown us *why* we need to bury this secret where no one will ever find it, no matter how hard they look. A hundred lives lost in exchange for the perpetuation of our species? Their sacrifice is monumental."

"It doesn't necessarily have to play out the way you envision. How many nuclear bombs have we built, but never used?"

"All it would take was the wrong country detonating one—just one—to trigger a chain reaction that would destroy the entire world."

The crown of Pike's head and his shoulders breached the water behind the whale-like nose of the RaveJet.

"This is different. If we did this the right way from the start, we could control the outcome. We could be the ones to isolate the proper traits and use them for the good of humanity."

"We could end up destroying it in the process."

Pike reached a point where he could stand, let the yellow unit sink, and splashed through the shallows toward them.

"A long time ago," Reaves said, "you and I embarked upon a quest to unravel the world's greatest mystery, knowing full well we might never do so. We've already accomplished more than we ever dreamed we would, but at what cost? We still have the opportunity to make amends, the opportunity to end this quest in the same spirit with which we began it. We can save the world, Graham. You and me. Right here. Right now."

Reaves stared his old friend dead in the eyes and proffered his hand.

"Get into the life raft," Pike said. "We don't have time to screw around."

"The two of us," Reaves said. "Just like it was in the beginning."

"You would stand by me?" Bradley said.

"Until the bitter end."

"Get in the damn boat!" Pike snapped.

Bradley hesitantly raised his hand from his side and reached for Reaves's, but Pike grabbed him by the arm and shoved him toward where the life raft tossed on the surf.

"You, too." Pike seized Reaves by his outstretched hand and jerked him into the water nearly hard enough to topple him to his knees. "We don't have all day."

Barnes staggered into the sea beside him, rubbing the sleep from his eyes. They were waist-deep in the ocean when they reached the boat and climbed up behind Bradley, who was already sitting on the taut fabric with his back against the inflatable ring, facing to the west. Pike threw his backpack in beside Bradley. The moment Reaves clambered aboard, he noticed the ragged gashes. The rain must have washed away all of the blood, but not the memories. He'd barely plopped down beside Bradley when he heard the whine of the RaveJet and the raft whipped in a half-circle, nearly throwing Barnes overboard. The computer technician crawled over beside them, and together they watched the *Huxley* growing larger against the smoky horizon. Pike was invisible beyond the point where the ropes angled into the water, save for the occasional yellow flicker beneath the waves.

Reaves glanced back at the island, and the fiery crown from which all of the smoke and ash originated. Perhaps this was nature's way of protecting her secret. Maybe the island would ultimately make the decision for them.

He could only hope so.

His hand trembled as he shifted the butt of the pistol against his abdomen.

In the end, he feared he wouldn't have the courage or the strength to do what needed to be done.

Seventy-Eight

Courtney could only stare at the *Trident*, the twin to the *Corellian* from the *Mayr*. The last time her life had been normal, she had stood just as she did now, imagining the journey ahead. Even though it had only been a matter of days, that felt like a lifetime ago...wedged into that cramped personnel sphere with Bishop at the helm and her brother right behind her. How much different would things have turned out if they hadn't gone down into the Basilisk Vent Field that day? If they had left five minutes sooner or later? If Ty's blasted armature had snapped off upon impact or if the hydraulic pincers had failed? If he hadn't filled the bioreactor or if its seal hadn't ruptured? She'd be working in the lab with her brother right now, poring over discoveries they hoped would revolutionize their fields. He'd still be alive. All of the others would still be alive. When she traced the course of events back to the beginning, the only actual choice that could have prevented this nightmare had belonged to the two of them in this hanger and the brother she would never see again. They had been in such a hurry to dive while there was a lull in the seismic activity that they hadn't stopped to think about the ramifications. What did the future hold for them from here, and what consequences did they risk by launching the *Trident* now?

These were foolish thoughts, she knew. There was nothing she could have or would have done differently at the time. No one could have known. It was as though they had been mere players in the first act of the tragedy to come, and they'd played their parts to perfection. From here on out, things would be different. They were in control now, and they would make sure that someone had to answer for all of this death, and that it would never happen again.

She'd watched the technicians ready the *Corellian* for launch a dozen times, but never this quickly, and never quite like this.

The *Trident* rested on an elevated steel platform with wheels like those of a train. They were already fitted to the rails, chocked, and braked. Cables and wires moored the submersible to its trolley. Bishop unfastened them one by one, then ascended the stairs against the hanger wall to the service platform, flush with the top of the *Trident*. Pipes as wide as her thighs climbed up the walls and crossed the ceiling, around the banks of useless lights. The exposed girders cast shadows so deep they were like pools of tar suspended overhead. Dribbles of water trickled through the roof and dripped onto the fixtures with a combination of pinging sounds and what could have passed for the scuttling noises of so many rats.

Bishop stepped from the platform and onto the *Trident*. His footsteps clanged on the closed hatch of the personnel sphere. He set to work disconnecting the various hoses and cables that recharged and fueled the myriad life support, propulsion, and navigation systems. She was a little worried about how he intended to launch the submersible without the power to operate the A-frame, which was nearly below the level of the water now as it was. And without electricity to power the trolley's drive train, they were expecting an awful lot of gravity if they hoped it would get seventeen tons of deep sea submersible rolling toward the sea, even with the brakes disengaged.

She walked around a toppled tool cabinet and its spilled contents to the front of the *Trident*, leaned over the armatures folded over its front, and peered through the circular window. Inside waited nothing but shadows. She shivered at the thought of cramming herself into that small space and immersing it under the ocean. Images of the isolation chamber flashed though her mind. The darkness. The slow suffocation. Bishop's grip on her hand loosening as consciousness abandoned him. The absolute certainty that she was going to die. She started to hyperventilate and had to turn away.

Breathing deeply of the smoky breeze, somewhat freshened by the gale winds blowing off the Pacific and into her face, she steadied her nerves and tried to chased away the stubborn memories.

"How much oxygen does it hold again?" she asked.

"Enough for forty hours with three passengers. We should have about sixty for the two of us." Bishop leaned over the edge of the sub and peered curiously at her. "You don't have to worry about that, Courtney. We can sail all the way to Namatanai on New

Ireland with the hatch open, if you want. Other than immediately following the launch, we don't need to be submerged at all."

"And just how do you plan to launch it?"

"Would you quit worrying and trust me?" He smirked, then ducked back out of sight. "Everything's under control."

She waited a long moment before she could finally bring herself to ask.

"Will you come back with me? After everything's over. Will you help me find my brother?"

He disconnected the lone remaining battery coupling, hopped back across to the platform, and descended the staircase.

The water dripping through the ceiling drummed a tinny rhythm on the housings of the lights, beneath which she heard more skritching sounds.

Bishop strode right up to her, wrapped his arms around her waist, and leaned his forehead against hers so that she had no choice but to look into his blue eyes.

"Try and stop me."

He kissed her until she was convinced, then turned her to face the west. The waves continued to grow taller and now nearly reached up the stern to the opening of the garage. The horizon was a churning mass of ash.

"Are you ready to go?"

There was a clattering sound behind her. She spun to see the hoses that dangled from the ceiling swaying from side to side.

"Yeah." She turned her face back into the gusting wind and toward salvation. It was hard to believe they were actually going to leave. She almost had herself believing that they were going to die on this island. Yet still, it felt like a betrayal, as though by escaping the island she was abandoning all hope for her brother, even though she fully intended to return and find him, if it took the rest of her life to do so. "But I swear, I'll be back."

"We'll be back, Courtney." Bishop took her by the hand and guided her back to the *Trident*. "I promise you. We'll be back."

Seventy-Nine

Pike cruised toward the open hull of the *Huxley* once more. His heart raced in anticipation. He allowed it to do so only long enough to flood his body with adrenaline before willing it to slow once he reached the gaping maw. With a flick of his thumb, he killed the motor and simply released his grip on the RaveJet. It fell away from him and settled into the silt, drawing its tethers tight. He kicked his way back to the surface and surveyed the scene. He could clearly see into the main level of the ship. There was no one looking back at him from the exposed aft portions of the main lab, the engineering room, or the corridor between them. Just as he had expected. Their approach had been quiet enough not to draw the attention of those inside, where he could hear the mechanical rumble of the *Trident* powering up.

Excellent. Not only had they made it in time, but Bishop had the submersible ready and waiting for him.

The three men in the raft looked expectantly at him. With their pale faces, the bags under their eyes, and the way they cowered in the bottom of the boat, shivering against the rain, he knew they wouldn't be any trouble.

They were already dead. They just didn't know it yet.

He looped his fist around one of the ropes and paddled toward the main lab. When he reached the bulkhead, he moored the raft to a bent piece of metal. The craft rose and fell dramatically on the swelling waves, which at their highest point brought the craft to within six feet of the main level floor. While the submersible's engine was running and surely echoing inside the hanger, he could risk speaking out loud without alerting those inside or raising suspicion with his own men by demanding silence.

"We climb up here," he said, pulling himself into the raft. "I'll go first and help the rest of you up."

He shouldered his backpack and turned toward the *Huxley*.

"It sounds like something's still running on the ship," Bradley said. "If there's power, maybe we can just call for help from here."

Pike looked back at him and smiled his warmest smile.

"There's no power on the ship. That sound you hear is my little surprise. It's how we're getting out of here."

"What is it?" Reaves asked. "When did you have the time to—?"

Pike turned his back on Reaves, leapt up to the ledge at the apex of a wave, and hauled himself aboard. He leaned back over the sharp metal edge and extended his arm for Bradley, whose head bobbed at the level of the slanted floor. The angle was even steeper than it had been when Pike was last here. When the reef finally gave, the stern was going to go down in a hurry.

"Grab my arms and kick off from the hull," he said. "I'll pull you the rest of the way up."

Bradley nodded and raised his arms. At the highest point of the next wave, Pike grabbed him around the wrists and heaved. Bradley thrashed and kicked against the ship. His shirt tore on the ragged steel lip as Pike tugged him onto the mess of broken glass and debris toward where the rainwater puddled against the wall to the divers locker room. He scurried back to the edge and repeated the process first with Barnes, and then with Reaves. He didn't like the look in the anthropologist's eyes. Something had changed inside of him when that pump of his got her neck ripped open. He had never known Reaves to be anything other than a passive, easygoing academic who was about as threatening as a housefly. Something was different now. An aura of repressed aggression radiated from him like so many of the zealots he had encountered during his various tours of duty. This recognition had saved his life on more than one occasion. When the time came to act, he was going to need to keep a close eye on Reaves.

The four of them stood on the steep floor. The waves beat against its underside with a thumping sound that reverberated into their legs.

"Follow me," Pike said.

With the door to the lab still attached to the forward portion of the ship, they were going to have to do this the hard way. He walked back to the ledge, leaned against the interior wall, and stepped out over the ocean. He planted his right foot in the hallway and swung his body around. The door to the stern deck stood ajar at the end of the sloped corridor, revealing nothing but water and the very top of the A-frame way out there. He helped Bradley around the wall and then left him to assist the others as he eased his way down to the hanger door. He placed his palm against it and felt the thrum of the *Trident*'s motor through it. With a quick glance back over his shoulder, he slipped his pistol from his bag and held it against his chest where the others couldn't see it.

He drew a deep breath and blew it out slowly in a practiced manner that allowed him to focus his senses and sharpen his reflexes.

His moment had finally arrived. Soon enough, he would be richer than God.

Pike leaned his shoulder into the door and slowly turned the knob. When he felt the latch release, he pushed it open just far enough that he could see into the enormous garage. There was no sign of anyone in the area directly to his left, just piles of debris at the foot of the stairs leading up to the control room. All of its windows had shattered, and its walls appeared to lean inward. The floor glistened with a steady stream of rainwater leaking through the ceiling. He pushed the door open a hair wider and saw the *Trident* across the room. All of the couplings had been disconnected and hung limply onto it like multicolored vines. The hatch of the personnel sphere stood open. Its fiberglass body shuddered with life. He heard voices, but couldn't decipher the words. There was no one on the platform above it. Either they were already inside the submersible or they were out of his range of sight behind the door to his right.

There was only one way to find out.

Pike took a two-handed grip on the pistol, lowered himself to a crouch, and ducked around the door. By the time it closed behind him, the Beretta was pointed into the rear corner at two startled faces.

He had Bishop and Martin in his sights.

Eighty

Bishop had just finished manually disengaging the trolley's brakes when the sudden movement caught his eye and he found himself staring at Pike down the barrel of an automatic pistol. He slowly reached back and drew Courtney behind him, keeping her out of the direct line of fire. He raised his palms so that Pike could clearly see he was unarmed.

How in the world had he gotten onto the ship?

Pike stepped to his right, away from the door.

"What's the *Trident*'s status?" Pike asked.

Bishop eased cautiously backward. If Pike so much as flinched, he would spin and tackle Courtney behind the sub.

"What's the goddamned status?"

"The batteries are fully charged. The fuel and oxygen reserves are at nearly one hundred percent. I haven't checked the instrumentation yet, but I see no reason that all systems shouldn't be fully online."

The door opened tentatively inward to Pike's left. He stayed clear of the door and out of sight as Bradley entered, followed closely by Reaves. Their faces registered surprise at the sight of Courtney and him.

"What's left to do?" Pike demanded. The pistol never wavered in his grasp. Bishop had seen enough men with guns to immediately recognize which ones were prepared to use them. He continued his careful retreat. Not only was this man capable of pulling the trigger, the look in his eyes suggested that he was eager to do so. "Move another inch and I'll put a bullet between the girl's pretty green eyes over your right shoulder."

Bishop stopped, but slowly raised his right shoulder. He hoped Courtney took the hint and ducked.

"What's going on here?" Bradley asked.

Pike ignored him.

"Kick out the chocks, climb in before she hits the water, and fire the thrusters," Bishop said. His eyes never left Pike's. "Unless you take on ballast, she'll float on her own from there."

Bradley stepped farther into the room and peered around the door to see Pike in his shooter's stance.

"What in the name of God are you doing?" he demanded.

Barnes was the last to enter the room. The door fell closed behind him with a resounding thud.

"I'm commandeering this vehicle," Pike said.

His stare locked with Bishop's, he swung his pistol quickly to his left, blindly aligned it with Barnes's startled face, and squeezed the trigger. Barnes's scorched face crumpled inward between his wide eyes. A ribbon of blood unraveled from the exit wound. Pike's sights were back on Bishop before Barnes's body even hit the floor.

"Jesus Christ!" Reaves shouted. He threw himself to the ground beside Barnes in the rapidly expanding puddle of blood. "What the hell did you just do?"

It had all happened so quickly that Bishop had been unable to act, but it was the nature of the violence that surprised him the most. Barnes had never seen it coming. Nor had Bradley or Reaves. Pike obviously had his own agenda, which didn't include any of the rest of them.

Pike must have identified Bishop as the greatest threat, and wasn't about to take his eyes off of him. If he made his move now, he'd be riddled with bullets before he could even turn around. Maybe his body would shield Courtney long enough for her to dive behind the *Trident*, but where could she possibly go from there?

"What are you doing, Roland?" Bradley asked. He held his hands up at his sides. "You don't have to do this."

Pike smiled and Bishop knew that none of them would be allowed to live.

"Yes," Pike said calmly. The Beretta leveled at Bishop's center mass. Pike's finger tightened almost imperceptibly on the trigger. "I do."

It was now or never.

Eighty-One

Reaves could only stare at the blood pouring from the back of Barnes's head. The exit wound was large enough to accommodate his fist. He tried not to look at the sloppy gray matter squeezing from the hair-lined hole in the cranium or the lines of blood tracing the contours of Barnes's face. Instead, he found himself focusing on the nearly black rivulets running down the sloped floor toward the sea, engulfing the spatters as they went.

The realization suddenly struck him. Pike had betrayed them all. None of them would ever be leaving this island. They were witnesses to a crime he had yet to commit.

Pike was keeping their Chaco Man all to himself, and heaven help the world if he planned on selling it to the highest bidder.

Heat expanded in his core, growing from an ember into a wildfire that coursed through his veins. It erupted as rage inside his head. His vision turned scarlet. He couldn't allow this to happen. There was too much at stake.

Reaves leapt to his feet and drew the pistol from his waistband in one swift motion. A bellow of anguish burst past his lips.

Pike turned toward him in slow motion as Reaves squeezed the trigger. The gun kicked in his hands hard enough to make him stumble backward.

A mist of blood burst from the back of Pike's left shoulder, followed by syrupy spatters that tracked the bullet's path to the wall, where it ricocheted with a spark.

And still Pike swiveled toward him, bringing the gun to bear on his chest.

From the corner of his eye, Reaves saw Bishop grab Courtney and lunge behind the *Trident*.

He squeezed the trigger again, but his arms were unprepared for the kick. The bullet flew high over Pike's head as he returned fire.

There was a flash from Pike's barrel, and he simultaneously felt something punch him in the gut, lifting him from the ground. He landed on his back and slid downhill through Barnes's blood. Or was it his own? Searing pain blossomed in his belly and streaked outward into his appendages. It wasn't until he pawed at the wound with both hands that he discovered he had lost his gun. Warmth sluiced between his fingers. He could already feel it trickling down his sides. He tried to sit up, but his body wanted nothing to do with it.

He raised his trembling right hand to see the sheer amount of blood. Through his fanned fingers, he watched Pike take aim at his face, his left arm hanging uselessly at his side, blood dripping from his fingertips.

The strength in Reaves's neck gave out and his head struck the ground with a crack that released the taste of copper from his sinuses.

His eyes rolled up to the rafters.

The shadows raced to consume him.

Through the darkness that constricted his vision, he saw Pike's silhouette looming over him.

He closed his eyes and bared his teeth against the pain, both what he already had and what was soon to come.

Eighty-Two

Bishop had tackled her behind the *Trident* the moment the first shot had been fired. She had heard two more in rapid succession as she tried to make sense of the chaos around her. These men had appeared from out of nowhere and all hell had broken loose.

She and Bishop crouched against the submersible, unable to see anything transpiring on the other side. Where could they possibly go? They'd be in the line of fire if they made a break for the ocean, and even if they made it, how far could they hope to get before the shooting commenced? They'd be sitting ducks for any kind of marksman while they struggled against the tall waves in an effort to clear the *Huxley* and head for open water. And she wasn't sure if she had enough strength left to make that swim again. She had barely made it to the ship in the first place.

"Get ready," Bishop said. "As soon as I pull the chocks, the sub's going to start to roll. We need to get inside of it as quickly as possible before it starts gaining momentum."

"We'll be totally exposed on top of it."

"He's not going to be expecting it. We'll catch him off-guard."

"He'll have a clean shot at us."

"At least we'll be moving targets. We can't just wait for him to take care of the others and come looking for us. We're dead if we stay here any longer." He turned to face her. "This is our only chance, Courtney."

She only vaguely felt herself nod her understanding. Her hands were shaking so badly that she wasn't even sure she'd be able to climb the side of the *Trident*. She imagined herself slipping and falling, watching the submersible roll toward the ocean, leaving her behind to face the wrath of the enraged man with the gun.

"On my mark," Bishop said. "Now!"

He dove forward, grabbed the rope attached to the chocks, and gave it a sharp tug.

Courtney leapt up onto the fiberglass shell. From the corner of her eye, she saw the chocks tumble away like dice, heard them clatter across the floor. The craft started to roll almost immediately. Her right foot found purchase on the hydraulic assembly of the starboard-side armature. She pushed off and grabbed for the roof.

A startled shout from the other side.

She kept climbing, certain she would hear the first report at any second.

Bishop was to her right, scurrying up the hull in a blur. He reached the rail just as she did. Across the roof, she could see the opposite wall passing...the staircase to the control console...the office with its shattered windows...and in the foreground, Pike sprinting toward them with his pistol aimed right at her face.

She ducked as a bullet ricocheted from the roof, cracking the fiberglass. The report echoed through the hanger.

The trolley was picking up speed, but not fast enough. And the impact with the water would slow it down significantly.

"Keep your head down!" Bishop shouted, even as he swung himself up onto the roof.

Courtney risked another peek. Bishop reached for the open hatch. He jerked his hand back as another bullet *whanged* from the shell. She could no longer see Pike on the other side, which could mean only one thing.

He had closed the distance to the *Trident* and was scaling the opposite side.

Bishop wasn't going to be able to reach the hatch before Pike had him dead to rights. Even if he did, she'd be any easy target trying to follow him.

To her right, the waves were approaching fast. Her grip wasn't strong enough to withstand a serious jolt.

They were never going to make it.

Eighty-Three

The moment he heard the clatter of the chocks, he'd known exactly what was happening. He'd forsaken the kill shot at Reaves's forehead and brayed in rage as he ran after the rolling vessel. He couldn't allow his only means of escape to sail without him. He'd fired repeatedly at the roof line to keep Bishop and Martin from reaching the hatch. If they managed to get inside, once they hit the water they'd be long gone.

He needed to gain control of the *Trident*. He could always swing back and finish them off, but not if he wasn't the first to get to the hatch.

He intercepted the vessel at a sprint and leapt up onto its flank. One solid kick with his right leg and he was over the top, just in time to see Bishop do the same thing from the other side. He was the first to his feet, and in one stride, towered over Bishop as the hanger sped past. Martin cowered beside him where she clung to the rail.

"You're not going anywhere," Pike said.

Bishop looked up at him with an expression of defiance.

Pike pointed the pistol right between Bishop's narrowed eyes.

Eighty-Four

There was no time to think, only react. Bishop rolled to his right and swung his left leg in a wide arc. His foot connected with Pike's ankle just solidly enough to knock him off-balance. He scurried behind the open hatch lid and heard bullets sing from the metal. The hatch lid wasn't nearly large enough to protect him from a second fusillade and he wouldn't be able to surprise Pike again. He lunged around the hatch and wrapped his arms around Pike's knees.

He felt as much as heard a *crack* on the back of his head and tasted blood in his mouth. The hanger swam around him. His grip around Pike's legs loosened, but the other man was already falling. They landed squarely on the roof, just as the *Trident* struck the water.

It was like hitting a brick wall.

Bishop made a desperate grab for Pike's pistol as he careened over the side. His fist closed around the smoldering barrel, which only slid out of his grasp.

He was weightless for an interminable moment. His right heel whipped past Courtney's cheek. She relinquished her grip on the submersible and fell away. The hanger floor rushed up to meet him. His shoulder crumpled beneath his weight and his head bounced from the ground.

His vision wavered as he craned his neck to see the *Trident* slowly advancing into the ocean, sinking as it went. The cold seawater washed over his legs and waist.

Pike knelt on the roof, his pistol aimed right at Bishop as he struggled to rise.

Eighty-Five

Bradley raised the gun. The butt was still slick with his old friend's blood. He'd fallen upon Reaves and tried to keep pressure on the wound, but Reaves had brushed his hands aside, nodded toward the gun, and burbled something incoherent through a mouthful of blood. The events had played out so quickly that by the time Bradley had mustered the courage to fire, Bishop had already been thrown from the roof and Pike stood alone, victorious, prepared to put an end to Bishop. All Pike had to do after that was duck down into the personnel sphere and ride the waves to freedom. Reaves would bleed to death in short measure. Bishop would be dead. And he and Dr. Martin would undoubtedly fall prey to the sea when the stern sank, if Pike didn't return to finish them off first.

All of this was his fault.

All of the pain.

All of the death.

And soon enough, Tyler Martin's mutated body would fall into the hands of men who would pay any price to tap into the awesome potential inside of it, men who would be gods, who would use the knowledge not for the benefit of mankind, but for its enslavement.

He couldn't allow his dream to become the world's nightmare.

His hands shook as he sighted Pike down the barrel. His longtime right hand man, in whom he had entrusted more than just his business secrets and his life. He had considered Pike a friend, a friend with whom he now aligned the barrel of a pistol.

Pike leaned forward to take the shot at Bishop. The ocean rose halfway up the sides of the submersible as it rolled toward the sea.

Bradley swallowed hard and closed his eyes. He couldn't bear to watch.

He squeezed the trigger and the gun bucked in his hands.

Eighty-Six

Courtney screamed and dove for Bishop. He was moving too slowly. He'd never get out of the way in time.

A shot rang out and she threw her body over his. She expected to feel the bullet snap ribs as it tore through her side, pierced her lungs, and pulverized her heart.

She glanced toward the *Trident* in time to see Pike stumble backward toward the hatch. His heels went over the lip of the hole.

Bradley fired again, well wide, just like the first shot.

Pike pinwheeled his arms for balance. When he was stable, he glanced down to take stock of the rising water and his current situation. The crests of the waves hurled brine against the open hatch lid.

He looked back at them and seemed to reach a decision.

"No!" Bishop yelled. He crawled out from beneath her and sprinted toward the wall of the hanger.

Pike lowered his legs into the personnel sphere, braced his hands on the rim of the hatch, and started down the rungs.

Bradley fired again. The report left her ears ringing. Above the tinny sound she heard Bishop rummaging through the contents of the overturned tool cabinet. He darted from her peripheral vision with a crowbar raised high over his head.

Pike locked eyes with her.

A smile split his face as he reached back for the hatch door and prepared to seal himself inside.

His smile never faltered as a silver shape reared up behind him from inside the sphere.

Eighty-Seven

Bishop sprinted into the waves, the crowbar poised in striking position. He couldn't let Pike pass the edge of the stern or they would never be able to catch him. Their only chance of escaping this island with their lives would be gone. Bradley fired wildly over his shoulder at the craft, which was now nearly submerged in the waves. If he allowed Pike to close the hatch, there would be no opening it again. The weight of the water would seal it like a tomb.

Pike leered down at him with an expression of pure triumph on his face, an expression that told Bishop everything he needed to know. Pike wasn't immediately heading toward open water. Once he was clear of the ship, he intended to make sure that no one else survived.

The water churning up into the air in front of his knees nearly obscured his view of the silver form that rose up over Pike. There was a sudden flash of movement and Pike's hideous smile twisted into a contortion of sheer agony. His eyes widened in terror. He reached for his throat, but not quickly enough. A mouth overflowing with hooked teeth opened over Pike's shoulder and latched onto the side of his neck. Blood burst from their union. A lone arterial spurt escaped the creature's mouth before it adjusted its grip and shook Pike's head from side to side.

Dear God.

The hatch door had been closed when they arrived. He remembered stepping down from the platform onto it. The swaying cables…they hadn't been blown by the wind, had they?

The creature had slipped into the submersible when they'd turned their backs on it, where it had waited for Courtney and him to climb in so it could tear them apart. It had known that the *Trident* was the only way off this island, and it had simply staked out the hanger and waited for them to come to it.

But he and Courtney had seen its corpse back at the mission. There was no doubt that it had been dead, which could only mean one thing.

There were two of them.

He recalled the footage of Tyler's graduate assistant hitting the emergency button and dragging Tyler through the smoke behind the isolation shield. Lanky, long-legged Devin...

If Lurch had been the first creature, then he knew exactly who they were up against now.

Bishop plunged into the ocean and stroked toward the *Trident*.

Pike swatted at the creature with his free hand to no avail. By the time he maneuvered the pistol to point back over his shoulder, it was already too late. The creature wrenched its head, with Pike's right along with it, to the side, and the shot clanged harmlessly from the hatch.

Bishop grabbed onto the tail of the submersible and dragged himself aboard. The water threatened to pull him right back down. Waves crested the personnel sphere and washed over the roof. He could hear it pouring inside and onto the cushioned pit at the bottom.

Pike opened his mouth to scream, but only a mouthful of blood came out. He pinched his eyes tightly closed in pain, unlike the creature's, which stared right at Bishop.

Never in his worst dreams had he seen such a frightening sight.

The creature's eyes had wide, vertical slits, reminiscent of a cat's. The slits were limned blue, like oblong black moons eclipsing twin cobalt suns, from which stray rays marbled the rest of the sclera. He had seen these eyes many times before, but never on a man.

They were the eyes of a great white shark.

It opened its mouth and Pike dropped down into the sphere. Bishop heard the body crumple to the padding inside, felt the submersible shake. The creature turned its full attention on him. Its teeth shimmered crimson. Chunks of flesh were stuck to its gray gums. Its gills fanned open at the base of its mandible.

Bishop crawled toward it as the waves crashed against the submersible. His heart rate accelerated. He moved from one slippery handhold to the next.

A scaled claw emerged from the hole and gripped the edge of the opening. In one sinewy movement, its shoulders were all the way out of the orifice.

Bishop lunged forward and swung the crowbar at its head.

The creature easily avoided his best effort. It ducked down into the sphere, like a serpent recoiling after a strike.

He wouldn't get a second shot at this.

Bishop dove toward the hatch before the creature could emerge again. He grabbed the lid and slammed it closed. It connected with the crown of the creature's head and nearly popped back open again. He threw his weight on top of it and started cranking the wheel to lock it in place. The ocean rose over the wheel and sprayed him in the face, yet he continued turning it until it was sealed.

The entire submersible rocked as the creature hurled itself against the hatch and the sides of the sphere. He could even hear the thrashing and banging sounds from beneath the waterline.

He fed the crowbar through the gaps in the steel wheel and wedged it in place.

The *Trident* continued to rock underneath him until the sea reached his waist and he was forced to stand. Inexorably, it continued its descent until it reached the end of the track. The sub bucked beneath him as the trolley met with the bumpers. Under normal conditions, this was the point where the *Trident* would be rigged to the A-frame, lifted out over the precipice, and lowered into the ocean. Instead, its momentum carried it forward and it slid off of the trolley. It tipped nose-down and dropped out from under his feet.

Bishop barely had time to draw a breath before he splashed into the ocean. The draft of the submersible pulled him down, but he kicked against it until he broke the surface. He coughed and spit out a lungful of saltwater. The rain-dimpled waves lifted him high and dropped him back down. He treaded water as he stared to the west, waiting for what he knew would happen next.

The smoke crawled over the sea like a fog. The ash formed a greasy film on the surface.

He could hear Courtney calling for him over the shrieking wind, but he couldn't bring himself to look away.

Not yet.

He felt it streaking toward the surface, a massive body displacing water as it fired up from the abyss. The *Trident* burst from the ocean, throwing up a wall of water. It submerged again before settling in to ride the waves, nearly completely underwater, save for the very uppermost portion of its spine. It had taken on so much water during the launch that it couldn't fully breach the surface, although he could see just enough of it to allow himself to breathe a sigh of relief.

The hatch was still closed and the crowbar was wedged just as he had left it.

He could hear the creature pounding inside as he turned and swam back toward the *Huxley*.

They weren't safe yet.

There was one more thing he needed to do.

And he needed to do it quickly.

Eighty-Eight

Bradley kept pressure on Reaves's abdominal wound. The bleeding had slowed significantly, but that didn't mean that they were anywhere close to out of the woods yet. It was a through-and-through shot, which meant that at least he didn't have to contend with the bullet. He'd cleaned it up and irrigated it as well as he could. The bullet had entered through the external oblique muscle and exited just lateral to the psoas muscle. Based on the trajectory, he was reasonably confident that it had missed all of the vital organs, but that didn't mean that it hadn't nicked a vessel or shredded the bowels. Beyond the blood loss, sepsis was a very real threat. Without antibiotics and fresh water to cleanse the wound, he was merely stalling the inevitable. He needed to get Reaves to a hospital, and the sooner the better. If they were able to do so, there was a good chance that Reaves would survive.

A part of him missed this. The actual physical treatment of patients, the ability to make a difference with his own two hands. He had abandoned the healing arts to pursue the greater good, and his fortune, so long ago now that he barely remembered what it was like to be an actual physician in practice, not just in name. The pharmaceuticals that his empire produced had saved countless lives and enhanced the overall health of millions, and yet somehow it just wasn't the same as getting in there and treating the sick and the injured on a more intimate level.

None of that mattered now. This tragedy would undoubtedly bankrupt GeNext, absolve him of his personal wealth, and possibly land him in prison, depending upon how everything played out once a thorough investigation of the events on this island was completed. He could always pay for the findings to be in his favor, but right now he was so tired...too tired to even contemplate the future.

The passion that he and Reaves had shared, that had consumed their lives for the last twelve years...this was where it had led them. To the wreckage of a ship preparing to sink into oblivion, on an island where nearly a hundred good men and women had lost their lives to the focus of their every waking thought, and for what? They had done exactly what they set out to do so long ago, yet they had nothing to show for it. There was no way they could explore the potential of the monster they had created. The world was simply not ready for that knowledge.

Reaves groaned and tried to say something, but the words came out a garble.

"Try not to exert yourself, old friend." He wiped the beaded sweat from Reaves's pallid face. His eyes fluttered open and he looked up at Bradley. "That was a very brave thing you did. He would have killed us all."

Reaves's face tightened with pain. He tugged meekly at Bradley's hand and swallowed hard. He tried to speak again. Bradley had to lean closer to hear him.

"...can't let anyone...find it," Reaves whispered.

"I know." Bradley looked Reaves in the eyes and gave his hand a reassuring squeeze. "We're not ready."

"Promise?"

Reaves pleaded with his eyes.

"You have my word, Brendan."

The ghost of a smile crossed Reaves's lips and his eyes gently closed. His grip on Bradley's hand relaxed.

Bradley raised his stare and looked to the west, where Bishop knelt on the back of the *Trident* like a native fisherman in a shallow dugout, silhouetted against the brutal waves. There was a loud hiss of air and the smoke above the submersible swirled upward on the sudden gust. Bishop stood upright as the *Trident* took on ballast and sank beneath him. A moment later, he was treading water where the vessel had once been.

Courtney stood knee-deep in the ocean on the stern. The waves now lapped into the mouth of the hanger. She simply stared out to sea at where the submersible had once been, her arms wrapped around her chest. He couldn't imagine what she must be feeling. He couldn't blame her for hating him. Whether intentionally or not, he had robbed her of one of the most important people in her life and then had her locked up in one of the cabins now on the ocean floor while he tried to determine how best to keep her silent. Would he have had her killed to keep their secret? He was glad he'd never been forced to actually make that decision. He wasn't certain he would have made the right choice. What happened to her brother hadn't been directly his fault, but it had been his responsibility. And while he couldn't bring Tyler back, he could at least make sure that his life, that his sacrifice, hadn't been in vain.

When the time arrived, he would fall on his sword and do what needed to be done.

He would do the noble thing.

The right thing.

He would lie through his teeth.

Eighty-Nine

Courtney swam ever downward toward the bottom of Tutum Bay. She had equipped herself in scuba gear from the divers locker room. The water was bitter cold, even through the wetsuit, but she couldn't feel it. She was physically and emotionally numb. Her arms paddled and her legs kicked of their own accord. Were it not for the weight belt, she probably wouldn't have the strength to reach her destination, but she needed to know. She couldn't leave this island without learning the truth. It would haunt her for the rest of her life if she did.

Bishop had offered to join her, if only for moral support. While she appreciated the gesture, this was something she had to do by herself. Although she did hope to see a lot more of him once their normal lives resumed.

She clicked on her headlamp and swam through the haze of silt, navigating the maze of coral formations that once would have held her enrapt for days on end. Maybe some other time, she thought, knowing that day would never come. She passed fish hiding in darkened enclaves under piles of metallic debris, past corpses nearly hidden in the reef, and through rising curtains of hydrogen sulfide and arsenic bubbles until she finally saw the *Trident*. It had sunken into the sediment to the point that the windows were mere feet above the ocean floor. It already looked as though it had been down here for years.

Courtney glided up to the port-side window, where her brother had been stationed on the *Corellian*, and knelt before it. She wiped away the accumulation of grime and brought her face close to the glass to shine her beam inside. A streak of dried blood bisected it at an angle from the other side. She could see the racks of equipment on the opposite wall, plastic faces broken, wires exposed. Monitors were cracked and shattered. Her breath caught in her chest. There was no one in there. It had somehow managed to escape. At this very second, it could be attacking the others on the ship.

And then she saw it, a hunched shape slouched down in the cushioned pit.

She placed her hand against the fiberglass hull, just to feel the vibrations, to know that oxygen was still being pumped into the sphere.

It didn't move at first. It merely stared back at her through eyes that reflected her beam as twin golden disks. The light shone dully on scaled skin that had taken on a sickly gray cast. She watched it even as it watched her. Its gills flared dramatically, exposing folds of pale tissue that no longer retracted like they should. Its mouth was closed, or as much as it could be with all of those teeth. Those that pierced its lips threw shadows across its chin and cheeks. Its respirations were agonal, gasping, reminding her of the goldfish she and her brother had shared as children. It had jumped out of its bowl and they had found it on the carpet, sucking desperately for even its dying breaths. She remembered the way Ty had cupped it carefully in both of his tiny hands and eased it gently back into the water. It hadn't taken more than a few minutes for it to die.

The figure rolled Pike's body off of its lap and pushed itself up from the cushions. It brought what at first looked like a dead snake to its mouth and took a long, deep breath that deflated the tube. She realized what it was with a start and glanced down at the hollow abdomen of Pike's corpse. When she looked back at the creature, it crawled forward until its face was only inches from the glass.

His hair was gone and his eyes were different, but the shape was the same. His mouth bulged and his nostrils appeared somehow too narrow, yet still she recognized him. She would have known her brother's face anywhere.

"I'm so sorry," she whispered into the mask.

As if he could hear her, Tyler nodded.

The scales on his face had peeled away in sections to expose the gray skin beneath. Lesions had opened along his cheek bones, brow, and chin. The pure oxygen had already started his deterioration, as Bradley had said it would. She looked deeply into his eyes in search of any of sign of the man he had once been, praying that she could stop this, but knowing in her heart that there was no way she could.

He inhaled again from Pike's bowels and his eyes widened in panic. He tried again and again before hurling the sloppy ropes across the sphere. She read desperation and fear in his stare.

She reached out and pressed her palm against the window.

Her brother matched her gesture. She could see the webbing between his fingers as though it were her own.

Courtney held her hand like that for several minutes.

This was how she would say goodbye.

Tears rolled from her eyes and pooled against the seal of the mask.

When she finally removed her hand, her brother attempted a smile and pointed upward repeatedly with one clawed finger. He wanted her to open the hatch. She couldn't even if she wanted to. Unless they brought the *Trident* back to the surface, it was sealed for good.

She shook her head.

The placid expression on his face metamorphosed into rage. He bared his teeth and struck at the window with his claws, over and over, until she had to turn away.

She sat down on the ground and leaned her back against the submersible, which rocked and shuddered as the creature continued to go berserk, hurling itself against the sides, rushing up and down the rungs to the hatch, throwing equipment...more animal than man.

"Goodbye, Ty," she whispered.

She would stay down here with him for as long as it took.

The frantic movement eventually stilled inside.

Courtney remembered sitting in the isolation chamber, waiting for her air to run out. The certainty of knowing that she was going to die was the worst part, but there came a point of acceptance. The rest...it was like just falling into a pleasant, dreamless sleep.

She would stay with her brother, right by his side.

There was no way she would leave him alone.

Not down here.

Not like this.

Not until he was finally asleep.

Ninety

Bishop found Courtney sitting on the starboard catwalk above the stern, her feet dangling in the ocean, staring off to the west, where the setting sun bled the cloud of smoke and ash crimson. He hadn't seen her return. The torrent had waned to a drizzle. No longer did the lightning flare overhead, and the thunder was just a distant grumble from across the sea. Behind them, the formerly long-dormant volcano continued to rumble and billow ash into the heavens, although with nowhere near the same ferocity. Lava slithered down through the forest as it cooled; however, no more danced above the caldera or boiled over its rim. The fires still advanced ever downward toward the shore, losing speed as they went. The ocean remained angry, hurling massive waves at them one after another, but it seemed as though even Neptune had blown off most of his steam.

Bishop climbed up to the railing and sat down beside her. She didn't appear to notice his arrival, so he just sat silently beside her. He hoped that maybe his presence alone would be enough.

"It didn't take as long as I thought it would," she said, still staring at the horizon. Despite her best efforts to hide it, her voice trembled. "I wonder if…in the end…a part of Tyler resurfaced."

"He's at peace now, Courtney."

"I just pray he didn't suffer."

Bishop held out his hand. She tore her gaze from the setting sun, took it in hers, and rested them both on her lap. They sat quietly for several minutes before she asked the question they were all thinking.

"What happens now?"

"We go back to the real world, back to our lives."

"How are we supposed to do that?"

"I suppose we take it one day at a time."

"And what about…?" She held up their hands. "What about this?"

"I can't wait to find out."

He traced circles on the back of her hand with his thumb.

She leaned against him and rested her head on his shoulder.

"What about everything that happened here? What are we supposed to do?"

"We can't change any of it. The best we can hope to do is make sure something like this never happens again."

"After everything we've been through, you're willing to let Bradley off the hook? He has to pay for what he's done."

"I have no doubt he'll pay, Courtney." He rested his cheek against her hair. "I just think that you and I are done paying. And I think that your brother is, too. Better he rest in peace here than end up on a dissection table somewhere, or, God forbid, that his remains be used to create more like him. And you know that's exactly what they'd do."

A black dot appeared in the distance where the sun settled into the ocean. It grew larger as he watched until he could clearly discern the wide bridge of the pilothouse and the T-shape of the satellite array crowning it.

"Well, it's about time," he said.

Courtney raised her head and looked to the west. Her grip tightened on his hand. She turned to face him with a mixture of conflicting emotions on her face.

"What are we going to tell them?"

"I guess we'd probably better figure that out before they get here." He shrugged. "But first things first."

He tipped up her chin, looked into her stunning shamrock eyes, and kissed her for everything he was worth.

MICHAEL McBRIDE

is the bestselling author of *Ancient Enemy, Bloodletting, Burial Ground, Fearful Symmetry, Innocents Lost, Sunblind,* and *The Coyote.* His novella *Snowblind* won the 2012 DarkFuse Readers Choice Award and received honorable mention in *The Best Horror of the Year.* He lives in Avalanche Territory with his wife and kids.

To explore the author's other works, please visit www.michaelmcbride.net.

Made in the USA
Las Vegas, NV
10 February 2021